THE GIRL AT ROSEWOOD HALL

THE GIRL AT ROSEWOOD HALL

A Lady Jane Mystery

ANNIS
BELL

TRANSLATED BY
EDWIN MILES

amazon crossing

Previously published as *Die Tote von Rosewood Hall (Lady Jane 1)* by Amazon Publishing in Germany in 2014. Translated from German by Edwin Miles in 2015. First published in English by AmazonCrossing in 2015.

Published by AmazonCrossing, Seattle

www.apub.com

Amazon, the Amazon logo, and AmazonCrossing are trademarks of Amazon.com, Inc., or its affiliates.

ISBN-13: 9781503944756
ISBN-10: 1503944751

Cover design by Scott Barrie

Printed in the United States of America

Where sunless rivers weep
Their waves into the deep,
She sleeps a charmèd sleep:
Awake her not . . .
Sleep that no pain shall wake;
Night that no morn shall break
Till joy shall overtake
Her perfect peace.

Christina Rossetti (1830–1894)

1.

Rosewood Hall, February 1860

Laughter, the clink of glasses, and scraps of conversation mingled with the lilt of the music and the swish of silk ball gowns as they glided over the parquet floor in time to a waltz. With every turn the dancers made, the magnificent jewels worn by the women sparkled and glittered in the glow of countless candles on the chandeliers in the ballroom. The exquisite buffet tempted even the most discerning palates, and Lord Pembroke had gone so far as to have the good champagne served.

Jane sighed. She knew that her uncle had gone to such lavish expense all for her sake. She leaned unhappily against a column and let her eyes wander over the lively gathering. After the death of her parents—both far too young, the victims of a cholera epidemic in India—her uncle Henry had taken her in. He could not have loved her any more had she been his own daughter. Jane gazed around the room anxiously, trying to see him. She knew her uncle was ill, seriously ill, although he tried to keep it hidden from her. In his sixties, he remained an impressive man, tall and slim and with a mane of silver hair, which she now spied among a group of older men on the far side of the ballroom. She was relieved to see that he had not yet withdrawn for the night, and turned her eyes to the guests.

The young, eligible women in attendance had gone to great lengths with their clothes and makeup. Some of them were so beautiful they could turn the head of any man there. Perhaps a goldfish or two would find its way into a net tonight. That's what this soiree was all about, after all. Her uncle wanted her—at long last—to find a suitable partner for marriage. Jane chewed her lip and nervously fluttered the fan in her hand. But who? What man would allow her the freedom that mattered so much to her? She wasn't one of those sugary creatures with a pretty face and an empty head. Not that she couldn't hold her own among the marriageable young ladies at the party. Her shining, red-brown hair was all the rage, and her daily routine of riding, walking, and swimming had given her an excellent figure. Perhaps her curves were not quite feminine enough, her chin too emphatic, and her green eyes too critical too often, but when she made an effort, she could bat her long eyelashes seductively and draw her full lips into a most enticing smile.

She fluttered the fan again. She had no desire to pander to vain fops who were only after her dowry and saw her as no more than a necessary evil. Not yet twenty-five, she was no old maid. But the danger zone was approaching.

"My gosh, Jane, if you go on frowning like that, your forehead will stay creased forever. Then we'll never find you a man!" Lady Alison was her best friend and, for the last year, the Baroness Latimer.

"Oh, Ally . . . do you really think I want to be with one of these men? I'd throw myself off a bridge first!" said Jane, swatting her friend's magnificent pink silk robe with her fan.

Alison was petite and blond, and her big blue eyes lent her an air of vulnerability that made her all the more attractive. But the impression was deceptive. Jane knew a sympathetic fighter's heart beat in her friend's breast. And she knew that she could trust Alison with her life.

Since Alison had married, they saw each other only on rare occasions, for Alison now had to care for her husband, her household, and her three-month-old twins. Jane missed her friend's vivacious company.

"Just wait, we'll find one for you. I see Lord Hargrave's here. Rich, attractive . . . if you like graying at the temples. He has a gorgeous townhouse in London, in Park Lane. I've seen it myself."

Jane followed Alison's discreet gaze and saw a giant of a man. There was something military about him, though he wore an elegant black suit and stood among the other guests. On second glance, his superficial handsomeness diminished. His mouth was too wide and was surrounded by deep lines, signs of a lack of restraint and a short temper. He seemed to realize that the women were looking at him, and when he caught Jane's eye, she immediately looked away.

"No, Alison, I don't like him. Was he in the military?"

Alison raised one shoulder coquettishly and continued to scan the room. "They say he was in various wars in India and Crimea, and doubled his fortune in the process. Well, you've only yourself to blame, because there are plenty of frogs in the pond today. Ah!"

Alison gave her friend a triumphant nudge. "There! He's the one! He just arrived ten minutes ago, and I asked Lady Dorchester about him. He comes from one of the best houses in England." Alison steered Jane's gaze past a row of pillars and a pyramid of champagne glasses.

The first thing Jane saw was the dress uniform of an officer. The man was tall and broad-shouldered and was standing somewhat ill at ease beside a group of young women who giggled behind their fans and stole covert glances at him. Their attentions, however, seemed to leave him completely cold. His black hair tumbled almost to his shoulders, framing striking cheekbones and a scar that ran from his right temple to his chin. His expression was unreadable and his dark eyes seemed to be scouring the room, coming to rest only when they caught sight of Jane's face.

For a brief moment, she held his gaze. He was at once dashing and inscrutable. Then she raised her chin slightly and turned to her friend. "Who is that, did you say?"

Alison grinned smugly. "I knew it! His name is Captain David Wescott. The youngest son of the Duke of St. Amand."

"*The* Amand?" Jane again turned her eyes in the direction of the officer, who was just then approached by Lord Albany. St. Amand was one of Queen Victoria's key advisors and famed for his covert diplomatic missions.

"The very same! Lady Dorchester also told me that Wescott and his father have fallen out. They haven't said a word to one another for years. He's just back from the war, poor man," said Alison sympathetically.

"Which explains the scar on his face?"

Alison nodded. "Apparently it's not the only scar he has." She cleared her throat in embarrassment and toyed absently with a lock of the blond hair that perfectly framed her well-proportioned face and was held in place at the back with pearl-studded combs. "He served in India and then in the Crimean War, in the terrible battle of Balaklava. Lady Dorchester says he was more dead than alive when they brought him back from the front."

"You don't see that now," Jane remarked. *But those dark eyes of his could be hiding wounds on the inside,* she thought. She observed Captain Wescott with renewed interest.

"Besides, he has a dubious reputation when it comes to women." Alison tilted her head. "Oh, look. Here comes your worthy cousin. No doubt he wants to ask you to dance."

Jane rolled her eyes and turned away, pulling Alison along with her. "It's enough that I have to see him every day. Him and his outrageous wife! Come, let's make ourselves scarce for a while."

"Jane, we can't do that!" Alison protested, following her friend uncertainly as Jane sneaked behind a column and out of the ballroom. "I promised Thomas the next dance!"

"Oh, Ally, just for a few minutes. I need some fresh air!" Jane knew every nook and cranny of the vast manor and could have found her way around it in pitch darkness. With determination, she made her way from the entrance hall into a small salon and from the salon into the conservatory.

In there, the sounds of the party were muted and seemed swallowed up by the enormous palms that towered to the top of the glass dome overhead. The conservatory smelled of rose, hibiscus, and lemon, and Jane took a deep breath. "Isn't it marvelous here? I love this place!"

Alison was panting a little. "Oh my, I'm out of breath." She stroked her tightly corseted waist. "This dress fit me, once upon a time. But ever since the twins were born, everything in my wardrobe seems to have shrunk."

Jane heard steps approaching and pulled her friend along with her. The expensive silk of their dresses rustled between planters and against the pedestal of a small fountain until Jane and Alison were standing at the doors that led outside. Jane pushed one of the French doors open and stepped out into the cold night air. In the silver moonlight, shrubs and topiary hedges cast bizarre shadows across the grass, and the clipped evergreen balls and tapers seemed to dance around the small statuette in the parterre. From the ballroom windows warm light fell onto the terrace, where a little snow still clung to the marble tiles.

Alison stopped in the doorway. "Come back. You'll catch your death out there!"

"A little cooling off will do me good." A deep sadness had come over Jane, as it had so often in recent weeks.

"Not me. I'm not as hardy as you. What is going on with you? Jane!"

It was so unfair! Why couldn't women own property of their own? "I wish I were a man," she said, giving voice to the thought in her head. "Then Matthew would have no power over me."

"But your uncle is still alive. He would never allow any injustice against you," said Alison, trying to calm Jane, but she just shook her head in despair.

"Uncle Henry is far more ill than he'll admit, and I'm deeply worried about him. Matthew knows it too. Why do you think he and his conniving wife moved in here? Oh, of course, they say they want to help. Matthew supposedly wants to assist Henry with the administration of the estates. Don't make me laugh! All he wants is a good look at his future property—including me. It makes me so angry! When Henry dies, Matthew will become my guardian."

Shivering, Alison reached a hand out to her friend. "Come back in, please. No one can take away your father's title. Isn't there a house in Cornwall that will belong to you when you marry?"

Jane looked out into the darkness. In her mind's eye she could clearly see the grounds surrounding Rosewood Hall, this place she loved so much. "I haven't been there since I was a child. In my bedroom hangs a small painting of Mulberry Park—that's its name. Henry hired a caretaker to look after it, but I have no idea how much the place brings in. Well . . ." Jane forced herself to smile. "I am not poor, but I am also not free. And I will never be free. Never."

"Don't say that, Jane. You make it sound as if we were all locked up," Alison objected.

"Aren't we? One way or another, all women live in prisons. One day, Alison, one day, we women will be allowed to decide for ourselves. I'm sure of it. Why else would the Lord above have given women a mind to think with?"

"Jane, that's enough now. I don't like it when you start talking like this. You know it makes me sad. There's a reason for everything, and it really isn't all that bad." Alison tugged disconsolately at a velvet purse dangling from her wrist.

"It's all right, Ally. I won't say any more," said Jane, but deep inside she was in turmoil. She felt a painful rebelliousness that she knew she would not be able to suppress for long when her uncle passed away. She would not allow Matthew to dictate anything in her life, and that fact would inevitably lead to more difficulties.

"Alison? Where are you hiding?" called a man's voice from inside the house.

With almost hysterical relief, Alison called to her husband. "I'm in the conservatory, Thomas. I'm coming!" She looked questioningly at Jane, who was still standing out in the cold.

"Go, Ally. I'd still like to be alone for a minute."

"Don't think about these things so much, Jane. We can't change the way they are." Alison turned and hurried off to her waiting husband.

Jane bit her lip, swallowed her tears, and murmured, "I will never give up on myself. I will die first."

Just then she became aware of a strange noise in the darkness, a kind of low whimper. A cat? Some injured animal? Jane lifted her skirts and took a step forward. The thin material of her shoes was soaked through instantly, but when she heard the pitiful mewling again, she realized it was the sound of crying, and she ran down the steps into the garden.

The crying was coming from near a statue, behind which grew a rhododendron. Jane didn't stop for a moment to consider that she might be putting herself in danger. During her childhood in India, she had learned to rely on her senses, to trust her instincts. Her instincts now told her that a human being was in need.

"Hello! Is someone there? Hello!" she called softly as she slowly approached the bush. Among Jane's peculiar gifts was the ability to see like a cat at night. This had led her first English nanny after her arrival in Wiltshire to call her half-wild and unnatural, an infernal little heathen. And although her uncle Henry had dismissed the nanny soon after that, Jane had learned early that it was often safer to conform than to stand out.

Without a second thought, she made soft, calming sounds, as she would with a skittish horse or anxious dog. "It's all right. No one wants to hurt you."

The crying sounded childlike, and when Jane peered cautiously beneath the rhododendron, she discovered a little heap of misery.

2.

What lay in the snow beneath the bush could easily have been mistaken for a pile of stinking rags. Jane pressed a handkerchief over her mouth and moved closer. The light of the full moon revealed a picture of wretchedness. A girl starved to mere skin and bones was curled there, cowering inside her torn rags. Jane touched the poor creature gently on the shoulder with her fan, and the girl turned her head and looked at her fearfully with wide, feverish eyes.

"Oh, my goodness! Now what on earth are we going to do with you?" Jane stood up and was taken aback to see Captain Wescott striding toward her.

"My lady, what are you doing out here alone?" A strand of dark hair fell over his face as he looked at her, and his expression was grim.

"This place is my home, and we have not yet been introduced, but now that you are here, you might be able to make yourself useful." She pointed fervently at the girl, who seemed more dead than alive. Only the soft rattle of her breath betrayed the fact that there was still some life in her body.

Without a moment's hesitation, Wescott went down on one knee, laid a hand on the child's forehead, and then lifted her effortlessly into his arms. As he stood up, a book fell from the girl's ragged shawl. Jane bent down and picked it up.

"Where can we take her?" asked Wescott. "Perhaps not the servants' wing. She has a high fever and could infect everyone there. Is there a separate room?"

"Yes. This way." Jane gathered her skirts and walked quickly back into the conservatory. Only now did she feel how cold her feet were, but there would be time later to remedy that. The glass conservatory had an extension where the gardener cultivated plants and, on occasion, stayed the night. Rosewood Hall was known for its grounds and gardens, with its exotic plants and extraordinary roses.

In her wide skirts, Jane pushed her way through an espalier of lemon and orange trees and opened the narrow door that led into the hothouse, or "infirmary," as her uncle liked to call it. A comfortable warmth rolled out to meet them. "In here. Uncle Henry loves plants. This is where he has them nursed back to health."

On wooden shelves stood a variety of orchids and other plants not hardy enough to survive the winter outside. In a corner of the long room stood a coal heater, and at the far end was the gardener's chamber.

"Your uncle's plants have it better than some people," Captain Wescott remarked.

Jane paused at the entrance to the chamber. Inside, a narrow cot stood along the wall. There was a table with a water jug and a washbasin; a chair completed the Spartan furnishings. On the cot was a thin mattress covered by a woolen blanket, which Jane pulled back. Captain Wescott laid the girl gently on the mattress and drew the blanket over her.

Jane set the girl's book on the table, then she poured water into the basin and took a cloth she found on the chair and moistened it. As she was about to bend down to the sick girl, Wescott took the damp cloth from her. "Let me. In war, one learns how to do such things."

As if it came naturally to him, he cleaned the girl's face and wiped down her thin arms and hands. Long blond hair tumbled from the hood of her shawl. Fascinated, Jane watched the captain and the girl. She couldn't look away from the girl's emaciated face. Her eyes were moving behind her closed eyelids, and then she suddenly opened her eyes wide and stared at Jane. When the girl saw Wescott, she began to tremble and pushed him away, but from her cracked lips came only unintelligible sounds.

"She's scared." Jane sat on the chair by the bed and took the girl's hand. "It's all right. No one will hurt you here."

The little hand in hers was simultaneously hot and cold, and the girl's cheeks glowed a febrile red. Deep, dark shadows ringed her blue eyes, and with every breath she drew, a rattling sounded deep in her lungs. Jane could feel the life draining from the wasted body with every tortured breath.

"Won't someone be missing her? We should send for help," Wescott suggested.

"She's dying. Can't you see that? I will not leave her alone." Full of sympathy for the poor creature that some whim of fate had led into her garden, Jane sat and stroked the little hand.

"Death is no stranger to me. I've encountered it far too many times. But you . . ." Wescott paused. Voices were coming from outside in the conservatory. "I'll deal with that."

Another woman in her position would doubtless have acted "correctly," Jane thought, then pressed her lips together and chided herself. She was behaving correctly! It was her Christian duty to tend to this poor soul. No one should have to die alone.

With a sigh, she took the damp cloth and laid it on the girl's forehead. Her breathing had become somewhat more even, and her blue eyes looked up at Jane.

"Mary, my Mary." Tears flowed from the girl's eyes. "They will come for her and . . . they mustn't do anything to hurt Mary! Please!"

The small hand gripped Jane's. "Find Mary! My only friend . . . you have to find Mary before the men come again."

The intonation and the way she said her *r*'s reminded Jane of the Cornish accent of her lady's maid, Hettie. An attack of coughing racked the girl, and when Jane held the cloth to the girl's mouth, she saw bloody sputum.

"Which men? What's your name? You have to help me so that I can find Mary! Where is she?"

The girl's large eyes were still on Jane, but their blue was becoming translucent and seemed already to see what Jane could not. "The book . . . our book . . . I always read to her from it when the others were asleep."

The girl reached out into the air with her other hand and, with her eyes wide open, whispered, "The devil is coming for our souls."

Struggling desperately for air, the starved body jolted upright, then slumped back with a horribly drawn-out sigh.

"May you find peace with God." Jane crossed herself and stood up.

"She's dead, isn't she?" asked Wescott softly behind her.

Jane took a deep breath and turned around. "Yes, I think . . ."

She let him by her and watched as he loosened the girl's shawl and felt her throat and inspected her carefully before closing her eyelids. He tried to pull the shawl quickly around the girl's throat again, but Jane had already seen the dark bruises ringing her larynx. Wescott looked thoughtfully at the dead girl, and then leaned forward again and raised the body slightly to look at the girl's back beneath her ragged clothes, which Jane now recognized as the ruins of a maid's dress. "Did she say anything before she died?" he asked.

It seemed to Jane that neither of them put too much store in social conventions, and she felt strangely secure in the captain's presence. She was not sure how else to describe the feeling. Normally, the company of potential suitors only bored her, or she felt ill at ease or downright repelled. But that was not the case with Wescott. The man radiated an unshakable calm and self-confidence, far removed from any affectation or arrogance. His expression remained inscrutable and revealed no particular emotion. *Not entirely,* Jane corrected herself. His eyes had been full of sympathy for the girl, and now that he had turned and was looking at her, she believed she could see in them something like acknowledgment.

Because it seemed important to the girl, Jane repeated word for word what she had said. "The book!"

She took the book from the table. The thin leather cover was worn and the pages discolored and tattered from being read many times. *The Vampyre. By John Polidori* was stamped into the cover in faded gold letters. She opened it and found the letters *P* and *M* on the first page. Underneath, someone had drawn a rose in a childish hand.

"The *M* could stand for Mary, and the *P* for the girl's name. What do you think?" Jane asked.

"Possibly." Wescott looked at her earnestly. He was standing one step from her now and was a head taller. His dark-blue dress uniform accentuated his powerful frame. She could see the muscles of his jaw tighten. "She has been abused."

The bruises on her throat, of course. As if wandering through the countryside in winter wasn't torture enough for the girl.

"Someone has strangled her, and her back is covered in wounds that might have been made by a whip. Considering the cold, it's a miracle she lived this long." Wescott pointed to the girl's wrists, where dark discolorations and abraded skin were also visible. "She's been tied up, too. My God, what . . ."

"Captain?" came a cautious voice from the door. A man wearing a brown suit was standing there. There was something unsettlingly intense about his eyes. The olive tone of his skin bore witness to a life spent under the southern sun.

"What is it, Blount?"

"Someone is asking for the lady," the man replied. He seemed to be the captain's valet. *Perhaps a former adjutant?* thought Jane, immediately noticing the camaraderie between the two men.

"Who is asking for me?" she asked.

"A Mr. Devereaux. It seems he was promised a dance." Blount smiled cautiously.

"Please extend the gentleman my apologies. I withdrew from the party because I was not feeling well."

"Very well, my lady," said Blount, and disappeared as quietly as he had come.

"Captain?" She looked inquiringly at Wescott.

"My apologies, my lady. Captain David Wescott. Your uncle was nice enough to invite me tonight, Lady Jane." He smiled at her, and she felt her heart beat a little faster, but his expression darkened again quickly. "The appropriate thing to do would be to inform the authorities."

"It would. But I don't want my uncle to be bothered with something like this, not this evening. He is terribly ill, and any excitement could damage his heart. Please, Captain Wescott. You know what high society's like. They pounce on scandal like a pack of hyenas. A mysterious dead girl in the park at Rosewood Hall will have them gossiping to no end. It would kill my uncle!"

Instinctively, Jane took hold of Wescott's hand, but released it instantly, as if she had burnt her fingers. "Forgive me! You must take me for someone with no . . ." Tears welled in her eyes.

Wescott took a handkerchief from his uniform jacket and handed it to Jane. "No. Far from it. I consider you an extraordinarily brave young woman. And society?" He laughed bitterly. "I don't give a damn about society! But I do hold your uncle in high regard, like you."

"He is my family," whispered Jane and wiped her eyes. Wescott looked at her. He seemed thoughtful.

Jane crumpled the handkerchief into a ball in her hands and said with determination, "She'll have a decent burial, and I will find out who Mary is. She seems to be in danger."

"I don't want to destroy your illusions, but that will be practically impossible. We know nothing about this poor girl." Wescott turned away from the cot and laid one hand lightly on Jane's back. "We should go out."

The warmth of his touch came as such a surprise that Jane stepped into the hothouse faster than she had intended and nearly stumbled over a box of earth.

"If we want to avoid a scandal, we shall need to come up with a plausible explanation for where we've been," said Jane. Lost in her thoughts, she moved toward the glazed connecting door that led back into the conservatory, and then stopped when she noticed guests strolling around the room. "My God, they're everywhere!"

"A ball is always a social event, and what could be more social than sniffing around other people's homes?" said Wescott with a mischievous smile.

"Well, if you . . ." Only then did she look at him and see the irony on his face. She sighed. "My maid, Hettie, is completely trustworthy. We'll say this girl was a distant relative of hers coming here for a visit . . . she lost her way and, unfortunately, she died." Jane thought of the rose drawn in the book she still held in her hand. "Rosie. Her name was Rosie."

"Good. I will instruct Blount to let no one into the room until tomorrow. Then we'll see where we go from there."

Relieved at having deflected a potentially life-threatening fuss from her uncle's attention, she suddenly felt exhausted, and so cold that her teeth began to chatter. "My shoes . . . I'm afraid I shall have to desert you, Captain."

Unbidden, Wescott took her by the arm and escorted her to the door. "The honor was mine, Lady Jane."

Jane left the conservatory like a sleepwalker, ignoring the curious looks of the guests there and paying no heed to the questions that came at her from all sides. In the entrance hall, she found her uncle deep in conversation with several gentlemen, one of whom was Mr. Devereaux. Lord Henry immediately broke off his conversation and approached her.

His custom-tailored black suit fit perfectly, and his posture gave no indication whatsoever of the state of his health. But Jane saw the deep lines that had formed beside his nose and mouth in recent weeks, and the haze of blue beneath his eyes. She realized that this evening had cost him more energy than he could afford.

"Aren't you well, my dear Jane?" Lord Henry asked his niece.

To which Mr. Devereaux unnecessarily added, "We were worried, my lady."

Charles Devereaux was certainly a good-looking man, tall and slim with fashionably trimmed light-brown hair and intense gray eyes, but Jane was unimpressed by his piercing gaze. She seemed to feel a natural aversion to the gentleman with his air of excessive self-confidence. She may have been doing him an injustice. High society was hard, and particularly remorseless when it came to the nouveau riche. It was therefore no surprise that someone like Devereaux had developed a thick skin. Still, Jane was quite sure that Devereaux's only interest in her had to do with her title.

"Just a little chill. I went out for some fresh air with Lady Alison. My shoes . . ." As evidence, she lifted the hem of her skirt to reveal the wet toe of one shoe. "We have more snow on the terrace than I realized."

She laid one hand on her uncle's and spoke so quietly that only he could hear, "I will find some dry shoes and come right back down. But are you all right, Uncle?"

He patted her hand and nodded. "Don't worry about me. I actually wanted to introduce you to someone. Where has he got to?"

Lord Henry looked around, and then shook his head. "A marvelous young man. Somewhat headstrong, but I believe you would like that in him . . ." His eyes sparkled. "Well, I will have harried him out of wherever he's hiding by the time you return."

Jane had an inkling she knew whom her uncle meant, and suppressed a smile.

"Don't forget our dance, Lady Jane!" she heard Devereaux say behind her as she made her way to the stairs.

3.

Mary

The shrill clang of the morning bell was followed by a general muttering and yawning and the shuffle of dozens of small feet on bare floorboards. Mary joined the girls lining up for the washroom. She was a little faster than the day before, which meant that only about twenty girls had washed in the tub by the time she reached it. If you were too sleepy and ended up last in line, you would have to climb into a stinking broth scummed with hair, snot, and bugs. And because Sister Susan insisted that the children immerse themselves up to their necks, it was better to be quick.

Mary scratched her head and arms. Lice and bedbugs felt right at home in the orphanage's dormitory, which made them the only creatures inside those drab, dank walls able to derive any enjoyment from their situation.

The sharp cut of a cane caught Mary on her upper arm. "Stop scratching at yourself, Mary! If you ever want to find a respectable position in a good household, you must learn a little self-control," Sister Susan snapped.

She was called "Sister" even though she was not a trained nurse and had only rudimentary medical knowledge. Master Ledford never took on qualified staff. That would have been far too expensive. Sister Susan was coarse and bony and had spent many years working on her parents' farm before she took the post in the orphanage. Unfortunately, she had a very short fuse and was notorious for boxing the children's ears. Her hard hands could grab hold of a child with brutal strength, and it was common enough for an orphan to show bruises in the evening. It was only after she grabbed you that you knew you had done something wrong or annoyed her.

"Yes, Sister Susan," said Mary softly. She did not look up.

Susan hated it if anyone stared at her. She had a knobby nose and yellowing teeth, which made her look like an old mare. She knew the children called her the "old camel" behind her back, and if she caught them looking at her too long, she quickly wiped any smile off their faces.

At six thirty, a washed and hungry Mary stepped into the refectory, which was even colder than the dormitory. None of the orphans owned more than two sets of clothing, and usually both were equally worn out. Clothes were washed once a week, and the unpleasant, stale odor of dirty laundry hung in the air permanently. The same was true of the rancid stink of oily, unwashed hair. Soap was a luxury reserved only for official visiting days. From time to time, representatives from the Poor Law Union came by, but such visits were always announced well in advance, so in the orphanage they saw, there was never anything to complain about.

The refectory was filled with low murmurings. The hungry children stood in rows at the counter where the food was dispensed, and then took their bowls and cups to one of the long tables. Mary sat on a bench next to Fiona, a girl with fiery red hair. Fiona had been living on the streets before being brought to the orphanage six months earlier. She didn't know where she had been born or how old she was. Her face was marked by her life on the streets, and her body was wiry and muscular, with no trace of a feminine curve. Because she was exactly as tall as Mary, she held fast to her claim that she could not be a day over ten.

Ever since Polly had gone away, Mary had forged an alliance with the streetwise Fiona, who knew how to defend herself from the assaults of Mr. Cooper and the night watchman better than the other girls.

"Good morning, Fiona," Mary whispered. Speaking during the meal was forbidden. She set her cup, which contained a whitish mixture of water and milk, onto the table and placed the bowl of porridge beside it. She stuffed the chunk of bread into the pocket of her skirt, saving it for later when the hunger would start to claw at her stomach.

" 'ave you seen the master this morning, Mary? 'e's in a wicked mood. Something's up," Fiona whispered and glanced sideways, toward the end of the hall where Master Ledford and the mistress stood in conversation with Miss Fannigan and Mr. Gaunt.

Mary slurped her porridge and swallowed the hard barley down without chewing it. "Mr. Gaunt's so nice. I hope they're not throwing him out!"

"Nice don't suit the master. Nice means a waste of time and money." Fiona lifted her cup to her mouth, but the slash of a cane smacked it viciously from her hand.

"On your feet!"

The girls sitting opposite Fiona and Mary went on eating with their heads down, not daring to raise their eyes. When Mr. Cooper, the master's right-hand man, swung his cane, no one wanted to stand out. Fiona stood at the table, her hands folded in front of her.

"Talking at table means you're not 'ungry. There'll be no midday meal for you. What's your name?"

"Fiona."

"You'll be at the workhouse. It's the ropes for you today," Cooper ordered. The man had the build of a former boxer. His eyes were close set and low beneath a square forehead that flaunted a deep scar. The lines of his face bore witness to a violent life.

Unraveling old hawsers was one of the standard jobs of the poorhouses, and was especially unpopular among the women. The ropes had become hardened by seawater, and twisting and pulling them apart left deep cuts in the skin. After a few hours of it, your palms were bloody and raw. The hemp material was then sold to shipbuilders, who mixed it with tar and used it to stuff holes in the hulls of ships.

Before Fiona climbed over the bench, Mary secretly pushed her chunk of bread into the pocket of Fiona's skirt. A working day was long, and the meager dinner wouldn't be served until six. With her head held high, Fiona moved around the end of the table, cast Mary a grateful glance, and left the refectory. The worst thing about Cooper was that you could never tell if he was close by or not. The man could creep around with terrifying silence. Mary observed the way Miss Fannigan shook her head and looked at Mr. Gaunt, but he simply shrugged. She quickly shoveled in the last of her own slimy porridge, rinsing it down with the milky water.

When breakfast was over, the bell rang and everyone stood. Master Ledford positioned himself at the podium at the end of the hall and intoned the daily prayer.

"Amen," he said, and his wife swung the bell again.

The children filed out of the dining hall. The boys ate at the two tables on the other side of the large room. Among them was Mary's brother, Tim. Every morning, Mary did her best to see to it that they left the hall together. This gave them an opportunity to talk. She was worried about Tim. He was two years older than she was and in recent months had changed a great deal. He was more often in contact with the people from the poorhouse next door. Apart from the permanent residents—the hopeless cases wasting away in the poorhouse with no hope of any other future—there were often vagabonds or women from the streets looking for a place to stay just for one night. The women especially were sources of news. They came from all parts of the country and brought with them stories of the world beyond the gates that sealed off the poorhouse from the rest of England.

As Tim stepped up beside her, their hands touched and she looked at him askance. His skin was pale, his eyes were ringed by dark shadows, and one throbbing vein was clearly visible at his temple. "Timmy, have you heard anything about Polly?"

"No. Maybe she's forgot about us. Maybe she's off living the high life in some fancy house." Her brother's lips were thin.

"She would never forget me. Timmy, she wanted to write to me. She promised! Something's wrong, and I'm scared."

"Stop it, Mary. Work hard and get better at reading and writing. Then you'll find a job with a well-to-do family. Or do you want to perish in some factory?"

"No," she whispered, but so low it was hard to hear. Factories were springing up everywhere, like mushrooms. Textile mills in particular. Everyone knew how bad the working conditions were, but for many it was the only path they had left, the last step before the poorhouse.

Polly was pretty and intelligent. She had learned to read and write faster than the others and had always encouraged Mary to do the same. But Mary was slower, and things didn't stick in her head as easily. But once she learned something properly, she never forgot it. Without Polly, things were harder, and she was afraid all the time. She was afraid of Mr. Cooper, the master, and Sister Susan. If you got on the wrong side of them, you could find yourself put on the list. Once you were on the list, sooner or later you disappeared.

"But Polly wasn't on the list, Timmy. She had herself a position. Why doesn't she write?"

They were standing out in the yard now, from where the boys and girls would go into their classrooms in the various buildings. The children had a few minutes free to play before the bell rang for the start of classes. One of the older boys, who came from the streets of London, wandered over to them.

"Oy, Tim. We're waiting." The boy was tall, and there was no longer anything boyish in his features. He nodded his head slightly toward a post where three other older boys were loitering.

"I'm coming, Amos. I have to talk to my sister."

Amos wandered off again, smiling disdainfully and walking his swaggering walk. There wasn't a week that went by without him tangling with Mr. Cooper and getting beaten or locked up. But his spirit seemed to be made of iron, impossible to break.

Tim took her by the shoulders and looked intently at her. "Mary, I can't stay here. Neither can Amos. We're on the list!" He whispered those last words.

Mary smothered a cry of fright with her hand. "How do you know?"

"Mr. Gaunt told us. I think he's in trouble anyway and knows they're going to give him the boot. So he told us. Do you understand?"

Not completely, thought Mary, but she nodded eagerly because she didn't want to look dumb. Tim glanced around quickly, then reached into the pocket of his trousers and took out a small wooden figure. He pressed it into Mary's hand. "It's a cat. Because you love cats so much. It'll remind you of me. We're taking off tonight, Mary."

"Take me with you, Timmy!" she pleaded as she squeezed the wooden cat between her fingers.

Her brother embraced her quickly and then immediately let her go, not wanting to draw attention. He rubbed at his eyes awkwardly with one hand. "That wouldn't be any kind of life for you, Mary. You're not built for the street. I couldn't bear it. Stay here and study hard, you hear? Promise me that. I want to be proud of you. One day, I'll come and find you. I'll find you, Mary!" Then he kissed her forehead and abruptly turned away and strolled off toward the other lads as if nothing had happened.

Mary stood there and watched him walk away. He didn't turn back.

4.

Jane slammed the door to her bedroom closed and let out a long sigh. "Phew. What an evening."

Her maid bustled through the door that connected the bedroom to the small salon and clapped her hands excitedly. "Oh, ma'am, tell me what is happening below! I can hear the music and I took a peek into the ballroom, but I didn't see you dancing! And there are so many fine men! You can take your pick!"

Six years earlier, Henrietta Beedle had come to her as a shy, half-starved creature, the fifth of eleven children from a fishing family in Cornwall. Tonight, no trace of that girl remained. Hettie, as she was known to all in the household, had developed into an attentive, lively young woman. Jane had seen to it that Hettie learned to read and write, for she believed a spirit could grow healthy only when sufficient nourishment was provided. Admittedly, she also did not want people around who could not at least partly understand her. It had become her habit to pass on to Hettie the books she herself had read and enjoyed, and this had led to them sharing many interesting conversations.

Hettie was shorter than Jane and had a real sweet tooth, which did little for her figure, but her round face was graced with a button nose and bright blue-green eyes. Her somewhat bristly sandy hair jutted perkily from beneath her white bonnet as she looked her mistress over and then dropped to her knees in front of her. "Your shoes are soaked through!"

"Wait until you hear why."

"Oh?" Hettie slid a chair across for her mistress and rubbed her cold feet dry with a towel. Then she produced a fresh pair of shoes. "Hmm. These may not go quite as well as the blue ones, but the ball is nearly over in any case."

Jane realized just how hard the death of the girl had hit her, and she described the incident and the request that went with it to her maid as briefly as she could. "Would you do that for me, Hettie?"

The young maid nodded eagerly. "Oh, yes, ma'am! Rosie was my fourth cousin and in a very bad way." She scratched her scalp beneath her bonnet. "Which is really not so much of a lie, for the poor girl really did suffer. But who would do something like that? How long had she been wandering out in the cold?"

Jane smoothed her skirt and stood up. "Thank you, Hettie. You're a good person, and very clever besides!"

Hettie's bright eyes beamed. "Is there anything else I can do for you? I think it's good you haven't said a word to the young master. Wouldn't he be thrilled to see your uncle upset and ill!"

Hettie could abide Matthew Pembroke no better than Jane, for he and his wife, Bridget, treated the servants with no respect whatsoever. Utter disregard was the friendliest gesture any of them could expect from Matthew and Bridget. If Lord Henry was not present, even the slightest mistake was severely punished.

"The captain sounds like a nice man," Hettie added as she straightened Jane's hair.

Jane went to the door with Hettie following her. "He will be staying until tomorrow, and it is good that he does. We have to take care of the burial and . . . but we will discuss everything else then."

With her quick, skillful fingers, Hettie had put her mistress back in order, and now she sprayed a hint of violet perfume over Jane.

"Enough now!" Jane slipped through the door, just managing to escape a second cloud of perfume, and ran back down to the ballroom.

Charles Devereaux seemed to have been waiting for her. He pounced on her immediately and led her to the dance floor.

"You promised me a waltz. And before you go disappearing into the snow again, I have decided to seize the moment!" He smiled disarmingly and whirled her elegantly among the other dancers. "Please forgive my impertinence, my lady, but I am surprised to find that such an enchanting woman has not yet tied the knot. No doubt you do not suffer from a lack of suitors."

Jane cleared her throat and avoided his eye. "My uncle is a very endearing man. He has never pressed me unduly in that regard."

"I imagine he enjoys your company and fears he will be robbed of that should you make up your mind to establish a family of your own. Isn't that rather too self-serving?"

Jane frowned. "Uncle Henry is my family, Mr. Devereaux, and I would never do anything to hurt him."

"Pardon me. I expressed myself clumsily. I will be in London until the end of the Season, when my business will require my return to India. Would you allow me, until then, to call on you?"

They had time for a final, vigorous turn around the dance floor before the music came to an end and the guests clapped politely.

Devereaux stood in front of Jane. "You have not given me an answer. Dare I hope? I do not appreciate being left hanging."

Jane recoiled from the businessman's hard eyes. "You are right not to. I'm the same. Please consider yourself relieved of any obligation toward me, Mr. Devereaux." Jane turned away forcefully and might well have stumbled had not the strong arms of Captain Wescott been there to catch her.

"There you are, Lady Jane! Devereaux, do you mind?" asked Wescott, although more for the sake of form, for it was clear he expected no reply.

The next dance was a slower waltz, a piece from Chopin, but Wescott danced no more than a few steps with Jane before he said, "I would like to talk to you."

She looked at him in surprise, then allowed him to lead her without further explanation through the ranks of chatting and laughing guests, whose cheeks were warmed by the champagne, the dancing, and the warmth of the ballroom, to the entrance hall. Several women stood fanning themselves for air and accepting refreshing drinks from their consorts.

"In there," said Jane, and turned in the direction of a small salon on the other side of the entrance hall.

Wescott swung the door behind them, giving them as much privacy as possible while, for the sake of etiquette, not closing it completely. A fire crackled in the fireplace and threw flickering shadows across the saffron-yellow damask wallpaper. The furniture and the paintings on the walls gave the room an air of the Orient.

Jane crossed to one of the paintings. It depicted a palace in Rajasthan and a procession of heavily adorned elephants. "We call this the Indian room." She touched the picture frame. "What did you want to tell me? Has it to do with the girl?"

Wescott shook his head almost imperceptibly and looked at the painting. "The painter caught the atmosphere well. The light in India, you know, is very different than it is here."

"I know. I lived there when I was young," Jane replied. "I remember the sun. It was wonderfully warm. And I rode on an elephant."

"How long were you there?" Wescott was standing beside her, and their shoulders were almost touching.

"My parents died when I was five. Cholera."

"You survived cholera as a child . . . a miracle. You were very lucky," Wescott said quietly.

"Probably," Jane whispered, feeling a deep, desperate sadness rising inside her as it had so often recently.

"You did survive."

"But for such a price."

"Lady Jane." He cleared his throat and looked at her.

Slowly, Jane turned to face him.

"I could not . . . well, earlier, before I followed you into the garden . . . I heard what you said to Lady Alison about marriage. And freedom." He fell silent and seemed to be searching for the right words.

Jane laughed bitterly. "We women have no freedom. You heard it! I cannot touch the fortune I have. My uncle is a wonderful man whom I love very much, but he is sick." She wrung her hands in despair. "He raised me. He gave me all the freedom I wanted, perhaps too much. But it is not all his fault. My parents were the same way. They did not draw distinctions and instead let me play with the local children . . . I know how things can be, and now I can't go back! Do you understand?"

Wescott looked at her for an endless moment before he spoke, and when he finally did, he spoke calmly, as if weighing every word. "I believe so, yes. And perhaps I am precisely the man to help you. I have no fortune, but I have a good name. My military career is at an end. The war in Crimea cost me much of my health." His face twisted bitterly. "This scar is just one of many."

Jane drew breath audibly. "Oh!"

But Wescott waved it off. "No cause for sympathy. Things are as they are. I have other talents and am looking for new duties. High social connections are certainly an advantage in such a search. You are a clever and practical woman. You proved that tonight. And you have a title and a fortune." He paused for a moment, and Jane waited for him to continue.

"Become my wife. I will give you your freedom. For you, it would mean no more than accompanying me to receptions from time to time and acting as the social framework for meetings with business contacts."

Jane stared at him in complete bewilderment. "How am I to understand that? You want my money?" She snorted. "I might as well marry Mr. Devereaux or some dowry hunter. They're all after my money, too! I have no illusions, Captain Wescott. At twenty-five, I am no longer the most desirable trophy on the market."

He shook his head. "No, you don't understand. I don't want your money. You can do or not do whatever you like with that. We can specify that contractually. I expect from you only what I have just described."

"Nothing more? No, um, marital obligations?" Jane plucked at her silk skirt.

His expression was again unreadable. "No. You would be completely free. As would I."

"I see." Confused, at a loss, she stood and looked at him. Never in her wildest dreams had she expected a proposal as unusual as this. "You don't want any heirs?"

"No. Unless you wish to have children? We could specify that as well. In case . . ."

But Jane shook her head vehemently. "No, no. Hmm. So our . . . contract would be limited to a business partnership?"

"No more."

"What line of business are you pursuing?"

"It is of a political nature."

"Do you plan to run for parliament?"

He hesitated for a moment. "No. But that's beside the point. I am an honest man, a man of my word."

"I don't know you! I know nothing about you at all!"

"Ask your uncle. He invited me. We know each other from the past." He did not smile, but his eyes were gentle.

"He's never mentioned you."

Wescott shrugged. "Perhaps you don't know everything about your uncle, or just as little as he knows about you."

Jane lowered her eyes, only to raise her head and look directly at him. "Are you trying to blackmail me?"

A jolt seemed to run through Wescott. His shoulders stiffened, and the look in his eyes grew hard and forbidding. "My lady, forget what I have just said to you. Blount, my valet, is making sure that no one enters the room where the dead girl is lying, and we can talk about the next steps to take tomorrow. A solution will be found, one your uncle . . ."

"Oh, now, don't act so affronted! Given the extraordinary circumstances and your unusual proposal, you can hardly say that my suspicion came out of thin air!" Jane hissed angrily.

A hint of a smile played on Wescott's lips, and he tilted his head slightly. "My apologies, my lady. In case you are considering my proposal, you should know that I am extremely sensitive when it comes to questions of honor."

She had touched a nerve. Beneath that hard exterior of military rigor and brusqueness was a vulnerable soul. And that made him human. She would probably regret it, but she trusted him. "How long will you be our guest?"

"I leave the day after tomorrow."

"Then you shall have my answer by then."

Jane heard the sound of steps and Alison's voice from the foyer. Wescott looked around and pointed to the door in the opposite wall. "I will go. Please don't worry, my lady."

He had just disappeared when the door from the foyer swung opened and Alison came in with her husband. They were accompanied by two more couples swinging their champagne glasses and obviously in a brilliant mood. Jane barely had time to pull herself together. She took a deep breath and put on a broad smile.

"Alison, darling. Where have you been? I've been looking for you! That dreadful Devereaux . . ." Jane looked past the heads of the guests. "He's not close by, is he?"

Lady Alison giggled. "No, he is not, and I must say he looked anything but happy after you danced with him. Tch, you really must tell me everything!" A strand of blond hair had escaped from Alison's artfully conceived coiffure, and she blew it out of her face. "What are you even doing here? You really should *not* be alone in here languishing in your memories. It's not healthy! No one should be sad, right, Thomas? Do say something!"

Lord Thomas took his tipsy wife's hand and lifted it to his lips. "It's late, and time we were going. Lord Henry seems rather tired. How are things with him, Jane?"

Jane saw with relief that the two couples merry on champagne were already weaving out of the salon. "Not so good, I fear. You're right. I'll go and see to him and make sure he gets to bed. When will we see each other again, Ally?"

"Oh, we're off to London tomorrow and won't be back for three or four weeks. That's right, isn't it, Thomas?" Lady Alison leaned heavily on the arm of her husband, who seemed not to mind at all as he looked lovingly at her.

Disappointed, Jane accompanied her friends out of the salon. She would have loved to have the chance to speak to Alison alone, but that was all but impossible now, and tomorrow her friend was traveling to London. In the end, though, no one could make this decision for her. It was her life that hung in the balance.

5.

It was well after midnight when Jane, in slippers and a dressing gown, made her way downstairs. She could not sleep and wanted to fetch a book from the library. When she saw light shining through the gap by the door, she quietly turned the knob and entered. She closed the door almost silently behind her and went toward the wing chair by the fireplace. The only sound was the sweep of her woolen dressing gown on the hardwood floor. A decanter of port stood on a table, and books were arranged in stacks around the chair. When she heard a grunt and saw the powerful body of a Great Dane stretched out on a Persian carpet, Jane, with some relief, stepped closer.

The Great Dane didn't even lift his head. He simply blinked at her and rolled onto his back. Jane crouched and scratched the magnificent gray dog on his belly.

"Jane? Is that you?" Her uncle's voice sounded sleepy.

"Yes. I didn't want to disturb you." She moved up beside the chair, laid her arm around her uncle's shoulders, and kissed him softly on his silver hair. "I couldn't sleep."

Lord Henry had on a deep-red velvet housecoat and comfortable slippers. Jane pulled up a leather seat cushion and settled herself at her uncle's feet. It was something she had done as a child, when her uncle had told her stories about India and her parents.

"Pour us a little port, my dear. The decanter's just there." He pointed to the table, an intricately wrought oriental piece.

"Are you allowed to? The doctor—" Jane objected, but her uncle clapped the book in his lap closed and gave a short, dry laugh.

"It makes no difference anymore. Let me have my little pleasures, and let us enjoy this moment of peace, just for us." Henry Pembroke, lord and peer and a close friend of Lord Melbourne before the prime minister's death, smiled mildly.

When he looked at his niece, his pale eyes were full of benevolence and love, and Jane had to keep a tight rein on her emotions to stop herself from bursting into tears. She hated to see her uncle as fragile as this. The evening had been more strenuous for him than he was willing to admit. The shadows around his eyes had a purple tinge, and his cheeks were noticeably sunken. But when he looked at her and smiled, he was radiant.

She poured the ruby-red port into two small glasses and handed one to her uncle.

"To you, my dear! The secret heart of the ball!" Henry Pembroke smiled and sipped at his glass.

"Oh?"

"It did not escape me that both Captain Wescott and Mr. Devereaux went to great pains to be close to you. Is there something you would like to tell me?"

Jane scratched the soft ears of the dog. "Well, Mr. Devereaux would certainly love to grace Rosewood Hall with his presence more often, but . . ."

"But? Could you fetch the humidor, please? Captain Wescott brought me some most excellent cigars." Lord Henry held his glass in his fingers and scrutinized the red shimmering liquid.

Jane stood again and crossed to a locked book cabinet. The key for the glass doors was hidden inside the base of a bronze sculpture. Hiding things had two purposes for her uncle: For one, it gave him a special pleasure. He also had good reason to keep his expensive cigars away from the staff and her venal cousin. They never talked about it, but Jane knew that profound differences separated Henry from his son. Matthew's jealousy of Jane was one reason father and son did not get along. His wife's spiteful nature was another.

Jane waited until her uncle, his eyes half-closed, drew on his cigar. The aromatic odor of the tobacco mixed with the smells of leather, paper, and burning wood. And of Rufus, Jane thought, casting a disapproving eye at the Great Dane. But the dog merely rolled onto his side.

"There is something about Mr. Devereaux that I can't abide."

"Did he try to make an advance on you?" Bluish rings of smoke rose toward the ceiling, and Lord Henry coughed a little.

"He tried, but I turned him down." Jane fumbled at the cords of her woolen gown. "Do you know Captain Wescott well, Uncle?"

Lord Henry looked at his cigar. "His father and I go back a long way. You wouldn't remember it—you were still a child—but we once visited the duke and his family."

"Really? How could I forget something like that!" Jane made an effort to find some memory of the visit, some image in her mind of Duke of St. Amand and the young David Wescott.

"It was just after you arrived here in England. St. Amand's Court was being rebuilt at the time. A beautiful estate south of Cambridge. You were particularly fond of the duck pond."

"Was the captain there?" asked Jane doubtfully.

"I don't remember exactly anymore, Jane, but I believe so. There were many children in the garden. What do you think of David Wescott?"

Surprised, she looked at her uncle, but he just continued to draw on his cigar, unconcerned. "He seems to be a man of honor."

Lord Henry nodded in agreement. "I know only a few men I would trust with my life, and Wescott is one of them. He has been through a very difficult time. I thought a soiree like tonight's would do him good, and . . ." He smiled. "And I hoped you would like him."

Jane's breath caught. Had she stepped into a well-set trap? Had Wescott perhaps arranged something with her uncle? She sat stiffly on her cushion and looked her uncle in the eye. "You hoped . . . ? Or have you already discussed the details of a marriage contract?" Her brown eyes sparkled furiously. "Wescott proposed to me! But you already knew that, didn't you?"

"What? No! Jane, my God, that makes me very happy! I mean, it's a surprise, and he never was a man to waste time, but . . ." Lord Henry coughed and had to drink something before he could say anything else. "It would make me happy to know that you are being cared for. Were I to pass away . . ."

"Don't say that, Uncle!" Jane's anger evaporated instantly.

Henry Pembroke sighed. "Things are what they are, my darling Jane, my daughter. I don't have much time left." He raised a placating hand and set down the cigar. "And I could make my peace with this life if I knew you were married."

He leaned forward and placed his left hand under his niece's chin. "You are well off, Jane. I have seen to it that you are financially secure, as a father ought to safeguard his daughter. You will never have to suffer any hardship, and even a husband could never have access to your entire fortune."

"But if I don't marry, there will always be a guardian," Jane whispered.

Henry sank back into his chair, his brow deeply furrowed. "Yes. That is the law. I can't do anything about that. Matthew would become your guardian. But he is your cousin, and you have known each other since you were both very small. He is not a bad man, Jane, as much as he likes to puff himself up."

"But Bridget is a beast!" Jane could not keep the words inside.

Her uncle rocked his head from side to side. "Unfortunately, Matthew made a genuinely bad choice there. But if you marry, Jane, your fortune will pass to you. Then you will have access to it without a guardian, and you know that Mulberry Park in Cornwall is part of that. You could move there. Your parents loved the place very much, and I have taken steps to ensure that it has been properly maintained."

"Oh, Uncle . . ." Jane laid her head on his knee.

He stroked her hair lovingly. "There are times I find it hard to believe how fast the time has flown. I still see the small, frightened girl with the sad eyes, looking at me with such accusation, such defiance, as only your father could. Jane, my angel, you brought sunshine into my life, and you too will be happy. Someday you will remember your old uncle, raise your glass of port, and say that I was right."

Jane smothered her tears in the velvet of Lord Henry's housecoat.

"Now, now. I'm still here, and I can still protect you. And what should I tell the young captain, should he ask for my permission?"

"Tell me what you know about him. How am I supposed to form any kind of judgment if I know nothing about the man?" Jane lamented through her tears.

Lord Henry cleared his throat and puffed on his cigar. "He has a good reputation, no debts as far as I know, and he has no notoriety as a gambler. He has fallen out with his father, however, but that carries little weight when it comes down to it; as the youngest son, he would inherit nothing regardless. His brother, Robert, will succeed to his father's title and lands." He thought for a moment in silence, and then went on. "I know practically nothing about the middle son, Lawrence. He studied theology or some such—something useless. And there are two sisters, one of whom is still unwed, from the duke's first marriage. Captain David Wescott is the only son from his second marriage. His mother died young. It was all very tragic, and the duke went into mourning for years. She was a real beauty, a Russian woman."

"Russian? Wasn't Wescott in the Crimean War?"

"That's right. That would be one of fate's ironies, wouldn't it? We didn't exactly cover ourselves with glory there." He swallowed a mouthful of his port.

"The captain was badly wounded and they repatriated him for that, didn't they?"

"A brave soldier, that's true. But there was something else . . . some sort of scandal that had to do with Lord Lucan. I can find out about that. Now, Lucan and his brother-in-law Cardigan have to answer before court for their failures on the Crimean Peninsula. The case is not over yet." Lord Henry was suddenly overcome by a fit of coughing, and Jane took the cigar out of his hand.

"You shouldn't be smoking! Where are your tablets?"

Her uncle flapped one arm helplessly toward the table and knocked the decanter onto the floor in the process. Rufus immediately leaped up and began barking.

It was a fraction of a second before the door flew open and Lord Henry's butler, Floyd, hurried in.

"You called, your lordship?" Floyd inquired, but more for the sake of form, for he took in the scene at a glance. Floyd had served his master for more than twenty years and was devoted to him. "Those cigars will be your death, my lord. Doctor Paterson expressly prohibited them."

Lord Henry struggled to catch his breath. Beads of sweat appeared on his forehead, and his face was ashen. Jane took hold of Rufus by the collar and pulled him aside to prevent him from injuring himself on the glass of the broken decanter.

"His medicine! Where is his medicine?" Jane cried desperately, as she managed to get the dog to lie down a safe distance away.

Floyd produced a small container from his coat pocket and took out a tablet, which he placed between Lord Henry's lips. "Try to swallow it, sir."

Jane fetched a jug of water standing on a credenza by the door and brought it to Floyd.

"That is good, my lady." Floyd gave his master a little water, then wiped his brow with a moist cloth. A few moments passed, then Lord Pembroke's breathing steadied and he slumped exhausted back into his chair.

Concerned, Jane looked to the butler. "He'll be all right, won't he?"

"Certainly, my lady. I will take him to bed and send for Doctor Paterson."

Lord Henry heard him and opened his eyes. In a hoarse voice he whispered, "Let the poor doctor sleep. Give me another tablet, then everyone can go to bed. Jane!"

She took hold of his hand and kneeled beside him. "Yes, Uncle?"

"Everything will be all right, my angel."

Jane slept restlessly. She tossed and turned, waking up repeatedly from nightmares, covered in sweat. In her dreams, the dead girl from the park pleaded for her help. Devereaux danced with Alison, who pulled free of his grasp and ran toward Jane. But Thomas stepped between them, and Wescott was suddenly standing in front of her, telling her that her uncle was dead.

After that last terrible dream, Jane decided she might as well get up. It was chilly in the bedroom, for the fire had burned down to a few dull embers. She stepped into her slippers, wrapped a plaid blanket around her shoulders, and went to the window. She had to breathe on the frosted pane several times to see outside. It was snowing! More snow meant more cold weather, more days she would have to spend inside. And then she recalled the dramatic events of the evening before.

"Hettie!" Jane wanted to take a hot bath and talk to Wescott about the girl before her uncle rose and got wind of the matter.

Her maid peeped through the door between their rooms. She was still tying her bonnet but already seemed wide awake and cheerful. "Good morning, ma'am. You're up early this morning."

Finished, Hettie swept into the room, pulled the curtains wide, and tied them back with cords attached beside the window. "Snowing again! If only spring would finally come. Oh, I was down below, and his lordship's butler told me about a strange man in the hothouse."

"That is Captain Wescott's valet. Hurry, I want to bathe and get dressed. Is the captain already up?"

"He was up and about very early and had his horse saddled. I don't believe he's back yet. Alma was going on about him." Hettie chatted on about the gossip among the servants, and Jane was amazed that anyone could pour out so many words so early in the morning.

"First tea, then the bath. And hurry, Hettie!"

An hour later, Jane, wearing a moss-green dress, stepped into the dining room, where breakfast had been set out. Her uncle was not yet out of bed. On the one hand, that made her feel relieved; on the other, it filled her with concern for the state of his health. She sat down and accepted a cup of tea. The table was covered with a huge variety of food, much of it from the previous evening's buffet. There was cold pheasant, mutton, baked and boiled ham, fried eggs and poached eggs, pickled beans and sardines, but Jane ignored it all and ate just toast and marmalade.

On days without visitors, Jane enjoyed a calm breakfast alone with her uncle. They would discuss the day ahead or chat about an article in the newspaper. Her uncle, against the grain of prevailing mores, had nothing against Jane knowing about the events of the day. Jane read the

Wiltshire Independent at the table. Her uncle usually read the *Wilts and Gloucester Standard* before getting out of bed.

The maid handling the tea service almost dropped a teacup when the door flew open and Matthew and his wife paraded in. Bridget, pregnant with her third child, waddled like a duck, and her eyes narrowed to slits when she saw Jane. Her sharp nose and small chin pointed forward. She had pasty white skin and dull brown hair. But what nature had denied her in physical endowments, it made up for in spitefulness and nagging. Their two children were away visiting Bridget's parents, and no one who had had the pleasure of dealing with the bad-mannered brats was unhappy at their absence.

"Good morning, Matthew, Bridget," said Jane politely, but without folding her newspaper.

Daisy, the housemaid, served steaming tea and murmured the obligatory "good morning" nervously.

Bridget sank wheezing onto a chair. "The tea is already cold. Take the pot and brew some fresh."

The girl made an unhappy face and lifted the teapot. "Pardon, madam, but it is boiling hot. I have just brought it up."

"I did not ask for your opinion, you oaf! Do what you are bidden and hold your tongue! Have I made myself clear?"

"Yes, madam," mumbled the maid, and took the pot away again.

"That was absolutely unnecessary, Bridget. The tea is hot!" said Jane, gesturing at the steam rising off it.

Matthew, meanwhile, walked around the table. He filled his plate with meat and beans and flicked at Jane's newspaper. "Give me that. That's nothing for a lady!"

"Pfff, as if she was one!" Bridget goaded, placing a sardine on her plate. "Where are the servants this morning? Lord, one has to do everything oneself!"

With exaggerated slowness, Jane folded the newspaper and set it beside her plate. "My guess would be that they are all down below clearing up the ballroom, Bridget dear."

Matthew reached across the table and took the newspaper. It was hard to imagine a father and son less alike than Lord Henry and Matthew. Matthew was shorter than his father and had stringy light-brown hair, a narrow, hawkish nose, and a receding chin. Lines had formed around his small mouth, lines that said more about his intemperate, impulsive character than any particular intelligence. He had studied various subjects at Oxford but left without graduating. And he loathed life in the country. He had no feeling whatsoever for his father's love of botany and made no secret of the fact that he considered the purchase of expensive orchids to be a waste of money. Even as a child, Jane had decided for herself that her uncle had raised another man's son.

"Servants are not born into the lower classes without reason," said Bridget, spoiling for a fight and staring at Jane.

Daisy returned with a fresh pot of tea, but Bridget ignored the girl.

"One is not born a servant. One is born a human being. Even you should have realized that by now." Before she had finished her sentence, Jane regretted her imprudence. Bridget's riposte was not long in coming.

"Easy for you to say, Jane! All you ever think about is your own pleasure. Here I am about to have my third child, and I'm three years younger than you! A woman's duty is to look after her husband, her home, and her children." Bridget placed one hand on the curve of her belly and leaned forward slightly. "Don't think for a moment that you can go on living as you have when your uncle is dead, Jane! Some things are going to change around here for you!"

The maid at the sideboard stiffened, then, with shaking hands, set more bread to toast.

"You won't even keep your rooms. An old maid does not need her own salon!" Bridget sputtered.

That seemed to be too much even for Matthew. Without looking up from his newspaper, he said, "Shut up, Bridget! Show some respect."

"I've lost my appetite. Please excuse me." With tears of rage and despair welling in her eyes, Jane stood up. She lifted her chin, took a deep breath, and looked over her cousin's head to the door, which swung open just at that moment.

When she saw Captain Wescott, a spark of hope kindled inside her. She would not let Bridget win in the end . . .

6.

Wescott's boots were still caked with dirt. He seemed to have come directly to the dining room from his errand. His dark hair, somewhat ruffled, fell over the scarf he wore outside his riding jacket. Whatever had happened, his face revealed nothing, and his dark eyes scanned those present only fleetingly before settling on Jane. "Good morning. Please excuse me for having to leave again immediately, but . . . Lady Jane . . ."

On her way out, Jane saw Bridget raise her teacup affectedly and heard her sneer, "What an uncouth man! Comes barging in here . . . it's high time you taught the people here some manners . . ."

Captain Wescott closed the door behind Jane and touched her arm. "You seem upset. Was there some trouble just now? Not because of the dead girl, I hope? Blount let nobody in, though they might well have wanted to lynch him for that."

"Just the usual." Jane managed a smile. "Who tried to get past your valet? Has my uncle heard anything?"

Wescott shook his head. "Not yet. I've just been to the village and spoken to the constable there."

"Oh?" Suddenly alert, she looked at him and followed him down the stairs.

Fearnham, the village, was no more than a collection of houses around a tiny church. Her uncle's estate was situated in Wiltshire, close to the Hampshire border. Salisbury lay a day's ride west and Southampton to the southeast. On Sundays, she and her uncle normally attended the service in the small parish church, and Lord Henry was popular not only for his generous donations. His farming tenants appreciated his willingness to listen to their travails and concerns. Jane thought often that all of this would change for the worse once Matthew became the new master of Rosewood.

Outside the dining room, the entrance hall was being swept and mopped, the carpets rolled up and set aside for beating, and the housemaids and servants were carrying silverware and dishes out of the ballroom under the watchful eye of the master's butler, Floyd. Seeing Jane and Wescott, he stopped what he was doing and bowed his head.

"Good morning, my lady."

Floyd stood very straight in a flawless black suit. He seemed to have something urgent on his mind.

"Good morning, Floyd. How is my uncle?" Jane asked.

"Better. The crisis has passed, but any further excitement should be avoided." The gray-haired man took a deep breath. "Which is why I would like to ask you about something." He glanced nervously at Captain Wescott.

"Please speak freely, Floyd," Jane encouraged him.

"Well, the captain's valet won't let anyone into the hothouse. Naturally, this is causing all kinds of speculation. Up to now . . ." Floyd looked unhappily from Wescott to Jane.

"There was an incident yesterday evening, and Captain Wescott was good enough to help me to . . ." Now it was Jane's turn to cast an inquiring glance at Wescott.

The captain provided a brief explanation to Floyd. "With the constable's consent, the girl will be brought to Fearnham and laid out there. The coffin has been ordered, and she will be given a pauper's grave."

Another servant, a young, good-looking man with intelligent but, Jane felt, rather calculating eyes, was standing just two paces from them holding a porcelain bowl in his hands.

Floyd's eyes grew wider with every word, and only once Wescott was finished did he notice the servant. "Why are you standing around here, Milton? Go and see Miss Gibbs and tell her I am busy and that she is to take over here. Sir, my lady." The butler looked around nervously. "Who is the girl of whom you speak? No one from the house seems to be missing, but I could . . ."

"Come with us," said the captain.

Jane and Floyd followed Captain Wescott into the conservatory. The butler kept turning back, and Jane heard him murmur, "I hope that Milton did not hear anything."

"Why? What's the matter with him?" Jane had never paid much attention to the man, who mainly attended Matthew. She clicked her tongue. "You think he'll go running to my cousin, don't you?"

"I'm afraid so, my lady," he said grimly.

Both of them knew what that meant, but they were already on their way through the hothouse, where they found the steadfast Blount at the door of the room where the dead girl lay.

The man still had on the brown suit from the evening before, but he did not seem tired. If anything, he seemed invigorated. "Nothing special to report, sir, other than that one of the servants was here and wanted to question me. He tried to get past." Blount grinned.

"Thank you, Blount!" Wescott clapped his valet on the shoulder and pushed the door open.

"Come inside, Floyd," said Jane. "Perhaps you know the girl, although I think that is unlikely." Jane let the butler go ahead, and Floyd crossed himself reverently at the sight of the dead girl.

Her hands were folded on her chest, and the shawl and blanket so arranged that only her face could be seen. Jane looked gratefully at Wescott, but he was watching the butler.

"Poor child. No, I don't know her. She's not someone I've seen here." Floyd looked up.

"I found her in the park last night in a sorry state. She was coughing her lungs out and died here just a few minutes later. Hettie says it could be a distant cousin of hers, someone she hasn't seen for years. It's possible. Her name is Rosie, she has no other relatives, and it seems she ran away from a bad situation." Jane cleared her throat and hoped the butler would swallow the white lie.

Floyd nodded, his expression serious and understanding. He looked first at Jane, then Wescott. "That must be it. That was very wise of you, my lady."

That was all he managed to say, for someone started shouting outside the door, and Jane heard the sounds of a scuffle and the smashing of glass and porcelain. Then a heavy wooden shelf crashed to the floor, and Blount shouted, "Captain!"

The door flew open and Matthew, his face bright red, barged in, closely followed by Milton. Matthew held a pistol in his right hand and was pointing it at Wescott. "What do you think you're doing? You are a guest in my house, and you dare conceal a crime behind my back? What is going on here? I demand an answer, on the spot!"

Jane leaned back against the table where the girl's book still lay. With presence of mind, she concealed the small volume in a fold of her skirts. "Everything is under control, Matthew. You don't need to storm in here and make such a commotion! And lower the damned pistol!"

"No one is trying to hide anything. Perhaps we could briefly acquaint you with the circumstances?" said Captain Wescott, his voice calm and clearly accustomed to giving orders. He was taller and more powerful than Matthew, and he radiated a natural authority.

As if it were the least he could do, Matthew lowered his weapon, but he seemed to sense an opportunity to finally act like the master of the house. "What pack of lies are you going to try to sell me? It's perfectly clear what happened here. You had your fun with the girl and went too far."

Jane saw with trepidation the unbridled fury that flared in Wescott's eyes.

"Stop it, Matthew!" Jane screamed at her cousin.

"Watch what you say, sir." Wescott's voice had lowered to a deep growl, and every muscle in his body seemed tensed, like a predatory cat about to pounce.

"Are you threatening me? Milton! You heard it! I've been threatened! And you, Jane, what are you even doing here, alone in the hothouse with this captain nobody knows? Not that it matters . . . nothing good was ever expected of you." Matthew's voice dripped with scorn and contempt.

"Captain Wescott is a better man than you will ever be. He is a man of honor and—" She paused for a barely perceptible moment. "And my fiancé."

"Ha!" Matthew spat derisively, but at the same time he looked confused. He stumbled back against the open door.

"What the devil is going on here?" thundered Lord Henry's voice from behind Matthew, who turned and was just able to catch himself on the door frame.

Jane silently cursed her self-serving cousin. With his ill-tempered outburst, he had brought about precisely what Jane had been hoping to avoid. Hardly had Jane caught sight of her uncle when she felt a painful stab in her belly. Lord Henry stood tall and impressive, sternly taking in the situation, but his face was marked by tension and fatigue.

• • •

A week after that extraordinary morning in Rosewood Hall, things had once more calmed down. For the time being known as Hettie's cousin, Rosie Gray, the unknown dead girl had found her final resting place in the village cemetery in Fearnham. Jane had presented the possible relationship to her lady's maid with the greatest reserve, to avoid anyone accusing her of deliberately lying later. The chances of clarifying Rosie's true identity were poor at best. Neither the girl's clothes nor a description that the constable had forwarded to other stations in the region brought any results. The girl had appeared out of nowhere, and apparently no one missed her.

February was coming to an end, and the next day, the first of March, would bring with it the hope of spring. Jane went for a walk with Rufus through the garden, where snow was still to be found in patches of shade. *One day*, she thought, *could change an entire life*. She could not forget the face of the girl, her delicate, damaged body, or her final request.

"Mary," Jane murmured into the midday air. It was still chilly, but the bitterness had gone out of the cold, and with it the winter.

The Great Dane turned its head, but Jane scratched his back. "Go on, then. Go for a run, Rufus. I'm just talking to myself."

She turned up the fur collar of her long coat and climbed a stone stairway up to the artificial ruins of a small temple. They were laid out picturesquely and situated exactly where strollers could stand and let their eyes roam out over the small river that wound through the landscape at the base of the hill. A carefully tended wood with exotic trees from every continent lay on the far side of the stream. Beyond that lay the village. Jane let her mind follow that line, eventually coming to Salisbury with its train station.

After the funeral for Rosie, Wescott had left on the train for London. The new railway line made the connection possible, and was far more comfortable than traveling by coach. Jane pushed her hands deep into the pockets of her coat and balled them into fists. She was now officially engaged to Captain Wescott. The news had made her uncle happy, and that made all the difference to Jane, for his health was deteriorating daily. He ought to leave the world with the knowledge that she had found a new home at the side of a respectable man. Everything else would work out.

Cousin Matthew, Lord Henry's own son, had puffed himself up and painted Jane as a liar. His wife, Matthew's equal in maliciousness, took great delight in insinuating that Jane was having an affair with Wescott. Jane could well imagine the gossip at the tea parties Bridget had begun hosting, and had immediately written a letter to Lady Alison to acquaint her with the situation. Jane kept the form of Wescott's proposal to herself. That was a matter between herself and Wescott, no one else. In less than a month, she would be his wife. Her uncle had insisted on the unusually short engagement, which only confirmed to Jane the validity of her fears for his health.

The day of her wedding would be a day of departure and of pain. Jane could not hold back her tears any longer, and leaned against one of the cold, white pillars of the artificial temple. Rosewood Hall would no longer be her home, but it made no difference: without her uncle, it would lose its soul.

Her cheerless thoughts were interrupted by Hettie, who came running breathlessly across the lawn and stopped at the bottom of the steps. "Ma'am, shouldn't we be going? The horses are already harnessed."

Rufus came galloping excitedly around a bush. He did not see the hare zigzagging away as fast as it could, but instead turned with interest to Hettie.

"Don't you jump up on me, you calf!" Hettie said, fending off the dog and holding her hands protectively in front of the lovely blue coat Jane had given her for Christmas. Rufus barked and trotted away.

Jane wiped her eyes with the back of her hand and came down from her lookout. She had ordered the coach to go into the village. Her uncle didn't want her hovering around him all the time and frequently hid himself away in his study. A local lawyer had been in with him since the early hours of the morning, helping him sort out his affairs. Jane only had to think about it and the tears began to blur her vision again.

"Oh, ma'am, please don't cry. I can't bear it when you're sad." Hettie fished in her bag for a handkerchief.

"It's all right, Hettie, thank you." Jane cleared her throat and whistled for Rufus. "We're going into the village to see if we can find out anything about Rosie."

"My cousin," said Hettie unnecessarily, giving her mistress a conspiratorial smile.

"We should mention the matter as little as possible. It's not like we want to lie deliberately."

"No, of course not. The poor thing's got a lovely grave beneath the lilacs. When it gets warm, the flowers there bloom a pretty white, and smell sweet." A gust of wind shook the ties on Hettie's bonnet, a meager covering, and Jane shivered.

Jane took great pleasure in giving Hettie items of clothing that Hettie herself could not afford. It rested on her, finally, if her lady's maid was not properly outfitted, but she mainly just enjoyed spoiling Hettie. The girl had grown up in poverty, but never complained about her background and always spoke warmly about her family in Cornwall. It was standard practice not to employ servants from the local area. Often enough, young girls entering domestic service for the first time were plagued by homesickness and simply ran away. If their parents lived close by, the risk of them absconding was higher. Moreover, separating the place of work from relatives by at least thirty miles made communication—and therefore gossip—more difficult. Before Rosie died, Jane had not been as aware of the mechanisms that controlled the lives of masters and servants, and she wondered if the time had come to rethink some things.

The coachman stood beside the team of horses and was chatting with one of the servants, the man Jane now knew to be Milton. The moment Milton saw her, however, he disappeared, and the coachman opened the door of the carriage for Jane.

"Did you see that, Hettie?" said Jane to her maid in a low voice. "I can't suffer that Milton much longer. He's always showing up where he ought not be. He seems to be spying on me. I'll bet a shilling he asked the driver where we're off to." Rufus was sniffing at the coach, and Jane shooed him back to the house before climbing inside.

"Then let's ask him!" Hettie whispered, and turned to the driver. "What did Milton want from you? Doesn't he have anything to do?"

The driver, a portly man with graying hair, scratched his scalp beneath his hat and mumbled between gappy teeth: "Nothing to do with you. Keep your nose out of men's business, darling."

With that, he slammed the door and swung himself up onto the box seat.

Hettie sat down opposite her mistress and pulled a face. "Rude man!"

"Might be, but might not be. Perhaps I'm seeing Matthew's allies everywhere." Jane sighed and looked out the window. From Rosewood Hall, it was a quarter-hour ride by horse or coach out to the road into Fearnham.

The Lord of Pembroke was a rich man. His estates lay in what, for Jane, was one of the most beautiful parts of England. The earth was fertile, and the gently rolling green hills were covered with forests that teemed with game. Matthew, it seemed, could wait no longer to come into his inheritance, and already saw himself as the master of Rosewood Hall. And Jane feared that her cousin would not settle only for that to which he was entitled.

7.

Mary

Mary had already been sitting in the tiny attic for three days. In winter, when the icy winds blew and the ice crept from the skylight out along the walls, those imprisoned here sometimes came down with a burning fever and cough that would not let up. After seven days of solitary confinement in there, weaker children were known to have died.

"But I'm not weak. I'm not! You won't get me," Mary murmured to herself.

Master Ledford had kept her shut inside the attic ever since Tim had fled. She would only be let out when she told them how he and his friends had accomplished their escape and where they had gone. No one believed that she didn't know.

She squatted on the sack of straw that served as both bed and seat, the scratchy woolen blanket pulled around her tightly. She leaned her back against the wooden wall and looked up at the ceiling. Through the skylight, she could see the night was clear and full of stars. Polly had known the names of the constellations. Mary sobbed. She missed her best friend terribly. She had been brought to the orphanage seven years earlier with her brother. Her father had already been dead a long time. Her mother worked in a textile factory until the coughing grew steadily worse. In the end, all she did was spit blood and fight just to breathe. It was horrible, having to stand by and watch when her mother sat up suddenly in bed, clutching at her throat and gasping like a dying fish. And then she simply fell back, eyes open, and never moved again. At that moment, she looked more peaceful than she ever had before.

Tim had covered their mother with a sheet and drummed it into his sister not to say a word to their neighbors, or both of them would be taken away. He was a good brother, but just six years old. How was a six-year-old supposed to feed his little sister and a baby? He had pillaged the neighbors' garbage, stolen, and begged. But the baby needed milk and soon grew weaker and weaker. Finally all she did was whimper and make small smacking sounds. *Like a little bird*, thought Mary, and cried.

It was her fault that the baby had died. She had promised her mother that she would look after the baby. In desperation, she had given the child her finger to suck on. When the little girl died, she laid her beside their dead mother. That same evening, the landlady had come to collect the rent. She saw immediately what had happened and called the police. Mother and the baby were thrown into a pauper's grave, and the people around them talked in whispers about her and Tim as the children of the devil.

Then the man who had fathered the baby appeared. All she could remember of him were his sideburns and the smell of tobacco that clung to his clothes. He paid off the landlady, who had wanted to sell the children to recover the rent she was owed. Then he sat Mary and her brother in a coach. When, after a long journey, she awoke, Master Ledford lifted her out of the coach and took her into the orphanage. She had been there ever since.

Mary looked up through her tears. A bat flitted over the garret window, a tiny, dark shadow. When she and Tim first arrived, the people at the orphanage had immediately separated them. That was what had hurt the most. She had been so alone, alone and frightened.

Polly was the same age as Tim, a beautiful blond angel. At the start, Polly had had little time for the small girl who followed her wherever she went and said nothing. The other girls laughed and made fun of Mary, but she stayed at Polly's side staunchly until Polly gave in and held out her hand to her. From that moment on, they had been inseparable.

In the dormitory, their beds stood side by side, and when the light was put out, Mary crept across and slid under the coverlet with Polly and snuggled close to her. Polly had whispered stories in her ear, stories about princesses and talking animals, about dragons and evil wizards. When Mary learned to read, together they read the books that Mr. Gaunt lent them. Polidori's *The Vampyre* had been Polly's favorite, and the teacher had given it to her when she left.

Polly had known that the time had come for her to leave. She was pretty and had a school education, so she got the chance to work in a grand house. Master Ledford had no doubt received a decent sum for Polly, but he said that raising, clothing, and feeding the children cost him a lot of money. It was only right and proper that he be reimbursed for that when they left.

Polly had been put in a coach, and then she disappeared. She had promised to write, but in the eight months that she had been gone, Mary had not heard so much as a word from her. Something was wrong, Mary was certain. But the moment she asked the master about Polly, he turned on her angrily and shouted that the girl was doing well, too well, in fact! It was always like that, he said. The moment the bird flew the nest, the past was forgotten. Mary should just get used to it.

A soft scratch at the door startled her out of her thoughts. "Is that you, Fiona?"

"Yeah. Come 'ere. I'm pushing some cheese and bacon under the door."

Mary jumped up immediately and kneeled by the door, under which, one after the other, slices of cheese and—a wonder!—a piece of bacon appeared. Mary greedily stuffed the food in her mouth. All they'd fed her since locking her in there was water and dry bread.

"That'll make you thirsty," Fiona whispered, "but I couldn't steal anything else."

"Mmm, it's all right. Thank you, thank you!" Mary murmured, and swallowed the delicious morsels.

"Psst, 'ush for a second!" Fiona hissed.

Mary held still and listened to the night-shrouded house. They were in the girls' building, with the classrooms and workshops on the ground floor and the dormitories upstairs. There were two large dormitories and two smaller ones, the sisters' room, a bathroom, and a laundry. Mary's cell was set above one of the smaller dormitories, from which light shone up between the floorboards. Now, she could make out muffled voices and groaning, then a smothered cry.

"The men are here. You're lucky you don't have breasts, Fiona," Mary whispered.

"Is that Sister Susan?"

"She takes the money and decides whose turn it is."

"Jeez, were you ever . . . ?"

"No. Nor Polly. They only take the ones who aren't supposed to go into service."

"It's filth. It's a 'orehouse, is what it is. I know, Mary. I lived in one once."

"I thought . . ."

"That I lived on the street the 'ole time? No, my mother's on the game, but she never forced me to be. I joined up with the kids on the streets and learned to pick pockets. That's useful to know." Fiona smothered a giggle behind her hand. The girls heard a thumping on the stairs, and Fiona gathered up her skirt. "Someone's coming. I 'ave to go. Tomorrow, Mary!"

Mary hurriedly jumped onto her sack of straw and pulled the blanket over her. When the door swung open and Master Ledford shone a lamp in her face, she squinted sleepily.

"Well. Thought it over, have you?"

"What do you mean?" she mumbled, rising to a crouch and pulling the blanket around her.

His hand swung around hard and hit her on the side of her head. Mary cried out in pain. Tears came instantly, and she slumped onto her side. Her cheek burned, but her ear hurt like it never had before.

"Stop being contrary! Talk! Am I supposed to beat the words out of you one at a time? Where's your damned brother? I saw you talking with him!" Master Ledford bawled.

In the flickering lamplight, his face, contorted with rage, was a diabolical sight.

But the pain in her ear was so overwhelming that Mary forgot her fear of her tormentor and rolled back and forth, wailing. It wasn't long before Sister Susan was there, too.

"What's going on here?"

"A little clip on the ear and look at her! She stays up here until she's had time to think about it!" the master barked, and stamped away.

The sister looked at Mary doubtfully. "Let me see that ear."

"No, no, it hurts so much!" Mary pressed her hand to her ear and felt the warm liquid. "It's bleeding!"

Sister Susan's forbidding expression softened. "Stand up! Mary, try to stand up."

When Mary tried to push herself up from the straw sack, she immediately grew dizzy, stumbled forward, then sank back.

"Lie down again!" Sister Susan ordered, then left. In a few minutes, she returned with her medical bag. First, she took out a bottle of laudanum and gave Mary two spoons of the numbing liquid. Then she swabbed the blood from her ear, dripped some liquid onto a piece of gauze, and stuffed it into the ear canal.

"I'll talk to the master. We'll put you back in your bed tomorrow. Why do you have to be so stubborn? Just tell him what he wants to know."

But Mary, her eyes closed, just wailed, "But I don't know, I don't know! Tim is just gone. He left me here alone."

There was a roaring in her head and the pain swelled again, but the laudanum began to take effect, sending her sliding into a bearable half sleep.

8.

Fearnham, County Wiltshire, February 29, 1860

The small parish church huddled beneath the protective branches of a mighty chestnut tree. In summer, the villagers gathered beneath the broad leaves offered by the old tree. Now, the bare branches presented a more sobering sight, and the plain little house of prayer looked unprotected. In the lee of the church stood the parsonage, built, like the church itself, from gray stone. Enclosed by a low wall was a garden, where the vicar's housekeeper was picking herbs.

"Dora!" Jane called and waved to the stout woman, who straightened up slowly and painfully.

"Lady Jane! How nice of you to drop by. Come in, the vicar's here." Dora trudged heavily through the snow and waited for Jane at the front door.

"How is your back, Dora?" Jane asked sympathetically.

The housekeeper, who had seen a lot in her fifty years, dismissed the question with a wave. "It pinches, and my legs hurt sometimes, but

I can't complain. I've got a roof over my head, and you could not ask for a better master than the vicar."

The woman made her way down the narrow corridor with practiced ease until she reached the roomy kitchen. Jane had drunk tea there many times with her uncle and the parish priest after the Sunday service.

"I've just made some tea. Hettie, give us a hand. There's some cake, but watch out for your nice coat." Dora, with a slightly waddling gait, the legacy of her considerable weight, went to the door and called, "Vicar, we've got company! Lady Jane is here!"

Jane unbuttoned her coat and sat on the proffered chair. "I don't mean to disturb you, Dora, but I can't stop thinking about the poor girl we laid to rest here so recently."

Dora prodded at the coals in the stove, making the fire flare. Her cheeks were red when she looked up again. Using a potholder, she lifted the cast-iron teapot from the stove. "A sorry story. Such a lost soul. What must she have gone through before she came here?"

While Hettie set a milk jug and plate of fruitcake on the table, Dora poured the strong, dark tea into four cups. Her graying hair was covered with a white bonnet, its ruffled brim bouncing with every movement. "There are so many girls who run away. My sister told me that another one's run off from Luton House. You know that's close to Exeter, my lady."

Jane nodded and accepted the tea gratefully. Coat and gloves could not keep out the cold, which had settled into the tight folds of her clothes. "Luton House? Is that a workhouse?"

The conditions in the so-called poorhouses or workhouses—little more than labor camps for the poorest of the poor—were notoriously appalling. Those who sought refuge there usually did so only as a last resort. They were referred to as inmates and treated like prisoners. Children, men, and women, all of them, without distinction, had to work for starvation wages. Most of their work was in manufacturing textiles. An eleven-hour day was the norm, with perhaps half a Saturday free and Christmas. Poor nutrition, cold, and abuse led to a high level of disease and mortality. Among the general populace, the workhouses were often compared to purgatory. Jane had never visited such a house, for her uncle had wanted to spare her having to face such misery.

The vicar, Herbert Smith, a slim man with a fringe of silver hair and friendly eyes behind round spectacles, entered the room and gave Jane a slight bow. "What an honor, my lady, to have you pay us a visit. Hettie, my dear, you look so full of life! Who would ever remember that skinny girl from Cornwall climbing out of the mail coach, so shy she spoke to no one?"

Hettie reddened slightly. "Oh, Vicar, that was a very long time ago."

"Did I hear someone mention Luton House?" the vicar asked, and sipped the tea that Dora pushed over to him. His black suit was clean, although the sleeves were worn and the collar frayed. Fearnham was one of those small village congregations that survived on contributions from local residents and the generosity of the patron. Under Matthew's patronage, Jane feared, the vicar could hardly count on any economic improvement.

"It is about the girl, Vicar. I am still thinking about her. Hettie believes she might have been her cousin, but she is not certain. What if she was a girl who ran away from a workhouse?" Jane asked, taking a small piece of cake. She sampled it and raised her forefinger approvingly. "It's wonderful, Dora!"

The housekeeper beamed and encouraged Jane to take another piece, but Jane thanked her and declined.

"It's difficult, my lady. The constable in Whiteparish went to some trouble. He telegraphed every police station in the district. You really can't do much more than that, unless you're prepared to ask every single person for ten miles around. She could have run away from almost anywhere." The vicar broke off a piece of cake, thought for a moment before popping it into his mouth, and said, "It happens all too often, I'm afraid, that children run away from homes and institutions like the Brentwood School."

Jane nodded. The scandal surrounding the Brentwood School in Essex was still fresh in her memory. "That was terrible!"

"What happened there, ma'am?" Hettie inquired.

Dora, puttering away at the stove, snapped disdainfully, "That's not something a decent young thing needs to know anything about."

"Well, I guess I'll just ask someone else," Hettie grumbled.

With a smile, Jane said, "Would you tell her about it, Vicar?"

The priest, well liked for his entertaining Sunday services, didn't need to be asked twice. He stroked his bushy sideburns and began, "It is sad enough that those in charge of such places repeatedly fail in their duties and betray the faith of those entrusted to them. Some people are simply too weak, and not up to the demands of the task. Caring for young, hungry, neglected children is a challenge each and every day. But . . ." Vicar Smith paused dramatically. "They have chosen the task, and they should complete it in a way that would please God. Now, without getting carried away with a sermon, I'll get to the school at Brentwood. The institution is both a home and a school for orphans, and was led by a very strict mistress. Punishment for disobedient children was always physical, and consistently more violent than anywhere else. Worst of all, apparently, was the nurse. I believe her name was Elizabeth Gillespie, yes . . ."

Mesmerized, Hettie listened to the vicar's tale. He took pleasure in building up the tension for her. "Miss Gillespie beat the children with a ruler, and black eyes and broken bones were an everyday occurrence. One day, a young girl fell down the stairs in the home and suffered such serious injuries that she had to be taken to an outside hospital. It was this 'accident' that led to the revelation that the girl had been pushed by Sister Gillespie!"

"No! The nurse did that?" Hettie cried in horror.

"It gets worse," the vicar continued in a grim tone. "The girl only dared to talk about the conditions at Brentwood once she was in the hospital. She was asked why no one complained about the beatings. All she said was that the girls knew that if the men went away, it would get even worse, so they held their tongues and put up with it."

"'The men'?" Hettie opened her eyes wide in confusion.

"It means the poor girls were rented out as prostitutes by Miss Gillespie, and that being a prostitute seemed more bearable to them than the beatings and abuse handed out by the sister," Jane explained, brushing some nonexistent crumbs from her coat.

Dora set the kettle down on the iron stovetop with a loud clank. "Now that's enough! Poor Hettie will have it hard enough tonight, trying to sleep. Brentwood was an exception. And that Miss Gillespie was a devil through and through. Something like that doesn't happen every day."

The vicar tugged at the hairs of his beard. "One would think so, yes. And we hope it's true, dear Dora. But there are also jobs from which the girls run away. Some of them are simply homesick."

Although Jane knew very well that this was not the case with Rosie, she only said, "Maids are also beaten by bad masters. Vicar, is there a house in your parish where that might be the case?"

"If there were, I would not be permitted to speak ill of it. But I honestly have no knowledge of such a situation. The usual small incidents, that goes without saying, but nothing particularly outrageous," the vicar assured her.

Jane realized that she would find no useful information here, and soon said a polite good-bye. With Hettie at her side, she walked down the main street of the village and, on the spur of the moment, stepped into the shop of the seamstress, Verna Morris.

V. Morris stood in curving letters on a sign above the shop, and Jane had often wondered why this elegant woman was here in remote, provincial Fearnham. The melodic tinkle of the bell on the door announced her entry.

Hettie sighed happily. "Isn't this pretty? I wish I had a shop like this!"

She ran her fingers over the bolts of fabric that lay on a long cutting table. On the shelves against the walls, all kinds of fabric were stored, and the choice quality of the material never ceased to amaze Jane. There were rolls of silk, linen, and expensive blended fabrics, the kinds one might find at an exclusive tailor in London. But there was simpler broadcloth as well, for the rural population could only rarely afford anything fancy.

"Be with you in a moment!" the seamstress called from the back room.

Jane examined a cream-colored silk cloth that would be suitable for a wedding dress, and she looked up when Mrs. Morris hurried out from behind the counter in a rush of skirts.

"Oh, my lady! What an honor! Is there anything in particular I can show you, or have you already found something special?"

Verna Morris was very thin and in her late forties. Her face was striking, with high cheekbones and slightly angular green eyes. She had dark hair parted in the middle and pinned at the back of her neck. In the bloom of her youth she must have been beautiful, and there were a great many rumors about her past.

Although Jane was happy to buy cloth in Mrs. Morris's store, she could never shake off the feeling that the woman looked down on her. But that might have just been the pride of a woman who had once occupied a better position. Jane smiled. "I'm looking for something for a wedding dress. But please keep that to yourself. No one knows about it, and that's how it should remain."

Verna looked at her warmly. "I'm happy for you. No need to worry, though. I keep my customers' confessions to myself."

Hettie giggled behind her hand and looked at a hat.

"That cloth would certainly be suitable. I also have other qualities in that color. Would you like to take a look? When would you be needing the dress?"

"In four weeks, almost," said Jane softly.

If the unusually short notice surprised Verna, she did not let it show. "That is certainly manageable. I have a new assistant, and she has turned out to be a real stroke of luck."

While Verna rolled out one length of cloth after another, Jane was painfully aware that the big day was drawing inevitably closer. "Mrs. Morris, no doubt you have heard about the unfortunate girl who was found in the park out at Rosewood Hall?"

The question was rhetorical. Everyone in Fearnham knew about the incident, of course.

Verna ran her hand over a length of silk brocade from Milan. "Oh, certainly. It was very good of you to give the girl a decent burial."

"Christian duty. But I can't help wondering where the poor creature came from, where she spent her nights. Have you heard anything? Have any of the farmers mentioned her sleeping in a barn? There are so many possibilities, and the people would certainly have talked about it. Perhaps not with you directly, but . . ." Jane left the question hanging in the air.

"This would be wonderful for the top, wouldn't it?" Verna held the silk brocade up to the light. "Just around the neck, and we'll use white silk for the rest. Unless . . ."

Ever since Queen Victoria's wedding, white wedding dresses had been in vogue, although only very well-off families could afford the luxury. Others chose a more subdued, less sensitive color, or had the dress dyed after the wedding to hide any stains that might appear.

"White like the Queen . . . no, I prefer a cream shade." The circumstances of her marriage were so unromantic that a white dress would be like putting a crown on the whole farce. "Do the people talk about the girl?" Jane pressed, and pointed to another roll of cloth.

The muscles of Verna's thin neck twitched, then she rolled out the raw silk. "Also an excellent choice, my lady. Yes, a person should stay true to one's own style. And . . . yes, a lot is being said. No one really knows anything. There are many runaways. It's nothing new. Sadie!" she called in a sharper voice.

"I'll just be a moment, ma'am," a hoarse voice said from the back room.

"Now!" Verna snapped back.

A gaunt young woman with tired, deep-set eyes and a red nose came running from the back of the shop. A handkerchief poked from her sleeve, and she held the back of her hand over her mouth to suppress a dry cough. Her dress was simple but in good condition, and she had slung a woolen wrap around her shoulders.

"Take that rag off! How many times have I told you not to come into the shop like that!" Verna said brusquely.

"I'm so cold, ma'am. Sorry, ma'am." Sadie laid the wrap on a stool and turned to Jane with a pitiable smile.

Verna hissed: "What have I told you?"

With lowered eyes, Sadie whispered, "No personal details in front of the customers."

"You're not from around here, Sadie?" Jane asked.

"She's from the same place as me, unless I'm much mistaken," said Hettie and smiled broadly, ignoring Verna's disapproving face.

Sadie's cold made it painful for her to speak, and she murmured, "Millpool, by Bodmin, ma'am."

She fidgeted at her dress with bony hands pricked all over from sewing. Her hair was thin and brittle. A decent meal and a few days in bed would have done the emaciated young woman good.

"Mrs. Morris has been praising your talent, Sadie." The seamstress's assistant widened her eyes with surprise. "I have to be going. Please send a preliminary design over to Rosewood Hall, Mrs. Morris. You have my measurements. If I like it, then you can work according to that."

"Very good, my lady. Thank you for honoring us with your visit. I will get started on it right away." Verna Morris held the door open until Jane and Hettie were back out on the street.

When they had walked a few steps, Hettie said, "Ma'am, I am very happy to be with you and not with Mrs. Morris."

"We've both been very fortunate, I think," said Jane and stopped walking as a hansom cab rolled by. "I would still like to stop in at the chemist's and pick up some herbs for my uncle."

The chemist's shop lay at the other end of the village, and when they arrived a boy in torn clothes came running out of the door and past them. He was holding a bottle of Godfrey's Cordial in his hands. The syrup, dosed with laudanum, was popular among nannies and mothers. The sweet sleep tonic settled children down quickly if they were upset or simply hungry.

Jane had almost reached the entrance door when, from between the houses beside them, someone coughed and called, "My lady!"

Hettie instantly moved close beside Jane, but relaxed when she saw Sadie shivering in the alley with only her thin woolen wrap.

"You'll catch your death. What are you doing here?" Jane stepped closer.

Sadie's lips were cracked and blue. "I 'eard what you asked my mistress. The dead girl was at Salisbury Station. Pete thinks she might 'ave been a stowaway from London."

"Who is Pete?"

"We were both in the workhouse in Salisbury. 'e was 'ere two days ago to tell me good-bye. 'e's found work in a cotton mill up north." Sadie's voice was husky; she was a picture of deep despair. "I can't go up there. I'm too sick. My lungs." She coughed again. "I worked in the textile factories when I was little. I 'ave to be getting back."

Jane had already fetched five shillings from her purse and pressed the money into Sadie's hand. "Thank you!"

The young woman stared into her open hand for a moment. Then she closed her fist and pressed it to her chest before hurrying away.

Jane was still thinking about this unexpected news when the coach rolled into the courtyard at Rosewood Hall, where the next surprise was already awaiting her.

9.

Jane had hardly stepped into the entrance hall when she heard Bridget call from upstairs, "Is she there? Send her up immediately!"

Moments later, Milton came trotting down the stairs, but her uncle's butler also seemed to have been waiting for her, for he appeared from the library, his expression grave.

Hettie helped Jane out of her coat and said softly, "I hope nothing has happened. They all seem very excited."

Jane thought the same. "What is it, Floyd?"

The butler was still a good five paces from her, and the younger, faster Milton had already reached the middle of the hall.

"Lady Bridget wishes to speak to you, ma'am," Milton stated in a tone that Jane found altogether too brisk.

What had the servant done to suddenly find himself in such high standing with Bridget and cousin Matthew? Ignoring Milton's request, Jane turned expectantly to Floyd.

"Your uncle awaits you, my lady," said the butler.

"Hettie, go upstairs and take a look at the fashion magazine I put out up there. Maybe you'll find a pattern for Verna," Jane said, and saw

Hettie's eyes light up. Her maid had a task to complete and would not allow herself to be interrogated by Bridget.

"Yes, ma'am. With pleasure!" With her coat over her arm, she left, and Jane followed the butler without so much as dignifying Milton with an answer.

"But my mistress wishes you to . . ." The servant made another attempt.

Jane turned to Floyd. "He seems unaware of his station."

The experienced butler nodded and turned briefly back to Milton, who stood below him in the domestic hierarchy. "Dismissed, Milton. We will discuss your disrespectful behavior later." Then, to Jane, he said, "I do apologize, my lady, for his importuning you, but ever since the wife of the young lord has been in the house . . . Please, your uncle is in the library."

Floyd opened the door to the library for her. Warmth and the smell of tobacco rose to meet Jane, and she would have been happy to see her uncle in the company of his old friend if only the mood in the room had been different. Samuel Jones was a London lawyer and notary public. That he had undertaken the long journey out here could not bode well. Jane had known the short, portly lawyer since her arrival in England twenty years earlier. It was he who had met her at Plymouth Harbor back then. His hair had turned white, his high forehead shone in the light of the afternoon sun, and he seemed to have put on a little weight around the middle. But in legal matters, few could hold a candle to Samuel Jones. His reputation for incorruptibility and sharp judgment preceded him.

As she entered, both men rose from their chairs at the large desk. Beside the hearty figure of Jones, Lord Henry looked terribly pale, but Jane hoped that it only had to do with the documents spread out on the table before him. She gave her uncle a kiss on the cheek before turning to receive a warm embrace from Samuel Jones.

Holding her in front of him at arm's length, Jones smiled and said, "I fell head over heels for you back when you were standing on the quay in Plymouth, all long plaits and with the most pigheaded look in your eyes." He released Jane and spread his arms wide in admiration. "And now look at this beautiful young woman! And soon to be a bride, I hear . . ."

Embarrassed, Jane moved beside her uncle and looked at the papers on the desk.

"Oh, Sam. Stop all that tomfoolery. You're as much a geriatric as I am," said Lord Henry and sank back onto his chair. Rufus lay on the floor behind them, letting out an occasional sigh in his sleep.

The lawyer cleared his throat, straightened the scarf around his neck, and smiled broadly, revealing teeth between which many a haunch of venison had met its end. Like his longtime friend, he was wearing a dark suit.

Floyd placed a chair for Jane beside her uncle and poured her a glass of wine. The men had eaten sandwiches, and the butler reached to offer them to Jane, but she raised her hand to stop him. "Thank you, Floyd. I'm not hungry."

"Jane," Lord Henry began, and she could hear the overwhelming emotion in his voice.

Samuel Jones came to his friend's aid. He placed one hand on the documents on the table in front of him. "I've come here to help your uncle make his last will and testament legally acceptable. You know that once you marry you are entitled to your parents' inheritance, and part of that is Mulberry Park."

Jane looked at the two men, her eyes wide. "Yes. But you already explained that to me, Uncle."

Lord Henry nodded slowly and frowned sadly. "I believed that everything was fixed and unimpeachable, but I had not reckoned with my daughter-in-law's greed."

The lawyer supported himself heavily on the wooden desk. "Matthew was in here this morning. He has claimed the property for himself unless you pay him back the money that your uncle has put into maintaining the place over the years."

"I'm so sorry, Jane. I never would have expected something like this from him. I've begun to question whether he is a true son of mine. I certainly never raised him to be such an embodiment of selfishness and greed," Lord Henry lamented, reaching for a small pill bottle that stood beside a water glass.

"I don't know what I'm supposed to say. Do I have to pay him back for your expenditure? Would I even be able to?" Jane had absolutely no desire to grapple with financial matters that she did not begin to understand. She looked unhappily from Samuel to her uncle.

"Henry wanted you to be aware of what you might have to face. Legally speaking, everything is protected, but Matthew could take you to court, and you never know which judge you'll find yourself facing . . . Nowhere are more lies told than in court, my dear Jane. This makes it so important that you have a husband who can support you and defend you, a man who will stand by you. Captain Wescott is an honorable man. We are both acquainted with his family, Henry even more than me. But there are secrets in every family, sleeping dogs one would rather let lie because waking them would cause a scandal." Samuel fell silent and looked to Henry, who had washed down his pill with a mouthful of water.

"Were my time on earth not so limited, I would go on protecting you from any and all hostilities, my dear child, but now it is . . . Wescott is an unconventional, reticent man. I think highly of him, believe me, or I would never have consented to your union with him. His mother was Russian. She died not long after his birth. She was a decent woman, very beautiful, and a scion of the Russian nobility." Lord Henry paused and searched for something among the papers on the desk. Finally, he found what he was looking for—a sealed document—and pushed it across to Jane.

Jane, surprised, turned the folded sheet of paper, sealed with wax, over in her hands. Her name stood on the front, and that was all.

"Should you ever have any doubts about your husband, then the person whose name and address you will find in this letter will be able to tell you about him." Her uncle looked at her intently. "Open it only if it is absolutely necessary, Jane. Promise me that, you hear? Promise me that!"

Trembling, she ran her fingers over the mysterious letter. "I promise," she said in a hoarse whisper.

"Guard the letter well, Jane. I could have deposited it with Samuel, but I wanted you to know that there is someone who will stand beside you when I no longer can, someone who knows Wescott better than his own father. Perhaps you will never have any need to pay that person a visit, but who can see into the future? I don't even know my own son."

Floyd had moved away to a vitrine. He seemed engrossed in organizing the books and jade figurines inside. Henry noticed Jane looking at him. "Floyd requested that I ask you whether you might take him over when I'm no longer . . ."

"Uncle, no! Don't say things like that!" Jane sobbed. Her uncle's approaching death suddenly hung over the room like a threat.

Henry Pembroke took his niece's hand in his and held on tightly. "Do him the favor. He will bring a new lease of life to Mulberry Park. No one can do that better than he can."

"Of course I will do that, but . . ." She looked at her uncle through a haze of tears. "But not too soon."

The conversation seemed to have made Lord Henry weary, for he closed his eyes tiredly for a moment. When he opened them again, they were dark and without hope. "I have telegraphed Wescott. He will be here tomorrow. There hasn't been a public announcement, Jane.

Forgive me. I know I'm asking a lot of you, but I would like to see you married. Then I can go."

Horrified, Jane sat up stiffly on her chair and stared at her uncle. "Tomorrow? Already? I have no wedding dress."

Lord Henry blinked weakly and managed a small smile. "That is not important, Jane, my dear. Please give us another moment alone. I will see you again at dinner."

Dazed at all she had heard, Jane stood up. She had to hold on to the desk because her knees were shaking. She embraced her uncle and pressed her face into the wool of his jacket, taking in the faint odor of tobacco and the tinge of aftershave, and kissed him on the cheek. Then she stroked his hair and turned away. She held the letter he had given her firmly in her hand. She walked straight to the door and left the library without turning around, for tears were streaming down her cheeks and she wanted to spare her uncle the sight.

Jane ran up the stairs, and from the corner of her eye she noticed one of the doors to Matthew's and Bridget's rooms swing open. She began to walk faster, and placed her hand on the knob of her bedroom door.

"Jane!" Bridget's unmistakable shrill voice rang down the hallway.

Sobbing, Jane pushed the door open, forcing her skirts through, and slammed the door behind her. "Hettie?"

Her maid appeared from the next room, a fashion magazine in her hand. "Yes, ma'am?" When she saw her distraught mistress, she cried out, "Oh, no . . . what's happened now?"

Jane threw herself onto her bed and pushed the sealed letter under her pillow. "Don't let anyone in, Hettie! I don't want to see anyone!"

There was a vigorous knocking at the door. "Jane! I know you're in there! I wish to speak with you!" Bridget demanded.

Hettie positioned herself behind the solid wooden door and said, "My mistress is indisposed and wishes to see no one."

"Outrageous! But she'll come down off her high horse faster than she thinks." With those foreboding words, Bridget's footsteps moved away.

"What a terrible person the lady is. I've stopped even trying to talk to her maid. Rena is a snake, just like her mistress." When Jane said nothing, Hettie went on chattering. "Would you like some tea, ma'am? I'll bring you a cup of hot tea. That will settle your nerves. Someone ought to slip the lady a little of that sleep syrup. It would be a blessing for everyone in this house."

Jane could hear Hettie setting up the teacups next door, and she got up from the bed. She splashed cold water on her face but avoided looking at herself in the mirror. Then she went and sat in the upholstered niche of the bay window. Rosewood Hall had many such bay windows where one could hide away. All you had to do was pull the curtains partly closed, and no one could see you. When she was younger, she had played hide-and-seek with Matthew all over the house. Today, those memories seemed like an imagined dream. What had become of the intrepid boy she had chased around the gardens, studied Latin with, and ridden with across the fields? His father had never denied him anything, had catered to his every whim. The most expensive horses, schools, clothes, travel: Pembroke's heir had wanted for nothing.

Jane looked out over the park, which was slowly disappearing in the twilight. With the growing darkness, the enormous ancient trees transformed into bizarre, shadowy forms . . . *that sometimes spat out dying girls*, thought Jane, and shuddered. "Mary," she murmured. "I have to find you. But how?"

Cold wind streamed in through the window, which stood ajar, and Jane felt a chill. "Mary, who are you? Where did your friend leave you? Or was she your sister?"

"So, time for a cup of fine English tea." The rattle of the teacup betrayed Hettie's return. Jane heard the maid pull up short for a moment before coming to the window. "You ought not to sit there, ma'am. It's still too cold."

Jane took the cup and raised it to her lips. The tea was strong, hot, and sweet, and instantly revived her spirits. "Thank you, Hettie."

The maid took the fashion magazine from a stool and opened it. "So many beautiful dresses. I don't think this one with the puffy top is very nice, but this one—"

"Hettie, I don't need a wedding dress."

"What?" Shocked, Hettie snapped the magazine closed.

"The wedding will take place tomorrow, if I understand my uncle correctly." Wescott was on his way. Why all the hurry otherwise?

"But that can't be! There's the engagement and the announcement and . . . ," began Hettie, who had been looking forward to a huge celebration and a new dress for herself.

Jane set down the cup and watched one of the servants lighting the torches down on the terrace. Without a doubt, Rosewood Hall was one of the most beautiful mansions in the country. And soon a new man would rule over this land and the people on it, a man who had never loved this place as his father had, and whose only interest was in having it for himself.

"Captain Wescott is expected for breakfast tomorrow, Hettie. Could you get out the lavender dress for me? White gloves, white shoes, and my mother's pearls."

"Lady Alison will be sorely disappointed," said Hettie as she put the magazine down on a chest of drawers.

"I don't doubt it for a minute. But I would rather weather her disappointment than my uncle's. It is his wish, his . . ." Jane's voice failed her.

"I understand, ma'am. What will become of us? Where will we go then?" Hettie asked, the practical nature of a girl from a plainer background prevailing.

"I will discuss that with Captain Wescott." Just saying that sentence cost Jane all her self-control. In front of her loomed a new phase of her life, and it looked to her like a walk through a moor: you never knew what awaited you, and stepping off the path might mean sinking into the bog. It was the kind of walk that sounded like an adventure at the outset, but when the time came to actually go, fear and uncertainty were your constant companions.

"Ma'am?" Hettie had apparently asked her a question.

"Yes?"

"The lavender dress is not pretty enough. If you ask me, it's a color more suitable for old women. The light green is beautiful. You shine when you wear it. But that is just my opinion." She pulled the curtain flat across the window.

Jane sighed. "I don't mind. But the pearls don't go with the green. Oh, I'll decide in the morning."

When Doctor Paterson arrived at Rosewood Hall in the early evening and disappeared into Lord Henry's bedroom, there could be no more doubt about the seriousness of her uncle's condition. The doctor later informed her that he had ordered strict bed rest and a sleeping powder for his patient. Without the presence of Samuel Jones, Jane would not have gone down for the evening meal, but the lawyer did his best to entertain her with amusing anecdotes from his eventful life. After eating, Matthew and the lawyer retired to the smoking room, and Bridget took the opportunity to block Jane's retreat upstairs.

"The old man's time has come, Jane. Have you packed your bags yet? I'll be sure to check that you take nothing away that does not belong to you." Bridget's cheeks were red, and her forehead shone greasily. She glared at Jane through eyes narrowed to slits. It seemed she had been waiting for this moment for a very long time.

"Let me pass, Bridget. You're a vicious, vindictive person. Remember that what you inflict on others will come back to haunt you." Jane pushed past the pregnant woman and continued up the stairs.

"I have nothing to be ashamed of. Absolutely nothing! All I'm doing is making sure my husband gets what he's entitled to! You pushed your way between him and his father. It's your fault that Lord Henry loves his son less than he loves you!" Puffing, Bridget tried to keep up with Jane.

"Does he really believe that? Poor Matthew! I haven't pushed my way in anywhere. My uncle took me in because I'm his brother's daughter. How could I ever take *anything* away from Matthew? I'm a woman. Have you forgotten that, Bridget? I am just a woman!"

Bridget was sweating, and her eyes were filled with wrath. "You never believed you were just a woman, Jane. You never played by the rules. You're different. You always were, and you think you're better for it, but you're not!"

"If you were not expecting, I would slap you," said Jane, but she understood that deep down Bridget envied her. What Bridget could not or would not say was that she begrudged Jane her strength and her irrepressible will. "But thank you, Bridget. I'll take that as a compliment. Good night."

10.

Mulberry Park, Cornwall, March 1860

The intense odor of seaweed and the ocean swept in with the spray from the waves crashing below the cliffs. Jane could hear the sea roaring against the rocks, and the mist rose as high as where she stood. Seagulls cried and a dog barked.

"Rufus!" Jane called. Since her arrival at Mulberry Park, she had gone on endless walks, exploring her new home and at the same time trying to find a way through the loss of her uncle.

The Great Dane came galloping over the green hill, giving Jane a dim sense of familiarity. It had all happened too fast. The events of the past weeks had swept her away and washed her up here on Cornwall's wild coast. Wescott had arrived that night at Rosewood Hall and spent a long time speaking with Samuel Jones and her uncle. Contracts were signed, her marriage contract among them. Her uncle had gone to great lengths to see that she was well provided for.

Jane stroked Rufus's fur, for the dog now trotted beside her, unhurried. "Matthew wanted to ban you to the stables . . ."

Rufus grunted.

Wescott had kept his word. At the end of the simple wedding ceremony in the village church, he had kissed her, but it was no more than the lightest brush of his lips against hers. He had taken her arm politely and led her to the coach. Inside, in privacy, he had asked her if she wanted to have their agreement about their life together set down in writing. But Jane had offered him her hand and said that his word was good enough for her. A handshake sealed the affair.

Because the wedding had been moved forward, Wescott said he would have to make his apologies and leave for his unfinished house in London. He had only recently moved into a respectable place in Seymour Street, but it was nothing luxurious and still required extensive work both inside and out before the house could meet their requirements, at least to some extent. He did not need to say any more for Jane to understand that he didn't want her in London, and Jane herself had suggested that she look after the necessary repairs at Mulberry Park. Wescott seemed relieved, and the rest of their journey back to Rosewood passed in an oppressive silence.

Wescott wanted to return to London the following morning, and Jane hoped to be able to spend a few more weeks with her uncle in Rosewood. But on the night of the wedding, Matthew got drunk and caused a scene with his father, accusing him of never loving him as much as he had Jane. That same evening, Lord Henry suffered a heart attack and passed away. In this terrible situation, Wescott proved himself an attentive husband, rigorously shielding Jane from any malice from Bridget or Matthew. He ensured that, with the help of Hettie and Floyd, her possessions were packed and transported to Mulberry Park. Only when he was certain that everything important to Jane was safely stowed did he ride beside her coach along the way that led from Rosewood out to the main road.

Floyd and Hettie sat with her in the coach. Bridget had forbidden the servants to wave good-bye, so no one was standing on the courtyard in front of Rosewood Hall when Jane left her home. When they reached the crossing where the road led west toward Cornwall and east to London, Captain Wescott stopped the coach and asked Jane to step out.

He took her by the arm and walked a few steps alone with her. "I had the greatest respect for your uncle, Jane. Give me a little time to get my affairs in order. Then I'll come to visit you in Mulberry Park, or you can come to London. But please don't hang back from contacting me should any problems arise. Of whatever nature! Promise me that, will you?"

She no longer remembered what she had said in reply, but she had not forgotten the look of concern in his dark eyes. David Wescott had shown himself to be a man of deep sympathy, and she admired him for that.

"And now we're alone, aren't we, Rufus?" The wind picked up, and Jane pulled her shawl tighter around her shoulders. Although temperature-wise, Cornwall was milder than the rest of the country, a cold, damp wind often blew in from the sea. Clothes absorbed the salty moisture and quickly became heavy and stiff. Jane rubbed her upper arms to keep them warm, and then she began to walk faster: the movement helped her circulation and warmed her limbs.

A pathway wound along the coast and was used by hikers, locals, and visitors, who mainly came to the seaside in summer. Jane, on her walks, had met herdsmen and residents of the villages hereabouts, and once an artist out from London. The man had brought his easel in defiance of the wind and the rain and gone on rapturously about painting *en plein air*.

She turned to face the wind and breathed in the salty air deeply. It was an unusual feeling to be the mistress of her own house, to do or not do whatever her fancy told her. Her newly gained freedom felt different than she had expected it to, and she was trying to find her feet in her new life.

Hettie, on the other hand, was overjoyed to discover that her cousin Jeanette lived close by. Jeanette's husband, Bob Piers, was a fisherman and had a small cottage outside Polperro. His boat was tied up in the harbor there.

After a hectic first week with plenty to do, Jane had given Hettie the day off to spend with Jeanette. She had no social obligations, and no one out here cared about how she was dressed. *Warm and dry*, thought Jane, *that's the main thing*, and she smiled.

Rufus slowed his pace and growled softly. Jane had no fear of wandering alone out over the meadows and fields separated by stone walls and hedgerows. But she was also not imprudent, and stayed within sight of the house. After a moment, she, too, heard the hoofbeats and saw a rider trot out from behind a bend in the path. The man was well dressed, and the closer he came, the more clearly she saw the English Thoroughbred he was riding. Her sudden move and mourning for her uncle had taken over everything, to the extent that she had not yet given much thought to any of her neighbors. It was about time she paid some courtesy visits. On the other hand, considering her loss, anyone would grant her her self-imposed solitude.

It wasn't long before the rider, with an elegant turn, brought his horse to a standstill in front of her. Lord Hargrave. He bowed his head and smiled winningly. "Good day, my lady. What an unexpected pleasure!"

Jane returned his smile and laid her hand on Rufus's neck. She'd forgotten the man owned a country house not far away, Bromfield Manor.

"Lord Hargrave, good day to you too."

"We are neighbors, my lady. Unfortunately, we were not formally introduced at your late uncle's ball. My sincere condolences on your loss. Lord Henry was an honest and thoroughly respected man."

Jane swallowed. She still found it difficult to talk about her uncle. "Thank you," she murmured, pulling herself together.

Although the rules of society did not require it, she wore a black dress, in keeping with the state of her emotions. Her coat was dark green with a black collar, and her shawl was also black.

The wind swept through Lord Hargrave's hair, and he made a nonchalant gesture. "I lost my hat along the way."

"Who could blame you for that? I'm sorry, I should have . . ."

"Oh, not to worry," Hargrave reassured her quickly. He was having trouble keeping his skittish horse under control. "Now that we've met, may I invite you for afternoon tea tomorrow? My sister, Violet, is here, and the Duke of Rutland and his wife will also be with us. Perhaps Mr. Devereaux will also come, but he could not say with certainty because he's tied up in London. Business." He looked at her expectantly.

"I, ah, that is very nice of you, but my husband is not here, and I . . . ," Jane replied uncertainly.

Hargrave smiled understandingly. "Unforgivable, leaving such a lovely young woman alone. I have no desire to embarrass you in any way, but my sister would certainly enjoy making your acquaintance. She lives in Bromfield Manor year-round, and is often there alone. The only variety she gets is through her charitable work with orphanages and whatnot."

His tone of voice was slightly deprecating, Jane felt. Even without knowing Hargrave's sister, Jane automatically sided with her. "Thank you. I would enjoy meeting your sister very much."

"Wonderful, then. Until tomorrow, my lady!" He nodded to her, clucked his tongue, and let his horse, a chestnut stallion, feel the spurs.

Because she had been standing still, Jane now felt the cold even more than before, and she set off again at a brisk walk. "I don't know what to make of the man yet, but his sister lives here the whole year. Maybe she's nice."

Trotting beside her, Rufus seemed to snort in answer. As they drew near to the trout pond that lay at the extreme end of the Mulberry Park gardens, he raised his head in happy expectation.

"No, Rufus, you don't go getting any fish now, or Mr. Roche will shoot you!"

The Great Dane barked and ran around the pond, but strutted back to Jane the second time she shouted "No!"

Bert and Martha Roche had been in charge of looking after the property all these years, and had greeted their new mistress with undisguised reserve, if not hostility. Jane sighed and walked around the pond. The extensive gardens of Mulberry Park were barely a shadow of the garden at Rosewood Hall, and one could sense the neglect. Many hedges and bushes were in need of trimming, and the vegetable beds needed to be redone. The lawn was patchy and the paths overgrown with weeds. A number of the mulberry trees that had given the place its name had been felled.

Mulberry Park itself was much smaller than Jane remembered it. The gray three-story manor house was functional and solid. Perched on a hilltop for a century, it had defied the storms that swept across the channel. It had not always been in Jane's family, and had even housed prisoners of war and smugglers. Smuggling belonged to the Cornish coast like salt to a kipper, as the people thereabouts liked to say.

Jane walked past the house's herb garden and looked in at the kitchen window. The red face of the cook, a plump, taciturn woman from the nearby village of Lansallos, leaned over a bowl. A shadow flitted past in the background, probably one of the kitchen maids. Jane had not yet gone through the housekeeper's books, nor had she spoken to all of the servants.

An impalpably gloomy atmosphere clung to Mulberry Park. Jane blamed it on her own state of mind, but as she pushed open the front door and stepped into the dim hallway, she decided that it was not just her. She tugged on the bell pull just inside the door.

A young footman rushed out frantically from behind the stairs, tugging his jacket straight. "Pardon, ma'am. You rang?"

"Is my maid back? Where is Floyd, ah, Mr. Coleman?" She had appointed Floyd as her butler, which set him above every other servant in the house. That, too, had come as a heavy blow to Mr. and Mrs. Roche in particular. "What was your name again?"

"Stuart, ma'am. Your maid has not yet come back, and Mr. Coleman is upstairs, ma'am." Stuart was of average height, had a nose that looked like it had been broken at some point, and one of his front teeth was missing, which indicated something of a tendency toward violence.

Jane nodded and was about to move past Stuart to the stairs when she heard a suppressed cry accompanied by the sound of breaking dishes. She hesitated for a moment, but Stuart quickly positioned himself in front of the passage that led to the kitchen and the servants' quarters.

"It's nothing, ma'am. The new kitchen hand is rather clumsy. Mrs. Roche will be taking care of that." In his attempt at a smile, the gap in his teeth showed more prominently, giving his face a somewhat devious appearance.

Jane immediately felt ashamed of her superficial judgment of the young man. After all, he could not help the way he looked. "I'm sure she will be. I would like to eat at seven this evening. And no fish."

"Yes, ma'am." He grinned again, and this time his expression was unmistakably malicious.

Since her arrival, she had eaten fish every single day. Smoked, fried, and boiled. Just the smell of it made her feel nauseous. She did not want to be impolite to the cook, but she'd had enough. Besides, the woman was not there just as some ornament of Jane's status. Jane would have to have a serious word with Mrs. Roche. *Soon,* thought Jane, and made her way wearily upstairs. Rufus, who had stood looking around in the hallway, followed her and trotted into her bedroom.

On the second floor there were two large bedrooms and a small one, connected by dressing rooms. A bathroom and a closet were located directly beside the stairs. The top floor was divided into five small rooms, of which two were occupied by two servant girls each. Jane had given Floyd the biggest room. Stuart and another servant slept in the attic. Mr. and Mrs. Roche lived in a small extension in the basement behind the kitchen.

"Floyd?" Jane called down the corridor, and the butler's familiar face appeared at the doorway of the second, larger bedroom.

"Ah, my lady! Wonderful to see you back. What would you say to our turning this room into your husband's bedroom?"

Jane went to Floyd and looked into a brightly lit room, slightly smaller than her own bedroom but with large floor-length windows exactly like hers. A door connected this room to her own. "Yes, why not. Tell me, Floyd, how are you getting on with Mr. and Mrs. Roche? Do you have the impression that they treat the staff here decently?"

Floyd scratched his chin. "I am not exactly in anyone's favor here, as you know."

"That will change fast enough. There seems to be a new girl in the kitchen. I want to be sure that she is being treated well. I heard a cry in the kitchen just now. Would you take care of that, Floyd?" Jane stepped out of the room and heard Hettie's cheery voice and laughter coming from the hallway below. Instinctively, she smiled. At least one person here had had a good day.

"Of course, my lady. And about the furnishings?" Floyd had followed her into the hall.

"I will leave that up to you, Floyd. Put in whatever you think is right. Oh, and tomorrow I will be driving to Bromfield Manor. Lord Hargrave has invited me to tea. His sister and the Duke of Rutland and his wife will also be there."

If Floyd was surprised, he did not show it. "Very well, my lady. I am familiar with Lord Hargrave and the duke from previous visits at your uncle's side, if you will allow me the observation."

"Oh?"

"Lord Hargrave enjoys the reputation of being a connoisseur. Valuable objets d'art and . . ." Floyd cleared his throat. "Well, he is known for his . . . profligate lifestyle. I only want you to be aware of that, my lady. But there are to be other guests in attendance, as you said."

"Thank you, Floyd. I really feel rather naïve."

Her butler looked at her sympathetically. "Oh, no, my lady. Your uncle would have told you the same, or your husband, if he were here."

She could not explain to him that her husband bore no blame at all, that she herself had come to this arrangement with him, for she heard the unspoken accusation in Floyd's words.

"Ma'am!" Hettie came up the stairs at a rush, her cheeks flushed. "There is so much to tell!"

11.

Mary

The sun shone warmly into the orphanage courtyard. It was a rare thing to hear the happy laughter of children from inside those walls, but on that day the youngsters romped across the patchy grass, playing tag and throwing balls. Mary and Fiona sat on a tree trunk that had been laid alongside a wall to serve as a bench, and let the sun simply shine down onto their pale faces.

" 'ow you feeling today, Mary?" Fiona asked, her red hair shimmering like flames in the bright light. She was plucking the petals of a tiny white flower and flicking them carelessly onto the grass.

Mary automatically raised one hand to her ear, from which a gauze wick soaked in lavender oil still protruded. The moment a draft of air or the cold found its way inside her injured ear, the pain began again. She had had to stay in bed a full six weeks. The pain had been unbearable, unlike anything she had ever experienced before. Her entire head had seemed about to explode. And then came the terrible attacks of dizziness.

"The dizzy feeling's gone most of the time now. There's just the buzzing. I hope that stops soon. It's worst when I'm in the workrooms. Hearing sounds from inside and outside drives me barmy." Mary looked at her friend uneasily, her eyes wide. "Am I going barmy?"

Fiona grinned. "No, silly. The master 'urt your ear, the old gobshite. That's what 'appens when you get hit really 'ard. Ratface, one of the boys in our gang, got whacked like that on 'is ear by a copper. But the poor bugger didn't 'ave a safe bed to rest in, so he numbed 'imself with sleep medicine. Till the day 'e didn't wake up again."

"Oh my gosh. Then we've got it good here." Mary plucked at the bow on her tattered skirt.

"I still don't want to stay 'ere, Mary. With Mr. Gaunt gone, it ain't the same," said Fiona.

"And Miss Fannigan's leaving soon, too. She's been so quiet, and she's changed since Mr. Gaunt left. She misses him. I think they rather fancied each other."

A ball landed at Fiona's feet, and she picked it up and threw it back to the boys. "The teachers and other staff aren't allowed to carry on. It's against the rules. As if anyone 'ere sticks to the rules. It wouldn't make no difference to no one if they 'ad something going."

"Maybe someone from the Poor Law Union was here and said something. Or the master was afraid they'd cut off his money if something like that got out," Mary conjectured.

"Codswallop! Just think of the men that Sister Susan lets into the dorm. The master's not afraid of nothing, not 'im." Fiona looked around for a moment, but there was no one close to them apart from the very small children. "Mr. Gaunt vanished overnight, right? They told us 'e'd found a better job up north. But I think it's something completely different. I saw Mr. Cooper stuffing Mr. Gaunt's jacket into a sack."

"He could have forgotten it," suggested Mary.

Fiona gave her a pitying look. "It was 'is good jacket."

"Oh. Where is he then?"

Sighing, Fiona stood up and held out her hand to help Mary up. When her friend was standing beside her, Fiona whispered in her healthy ear, "I'd like to know that, too, but I'm afraid to find out . . ."

The bell rang to signal the next hour, and Fiona took Mary's hand in hers.

After the usual evening meal of old bread, a piece of cheese, and a cup of milky tea so thin you could hardly taste it, Fiona and Mary stood at the window of their dormitory and looked out onto the street. The entire complex of buildings was surrounded by a grass verge and a wall. Sharpened iron spikes on top of the six-foot wall were supposed to keep the inmates inside and uninvited guests out. A porter at the main gate was the eye of the needle that anyone wanting to enter any of the buildings had to pass through.

With the warmth of spring, the days had begun to grow longer. Nature reawakened, insects whirred through the air, and bats fluttered among the gables in the twilight.

The two girls stood shoulder to shoulder at the open window, and Fiona furtively produced a wrinkled apple from the pocket of her skirt. She held the apple closely under Mary's nose to prevent the other children, most of whom had already fallen into an exhausted sleep in their beds, from seeing it.

With her eyes closed, Mary inhaled the delicious smell. It was an odor she only rarely had the chance to enjoy. "Where did you get that?" she whispered.

Fiona grinned, bit off a chunk, and handed the apple to Mary, making a gesture with her hands as she did so, like a street magician talking up a trick. But her attention was suddenly caught by a movement on the street. "Look! A coach!"

Coaches only rarely pulled up at the orphanage, and as good as never at the poorhouse. When they did, it was normally a representative from the Poor Law Union, and they didn't come at night.

"The men were here just yesterday. Who can it be?" Mary murmured and handed the apple back to Fiona. The sweet taste of the overripe fruit was delicious, and she kept the flesh of the apple in her mouth as long as she possibly could.

Mary and Fiona were the eldest of thirty girls in this dormitory. They were expected to look after the little ones if they woke up at night and began to cry. They were also expected to know when the smallest children needed to use the pot. But knowing that was plain impossible and if, in the morning, one of the beds stank of urine, then Mary or Fiona was caned on the hands or calves for it. But they took it all in stride, and gladly so. Anything was better than having to go into the small dormitory where the men came to visit.

"I meant to tell you, Mary." Fiona, when she wanted to, could put on the cockney accent of London's working class. She used the talent to talk to the men and women from London that she met in the workhouse, to find out news from the capital.

"There was a cobbler in over there last night. 'e'd come from London looking for work, and 'is family lives on the coast. Anyway, 'e told me that there was a story in the papers about a lass who suddenly appeared at some lord's place in Wiltshire and then promptly died. The young lady of the 'ouse went to a lot of trouble and paid for 'er to be buried in the village cemetery. 'e said it stuck in 'is mind 'cause 'e'd been working for a shoemaker in Salisbury at the time." Fiona nibbled on a morsel of apple and passed the rest back to Mary. " 'ere, finish it off. Oh, yes, and the lady who lives there is called Lady Jane. That's a pretty name . . . The cobbler said she was well-liked, and the people there felt sorry for 'er 'cause after that, 'er uncle, the old lord, died and—" Fiona stared at the gate. "That coach is driving in! Well, if that ain't some lord or other. Lovely 'orses."

Mary chewed every single apple seed with delight. She found them sweet, and they tasted of almonds. "And?"

"I don't remember much more. Something about the lord's son. Don't make no difference, they'll get along. They've all got their upkeep taken care of. Look at the man getting out!" Fiona whistled through her teeth. "Now that's a fine gentleman. No, 'ang on, the gentleman's still sitting inside. That's just 'is servant. Talk about class!"

Master Ledford bowed at the open door of the coach, and Mary giggled. "If the master grovels any lower, his nose will touch his shoes."

Now the mistress joined him and curtsied nicely, but her husband shooed her back into the house. The girls waited excitedly for what would happen next, but the coach simply stood where it was. The coachman climbed down, gave the horses some oats, then took his place back on the seat.

"Why did you tell me that about the girl in Wiltshire, Fiona?" It suddenly occurred to Mary to ask. A dark suspicion made her stomach tighten.

"The cobbler said there was rumors flying 'round that the girl might've been an orphan who took off from an 'ousehold. He was talking to a worker at the station in Salisbury." Fiona paused and took Mary's hand. "The girl 'ad blond hair and blue eyes, and she's supposed to 'ave said something about a Mary."

Mary groaned aloud and shook her head. "No. No, Fiona! It can't be true, never. That wasn't my Polly. That's what you were trying to say, wasn't it? You think it was Polly? No, Polly's in a nice house and helps in the kitchen or carries white lace up to the rooms."

"Mary." Fiona squeezed her hand. "I wanted to tell you so you'd know what might 'ave 'appened. Maybe a letter from Polly will come tomorrow, and we'll see we've been fretting for nothing."

"Look, Fiona! They're taking Molly out!"

Both girls gazed spellbound out the window and watched as Master Ledford hauled petite Molly, twelve years old and with her head bowed, from the dormitory nearest the coach. The gentleman remained out of sight. All Mary and Fiona could see was one white glove reaching out through the door. The glove gestured to Molly to turn around so that the gentleman could see her from all sides. She even had to show her teeth.

"They give us the once-over like we're cows. That's all we are, ain't we? Cattle to be bought," Fiona said bitterly, growling through her teeth.

"I bet he's looking for a new servant girl. Molly's in luck, Fiona!" Mary said as she gazed at the beautiful coach and the nervous, prancing horses. "Oh, I would love to get a position in a lovely house one day and not have to live in this filth anymore."

Just then, the lice in Mary's hair bit into her scalp, as if they had heard her, making her scratch. The stink of her old clothes suddenly seemed unbearable, and she hated the bugs that crawled out of their lairs in the dark and attacked her. The screams of the little ones who didn't know what it was nipping them in their diapers, and those who scratched their little arms until they bled, the nauseating stench from the chamber pots, and the green meat that was the only meat they had to eat—all of it made her choke. Why shouldn't it get better if they entered domestic service somewhere? It could not be worse than here, surely! And she pushed aside any thoughts that leaving the orphanage had perhaps not turned out as well for Polly as she had hoped.

12.

While Hettie helped her mistress undress, she babbled away with all her news. Jane listened to stories about countless family members and was happy for the young woman, whom she had not seen this merry in a long time. The black skirt was set out to be dried and brushed on a wooden frame.

"You want to invite Lady Alison to visit, ma'am. She's your friend, after all. Then you would have someone to talk to. Lady Alison is always so lively," said Hettie, who suddenly seemed to realize that Jane was very quiet.

"Hmm, yes. But later. This house still has all the charm of a mausoleum," Jane replied as she slipped into a plain black housedress.

"Now that you say that, ma'am, about the mausoleum, well, Jeannie told me something that came as a real shock, I can tell you. I told her about the dead girl, and she looked at me and turned white as a whitewashed wall. 'Well, I never,' she said. Over St. Winnow way, not six months back, there was also a young girl found. She was already dead, but very young, and no one knew where she came from. It was a strange affair, said Jeannie, and everyone felt sorry for the poor thing.

She was starved thin, and it looked like she'd been mistreated, because there were signs she'd been beaten."

"My goodness! Was there an investigation?" Hettie knew nothing of the marks of ill treatment on the body of the girl at Rosewood Hall, and it was better that way.

"There's an orphanage in Bodmin. It seems they asked there, but no one knew the girl. Ma'am, there are many orphanages and homes. They can't ask everywhere, and who's interested in such a poor thing? It's sad but true, says Jeannie."

"St. Winnow. Where is that?"

"A few miles up the river on the way to Bodmin."

"Hettie, tomorrow I've been invited to Bromfield Manor. You're to accompany me, and while we're there you can chat with the maid of Lord Hargrave's sister, Violet. She's supposed to have an interest in the orphanages hereabouts. I ought to be able to find out more about it from her, don't you think?"

Hettie's eyes lit up expectantly. "How nice! Oh, but what will you put on? Not this horrible black dress?"

Jane thought for a moment. "The black-violet will do. With the velvet ribbon and the cross."

The following afternoon, wearing the elegant and expensive black-violet silk dress, Jane found herself standing in the entrance hall talking to Floyd while she waited for her coach to come around.

"The new kitchen girl seems anxious, but that is normal, my lady. This is her first time in a manor house," Floyd explained quietly, and then cleared his throat distinctly.

A stocky man with a balding pate and surly expression was trying to make his way unnoticed to the kitchen and laundry area from the corridor that led down to the larder.

"Mr. Roche, a word, please!" Jane called the caretaker back.

A jolt seemed to run through the man. He turned around reluctantly and came over to her. "Yes, ma'am?"

Mr. Roche had a beefy face and drooping eyelids, and his expression was not only surly but also guilty. He wore a leather vest over his jacket, and a pheasant feather protruded from one pocket.

"No one in this house is to be reprimanded with violence. No beatings! Anyone working for me should be happy to work here. If there are problems, they should be directed to Mr. Coleman." Jane looked firmly at the man, who was at least thirty years her senior.

"Yes, ma'am. Will that be all, ma'am?" Roche grumbled.

"For the time being. Tomorrow morning, the entire staff is to assemble in the kitchen. I would like to speak to you all."

"As you wish, ma'am." Roche considered himself discharged and lumbered away.

From the outside, Stuart opened the front door and held it for her. "The coach has arrived, ma'am."

"I'll be along directly." Jane turned back to Floyd and said, "Did you see the feather and the blood on his jacket? Check and see how much game they bag and dress here. Most of it gets sold outside, I'm guessing."

Floyd grinned. "I already suspected as much, my lady. One of the tenants was in the kitchen this morning, and the cook often disappears into the village with a full basket."

"What's her name again?"

"Becky Thomas. She lives with her family in Lansallos. Everyone there seems to be related. The blacksmith's a Thomas, as is the miller, Becky's brother . . ." Floyd shrugged. "I shall be ruffling some feathers there soon."

"Thank you, Floyd. I am very glad to have you with me."

Her loyal butler looked toward the door. "Your coach awaits, my lady. I wish you a pleasant afternoon."

Hettie came running down the stairs, the ribbons on her hat flying.

A light drizzle obscured the view of the gray-green hill. It took the warmth of the first sun of spring to call forth the succulent green that would later blanket the meadows and fields. Here and there, the first delicate buds were appearing on hedges and trees, but for now the gloomy, overcast sky promised no change.

The coach drove along a low stone wall, sheep grazing on the other side. The wall came to a sudden end, and they turned onto a single-lane track heading unswervingly toward a mansion. With its gray, ivy-covered walls and squat, inelegant proportions, the house did not make a particularly inviting sight.

"I am very glad we won't have to spend the night here," said Hettie.

"Sometimes a facade is forbidding but looks much different from the other side." Jane tried to drum up some courage for both her maid and herself, though her words did not sound very convincing even to herself.

"When is the captain going to come home, ma'am?"

The coach pulled up at a weathered stairway flanked by stone lions. A uniformed servant, who had obviously been waiting for her, opened the door of the coach.

"What makes you ask, Hettie? I've told you that Captain Wescott spends much of his time in London." They climbed out. Jane handed the servant her visiting card, and they followed him into a brightly lit vestibule furnished in surprisingly good taste.

"Yes, ma'am," Hettie whispered, close beside her. "I was just wondering."

Facing an unknown house and a host with a dubious reputation, Jane would certainly have felt more secure at her husband's side. But their arrangement was the way it was.

The servant had just relieved her of her coat when the butler, a thin man with a crooked back and imperious lines, appeared. Jane could instantly see that he was a man used to giving orders.

"Welcome . . ." The butler cast a practiced glance at the card the servant held out to him. "Lady Jane. You are expected in the salon. Your maid will be so kind as to follow the footman."

Jane and Hettie exchanged a brief, telling glance before going their separate ways. The butler led her past lush potted palms and landscape paintings into a bright salon. The men were seated in armchairs arranged at one end of the room before a fireplace. Two women sat on a sofa in front of the high windows, and an afternoon buffet had been set up opposite them.

"Lady Jane!" the butler announced formally.

The men immediately jumped up from their chairs, and Lord Hargrave greeted her with an amused smile. "Wonderful that you could make it, Lady Jane. Allow me to introduce my dear sister, Mrs. Violet Sutton, and her friend Lady Florence."

Violet was the opposite of her brother in every way. Her face was narrow and pale, framed by thin ash-blond hair. Her light-blue eyes seemed somewhat absent, and the delicate hand she offered Jane was cold and feeble. She was not unattractive, but her lips were too thin, and she radiated the air of someone who had withdrawn into a different sphere of existence. *She lives in her own world,* thought Jane, and turned from her to Rutland's wife.

Lady Florence was powerfully built and gave the impression of an unmitigated woman of pleasure. She had applied too much color to her cheeks, and her eyes were strikingly dark. Expensive rings glittered on her fingers, and her entire appearance could only be described as excessively flamboyant for an afternoon tea. But she smiled welcomingly. "You are still in mourning, Lady Jane?"

"I miss my uncle very much, thank you, my lady." She mentally noted Violet Sutton's brown and black dress, but did not ask about a possible bereavement in the family.

Finally, Hargrave introduced her to the Duke of Rutland, who bowed briefly to her before raising her hand almost to his lips. As a man, Sidney Rutland was similar to Hargrave, perhaps somewhat older and more benevolent, as Jane would have expected of a peer and advisor to the Queen. His beard was trimmed close on his cheeks and tapered to a neat point on his chin. Not a good-looking man, but one whose appearance left a strong impression.

"A pity you did not bring your husband with you, Lady Jane," said Rutland.

"He is in London, on business. My uncle's sudden passing threw our plans into some disarray, my lord," Jane replied, not without a certain sharp edge.

"Of course, of course. I can imagine. How do you like it down here? Not everyone's cup of tea, eh, Florence?" Rutland laughed out loud.

Florence Rutland had taken her seat on the sofa again and screwed up her nose. "Not much to do here at this time of year. You must have noticed that, Lady Jane? The horrible, damp wind, the fog. And these drafty old houses! In London, one has no end of distractions, but here, well, you'd have to be born here to put up with it."

Violet cast her a reproachful glance, and Florence patted her hand. "All right, if you happen to be a saint, you'll find something to do wherever you are."

"Florence, of course, is referring to the sacrifices my sister makes through her work for the poor. I always say you can't help everyone, and that some of them don't deserve it at all, but . . ." Hargrave gave a quick shrug. "She doesn't believe me, though she's been let down often enough."

"Oh, Robert, stop it! That is not true at all!" Violet defended herself in a reedy voice. Her skin was pale and so transparent that Jane could see the veins beneath it. Violet's hands lay folded primly on her lap.

"Let me think . . ." Hargrave made a show of thinking hard, obviously amused at his sister's unease. "Oh, yes, there was this lovely young girl from Tavistock, for whom you found a position with Florence. Who was it that she ran off with? The boot boy?"

Florence giggled but said, "Robert, stop it."

"Wait! What about the short one with the blond curls? Pretty little thing, could even read and write and might have made it to governess. But no, Violet picks her up from the gutter and finds her a job in London, and not more than six months later she purloins her mistress's jewels and disappears quick smart. Shall I go on? Oh, my dear Lady Jane, all we're trying to do is show my sister the real world!"

Jane moved over to stand beside the couch where the women were sitting. "Is it wrong to believe in the good in people? Isn't it far more objectionable to judge someone based on their origins? I can understand your sister only too well. My own maid comes from the most humble of circumstances, and I don't regret for a moment taking her on."

Hargrave and Rutland exchanged a meaningful look, the slightly lewd nature of which did not appeal to Jane at all. Her host remarked, "You do not shy away from expressing your opinion, Lady Jane. Let us hope, for your own sake, that you do not find yourself let down."

"Don't give yourself a headache on my account, my lord," Jane shot back.

"A lion in a lambskin. How charming!" said Rutland with a broad grin.

Before Jane could continue the exchange of blows, Florence Rutland interrupted. "My dear, join us. We'll leave the gentlemen to enjoy a cigar. Violet has an outstanding cook. We really only come here for the food." Florence laughed a touch too loud at her own joke.

Violet, who was looking up doubtfully at Jane, picked up on her friend's suggestion and waved to the maid waiting beside the buffet. "Bring us an assortment. What would you like to drink, my lady? Tea, sherry, champagne?"

Florence laughed. "We don't stand on ceremony this far out. Champagne is good at any time of day!"

With a nod, Violet sent the maid off to the buffet. Jane thought that, in this house, there were a number of things they didn't stand on ceremony about, and she could not say that she felt particularly comfortable. Still, her social experience was limited to a handful of balls during the London Season, visits to the theater, and occasional outings with Alison or her uncle. With a sigh, she took a champagne glass from the silver tray the maid held in front of her.

"We are quite impossible," said Florence. "Please forgive us, Lady Jane!" Florence and Violet raised their glasses and smiled at her.

"But once you get to know us, you'll change your mind," Violet added.

"We're even worse!" Florence laughed.

Jane smiled and clinked glasses with her new friends. The men, meanwhile, were deep in conversation by the fireplace.

"So, tell us, what is the story with your husband? We are dying to make his acquaintance, Lady Jane. You've hooked yourself a terribly attractive man, title or not. On any account, you've a title yourself!" Florence seemed more and more in her element. Her ample bosom threatened the embroidered neckline of her top every time she laughed, and her cheeks were growing redder. It occurred to Jane that Florence Rutland was already well acquainted with the champagne.

"Florence!" said Violet in a chiding tone. "You must not take everything dear Florence says so seriously. The loss of your uncle must be painful for you. You grew up with him, didn't you?"

"I spent my youngest years with my parents in India. After they died, Uncle Henry took me into his home, Rosewood Hall," Jane said, as plainly as she could.

"A magnificent estate. Sidney and I were there once, many years ago. Oh, and wasn't there an incident there not long ago? A peasant girl who died? Gossip spreads at an alarming rate. Even faster out in the country, believe me, because there's nothing else worth talking about." Florence looked at her expectantly.

Jane cleared her throat and selected a small sandwich offered to her on a tray. "The unfortunate girl was laid to rest in the village cemetery," she said, and bit into the sandwich.

"Who was she?" Violet asked as she laid a slice of buttered bread on her plate.

"That could not be established," Jane admitted.

The men had been helping themselves to the buffet, and Hargrave stopped and stood in front of the women. "Which confirms my theory: another runaway from service."

"Nonsense," Jane retorted. "No one knows the first thing about her! And something could have happened to her. There are a thousand reasons for a girl to run away, and not all jobs are respectable. What about the dead girl at St. Winnow?"

"You heard about that?" Hargrave raised his eyebrows in surprise and sipped from his glass.

"News travels fast out here in the country," Jane said and smiled, earning an approving nod from Lady Florence.

Hargrave's brow furrowed. "Well, these are hardly topics of conversation for sensitive ladies."

Florence giggled and Violet lowered her eyes. *What illustrious company I'm in,* thought Jane, and glanced at the clock above the fireplace. "You're active with the orphanages in this region, Mrs. Sutton?"

Violet looked at her almost in shock. "Uh, yes. I pay regular visits to the homes in Bodmin and St. Austell. And I go out to Newbridge, but rather less often. Are you interested in charitable work?"

"Yes. Very, in fact." Jane's reply came spontaneously.

"You can come with me, if you like. I'll be driving to St. Austell next week. They mine the china clay there, which means work, but the children are often very sick. You could see for yourself what it's like."

They had been mining the clay around St. Austell for the porcelain industry for many years. Until clay was discovered there, only China could provide material of similar quality and quantity. The enormous spoil heaps had become characteristic of the region.

"With pleasure!" Jane assured her.

A few minutes later, she said her good-byes. Better not to extend the first visit unduly, Jane reasoned. Besides, she had the feeling that she had gotten somewhere with Violet, and Florence was growing increasingly talkative, and lewd.

When she was finally alone with Hettie in her coach, she sank back into the upholstered seat with relief. "Did you have a pleasant afternoon, Hettie?"

"Not especially enjoyable, ma'am, but informative," her maid replied slyly.

As the coach rolled slowly away from the house, Jane saw Hargrave walking with a young man around the side of the house. The clothes of the younger man indicated he was a hunting tenant, but the two men seemed better acquainted than such an owner-tenant relationship would have allowed.

13.

Hettie, her eyes gleaming with excitement, sat opposite Jane. "Well, the kitchen in Bromfield is huge, really, and the cook knows her business. Mrs. Roche could send our cook over there to apprentice. For dinner, they've prepared artichoke soup, lamb, and raisin pudding."

"Hettie!" Jane warned. Her maid was quick to forget herself where food was concerned.

"Mrs. Violet's maid is Nancy, and very curious she is, I can tell you. Twice as old as me and with a nose that's always sniffing around. But I'm smarter, and did not let her sound me out about you!" Hettie said proudly.

"Good girl," Jane praised.

"Mrs. Violet has been living in Bromfield ever since her husband passed on, six years ago. It seems she took his death very hard. He was twenty years older, an officer, and he died in Crimea a few months after they married. Nancy says Lord Hargrave had never been able to abide Mr. Sutton. But his sister was no longer young and wanted desperately to marry the man. She was in a family way when Sutton went away to the war. Poor woman . . ." Hettie shook her head. "Her husband fell in the war, and her baby was stillborn. After that, she retreated here to

Cornwall. The house used to belong to her parents, and now it's Lord Hargrave's. Sutton had no fortune to speak of, which left Mrs. Violet dependent on her brother. The servants say she looks after the orphans only because she herself wasn't able to have children."

"Why do they say that? It doesn't sound very nice," said Jane.

"No, but the mistress is not especially nice either, apparently. She makes out like she's a saint, but she's moody and screams a lot. They say she's a right terror when the lord's away. No one stays at Bromfield long, it seems. Or so Nancy says, at least."

"So why is Nancy still there?"

"She says she's had worse positions, and I think she's got something going with Lord Hargrave's valet. He came into the kitchen for a minute and whispered with her, then went off again. A good-looking chap he is, but not one to miss an opportunity, if you know what I mean," said Hettie with a telling look, and she leaned back, satisfied.

Jane suppressed a smile. "You really shouldn't talk like that, Hettie. It isn't proper for a young lady."

"But I'm not a young lady, ma'am. I'm just a maid." Hettie grinned.

"And what do they say about the lord of the manor?"

"That he's mostly away at one of his other properties or in London. He's known for the parties he throws." Hettie giggled. "His valet seems well suited to him. Because of the many women, I mean. The duke's often part of the show, too. Florence comes to visit Mrs. Sutton quite a bit. That's all I found out."

Jane nodded. "That's certainly a lot, Hettie. Well done!"

The young woman gave Jane a contented smile. Jane thought that she could count herself lucky not to have ended up with a man like Hargrave or Rutland. She would have hated it if her husband constantly amused himself with other women. But what did she really know about Wescott? Perhaps he was no different, just more discreet. Still, the women had made no veiled comments about any amorous adventures on her husband's part. If they had had the opportunity to do so, they would certainly not have wasted it. But thinking about it made no difference. She and Wescott had an agreement, and discretion was part of that.

"I'll be accompanying Mrs. Sutton to the orphanage in St. Austell next week." Jane had determined to visit the orphanages in the area one at a time and ask about two girls, one of whom was named Mary. She would take the book by John Polidori with her. One never knew, after all, when coincidence would play in one's favor.

No fish was served in Mulberry Park that evening, but the mushy peas were tasteless and the roast beef tough. Jane finished her lonely meal and gave the leftovers to Rufus, then left the joyless dining room that bordered the laundry. She passed through the entrance hall and entered the library and a salon that opened onto a lovely terrace overlooking the garden. *I could make something of this room,* Jane thought. The portraits of her parents and her uncle, as well as the Indian painting, were already hanging on the walls, which were papered in pale green.

Two young girls, one of whom owned a book about vampires . . . it must be possible to find them, Jane thought. She was becoming more and more convinced that Rosie and Mary had lived together in a home or an orphanage. They had been friends, and the more Jane heard the local people speak, the more convinced she became that Rosie had come from this corner of England.

Jane tugged on the bell pull to call a servant. Rufus had stretched out in front of the fireplace to digest the tough roast. There was a short wait, then Mrs. Roche appeared in person.

The woman's expression was like a wall. Her gray dress was clean and immaculately ironed, and the white collar starched and stiff. She was probably around fifty, with a sturdy build, and her pinched mouth reflected her aversion to the new mistress of the house. "The new girl's just spilled soup over her dress, so I've come myself, my lady."

"That's very nice of you, Mrs. Roche. Please go and fetch Mr. Coleman," Jane said. "Oh, and there was something else. The cook . . ."

Mrs. Roche's eyes narrowed to slits. "Yes, my lady?"

"Has she been here long?"

"No. We used to do the cooking ourselves. There was never any company here, and the late Lord Henry didn't put much store in big dinners when he came to visit." Mrs. Roche spoke coolly, her chin raised. "We had to find a cook right quick, my lady. Mrs. Thomas is from Lansallos and happened to be available. She used to cook for the parson."

"How could he bring himself to part with such a find?" Jane's words dripped irony.

Mrs. Roche scraped one foot nervously on the floor. "He let her go."

"I assume that had to do with the fish. Please start searching immediately for a new cook with decent references. Mrs. Thomas can remain until the new cook arrives, but not a day longer."

"As you wish, my lady. But if you'll allow me the observation, it won't do no good to ruin things with the folks in the village." Mrs. Roche raised her eyes.

"Why? Was the parson struck dead?"

"Not exactly dead, my lady. He had himself transferred."

Jane raised her eyebrows in surprise. "He felt threatened by the people who live in the village?"

"That I wouldn't know, my lady. I just wanted to say it." The woman's thin-lipped mouth twitched, but she said no more.

"Thank you. I won't let myself be intimidated. Those who don't do their job well must live with the consequences. Mrs. Thomas will receive her full month's pay plus an extra week. Now fetch Mr. Coleman."

Instead of obeying the request, Mrs. Roche replied, "Mr. Coleman's been putting around a lot of questions, my lady. He might be the new butler, but he's no right to go spying on us behind our backs. We've managed this household to your uncle's satisfaction for many years."

Floyd had begun asking questions among the staff. Of course that didn't suit them, which could really only mean they had something to hide. "Mr. Coleman is not spying, he is checking the facts. You will have to make the best of it. Thank you!"

Jane detested having to resort to such heavy-handedness, but it was imperative for her to gain the respect of her domestic staff. She was the new mistress of Mulberry Park, and she would tolerate no lies or intrigues behind her back. It would have been easier with a husband at her side. Jane automatically straightened her shoulders and eyed Mrs. Roche coolly.

Without a word, the woman turned and left. When, a moment later, the familiar face of Floyd appeared, Jane let out a sigh of relief. "You would not believe how happy I am to see you. Please, take a glass of sherry or whatever's there on the sideboard and tell me what you've found out."

Her loyal butler bowed his head and smiled politely. "I will gladly bring you a glass, my lady, but I would prefer to do without."

Jane waved it off. "As you like." Floyd poured a glass of port and handed it to her while she briefly related her discussion with Mrs. Roche. He always knew exactly what was needed, Jane thought, as she swallowed a mouthful of the sweet wine.

"You have made the right decision, my lady. I have been looking into the Thomas clan, and I don't like what I hear. The cook's brother has been behind bars a number of times for smuggling and fighting, and their father was sent to Australia for blackmail."

Jane nearly dropped her glass. "What? Good God!"

Floyd's face grew serious. "The cook's sister is married to the owner of the guesthouse in the village."

"Those baskets she's been taking from our kitchen! We would only have to prove it, although . . . she has been dismissed now. Perhaps we should leave it at that. What do you think, Floyd?"

"I believe that would be the more elegant solution," the butler replied. "Anything else will only cause bad blood. That still leaves the tenants. Poaching is a serious crime. No one has a disparaging word to say about Mr. Roche and his wife. They're not from around here, in any case, but from Norfolk. I could make some inquiries, of course, but I believe your uncle did that when he hired them. They have been working here for more than twenty years."

"A lot can happen in twenty years, and people change," said Jane grimly, and looked out the window into the darkness. "We should light lamps outside, like we did in Rosewood."

"Yes. I'll see to it," Floyd said, and his voice took on a sympathetic tone. "Perhaps Lady Alison has time to visit you? The house is not yet especially livable, and very big . . . Well, Captain Wescott will come soon, no doubt."

Jane sighed. "Oh, Floyd, I fear my husband's business will keep him tied up in London, and it will be quite a while before he visits us."

She turned the glass between her hands and watched the ruby-red liquid gleam in the lamplight. A tear rolled down her cheek. "My uncle loved port . . . do you remember, Floyd?"

"Naturally, my lady. He is sorely missed."

Jane looked up and saw a telling gleam in Floyd's eyes, but the butler quickly brought himself back under control. He stood before her, as dutiful as ever, providing the sense of security so familiar to her at Rosewood.

"Thank you, Floyd."

The butler blinked and turned to the Indian painting. "We could decorate this salon with the colonial items you brought with you from India. There is still that unopened crate full of them upstairs."

"That is an excellent suggestion. But I don't like this light green at all." She smiled crookedly.

Floyd nodded. "Curry, possibly?"

Jane's eyes lit up. "A solid curry or saffron tone would lend the room more warmth."

"An Indian salon," said the butler.

• • •

The next day was noticeably milder, the sky a patchy blue, and the birds were twittering in the trees. Luna, the mare Jane rode, had gray-white hair reminiscent of the light of the full moon. She trotted sedately toward the village, which lay in the hollow behind the patch of woods. It was three miles from her land to the village. A third of the woods here belonged to Mulberry Park, the rest to Bromfield Manor. The inhabitants of the village were expecting her visit, as were her tenants. They would be wondering who the new mistress of Mulberry Park was, though the estate was small and not really very grand. Rufus romped over the fields and chased the sheep. Jane whistled twice, and the Great Dane turned and covered the distance between them in a few bounds. Jane clucked her tongue and urged the mare into a fast trot. More than anything, she had been looking for an excuse to get out of the house for a few hours.

The oppressive atmosphere about the house stemmed not only from its size and emptiness, but also from the memories associated with the many items in the boxes she had not yet unpacked. Sooner or later, she would fill the place with life—with friends and guests—but she was not yet ready to do that. She still did not feel like the mistress of Mulberry Park. First, she knew she had to win the respect of the Roches; the couple had managed the house alone for too long.

Suddenly, Rufus barked and dashed into the undergrowth. The woods were dense, and the dog disappeared among the trees after just a few yards. Jane listened briefly, then turned Luna onto a trail that led off through the woods. The River Fowey lay in that direction, and opened into the estuary farther down.

As she road along the trail, she called for the dog several times without success, and soon heard what sounded like a water wheel. *The miller,* she immediately thought. The brother of the cook? A cracking noise in the forest to her right made Jane jump. *I should have brought a gun,* she thought. She was a good shot, after all.

"Is anyone there?" she shouted.

Again, she heard the cracking sound, this time followed by rustling and the clear sound of someone running away. "Hello! Who's there?"

Cursing silently, she drove the horse forward, ducking under low-hanging twigs, until the trees thinned out and the sound of the water wheel grew very loud, and she could see the mill ahead.

"Stinking mongrel!" someone shouted and Rufus yelped.

It sounded as if the dog had been hit, for she now heard Rufus growling and the man swearing and yelling even louder.

Jane gave Luna a sharp jab with her boots, and the horse leaped over bushes and a stone wall and landed at the top of a precipitous drop. Any farther and she and the horse would have plummeted into the waterway beneath the mill wheel.

"What the . . . ? Get off my land, damn it!" bellowed a man in work clothes and an apron. Both man and clothes were covered in flour. He held a club in his hands and was threatening Rufus with it; the dog was holding a dead rabbit in his mouth.

Rufus's head was bloody, and Jane saw another bleeding wound on the Great Dane's back. "Stop it, immediately! Rufus, drop it!"

The dog was in shock but instantly dropped the rabbit and trotted to Jane, who stayed in the saddle and glared furiously at the man, who was obviously the miller himself. "What do you think you're doing, beating my dog?!"

"Your mongrel, is it? It killed my rabbit and tried to attack me." The man paused. He was of medium height but muscular, in his late thirties, with a calculating face and a wide mouth. Clearly, not many women on the backs of stately horses came through this way. He finally put two and two together and swept the cap from his head. "Lady Allen?"

"Are you the miller Thomas, related to the cook, Becky Thomas?" Jane asked sharply.

"Yes, ma'am. I'm her brother."

Jane inhaled sharply. "So how does that work? Running a mill when you're sitting in prison, I mean?"

The man's chin jutted forward angrily. "That weren't me, ma'am, that was our brother Fred. I'm an honest man. I've run this mill for years, and I've never 'ad no problems with the law."

"My apologies, Mr. Thomas," Jane said, though she had serious reservations about the honesty of anyone from this family. "How is it that my dog caught a rabbit? Rufus is a Great Dane, not a hunting dog. Any halfway healthy rabbit can outrun him."

"I couldn't say, ma'am. Maybe the dog got lucky. It 'appens." The miller twisted his mouth into a hateful grin and leaned on his club.

"Don't be impudent, sir. Should I dismount and check whether that rabbit's been shot?" Jane leaned forward, but just then a second man appeared from the woods and jumped effortlessly over the stone wall.

The family resemblance was unmistakable, though the newcomer wore tattered clothes, boots, and a hat that he had pulled low over his forehead. A leather belt crossed his chest, holding cartridges and a knife. His hands were grazed and he'd wiped blood on his thigh. The man looked shiftily from the miller to Jane. "What's goin' on, Will?"

"You're an idiot, Fred!" the miller hissed at him. "Skedaddle!"

Fred finally seemed to comprehend the situation, then ducked and ran off into the undergrowth.

"Looks to me like your brother is poaching on my property."

"That's something you would 'ave to prove." But the miller suddenly sounded much less sure of himself.

Jane looked at the injured Rufus, then turned angrily back to the miller. "I'm giving you one chance to stop your brother from poaching.

Should I or one of my people catch him at it again, the police will be informed."

Will Thomas relaxed a little and looked relieved.

"A sack of your best flour! Tomorrow!"

The miller narrowed his eyes and nodded curtly. "Yes, ma'am."

Jane steered her horse around the mill and back onto the trail. She would not ride to the village with Rufus injured. His wounds would have to be tended, and she had lost all interest in meeting any further members of the Thomas family.

14.

That same afternoon, Jane sat in the library, spoiling Rufus with morsels of fish. She had tended to his injuries herself. At Rosewood, she had not only learned how to ride and hunt, but had also spent time with the gamekeeper helping to look after the dogs and the animal pens. She had assisted at the birth of pups and lambs, and the sight of blood made no difference to her. If an injured animal needed attention, Jane—under the gamekeeper's direction—had cleaned wounds and even stitched cuts.

Floyd approached carrying a silver tray on which two letters lay. Jane would have just as well have dispensed with such cumbersome formalities, but that would have injured Floyd's standing, and his spotless behavior served as an example to the other servants.

"Thank you, Floyd," she said, and tore open the first envelope. "Please, stay."

Jane quickly scanned the letter, which had been written in a flowing hand, and then read it aloud to him:

Dear Lady Jane,

Sadie has asked me to write you this letter. We are all mourning with you for the loss of the honorable Lord Henry, for your uncle was deeply beloved. Your uncle and you yourself, dear Lady Jane, have always provided, as Christians, for the needy, as you did for the poor soul of the young girl to whom you gave a dignified burial. It is therefore of necessity that I inform you of recent events.

Fearnham is not large, and strangers are quickly remarked. Sadie mentioned to me that a man suddenly appeared in town and was asking questions about the girl who died at Rosewood Hall. A strange fellow—Sadie called him a crook—with his roots in the same region as hers. When she asked him from where he came, he said Millpool, but that cannot be true because Sadie knows the people there. She thinks he had something to do with the girl but did not want to admit it, and then he was gone again. I did not speak to the man personally, but Sadie said he was over forty, neither fat nor thin, and he was missing half the little finger on his left hand.

After that came salutations and the signature of Verna Morris.

"Very odd," said Floyd thoughtfully.

"Isn't it? But what do we do with this news?" Jane chewed at her bottom lip. "Perhaps I should inform the captain."

"I consider that an outstanding idea. And you should not undertake anything yourself. It seems to me that there might be more to the death of that poor girl than we thought," Floyd cautiously put forward.

"And somewhere there is another poor girl named Mary waiting for someone to come and help her. Maybe I am her only hope. If she is even still alive . . ." Jane had taken the second letter and immediately recognized the wax seal of the Pembrokes. She snapped the seal and read what her cousin Matthew had written:

Dear cousin,

I warned you not to make yourself too comfortable in Mulberry Park. You have no right to the house, for my father has maintained it with his own money all these years. You have received far more than your due. Now fate has played into my hands and put me in a position to take what belongs to me, and I will not hesitate to enforce my claims against you. In court, if need be. But when you read what I have found, I am sure we will not need to put a lawyer to all that trouble.

While going through my father's papers, I came upon an old bundle of letters. Letters from your parents in Rajasthan. Your father, James, considered himself a humanitarian and refused to support the opium trade through his trading post. Of course, we all know that the East India Company would never have been as successful as it was without the opium trade, but be that as it may. Your good father went looking for trouble among the local dealers and repeatedly lost cargo consignments and orders. This all began some three years before his death. By 1837, he was up to his neck, and he asked my father for a loan. Naturally, my father helped his incompetent brother and bought up his debts.

Jane's hands shook. She knew what was coming next.

The promissory notes, dearest cousin, had been laid away carefully, still clean and fresh, among the letters. An old man's sentimentality, perhaps. Stupidity, I'd say, or simple forgetfulness. Whatever the case may be, the sum of those notes is considerable. I would give a great deal to be able to see your face right now, dear Jane. Always so self-righteous and upstanding. I do know approximately how much my father bequeathed you, and if my view of your financial situation is not mistaken, you can either sell Mulberry Park and live respectably from what is left once you have paid off these debts, or you can pay off the same from your existing assets. But in that case you will have hardly enough left over to maintain that old hovel in Cornwall.

Oh, of course, you are married now, but the way I hear it your husband is a war veteran and amuses himself alone in London. Sadly, he has fallen out with his stinking-rich family, so not much to expect from that side, it would seem. If I know you, though, Jane, old girl, you will find a solution to your dilemma.

In case you have any doubt as to the authenticity of the promissory notes, feel free to send old Samuel Jones over. Please understand, though, that I will not let them out of my sight. One can never be too careful.

Matthew had signed the letter with all of the titles he was entitled to as the new Lord of Pembroke.

"This cannot be true!" Jane whispered. "You knew my uncle. Did he ever say anything about this? Here, read it for yourself!"

Floyd took the letter from her and, as he read, grew paler and paler. Slowly, he looked up at Jane and folded the calamitous letter. "You would do best to inform your husband about this immediately. The consoling words of a butler can't help you, my lady. I regret that very much." Shaking his head, Floyd laid the letter on the table at which

Jane was standing. "His lordship was always proud of his son. It is his wife's influence that has driven Matthew to such base behavior. I can't explain it any other way."

Jane leaned heavily on the table for support and stared at the letter. "Jealousy, Floyd. Matthew hates me because he thinks his father loved me more than he did him. There's nothing I can do to fight that."

Despair coupled with the fear of losing her livelihood rose in Jane, cold and paralyzing. Her financial independence was everything she possessed, and if Matthew took that away from her, she would be in precisely the situation she had feared her entire life. Wescott might separate from her and go in search of some other rich heiress. Their arrangement would no longer be valid because she would be unable to keep up her side of the bargain, to offer him the particular social background he needed.

"My lady?" Floyd was looking at her with concern. "Can I do anything else for you?"

"Take the letter I'm about to write and have it delivered to the post office immediately." Jane took the two letters and went over to her secretaire, which stood at a window in one corner of the room.

It had never been easy for Jane to ask for help, and it was even more difficult for her to set out her situation to Wescott. She respected him, but when it came down to it, she hardly knew the man. She weighed every word carefully, openly admitting that she feared his reaction. Although she took care to ensure that Hettie never laced her corset too tightly, it seemed today to be taking her breath away. *What idiocy it is to crush women into cages of whalebone and wire,* thought Jane. One was literally forced to do practically nothing. But obstacles were there to be overcome, her uncle had always said, and Jane's fighting spirit had been rekindled.

She signed the letter with a polite and familiar "your faithful Jane," folded the letter, and sealed it with wax. The crest of the Allens united a swan and a stylized rose. Finally, she addressed the letter and handed it to her patiently waiting butler.

"Rest assured, my lady, that this letter will reach its destination as fast as possible."

"Thank you, Floyd." Jane went to the window and, minutes later, saw a mounted servant riding out of the courtyard.

Rufus whined and tried in vain to reach the wound on his back with his tongue.

"No, Rufus. That has to heal. It's all right." Jane crouched beside the dog and stroked him until he relaxed, stretched, and fell asleep.

With a final look at the injured dog, Jane left the salon and passed through the entrance hall on her way to the domestic rooms. Stuart, the servant with the missing tooth, put his broom aside, patted down the sleeves of his dark-blue jacket, and looked at her in anticipation.

"I would like to speak with Becky Thomas. Is she preparing the evening meal?" Without waiting for a reply from the confused servant, Jane moved past him and opened the door to the domestic wing herself.

"Ma'am, I can fetch the cook for you, you don't need . . . ," said Stuart and followed her into the corridor, where it smelled of cabbage and potatoes.

When she first arrived, she had made a quick tour of the entire house but had taken little notice of the kitchen. Now it was high time to get to the bottom of things. Jane encountered a young kitchen maid who instantly sank into a deep, shocked curtsy and hid her wet hands in her dirty apron. To the right was a pantry, and next to that the laundry. From inside came the squeak of the rollers on a mangle.

Undaunted, Jane continued on her way and entered the kitchen. Becky Thomas was standing at the stove and stirring something in a pot with a long wooden spoon. Another girl was chopping onions at a table, while a skinned rabbit lay on a wooden board beside her. At the sight of Jane, the knife fell from the girl's hand, and she froze, awestruck.

When the sound of chopping suddenly ceased, the cook turned her head. When she saw Jane, her dour face darkened. "Ma'am."

No more than that came from between her gritted teeth. Jane searched the cook's round face, red from the heat of the fire in the stove, for any resemblance to Will or Fred, and found the same belligerent lines around her mouth and eyes. Understandably, the cook, now dismissed, was not well disposed toward her, but one who delivered poor work had to live with the consequences.

"I was at the mill today, Becky. Your brothers were there," said Jane, and waited for Becky's reaction.

"Will's the miller. What do you mean by 'brothers'?" Becky asked cautiously.

"Don't you have a brother by the name of Fred? I caught him poaching."

The kitchen suddenly grew deathly quiet. The only sound was the bubbling and hissing from the stove.

The cook wiped her sweating forehead with the back of her hand. "I don't know nothing about that."

"Really?"

Becky Thomas's cheeks turned deep red, and she planted her hands defiantly on her hips. "I know what you're on about! Our Fred's been in a fight and 'ad to do his time for it. But the likes of us are easy to judge. Don't matter who else was in that fight, oh no! If you've got a white collar and rich friends, no 'arm done."

"Your brother's a known smuggler, and I'm talking about poaching. Those are not trivial offenses!" Jane insisted, not letting the hate-filled eyes of the cook intimidate her.

"You've no idea what it means to be poor!" Becky ranted. "With the little 'uns at 'ome crying with 'unger and—"

"Becky Thomas!" The sharp, authoritarian voice of Mrs. Roche rang through the kitchen, and the housekeeper was with them in a few steps. "My lady, can I help? I thought we had settled the matter."

"I did not know yesterday that Becky's brother Fred was poaching on my land or that her brother Will, the miller, wanted to beat my dog to death," said Jane, her voice cold.

Mrs. Roche smacked her hand to her mouth in horror. If she were faking her surprise, then she had missed her calling and should have gone into the theater. "How horrible! And I thought I was doing something good by helping her out. One ought not judge the children by the father . . ."

"Your Christian efforts are to be applauded, Mrs. Roche, but Becky is not a good cook, or I wouldn't have said anything. All I really want to know now is whether meat and other food from this kitchen and from my land has found its way into the pots of your family, Becky. What about your sister's guesthouse? Do they serve game from my woods there?"

Steps sounded from the hallway, and the butler ran into the kitchen. "My lady, is everything in order?" Floyd looked around in concern, and his eyes settled on the cook.

Jane nodded. "It is high time that someone sorted things out. My uncle gave everyone here a free hand for too long."

Mrs. Roche lifted her chin and muttered, "His lordship never had any cause for complaint. We've managed this estate to his full satisfaction for many years."

"Then let's leave it at that. Hand over the housekeeping books to Mr. Coleman, and I want the gamekeeper to come by. Becky, you will leave this house today. Mrs. Roche will pay you the agreed wages," Jane ordered.

"Yes, ma'am," Becky murmured, her expression grim. "But you won't turn up another cook fast! When word of 'ow you treat your people 'ere gets 'round, you won't turn up another one at all . . ."

"Hold your tongue! I will not allow you to threaten me. Floyd, please make sure that this person vacates these premises immediately." With that, Jane turned and left the kitchen.

As she left the domestic wing, she breathed in and out deeply to bring her shaking knees under control. With great concentration, she made her way up the stairs, went into her room, and leaned against the door frame inside with a heavy sigh.

Hettie came from the next room. "Ma'am, you're very pale. Is something wrong with Rufus?"

"No, no, it was this Becky Thomas. Hettie, I've never come across such a devious family!"

"Yes. Stuart said the same thing. They are not suffered happily in the village, but no one says anything because they're all afraid of them," Hattie remarked wide-eyed.

"Stuart? What are you doing dallying with him? Watch out, Hettie. You're still too young to be flirting with men."

Hettie shrugged it off. "I know that. I don't want a big belly. Then I'd have to leave you. No, ma'am, you don't have to worry about me."

"Good. Oh, Hettie, I really have enough to worry about!" Jane briefly summarized the content of the two letters.

Shaken, Hettie stood and stared at her. "Lightning ought to strike your cousin dead!"

15.

Mary

"More water!" Sister Susan shouted, pouring a torrent of soapy water onto the floor.

Mary slid back and forth on her knees, wiping away as much filth as she could with a cloth and wringing the stinking rag into a bucket. Since early morning, she had been hard at work scrubbing the orphanage floors. How was it possible for such small feet to track in so much muck? Puffing, she wiped her forehead with the back of her hand.

"This place will be clean as a whistle when the committee gets here tomorrow. Back there, that corner is still black! Mary, didn't you see that?" Sister Susan was pointing to one corner of the dormitory where black spots looked to be spreading across the plaster. The floorboards below were also discolored and smelled moldy.

"It won't come off, Sister! I've already scrubbed it." Mary stood up in her soaking dress and trudged over to the corner, which was constantly damp because the outside wall had a crack at that point. "The corner's always wet. You can feel it!"

Sister Susan's eyes narrowed to slits, and the cane in her hand whizzed through the air. Mary was quick enough to throw up her arms protectively over her head, and the first stroke hit her on the forearms. Again and again, the cane slashed down remorselessly on her delicate, childish skin, which finally gave way and split open. Mary felt the warmth of her own blood.

The blows stopped. "Look at the mess you're in, girl! It's all your fault! You're a stubborn, unteachable child. I don't know why the master lets you stay on here."

Mary stood trembling before the angry sister.

"Take your arms down and look at me when I speak to you!" the sister snarled.

The other children had fallen silent, and the only sound heard was the soft scrubbing of washcloths on the wet wooden floors. It was almost as if everyone had stopped breathing. Mary knew that if it were possible, they would have made themselves invisible.

One of the new girls began to cry softly, and Mary hoped that Fiona would be able to distract the child. "Stop whining, you useless little glutton!" screamed the sister. She was obviously very nervous today, and much more impatient than usual. She swished the cane through the air with a hiss, and a moment later the silence returned.

Mary simply stood there and looked at the blood running from the cuts on her arm onto the floor. It mixed with the wash water and ran into the gaps between the boards. *How much blood has seeped into this wood?* she wondered. Blood and tears. This place was a sea of blood and tears.

"What's the matter? Are you deaf?"

Mary, suddenly frightened, opened her mouth to speak, but no sound came out. She had wanted to say that, yes, she was deaf in one ear, but then thought better of it. Instead, she raised her arms and said, "Please, Sister Susan, may I fetch a bandage? Then I'll clean the corner."

The sister's lips pulled back from her yellow teeth scornfully. "Why not, Mary? We'll make a decent maid out of you yet. Go. I'll be back in one hour, and I don't want to see a speck of dust. And the beds must be made!"

In a panic, Mary ran down the corridor to the nurses' room, where there was a box of torn rags that served as bandages. Sister Susan wasn't always as mean as she was today. Usually her ill temper had something to do with the master and special visitors—perhaps the committee, a group of rich women who came by once a year, strolled through the rooms with their noses turned up sighing, "How dreadful" and "Bless me," then went into the private salon of the master and mistress to drink tea before disappearing again.

Once, Mary had received an orange from one of the women, and at Christmas they sent clothes and toys. The good items were separated and stored away for those who were meant to take up a position somewhere. Mary wrapped a strip of linen around one arm, held it firmly in her teeth, and tucked it in provisionally to keep it tight until she could get help with it. Then she did the same with the other arm and ran as fast as she could back to the dormitory, where Fiona was already waiting for her, her eyes wide with anxiety. "What was all that? Why did she give you a hiding like that? Come on, I'll help you."

Fiona wrapped the cloths tighter around her friend's arms, tore the end of each cloth down the middle, and knotted the makeshift bandages.

"Something's up. The committee's coming, but that's not it. At least, I don't think so. Those women have come here lots of times, and the old camel's never been this ruffled," said Mary. She went to a little girl who was squatting unhappily in the water and reaching at the air with her hands. "Little grub. She can't even speak," said Mary, picking her up. She hugged the girl to her and stroked her hair. The little girl was three years old and smiled and made smacking noises with her lips. Mary set her down again, for the sight of the girl reminded her too much of the baby. It had been a girl, but Mary had forgotten her name. Her memory only allowed for the baby she had let die. "I don't have anything for you to eat."

"She'll learn 'ow to speak one day. That's 'ow it is sometimes. It takes longer. Come on, we have to dry the floor. But what about the corner back there? 'ow are we supposed to get that clean?"

"We can scrub the boards with sand, but what about the plaster?" Mary looked around in despair.

"I've got an idea!" said Fiona. "There's lime in the workshop. We'll paint that over. You keep going 'ere and I'll fetch it."

"What would I do without you?" said Mary, and kneeled on the floor.

"Don't forget me when things get better, Mary."

But the final gleam of Mary's hope was fading.

The sun spent the whole day hidden behind a heavy blanket of clouds. Now and then it started to drizzle, and gusts of wind swept salty air over from the sea. *Just once, to see the sea,* thought Mary, while she spread sand on the floorboards and rubbed it into the wood with a hard brush.

From outside came the regular knocking of the men who were smashing stones with hammers. Breaking rocks exhausted the men physically, but it was also degrading, just like taking apart the old hawsers. It was draining, soul-destroying work, the work you did when you were at the end, when there was nothing else to do to earn a bed for a night and a lukewarm meal.

Fiona returned from the workshop, where she'd managed to get some lime. They stirred it into a creamy mass in a bowl and smeared it over the discolored wall with their hands. The result was surprisingly good, and the girls looked at each other proudly.

"But it's wet," said Mary.

"Can't be 'elped. You were supposed to wash the wall anyway, right?"

"But they'll notice."

"No, they won't. Listen!"

From the open window came loud voices and the cries of children from the courtyard on the street side. The other children tried to run to the window to see what was going on, but Mary told them, "Better stay out of sight. The camel's in a bad mood today. Wash your hands, and then we'll play something."

Fiona and Mary went to the window in time to see Sister Susan take a child from the arms of a woman—a laborer, judging from her humble clothes—and pass the child to a maidservant who worked for the master and his wife.

"And will my little one be treated well here?" the woman asked despairingly, reaching out one hand toward her child, who began to scream and was carried away by the servant.

Sister Susan looked quite impressive in her light-blue dress and white bonnet, and instilled a feeling of trust in strangers. "My life is dedicated to these children, and I can assure you that none of them lack for anything. It all looks rather untidy now, certainly, but that's because we are in the middle of preparing for a visit from some eminent patrons. If you really want, I can show you one of our classrooms and the dormitory."

But the way Sister Susan said it, it was clear that she was telling the woman to get lost, and the sooner the better.

"No, no, don't trouble yourself. I've a train to catch and can't stay. But I'll come back and fetch my little one as soon as I've found some work and money." She pressed a few coins into the sister's hand. "Here, take this. I don't have any more right now." Sister Susan put the money in her pocket without a word.

Then the woman ran off as if the Furies themselves were after her. Sister Susan was still standing in the courtyard watching as the porter closed the gate when the mistress approached her. She spoke in a low voice, and Mary and Fiona could not catch every word.

"How many do we have for the transport to . . . ?" the mistress asked.

"Five can go tomorrow. This new one, too," the sister replied.

"Are you sure? The mother agreed?"

The camel gave a dry laugh. "You know how it works. If she comes back, then, dearie me, we lost the little one to the fever."

Suddenly, Sister Susan turned and stared up at the window. Mary and Fiona ducked instantly.

"What transport?" Mary whispered.

Fiona looked at her solemnly. "It sure as heck ain't good."

16.

Jane had lost her appetite for dinner and had bread and cheese brought to her bedroom. The room was large, with space for a table and chairs in front of the window. A small lockable desk with various compartments crouched in one corner. It was where Jane kept her personal documents and letters. Wearing a comfortable housedress, she sat at the desk, folded her cousin's letter, and placed it in one of the narrow compartments. Above the compartments, she had stood the book the dead girl had left behind, and she withdrew it and put it on the desk in front of her. Gently, she stroked the worn cover with its stamped gold letters.

After Jane ate, Hettie cleared Jane's meager dinner. Rufus lay stretched out on his mat beside Jane's bed. Hettie gave him a piece of bread, and Jane heard the loud smacking noises he made as he ate. "Don't spoil him too much, Hettie, or he'll get fat."

"Oh, no, the poor thing. He's earned it." The maid scratched Rufus's huge, bony head.

Jane leafed slowly through the thin volume, page by page, hoping to stumble across some clue she had so far overlooked. But the pages were unmarked. No scribbling in the margins, no notes tucked between the pages. There were only the initials *M & P* and the sketch of the rose in the front. Finally, she turned to the last page and ran her fingertips over the marbled paper, as if it might reveal something about the two girls for whom this book had meant so much. The last page was thicker than the others, and as she rubbed the paper between her fingers, it separated from the patterned flyleaf that reinforced the inside of the cover. It looked as if the last page and the flyleaf had got wet at some point, but some faded and partly illegible handwriting remained. It was not a child's hand, but rather a bureaucratic entry, something a librarian would write: *Ga . . .* and *Orp . . . age* and *Cornwall* could still be read.

Jane slapped one hand on the desk in triumph. "An orphanage in Cornwall! This is proof! Hettie, look at this!"

The maid read the fragmentary inscription and said, "But where do we start, ma'am?"

Jane laughed for the first time that terrible day. "In Bodmin, Hettie. That's where the main administration is. Tomorrow!"

They left Mulberry Park in the early hours of the morning. Thick wraiths of sea fog swept miles inland, revealing only occasional glimpses of craggy hills, forests, and lonely farmhouses out on barren meadows. The coachman was of Cornish stock and steered the horses surely along the muddy roads, where stones and potholes lurked. Only a few villages lay along their route, which took them up the east side of the River Fowey.

"Once we cross the Fowey, the moor begins, ma'am," said Hettie. "Actually, it starts lower down, but between Bodmin and Liskeard and then up to the north stretches what we call the wild moor. One of my uncles lives in Churchtown, not far from Brown Willy."

"Brown Willy?" asked Jane. She was glad the coach was closed. Rain had begun to beat against the windows.

"It's the mountain in the moor. You can see clear to the coast from up there, and to the white mountains near St. Austell. It's awfully bleak. My uncle's lost a lot of animals to the moor."

"A terrible way for a poor beast to die. Didn't Mrs. Morris's Sadie come from Millpool? That's north of Bodmin."

"That's right. It's not a pretty place, I can tell you that," said Hettie.

Jane thought for a moment. "I hope the orphanage administration in Bodmin can help us. 'Ga' could be almost anything. It would make things easy, of course, if there were an orphanage with 'Ga' at the start of its name, but I doubt that's the case." With a sigh, Jane sank back onto the seat and let her thoughts wander to the juddering rhythm of the coach.

There was something soporific about the pattering of the raindrops, and Jane's eyelids grew heavier until she fell into a shallow sleep. Images from her young life in India mixed with the last ball at Rosewood Hall. Her uncle was talking to Wescott, and Lord Hargrave wanted to dance with her and quarreled with Mr. Devereaux. She ran from the scene and found the dying girl in the garden. The girl begged Jane to help her. Suddenly, Matthew and Bridget appeared, laughing and sneering, banishing her from the house. The next thing she knew, she was standing alone in the barren solitude of a moor, at the foot of a mountain. She stared at her feet, beneath which the ground suddenly gave way. She reached for a branch to hold on to, but could not get hold of it because a man in a dark cloak appeared and pushed her back with his walking stick.

"Ma'am, wake up! You've been dreaming!" Hettie's concerned voice penetrated the forbidding images, and Jane opened her eyes in fright.

"A nightmare," she murmured.

After two brief stops, they reached Bodmin in the early afternoon. The small town was the administrative center of the county and notorious for its prison and asylum. The rain had stopped, but the sky was still heavy with clouds, and a chill wind swept through the narrow alleys. The people went about their business hunched inside waxed cloaks, wearing expressions that invited no contact. Many of the faces were marked by a hard life and the harsh climate. The wheels of the coach clattered over cobblestones, past the town hall, market square, and a number of churches. The mortal relics of St. Petroc had rested here since the middle ages, and as a result the town was considered the religious heart of Cornwall.

As the coach slowed and came almost to a standstill, Jane peered out the window and saw a crowd pushing through an arched gateway in front of a grim-looking complex of buildings.

A street trader carrying a hawker's tray of haberdashery walked past. Jane opened the window and stopped him. "What is going on there?" she asked.

The man grinned. "It's a 'anging, ma'am. Do you want to watch? I can get you a good place."

Repulsed, Jane shook her head and knocked on the coachman's seat from inside. The coachman cracked the whip several times, and the crowd, cursing, made way. Past low houses of gray stone, the road led westward, heading out of the town. A weathered wooden sign pointed toward a side street, and Jane recoiled at the sight: WESTHEATH ASYLUM. Beneath it was a sign for the orphanage.

"Let's hope the poor children don't share a building with the lunatics," said Hettie gloomily, and gazed up at the Elizabethan building that loomed behind an iron fence.

The coach rolled to a stop at a high gate where a man in uniform stood. The coachman exchanged a few words with the guard, who pointed farther on to the next entrance. The orphanage turned out to be a smaller secondary building, but still part of the asylum complex and no more cheerful, save for a brief burst of child's laughter that instantly fell silent.

As Jane and Hettie climbed out of the coach, they instinctively felt they were being observed. Jane looked up to the windows of the orphanage, where the pale faces of children pressed against the panes of glass. Then she turned to the three-story hulk of the insane asylum, which seemed as though it were about to swallow the orphanage like a dark shadow. She heard horrible, inhuman cries and mad laughter from inside, and it chilled the blood in her veins.

Hettie bustled close to her mistress and whispered, "I'm not about to go in over there, ma'am. Not there!"

"They're still human beings, Hettie. Tortured souls beyond any help," said Jane in an effort to calm her maid, and she marched with less resolve than she felt toward the door at the entrance to the orphanage, which now opened.

Miss Shepard, a friendly young governess and the deputy mistress of the home, greeted Jane and led her into her office. As Jane took a seat on the chair the young woman in the gray dress offered, she heard the scrape of many small feet outside the door. Miss Shepard smiled apologetically. "You must excuse the curiosity of our children, but every visit means change, at least for some of them. How can I help you, my lady? Are you looking for staff? We have a number of very charming young women."

"No, no, that's not why I'm here," Jane said, and wondered how best to present her reason for being there.

Miss Shepard moved behind her desk and seated herself. "An unfulfilled wish for children? We have one young boy who is just six months old. His mother is healthy, but unmarried, you understand."

Jane cleared her throat. "No. I'm here for a completely different reason. I'm looking for a girl . . . well, two, actually . . ." She outlined the facts of the case to the governess, whose interest grew as she listened.

Finally, Jane took out Polidori's novel. "Here. You can see for yourself."

The young woman before her seemed honest and trustworthy. She looked at the initials in the book and the blurred handwriting and handed the book back to Jane. "As sad as it makes me to say so,

I'm afraid I can't help you, Lady Jane. We do have a classroom where a number of books are kept, but this one was definitely not among them."

Jane nodded, but she was disappointed. "It is like looking for the needle in the proverbial haystack, but I had to try."

There was a knock at the door, and when Miss Shepard called, "Come in!" a young boy poked his head around the door.

He was far too thin for his age, and his large, dark eyes looked emptied of hope. "Amy has a high fever, miss, and the new baby is crying, and Louisa has no more sleep medicine."

"Oh, no . . . all right, Thomas, I'm coming. Where is Mr. Tobin . . . oh, the execution," Miss Shepard murmured. "Go to the kitchen and fetch milk for the baby. And if Ethel doesn't want to give you any, tell her I gave you express permission."

"Yes, miss." The boy cast a quick, curious glance at Jane before quietly pulling the door closed behind him.

Miss Shepard turned back to Jane. "That's how it is here, my lady. We're short of everything, wherever you look. Every week there's a new foundling left at our door. Milk is expensive." The governess wrung her hands. "Just two weeks past, we got tainted milk, and not for the first time. Two babies died of the colic."

"But I don't understand. Lord Hargrave's sister is one of the patrons here, isn't she?" Jane objected.

The governess's face reflected the turmoil of emotions going on inside her. Finally, she said, "It is true that Mrs. Sutton often comes here. She is also on the committee of the Friends Association. She . . . well, she really only ever speaks with Mr. Tobin."

"The director of the home?"

"He and his deceased wife founded this orphanage. He is also the director of the asylum," Miss Shepard explained.

"That explains why the orphanage is here."

"Yes. It isn't the most fortuitous solution, but one can't be too picky. But what I wanted to say is that ladies like Mrs. Sutton never actually see the destitution of the children directly, and Mr. Tobin is the one who decides what the money gets used for."

"I see." Jane spontaneously took out her purse and laid five pounds on the desk. "I don't need a receipt for that. Please use it to buy milk and medicine."

"My lady, thank you! That is extremely generous of you." Miss Shepard quickly tucked the note away in the pocket of her skirt. "I will buy the milk myself. Then I know that it's good."

As Jane stood, there was another knock at the door.

"My lady," said Miss Shepard, who had also stood. "I wouldn't put too much store in the book. 'Ga' most certainly does not stand for the name of an orphanage. I know all of them. It could only refer to the name of whoever donated it, or perhaps a teacher who gave the book to the children. I will ask around."

Another knock, and Miss Shepard sighed. "Yes?"

The same young boy peeked self-consciously through the gap in the door. "The baby's crying real bad, and the others, too."

"Thank you so much for your assistance, Miss Shepard." Jane did not want to keep the busy young woman any longer.

She smiled. "I should be thanking you. Do you still have far to drive?"

"We intend to spend the night here, actually. Can you recommend somewhere?"

Miss Shepard looked down in embarrassment. "I only know the simpler lodgings, my lady. But the Coach Inn beside St. Lawrence Church is supposed to have clean rooms and good, simple food."

"Good-bye, then." She gave the governess her card. "Please write to me if you hear anything. But please don't breathe a word to anyone else."

"Of course not, my lady."

Jane and Hettie left the small office and, in the dim light of the corridor, saw the outlines of waiting children, pressed together.

"If only one could do more," said Jane softly and with Hettie stepped out into the afternoon sun, now showing itself between the clouds.

The coachman was waiting for them outside beside a high iron fence, behind which was the courtyard of the asylum. Benches stood there among the trees, but no one was sitting on them. It was indeed cold and damp, but Jane had the feeling that even in good weather few would be using the benches. When the coachman saw her coming, he jumped down from his seat and held open the door for them. Jane had just set one foot on the step when a movement on the other side of the street caught her eye. A man was loitering in the entrance of a building and staring across at her.

He was shabbily dressed in dark clothing, as far as she could see, and wore a cap pulled low over his forehead. His hands were buried deep in the pockets of his woolen coat, and he gave the impression that he'd been standing there for a long time. A dark suspicion came over Jane, and she stepped back down from the coach.

"Rogers, would you ask that man over there why he's staring at us?"

The coachman turned and caught sight of the stranger, then quickly strode across the street toward the man, who suddenly seemed to come to life. He leapt from the cover of the entrance and ran down the street. The coachman lumbered after him but gave up the chase after a few yards and returned to the coach, out of breath.

"The man is used to a quick dash, ma'am. I'm not, I'm sorry to say."

Hettie observed the scene and voiced Jane's suspicions. "Maybe it was the man from Fearnham, is that it? The one that Sadie met?"

"Let's not lose our heads, Hettie. Rogers, to the Coach Inn, please."

Miss Shepard's recommendation turned out to be a good one. The guesthouse offered small, clean chambers, and set out eggs and ham, potatoes, and a bread pudding for dinner. Jane and Hettie shared a room and, worn out from the long drive, retired early.

• • •

The next morning, they were sitting in the small restaurant, eating breakfast, when a messenger came with a letter for Jane. The boy was a street urchin, one of the many who struggled to keep themselves alive in the cities and large towns. His hollow face and shifty eyes had no doubt seen more violence and misery than either Jane or Hettie could imagine. With dirty fingers, he held out an envelope to Jane.

"You're the lady who was by the orphans' 'ome yesterday, ain't you?" he asked in a broad Cornish dialect.

The innkeeper was watching the scene and approached their table. "If this young crook is bothering you, I'll have him thrown out."

"I think he just wants to give me something," said Jane. She took sixpence out of her bag and gave it to the boy, who then dropped the envelope on the table and took off at a run.

"Vermin. They'll pick your pocket soon as look at you," the innkeeper grumbled and stomped away.

Jane opened the letter, a folded sheet of paper sealed with candle wax, while Hettie looked on curiously. There was no name on the outside.

"Something from Miss Shepard?"

Jane quickly read the letter, just a few lines written in a flowing hand, and her expression hardened. "No, most certainly not." She showed it to Hettie.

"A poem?" asked Hettie, and read the lines in a low voice.

> *Death found strange beauty on that cherub brow*
> *And dash'd it out . . .*
> *There was a tint of rose . . .*
> *And the rose faded*

The maid looked at Jane uncertainly. "That's the elegy that Lydia Sigourney wrote. But that's not how it goes, not exactly."

The poetic lines about the death of a child were beloved by many and familiar to most. A shudder passed through Jane. "This is a threat, Hettie. Someone doesn't want me asking questions."

"Oh, ma'am, no. A threat? But . . ." The young girl bit her bottom lip and blinked nervously. "What do we do?"

Jane folded the letter carefully and stowed it in her bag. Then she looked intently at the other guests, but none of them seemed interested in her. They were focused on their breakfasts or were chatting away to their neighbors. No one was observing her.

"I will not let anyone intimidate me!" said Jane with determination, and she stood up. "We're going home, then we'll see where we go from there."

17.

They left Bodmin with the oppressive feeling of having stumbled upon something important without knowing exactly what. But Jane trusted her instincts, and they told her that without an armed man beside them, it was too dangerous to continue their investigations. It would be willfully stupid to ignore such a threat, though it galled her to leave Bodmin, and she had the feeling that the sender of the letter was mocking her with those few lyrical lines. *One should never underestimate one's enemy,* thought Jane. *But that goes for both sides.*

The drive back to Mulberry Park took place with no incidents of note, save a few rain showers and the wind. The closer they came to the coast, the stronger the wind blew, with occasional storm gusts. The trees bent, and the gorse bushes, the yellow flowers of which were the first to drive out the winter, whooshed and rustled beside the road. Jane could taste the sea salt on her lips as they approached home. What had moved her father to buy these gray walls so close to the sea? She was sorry she had been too young to really know her parents. But more than that, she regretted that her uncle had not spoken to her about his brother more often. Perhaps there were more dark shadows in her father's life than just the debts he owed?

The coach rolled through the gate at the end of the driveway that led to the house. *We have to plant more mulberry trees,* thought Jane, looking at the massive stumps that remained alongside the driveway. She saw Rufus from some distance away. He was still suffering some tenderness, but his tail wagged happily from side to side. The coachman slowed the team, and they eventually came to a stop at the main entrance. Jane climbed out and greeted Rufus, who threw himself at her. She looked up, expecting to see Floyd. Instead, she saw Mrs. Roche approaching, looking downcast.

"Good day, my lady. Did you have a good trip?" asked Mrs. Roche, her voice suspiciously brittle.

"Yes, thank you. Where is Mr. Coleman?" Jane looked around.

"In his room, my lady. He has gone to bed. Please, come inside. Stuart will take care of the baggage."

"Gone to bed? Is he sick?" Jane's stomach tightened. *Not Floyd,* she thought. *Nothing can happen to Floyd!*

Mrs. Roche bustled ahead up the stairs. A lamp had been lit in the entrance hall, and the smell of roast meat came from the domestic wing.

"Do we have a new cook already?" asked Jane warily.

"No, my lady. I'm working on that. One of the kitchen maids is very good, and we are getting by. Mr. Coleman had an accident. The doctor is with him right now."

"What? My God! Why didn't you say so?" Jane gathered her skirts and ran up the stairs. On the landing, she took off her cape and threw it to Hettie, who was close behind her.

Followed by Mrs. Roche, she ascended to the top floor. "What happened?"

"Yesterday afternoon, Mr. Coleman rode out to pay a visit to the tenants. He wanted to speak to Jacob Blythe, the gamekeeper. It must have happened on the way back. Mr. Coleman's horse shied and bolted and threw him off. He is still unconscious, and his leg is broken."

They had nearly reached the door to Floyd's room. "Who found him?"

"The horse came back here alone. As soon as we saw it, my husband rode out with Stuart, and they found Mr. Coleman at the edge of the woods, just by the gate that leads to the lower meadow." Mrs. Roche kneaded her hands nervously. "No one can say how it happened. Such a terrible accident."

Yes, thought Jane grimly. *And I'm sure what you regret most is that Floyd can't check up on you anymore.* She knocked and turned the door handle. She stopped momentarily, as if paralyzed at the sight that met her eyes, but quickly pulled herself together and stepped into Floyd's room.

The doctor was a man of medium height with blond hair and penetrating blue eyes. He washed his hands in a bowl and dried them. "Lady Jane, I'm Doctor Woodfall. I'm sorry to have to make your acquaintance like this."

Jane nodded absently. She only had eyes for Floyd, who lay motionless on his bed. His forehead was red and swollen, and his cheek badly grazed. His breathing was shallow and irregular, but it was his leg that shocked Jane most. Blood had seeped through a tight bandage on his thigh, and a bowl of bloody water stood on a table beside the bed. Beside the bowl lay medical instruments and an old bandage with an unpleasant smell.

"An open fracture?" asked Jane flatly and stroked Floyd's hand.

The doctor raised his eyebrows. "Are you one of Florence Nightingale's nurses?"

"No. That experience was never mine, I'm sorry to say, but I've seen my share of injuries. More with animals, but still . . ."

She heard a whistle behind her, followed by a wheezing sound. "Blood. I can't stand to see blood," said Mrs. Roche, standing in the doorway.

"Fetch us a bottle of whisky and fresh towels," said Jane. "And hot water?" When the doctor nodded, Jane gave the housekeeper a wave, and the woman hurriedly left again.

"Has he been unconscious the whole time?" asked Jane.

"No. But his pain was so bad that I gave him laudanum. The swelling on his forehead would have come from the horse throwing back its head. Your butler was lucky. I've seen similar accidents leave the rider dead or paralyzed."

"Then there's hope that he'll recover fully?" Jane looked at the familiar face of her loyal butler and felt a sharp pang in her chest. "He's practically part of the family."

Woodfall smiled. "He seems a robust chap. If no gangrene sets in, his chances are good. I was able to set the bone, but I won't splint the leg until his wounds have closed."

The doctor knows what he's doing and has had experience with traumatic injuries, thought Jane. "What is someone with your knowledge doing out here in the country? You were in Crimea, I presume?"

"Sebastopol. Balaklava. I was there, and I stitched the soldiers back together. My wife comes from St. Austell. Part of the land where they mine the clay belongs to her family."

"Then they've called you here all the way from St. Austell?"

"No. We have our own place in Looe. Keeping a little distance between us and her family has its advantages. I've had enough of battlegrounds." The doctor grinned.

"I understand. My husband says the same. He was in Crimea, too. Captain Wescott."

"Really? I know him! He was on my table!" Woodfall paused. "I beg your pardon. In war, social strata are of less importance, and can be fatal."

"You mean what happened with Lord Lucan?" People still talked about the terrible defeat at Balaklava, the direct result of the general's incompetence.

"That, too. My lady, may I ask when your husband is expected? It would make me very happy to see him again."

There was a knock at the door, and Mrs. Roche and a housemaid brought whisky, towels, and hot water.

Once Jane knew Floyd was in good hands, she left the doctor to his work. "When you have finished up here, please join me for dinner, Doctor Woodfall."

When Jane stepped into her bedroom, all the tension she had been feeling suddenly slackened, and the strain of the events of the day caught up with her. Exhausted, she let Hettie help her out of her dress. "Bring me a cup of hot tea, then have them draw me a bath," she said. "Put out the violet dress. Doctor Woodfall is staying for dinner."

"Yes, ma'am. I've spoken to Stuart. He told me that the horse Mr. Coleman was riding came back very nervous, and it's normally a completely unflappable beast."

"Then it must have gotten a fright. Maybe someone was shooting. Not all horses are gun proof."

"That's true, but who would be shooting? The gamekeeper was in his house, and no one else is allowed to shoot anything around here."

Jane slipped into her dressing gown and slumped onto a chair. Through the window, she had a sweeping view over the park. "Unless someone's poaching again. I wouldn't put anything past that Fred Thomas. It was probably a mistake to dismiss the cook, but she was simply unbearable."

"I'll get the tea, ma'am. You made the right decision. Mrs. Roche doesn't like the Thomas clan any more than you, but she and her husband are afraid of them. I have yet to find out why, though."

Jane pulled the longest pins from her hair and shook it loose. The embroidered bag in which she kept her money and powder lay on a stool within easy reach. Pensive, she retrieved the letter the grimy boy had handed her that morning and unfolded it again.

"'Death found strange beauty on that cherub brow . . . and the rose faded,'" Jane murmured. The death threat could be meant for her, or just as easily the second girl, Mary. She felt she could safely assume that whoever was following her also knew about the two girls. "P. and Mary, where did you live? Where did you come from on that cold winter night?"

Not directly from an orphanage, that much was clear. The girl had been wearing the plain outfit of a simple maid. Miss Shepard knew of no girl who had found a position in a household only to disappear, and if Mary had still been in the orphanage in Bodmin, then Miss Shepard would no doubt have thought of two inseparable girls immediately. Something like that would stand out. On top of everything came Floyd's strange accident, utterly unlike anything that should happen to such a cautious man.

The table was set festively, the lamps lit, and a fire crackled in the fireplace. With the dark-green curtains and the landscape paintings Jane had brought with her from Rosewood Hall, she had to admit that the dining room looked thoroughly presentable. The sideboard and the silver had been polished, and the étagère in the center of the dining table had been filled with fruit. *Mrs. Roche has outdone herself*, thought Jane, and she smiled at Doctor Woodfall, who had seated himself on her right at the table. Rufus lay in front of the fire and stretched.

A maid that Jane had not previously seen served the oxtail soup, which was surprisingly tasty. Jane lifted her glass of red wine. "Your health, Doctor. I'm very glad you were close by and able to attend to Floyd."

"Thank you, Lady Jane, the pleasure is all mine," Woodfall replied.

They turned their attention to the soup, and Woodfall reassured Jane that Floyd was on the road to recovery. The main course consisted of roast venison, mashed potatoes, and carrots, and Jane nodded appreciatively when she tried the gravy.

"You have an outstanding cook, Lady Jane," Woodfall remarked.

"Hmm. Well, the truth is that I don't have a cook at all. I believe the praise is due my housekeeper, who has jumped in for the time being. Unfortunately, I had to dismiss the previous cook. I haven't been at Mulberry Park long." She drank some wine and looked at Woodfall directly. "I assume you heard of the death of my uncle. The captain and I brought our wedding forward for his sake, which is why not everything in this house is as it ought to be. There simply hasn't been time to do it all."

Woodfall set down his cutlery and dabbed at his mouth with the napkin. His blond hair was graying at the temples, Jane noted, and he could have been a few years older than Wescott. Life as a doctor at the front had left its legacy on him. Social decorum was the last thing that interested this man.

"Outstanding, Lady Jane. Please, don't give a second thought to formalities. In the war, we were thankful for clean water and a piece of bread that wasn't moldy. You mentioned Lord Lucan. I have to admit that when I hear that name, everything in me boils up. So much arrogance and stupidity in one man makes me furious, in particular when this man is able to order a brigade to ride into certain death."

"That must have been a terrible experience. I don't think anyone who has not been to war can really understand what it is like. And my husband actually found himself wounded on your operating table?" Jane asked, hoping to find out more about Wescott.

Their conversation paused as the maid cleared away the plates and set a cheese plate on the table.

"Without wanting to go into great detail about the battle, Lady Jane, the captain was among the wounded of the Eleventh Hussars. His horse made it to the edge of the battlefield before collapsing, fatally wounded. If memory serves, the captain was rescued by his adjutant, who immediately brought him to me in the field hospital."

"Blount," Jane whispered.

"Right. That was the man's name. Headstrong type, came from a Hungarian gypsy family. I would not have trusted him myself, but the captain wouldn't hear a word against him. Your husband's wounds were serious. I had little hope at the start that he would even survive." When he saw Jane's horrified face, the doctor smiled. "But he proved us all wrong. I provided the initial treatment, but at some point I had to move on to the next patient. His adjutant took care of him after that. I never understood why he stayed on in Crimea. With the wounds he suffered, he could have been given an honorable discharge and immediately sent back home."

Jane had come to believe that the quarrel with his father was what had kept Wescott away from England for so long, but she kept that to herself. To the doctor, she said, "Do you need to be going, or can I offer you a room for the night?"

Outside darkness was falling, and it would soon be too late to ride anywhere.

Doctor Woodfall stood and went to the window. "Hmm. Perhaps it's really for the best if I spend the night here. Then I can change your butler's dressing once more before I leave in the morning."

Jane, too, had stood, and said to the serving girl waiting by the sideboard, "Bring us a carafe of fresh water in the library. Doctor, would you keep me company a little longer?"

"It would be my pleasure." He offered her his arm and then scratched Rufus's ear, for the dog immediately positioned himself at the doctor's side. "He's hurt. It looks like he's been hit."

"Yes. An unfortunate story." Jane told him about the incident at the mill, and did not omit the miller's relationship to the dismissed cook.

Thoughtful, the doctor led her down the hallway. "The Thomas clan does not have a good reputation. I'm surprised that your housekeeper employed Becky in the first place. The father is said to be a very bad egg. No one shed any tears when he was transported. I hear bits and pieces on my rounds in the area. Being a doctor also makes you something of a pastor."

In the library, Woodfall lit a cigar to accompany his whisky, and Jane settled into an armchair with a glass of port. It was pleasant to spend the evening in the company of an eloquent man. Perhaps she should push ahead with the renovations and invite guests more often. Violet Sutton and Lord Hargrave, at least, were expecting a return invitation.

18.

Mulberry Park, Cornwall, April 1860

Two days after Jane's return to her new home, Floyd's condition had improved considerably. He required very little laudanum, and the wound on his thigh had not become infected, which allowed Doctor Woodfall to strap on a splint. The doctor ordered absolute bed rest for his patient to give the bone time to knit, a stipulation that Floyd accepted only with the greatest reluctance.

Jane set the estate's books on the table beside Floyd's bed. "If you don't do what the doctor says, I will be extremely disappointed in you, Floyd. We're lucky to have such a skilled doctor in the neighborhood, and we should follow his instructions. Promise me that, will you?"

The butler grumbled something and tried to reach for a cushion, but Jane was faster and pushed it behind his back.

"My lady, please, that is not your job. I'm supposed to be taking care of you!"

"Maybe. But the fact of the matter is that you're the one with the broken leg. When you're healthy again, you can look after me. Until that time, I'm in charge!" She smiled and looked to the open door. "Stuart will be bringing up some chicken soup soon, and there'll be tea and fruitcake later. I don't really know who in the kitchen is responsible for that miracle, but Mrs. Roche seems to be trying, in her own way, to apologize for all the unpleasantness caused by that Becky Thomas. Now, tell me again how the accident happened, and don't leave out a thing."

With a sigh, Floyd folded his hands on top of the blanket. He was very pale, and despite his reluctance to take laudanum, it was clear that he was still in pain. "I paid a visit to Jacob Blythe, the gamekeeper. I'm not yet done with him, my lady. I am certain he has something to hide. He has pens full of partridges and pheasants and, as far as I could see, a large number of tame deer besides. Far more than what we would ever use in the house, and none of it is entered in the books." The butler closed his eyes. Even talking was a strain. "I left things at that for the time being, just a talk, and rode back through the woods. Then there was a shot, just before I reached the edge of the woods, and it sounded very close. My horse went mad. It reared up, then galloped off with me. After that, I don't remember much at all."

There was a soft knock, and Stuart entered with a tray. "Here's the soup for Mr. Coleman, and lunch can be served down below, ma'am. Oh, and there's a letter for you."

Jane took the envelope. Her name and the Mulberry Park address were written on the front in a delicate hand. "I'll come to check on you a little later, Floyd. Stuart, he is forbidden to leave the bed!"

"Yes, ma'am."

Jane did not open the letter until she was in her room. It was from Miss Shepard! After the usual formalities came the sentence that really mattered: "... *asked after teachers whose surnames begin with 'Ga,' and I have had some success. Until a year ago, a Miss Hope Gardner taught*

148

in St. Austell, and the same agency that listed me also had a Peter Gaunt on their books. He was in Plymouth, and most recently in London in an institute in Fleet Lane. I very much hope that I have been able to assist you in your search."

Hettie came into the room, and Jane showed her the letter. "Well, if that isn't a coincidence! St. Austell! Isn't that where you wanted to go with Mrs. Sutton?"

"I would most like to drive over there immediately, but under the circumstances, I think it best to go with Lord Hargrave's sister," said Jane, still very much aware of the threat she had received in Bodmin. "Send Mrs. Sutton a message to say that I am looking forward to our excursion together. Perhaps that will speed up her plans."

Jane spent the following week in anxious expectation of word from Mrs. Sutton and from Captain Wescott, from whom she expected at least a short reply to her letter. Her days were filled with looking after Floyd and the visits of the doctor, whose company at dinner she found herself looking forward to more and more. He told the most adventurous stories from his army days in Russia and on the Crimean Peninsula.

Spring brought milder temperatures and showed its face more and more often. Jane had the terrace in front of the dining room cleaned and all of the weeds removed. She did not want to go to great expense with the park yet, at least not until Matthew's demand for repayment of her father's debts had been sorted out. But she had approved the purchase of whatever the gardener needed to restore the vegetable beds and planters all around the house. She hoped a few daubs of color would improve not only the house but also her mood. As things turned out, however, improvements to her mood would have to wait.

Jane returned cheerfully from a morning walk by the sea and playfully let Rufus tug and tear at her wrap. Her eyes turned from a barberry bush, its orange berries almost luminous in the sunlight, to a splash of radiant yellow euphorbia beneath a hazel bush beside the front entrance. The idyll, however, was shattered by Hettie, who was waving excitedly.

Jane's maid was brandishing a newspaper. "Ma'am! Come quickly! Oh, ma'am!"

I can't bear any more bad news, thought Jane, then berated herself for being a coward and began to walk more quickly. "What is it, Hettie?"

"Take a look! The newspaper came an hour ago. Oh, it's terrible. Poor Miss Shepard." Hettie held the article under Jane's nose.

It was the story of a young teacher from the orphanage in Bodmin, found dead by the river. The writer regretted the loss of the young woman, who had clearly taken her own life because she was carrying a child. She shared the fate of many fallen women who knew only one way out of their predicament, namely, to drown themselves. Beside the short report was an etching of the George Frederic Watts painting that depicted the corpse of a young woman on the shore of a river and bore the sad title *Found Drowned.*

"It has to be Miss Shepard, doesn't it? Who else could it be?" Hettie asked breathlessly.

Tears rolled over Jane's cheeks, and her trembling hands clutched the newspaper. "I'm afraid it most likely is. What's going on here? Who would do something like that?"

"You don't think she drowned herself, do you?"

"No! She wasn't . . ." But did she really know that? Perhaps Miss Shepard had really been pregnant. Under such ample skirts, a pregnancy could be kept hidden for a long time. "And maybe it isn't Miss Shepard at all!"

But how many young female teachers were there in the orphanage at Bodmin? "I shall write a letter to Mr. Tobin, and then we will know for certain."

Rufus left off tearing at her wrap and suddenly stormed across the courtyard and down to the street. They heard his excited barking, and it wasn't long before two riders trotted between the two enormous mulberry trees that still flanked the courtyard entrance. Jane caught her breath and wiped a hand across her teary face.

"Wescott."

Captain Wescott, riding a powerful brown and black stallion, pulled up directly in front of her, slid from his mount's back, and handed the reins up to Blount. The adjutant immediately rode off in the direction of the stables, the stallion in tow. Wescott wore no hat, and the wind had tousled his dark hair. Beneath his tweed jacket was a white shirt, and he carried a pistol in his belt. *He looks more like a highwayman than a gentleman,* thought Jane and swallowed.

She was so relieved to see him that she could not stop her eyes from once again filling with tears. "Captain . . . ," she managed to croak, and she reached out to him with her free hand.

Wescott's smile froze. He took her hand and pulled her to him tightly. He held her against him for a moment, and Jane felt the rough material against her cheek. There was something consoling about the odor of horse, dust, and man, something that reminded her of her uncle. She could hear his heart beating strongly in his breast, and as he held her away from him to look into her face, his own was filled with concern. "You're crying! What's happened? Has your cousin made some new demand?"

Jane sniffed and wiped her nose with the back of her hand. "What you must think of me. Every time we see each other, I'm crying."

Wescott almost smiled. "We always seem to see each other in unusual circumstances. You are one of the most courageous women I know, and if you are crying, then there must be a good reason for it. That's what worries me, Jane."

He said Jane. Not "Lady Jane" or "my lady." What was he expecting of her? Should she call him by his first name? That felt far too bold to her. She turned to her maid, who was looking at them wide-eyed. "Hettie, go in the house and tell Mrs. Roche that the captain is here."

"Yes, ma'am, Captain." She curtsied politely and hurried off.

"Captain . . . ," Jane began, but Wescott took her hand and held it firmly.

"Wouldn't it be fitting to call me by my Christian name? What would the people here think of our marriage otherwise?" He smiled encouragingly.

"David," she said quietly, and felt him squeeze her hand and let go. She handed him the newspaper. "I discovered this just now."

As succinctly as she could, she outlined the events of recent days. Wescott's expression grew increasingly grim. She finished by saying, "I think you can see that Matthew's outrageous demands are the least of my worries at this moment."

"My dear Jane, I can hardly believe what you've told me. It's monstrous! And it is unconscionable that you have put yourself at such risk, alone!"

"But I could not have known about it!" she defended herself indignantly. "Everything has come to a head in the last few days, and who can say that these events are even connected?"

He raised one skeptical eyebrow. "Oh, Jane. We both know what this is all about. The girl at Rosewood Hall!"

A raindrop landed on Jane's forehead. She had not noticed the dark clouds rolling in from the sea. She looked up at the sky. They would not get much more than a shower. Since her arrival, she had learned something of the local weather, which was heavily dependent on the tides. "Come, let's go inside. What do you think of Mulberry Park? There's still a lot of work to be done, of course. The whole estate needs some care and attention."

David Wescott placed his hands on his slim hips and gazed up at the old walls of the house. "It fits the harsh landscape. I only hope it looks a little friendlier on the inside. You know, Jane," he said as they climbed the stairs side by side, "I've never had much use for such grand old boxes. Maybe it's because I grew up in one. Too many rooms for too few people and too many staff, and all of it has to be managed constantly. One has no real privacy. When you visit my townhouse in London, you'll see what I mean. It's small but livable. And it doesn't cost a fortune to heat, not even in winter."

"Hmm. You may be right. I've never had to pay any attention to expenses before." She sighed. "Let's hope that the whole thing with Matthew can be settled."

Stuart held the door open for them, and Wescott greeted him with a nod. *He has an observant way of dealing with people,* Jane thought. Not trusting exactly, but respectful.

"Please set up the captain's bedroom, and a room on the top floor for Mr. Blount," Jane told Stuart.

The servant nodded and disappeared.

"What about some tea? Or would you prefer to get changed? It will be a while till lunch is ready. I didn't see any luggage," said Jane, talking to conceal her nervousness.

"We've brought only the most necessary things in saddlebags. We won't be staying long."

• • •

After lunch, Jane and Wescott sat together in the library, where he went through the letters she had recently received. He was particularly interested in the lines that Miss Shepard had penned.

"This seems to me an important clue and perhaps the reason for the death of the poor woman mentioned in that article, if it really is her," Wescott said, stretching his long legs toward the fire.

Rufus had sprawled between them; he seemed willing to accept Wescott as a new member of the household. Wescott was still wearing his riding breeches and boots but had put on a fresh shirt. He rubbed the scar on his cheek occasionally, which reminded Jane of Doctor Woodfall's remarks about the Crimean War. One day, Jane hoped, Wescott himself would tell her what he had been through, and she would understand him better for doing so. Behind his somber and serious facade, Jane believed there was a vulnerable man hidden, but she had no choice but to wait for what time would bring.

"I don't know who else from the Bodmin orphanage it might be, but of course I could be mistaken. Perhaps there are other staff members there that I didn't see. I'm going to write a letter to Mr. Tobin, the director. Then we will have some certainty." She had said "we," although she did not even know if Wescott wanted to bother himself with the matter any longer. She looked at him inquiringly.

He laid the letter on the table and reached for the sheet of paper containing the threat. "That's a good idea, Jane. Do that. And about this . . ." He flicked his fingers against the paper. ". . . this is a riddle to me. If we assume this person doesn't like you asking questions, and is willing and able to kill a woman over it, then such a poetic threat surprises me. After all, you might have misunderstood the lines and dismissed them as a silly joke."

"Don't forget the man who was watching me outside the orphanage. He knew that I'd spotted him. Rogers, the coachman, went after him, but could not catch him." Jane propped her chin on her hands and toyed with a strand of hair that had worked its way loose.

"Miss Shepard was killed only after she'd found out the names of the two teachers. It looks as if she went too far by asking about them." Lost in thought, Jane chewed at the strand of hair. "If only I hadn't asked about the name . . ."

Wescott laid the strange poem on top of the letters and slapped his hand loudly against the tabletop. Rufus jumped to his feet, and Jane looked at Wescott in alarm. "I think the same way. Driving around asking complete strangers about orphan girls who've disappeared seems to be a dangerous pastime. Too dangerous for you, Jane!"

"But I'm not going to stop now. It would mean that whoever murdered Miss Shepard has won. No, it's out of the question!" Jane retorted.

A hint of a smile played around the corners of Wescott's mouth. "I would not have expected anything else of you. But I promised your uncle that I would take care of you and protect you, if necessary. And now it's necessary."

Jane snorted. "I can look after myself, thank you very much!"

"I can see that. What about your butler?"

"An accident."

"And your dog?"

"Also an accident. The miller didn't know who I was. I have forbidden his criminal brother from ever setting foot on my land," she answered quickly.

"And do you have trained, trustworthy staff, familiar with firearms, who can act against a poacher willing to use violence?" Wescott asked. He spoke softly and thoughtfully. There was no criticism in his voice, only questions about the situation.

"I, well, I haven't found the time yet." Jane sank back into her chair and capitulated. "No, I don't. But . . ."

"Yes?" His dark eyes, sparkling with good humor, watched her.

"I would have taken on new staff if Matthew hadn't attacked me with his unspeakable demands. What am I supposed to do? I don't even know how much I have left or if I'll be able to keep this house at all."

"It's certainly a difficult spot you're in. We're in." He paused and seemed to be waiting for a comment from her, but Jane merely shrugged helplessly. "Does this house mean much to you?"

"What? Yes, of course! It belonged to my parents. I know I didn't grow up here, but it's now my home, or at least the one after Rosewood Hall. My uncle invested a large sum of money in Mulberry Park, all to be able to leave it to me one day. I . . . yes . . . it means a lot to me! My uncle was my family, Rosewood Hall my home. I would like to build a new home here." The words came out more vehemently than she'd intended.

Wescott was silent for a moment before finally saying, "In that case, we should do everything we can to ensure that your cousin's demands come to nothing."

"But how?"

"The easiest way would be if those promissory notes he has were to disappear." Wescott grinned.

Jane frowned. "If I know Matthew, he's stashed them in some secret hideaway or carries them with him day and night. Besides, I'd be the first one he'd suspect if anyone stole them, wouldn't I?"

"I was just being facetious. Of course you shouldn't become a thief. Though you certainly have what it takes."

"Excuse me?"

Wescott laughed. "To be a successful thief takes intelligence, skill, courage, and ruthlessness. You have demonstrated all of those qualities, but that's just by and by. You should visit your cousin and talk to him. Then we'll see where we go from there."

"Alone?"

"Afraid?"

"Of course not!"

"When I leave, Blount will stay here with you. He will ensure your safety. I would trust him with my life."

"Are you trying to saddle me with a bodyguard?"

"An escort. There's a big difference. And only for the time being, until we know what game is being played here." He pulled back his legs and looked at Rufus. "Now I'm going to go and have a word with your gamekeeper."

19.

Mary

"Yes, Mary?" Miss Fannigan was still sitting at her desk, organizing the workbooks from the test the pupils had just taken.

There were more than forty children in the class, and their level of education varied so much that it made practically no sense at all to test them. But rules were rules, so the children, from four to twelve years old, scribbled more or less sensible rows of letters in their books.

The other children had already run out into the courtyard, but Mary had something she had to get off her chest. Miss Fannigan was no longer very young, but not yet old, either. She was petite, with brown hair and brown eyes that had seemed heavy with sadness since the departure of Mr. Gaunt. The teacher seemed to have lost her smile completely; she was a shadow of who she had been.

Mary scuffed her feet over the floor, which was still relatively clean since their marathon scrubbing. It had not been in vain, then, although the committee had failed to appear. Mary suspected that the master deliberately announced such phantom visits just so everyone would do their utmost to give the home a thorough cleaning. The weather had grown warmer, and Mary wore her short-sleeved dress. The welts on her forearms were healing slowly, and were still easy to see.

"Miss, you're not going to leave us, are you?"

The teacher let her thin hands rest atop a pile of books and looked at Mary sadly. "Why do you ask that, Mary?"

"I thought that now that Mr. Gaunt is gone, you might also go away. That wouldn't be nice. We all like you very much, miss."

A warm smile made Miss Fannigan's face light up for a few moments. "And I like all of you, Mary. Very much. You've all become very dear to me in the year I've been here." The smile faded, and Mary knew what was coming next. "But it is time for me to move on. Other children need me too, Mary. You understand that, don't you?"

Mary shook her head vehemently. "No! We need you, miss. Where did Mr. Gaunt go?"

"He decided to try his luck in America. Imagine that! He didn't breathe so much as a word about it to me!" With a sigh, Miss Fannigan pushed the books into one pile. "I would have gone with him. It didn't matter where, I would have gone."

"Then why did he leave you behind?"

"Oh, Mary, who knows what men are thinking! When you're older, you'll understand these things better."

"I think I already understand some things, miss. My brother also up and left, just like that, and left me behind by myself."

"That's something different, Mary. I'm sure he didn't mean to hurt you by doing so. He loves you, I've always believed that. For the boys, it can be more difficult to fit in here. This is certainly not the nicest place to live for a child without parents. But it is not the worst, either." The teacher's hair was parted down the middle and held at her neck by a pretty comb, and as she talked, she adjusted the comb with practiced ease.

Miss Fannigan surely did not know about the men that Sister Susan let into the dormitory at night. She lived in the village and was not able to hear what went on in the orphanage after hours. She probably didn't know about the transports, either, and Mary decided not to ask her about those.

"How do you know that Mr. Gaunt wanted to go to America? Did he write? Did he write to us, too? Has he heard anything about Polly?" she asked quickly, for she could see that Miss Fannigan was about to stand up and go home.

"You're very curious, Mary. But why shouldn't I tell you? He wrote a letter to the master; that's how I found out. He said hello to all of you, too."

That was a lie. Mary could tell by the way the teacher lowered her eyes when she said it. "Then why didn't he take his good jacket and his good pair of shoes with him? I would take my good things along with me on such a long journey." With her large, innocent eyes, she gazed unwaveringly at Miss Fannigan.

"Pardon me? What makes you say that?" Suspicion was followed quickly by fear, and Miss Fannigan looked first to the window and then to the half-open door.

"I saw Mr. Cooper putting Mr. Gaunt's things into a sack."

A smothered cry escaped Miss Fannigan, who jumped up and came around the desk to Mary. She took the small girl by the shoulders and kneeled in front of her to look her straight in the eye. "Have you told that to anyone else, Mary?"

Without hesitation, Mary answered, "No."

"Really not?"

"No, not a soul. I didn't think it was important, but now that you told me that Mr. Gaunt went to America, I remembered it." She had learned a lot of things from Fiona, and one of them was that it was better to tell a lie than betray a friend. You never really knew who was an enemy and who an ally. Even though she was fairly sure that Miss Fannigan was not an enemy, Mary decided it was better to play it safe: you never knew.

"That's good. Are you sure it was Mr. Gaunt's jacket and shoes?"

"Oh, of course! It was that brown jacket with the nice leather patches on the sleeves."

Miss Fannigan's eyes shone. She was close to tears. "Yes, that's right. He loved wearing that jacket. Mary, you're a very bright, observant girl. Promise me you won't talk about this with anyone. I will ask the master what it means, and then we'll see."

Both the girl and the teacher jumped in alarm when steps sounded out in the hallway. The door suddenly flew open, and Sister Susan stepped into the room. She had the detested cane jammed under her belt. "What's going on here, Miss Fannigan? Is this little pest causing trouble again?" She turned to Mary. "Didn't you learn from the last thrashing?"

Mary immediately hid her arms behind her back and took two steps backward.

"You're too tenderhearted, Miss Fannigan. These little vandals crawl out of the sewers and don't know the first thing about manners or morals. The only way is to beat it into them. They'll lie as soon as open their mouths," said Sister Susan, without so much as a second glance at Mary.

Miss Fannigan, who had stood up the moment Sister Susan entered, patted down her skirt and moved behind her desk. "That may be your view, Sister. I have my own opinions as far as these children are concerned."

The camel contorted her mouth into a sneer. "Of course. No doubt that was the reason for Mr. Gaunt leaving us, wasn't it? And now you are, too."

"There are different approaches to raising children and, in my opinion, Master Ledford is not particularly up-to-date. I have already made inquiries at a school with a more progressive approach, and which will appreciate my work. Mary, you may go. And don't forget what I told you."

"Yes, miss. Thank you!" Mary curtsied and ran off.

It was still some time before the evening meal, and she found Fiona in the corner of the walled courtyard that bordered the yard of the poorhouse next door. There was an oak tree there, and thick bushes and ivy covered the old walls. Fiona had discovered a hole there in the wall that was just big enough for a thin girl like her who could twist like an eel. The heavy foliage of the oak protected them from the prying eyes in the windows of the surrounding buildings.

She squatted next to Fiona, who took out an old newspaper from under the bushes. "Ta-da! The latest news from the outside world! Ain't I a star?"

"You're the best, Fiona, but listen . . ." Mary told her what had just happened in the classroom.

"And you didn't mention me?"

"No, I already told you!"

"Good! I just wanted to make sure! I don't want the camel or that bastard Cooper dragging me out of bed at night, stuffing me in a sack, and dumping me in the river!"

"Stop it, you're scaring me!" Mary spread out the newspaper. There were stories about sittings of parliament, the uprising in Poland, newly opened railway lines, the launch of the navy's biggest three-master, and a drowned teacher in Cornwall.

"Fiona, look!" Mary pointed excitedly at the little article about the death of a teacher from the orphanage in Bodmin.

Fiona read through the short article quickly. "Tch, poor lass. Left in the lurch and would rather throw 'erself in the drink than live in shame. What's it to you?"

"Maybe it isn't just that. I was thinking of poor Miss Fannigan. I mean, I told her about the things that Cooper put in the sack, and if she goes to the master now . . . I'm afraid, Fiona." Mary rubbed her hand on her belly. "It hurts in here, and I can't do anything about it. That's fear!"

For a moment, the two girls sat side by side in silence. Finally, Fiona said, "Let's wait and see. If we get all barmy about this, it ain't going to 'elp nobody. They mustn't know what we're thinking. You know what they'll do with us then."

"And what about the transport? Where do they send the children?" Mary asked quietly.

"Oh, I've been asking round over there. I was talking to a poor sod from Launceston who was breaking stones, and 'e told me 'e knows about ships that sail English children off to the colonies. Off to America, Africa, and Australia, 'e said. They say it's 'cause they're better off over there, but people say it's just a way to get cheap workers. They're sold by the Salvation Army and the orphanages."

"But the girl from yesterday was so small!"

Fiona shrugged. "Don't matter to them. The trip takes ages anyway, so they're nearly a year older by the time they arrive." She laughed bitterly. "We're goods, Mary, no more than cheap goods. But I'll tell you one thing, no one's shipping me off nowhere! I know my way round 'ere. If you're poor, the world's a shit 'ole wherever you go. Them in America, they're no better than the ones 'ere. Take my word for it!"

"How do you know that? Maybe it really is nicer over there."

"Why should it be? Where did the people who live there come from? From 'ere, all of 'em! No, Mary. I'm staying in the shit 'ole I know."

20.

"The captain is a handsome man, ma'am, if I may say so." Hettie was kneeling before Jane, helping her unlace her boots. After Wescott rode off to visit the gamekeeper, Jane had gone out for another walk, and her boots were wet and dirty from her trek across the fields.

Jane was working on the fasteners on her jacket, but the tiny, cloth-covered buttons had also gotten damp and were almost impossible to push through their loops. "He wanted to speak to Blythe." She sniffed. "I would have done it myself, but no sooner does he arrive than he starts interfering."

With a skillful twist, Hettie pulled off the first boot. "He's your husband, and he's worried about you."

"We have—," Jane began, then stopped. Hettie knew a lot about her and was her confidante in most matters, but Jane had spoken to no one about the special circumstances of her marriage to Wescott. Even Alison, her best friend, didn't know. After the death of her uncle, it was one thing on top of another, and a matter like that was not something to write about in a letter. She would have to invite Alison to visit, soon.

"He has his life and I have mine, Hettie. That's the way it is."

Hettie looked up in surprise. "He won't be staying? I mean, you've had no time at all together, no honeymoon." She grinned. "And I was hoping so much that you would travel to Italy, like the fine people do. Lady Alison was in Rome, wasn't she?"

Jane tugged nervously at the buttons, accidentally ripping one off. She threw it angrily onto the dressing table. "Oh, to blazes with it! No, get that out of your head. There will be no honeymoon! I really have other things on my mind. Where is your head?"

Shocked at her mistress's unaccustomed outburst, Hettie lowered her head and pulled off the other boot. "May I help you with those?" Gingerly, she reached for the lowest button on the damp woolen cloth.

Jane leaned back to make it easier for Hettie. "Cousin Matthew's demands are deeply unsettling, Hettie. Then Floyd's accident, and the whole matter of the dead girl, and Miss Shepard, and, oh, it's all just too much!"

"But isn't it good to have some support?" Hettie cautiously interjected.

With a sigh, Jane relented. "Perhaps. It's a new situation for me. I have to get used to it first."

Wescott was little more than a stranger, and she hoped very much that she would not have cause to regret her impulsive decision to marry him. On the other hand, she trusted her instincts about people—they had never let her down. Whatever secrets he might be harboring, he was no fraud.

"How is Floyd? Has he eaten?"

"Yes, ma'am. He said he'd get fat if we kept stuffing him like that, but he is following the doctor's orders. Oh, look, there he is now!" Hettie was standing closer to the window and could look down onto the yard.

"Wescott?" Jane's breathing grew a touch faster.

"No, the doctor."

"Ah, good. He should stay for dinner." Jane let Hettie help her out of the tight bodice and stood up. While Hettie unlaced the corset, Jane told her, "Run down to Mrs. Roche and tell her that we will be having two guests for dinner. Her meals are excellent. I don't think I'm going to be needing a new cook after all."

"I won't be telling her *that*, ma'am!" said Hettie. "Shall I draw a bath?"

"Yes, do that."

Once Hettie was gone, Jane stepped in front of the full-length mirror and ran her hands over the contours of her narrow hips. Would a man be pleased with what he saw here? Her body was firm, her breasts small and round, perhaps not quite ample enough, but her legs were slim. Horses with slim fetlocks were valued, and if they had a little temperament as well, it was considered a good mixture. *Not for women, though,* thought Jane and turned away. But then again . . . No, no man would look twice at her, because no man could tell her how to live her life. She lifted her chin, threw her long locks back over her shoulders, and stepped over to the window.

Wisps of fog swept over the land from the sea, and the sun gleamed weakly behind an overcast sky. The smell of the sea mingled with the cries of gulls. Jane felt already that she had formed a deep attachment to the region. The house may not have been the most beautiful, nor the grounds, but it was her land and her house. Her parents had bought it as a place to live one day. Matthew could not be allowed to take it from her!

Shortly before eight, Hettie plucked at the velvet trim of Jane's exquisite evening dress. It was a deep violet and shimmered like mother-of-pearl, a compromise during this time of mourning to which Jane still felt herself bound. A "Swiss belt" was the name for the broad serrated waistband, adorned with silken tassels, that emphasized Jane's slender midriff.

"You look especially beautiful tonight, ma'am. The captain won't be able to keep his eyes off you." Her maid stepped back and put her clasped hands to her lips.

"Thank you, Hettie. Take Rufus outside for a little while, and ask Floyd if he needs anything. No, even better, just take him a whisky and something to nibble. That will cheer him up. The poor man has been so fidgety since he's been confined to bed."

"Yes, ma'am." As if he had understood Jane's words, Rufus snuffled and stood up. He trotted obediently to the door with Hettie, and Jane held it open for them.

Jane opened the jewelry box on her dressing table. She was considering what would go best with the solemn dress when she heard a knock at the door. "It's open, Hettie, come in!" she called, without turning.

The door opened and closed, but the steps didn't sound like Hettie's. Jane froze for a moment, then turned around so fast she knocked a hairbrush from the table. *These sweeping skirts make it impossible to move normally,* Jane thought, as she bent to pick up the brush. Wescott was faster.

"I'm sorry. I didn't mean to give you a fright," he said as he deftly fished the silver brush from behind the leg of a chair and placed it back on the table beside Jane. His voice was husky and full of warmth.

She noticed that he had taken a bath. His hair was still wet, and he had shaved and changed his clothes. He now wore a dark frock coat and matching trousers. Only the brown velvet vest and loosely knotted scarf around his neck showed that he was traveling lightly, and also that he placed little store in formalities.

Jane pulled herself together. She closed the lid of the jewelry box and took a step to the side. "Captain."

"Jane, I wanted to talk to you before dinner. Doctor Woodfall will be joining us, won't he?"

"Yes, I thought he might. Are you looking forward to that?"

Wescott nodded. His eyes roamed the room and came to rest on hers. "We knew each other in another time, Jane, in Crimea. In war, everything is turned on its head. The whole world feels out of joint. Nothing is the way it was before, nor will it ever be the same again." He touched his cheek, then let his hand fall and went across to the window. "A wonderful view. This estate has potential."

"There's still an awful lot to be done. I hope your room is all right for now," she said, self-consciously checking the line of her wide décolletage.

"Thank you. I have everything I need." He turned back to her. "I've spoken to the gamekeeper, Blythe."

"Oh, yes?"

"He keeps very much to himself, but I don't think there's anything wrong with him. That said, he keeps quite a few pens of deer, pheasants, and partridges. Do they organize a lot of hunts here? That ought to be checked, at least. He seemed genuinely appalled at your butler's accident. He thinks someone fired a shot to startle the horse intentionally."

"I've been thinking the same."

"He believes the miller's brother is responsible. Perhaps avenging his sister. By dismissing the cook, you seem to have slighted the entire Thomas clan."

"I will not allow myself to be intimidated!"

Wescott smiled. "No, clearly not. If you ask me, the people here don't know who they're dealing with."

"Don't make fun of me, sir," Jane snapped back.

"That was never my intent. I would not be standing here if I did not have the greatest respect for you." He took a step toward her, took her hand, and held it between them for a moment. He seemed to be having difficulty finding words. "Our agreement requires us to appear and to act as a married couple would, and I would ask you not to address me formally. If that would be acceptable to you, Jane?"

She pulled her hand free and looked at him doubtfully. What did he really want? Was this a trick to seduce her, to wrap her up and force her to submit to his will?

He seemed to read her thoughts, for he tipped his head to one side and grinned. "Don't worry, my intentions are entirely honorable. It is just that I know Richard Woodfall well and am on very familiar terms with him. It would seem strange if you and I were to address each other with anything other than our given names."

Jane sighed with relief. "Of course. I understand. And what are we to do about Fred Thomas? Should I inform the police? If I do that, I'll no doubt turn the whole village against me."

"That would certainly not be helpful. Perhaps you should come with me to London for a time."

"No!"

He frowned. "You're in danger here, Jane. Are you not aware of that?"

"There is no solid proof of that, not yet. Just suspicions. And I will not let anyone drive me away from here! Certainly not now. Do you understand that, David?" There was a pleading edge to her words.

Wescott gestured toward the door. "Shall we go down? We don't want the doctor to starve for our sake." He offered her his arm, and Jane placed her hand on his sleeve. "By the way, you look absolutely captivating, if I may say so."

"That is not an answer," she said, her voice now lower as they stepped out into the hallway.

"If the question was whether I understood you, then an answer is unnecessary, isn't it?"

She glanced angrily at him from the corner of her eye, and they descended the stairs in silence. As they entered the dining room, where the doctor was already waiting for them, she greeted her guest with a smile. "My apologies, Doctor. We've kept you waiting. I hope I can make up for it by bringing an old friend along."

Richard Woodfall was overjoyed to see Wescott again, and the two men embraced in a hearty greeting.

"My God, David, how long has it been? You look fantastic! Who would have thought? Excuse me, my lady, but I saw your husband in such a state that I hardly hoped to—"

Wescott cut him off with a dismissive gesture. When he spoke, there was a certain warning in his words. "Let's drop it, Richard. No war stories, not when there are ladies present."

The doctor eyed his old friend and then said, "Where are my manners? Your butler is doing much better, my lady. No infection, and the break is healing cleanly. If he's careful, he can even take a few steps. He is beset with the idea of resuming his duties."

Jane laughed. "Yes, that's our Floyd. I am so happy that he's recovering. Please, let's sit down."

She let Wescott guide her to a chair, and as she sat his fingers touched her bare back. The touch was so brief, little more than a whisper of air, but it felt to Jane like an apology, and her anger at her husband evaporated.

Jane noted the care that had been put into setting the table: a tiered dish lavishly filled with candied and fresh fruit, the silverware freshly polished, glasses gleaming. Without being asked, the serving girl poured champagne that Jane did not even know they had. Hors d'oeuvres were tasty fried oysters, which raised Jane's hopes for the course of the evening. She had discussed the menu only briefly with Mrs. Roche. The letter to Mr. Tobin had seemed more important.

"It's a damn scandal they let Lucan off the hook," said Woodfall and drained his glass of champagne.

"But you could see it coming. The commanders get off scot-free every time. It makes no difference how many soldiers die from their incompetence," Wescott answered bitterly.

"At least Lucan has left active service."

Wescott's mouth twisted in disgust. "There are enough others out there. Another one will get promoted, and it will happen all over again in the next battle. There will always be inept, puffed-up idiots like Lucan, and unfortunately their families have most of the money."

Jane looked at her husband curiously. His father, after all, was among England's richest men. Then she turned to the doctor. "Is that why you turned your back on the army, Doctor? Because you saw how senseless all that sacrifice was?"

Woodfall leaned back and turned his glass back and forth. "I studied medicine because I wanted to help people. We don't understand misery and disease enough without a war, my lady. Where's the sense in robbing a family of its breadwinner? It doesn't matter which country."

"Careful, Richard. That sounds awfully close to treason. You haven't been in London for quite a while, have you?"

Woodfall ran his hand through his blond hair. "I don't miss it. Well, perhaps the theater season. My wife would love to spend more time there, but the sea air is better for her." A shadow settled over his face.

"Is your wife sick? I'm sorry," said Jane with sympathy.

"What? No. I mean, she is not well, but it's in her family. Nerves." He looked at her, his face dejected. "Maybe you can come and visit us sometime, then you'll see for yourself. My wife is afflicted with epilepsy, and the only thing that can ease her suffering is morphine."

It did not escape Jane that Woodfall and Wescott exchanged a glance, as if they shared a secret. Epilepsy was a rather dramatic disease and was generally considered incurable.

"And what a blessing it is . . . a medicine that has helped so many cope with such serious pain." Jane waved to the waiting maid to serve the next course.

Wescott's expression grew darker, and Woodfall said, "I would not talk about morphine as a blessing, my lady. It certainly has its advantages, but it quickly becomes a habit among patients, which leads to new problems. But we don't want to spoil our evening with such depressing topics, do we? Where did you two get off to on your honeymoon? I wish I could travel down to Rome this summer! I love the coast down there. Blue water, colorful houses, and the sun shines the whole day!"

Jane laughed. "I'm starting to understand why everyone here is so mad about the sun! I must say, though, when it does come out, I find this area absolutely stunning."

"We haven't yet had the time to travel anywhere, Richard. Jane's uncle passed away very suddenly," Wescott said.

There was a scratching at the door, and when the maid opened it, Rufus pushed his big head through the gap. Jane clicked her tongue, and the huge dog trotted over and lay on the carpet beside her.

"Should I arrange a room for you after dinner, Doctor, or will you have to be going this evening?" Jane asked.

"As sorry as it makes me to say it, I really will have to get on. Lord Hargrave's sister is expecting me. I check on her regularly when I do my rounds."

"Anyone seeing Mrs. Sutton and her brother would never believe they are related. They are so different!" Jane helped herself to a few morsels of pheasant and vegetables. "But Lady Rutland seems to keep Mrs. Sutton's spirits up. She seems very energetic."

"You know the Rutlands?" Wescott asked.

"They were there when I went to visit Violet Sutton and her brother. Didn't I mention that?"

"It must have slipped my mind. Sidney and Florence Rutland are rather illustrious characters in the London nightlife crowd, my dear. Lord Hargrave, too," said Wescott, looking at Jane with raised eyebrows.

"Well, not being in London often, I couldn't know that. Out here in the country, one welcomes any diversion that comes along. Don't you agree, Doctor?"

Woodfall swallowed and smiled wryly. "Mrs. Sutton is a nice person, a widow. She sacrifices a lot for children in need. Very noble."

Since her recent visit to Bodmin, Jane had been thinking that Mrs. Sutton's work with needy children did not involve much sacrifice at all. But the charitable work itself was certainly worthy of praise. "I'm going away with her next week," she said. "To the orphanage in St. Austell."

As she said this, she looked belligerently at Wescott, but his expression remained inscrutable. Only the muscles in his jaw stood out noticeably as he chewed. Jane feared he would raise the subject again later, and she raised her chin defiantly.

21.

"Mrs. Roche, you have truly outdone yourself. I have not eaten better, not even at Lord Hargrave's house," said Jane to the housekeeper, who was still standing in the kitchen in her apron and bonnet.

"Thank you very much, ma'am. It's very nice of you to say so. I was to blame for choosing the last cook." Mrs. Roche, usually so forbidding, looked at Jane with some embarrassment. "My husband would like to speak with you, ma'am. Tomorrow morning, if that's all right?"

It was already late, and Jane was tired from the long day behind her. Her strained relationship with Wescott was gnawing at her, as well. "I'll expect him after breakfast in the library. Was there anything else?"

"I've lodged the opening for a cook with an agency in London, ma'am. My sister works at the agency and can check the suitability of any prospects there. If that's not to your liking and you'd rather . . ."

For some time, it had been the fashion to find servants through agencies, which were springing up everywhere in response to the demand. The process guaranteed a certain level of quality, and one saved the cost of advertising in the newspapers. Even better was to find staff from a friend's recommendation, but Jane did not want to bother Lady Alison with her situation. Not yet.

"No, that sounds sensible. Thank you, Mrs. Roche. Good night!" Jane left the kitchen and found Rufus waiting for her by the door. The dog accompanied her up the stairs.

"Well, old friend?" She stroked a hand over Rufus's short fur and checked his wounds. "That's looking much better. Don't let anyone beat you like that again! We'll catch that rogue out yet."

She scratched the Great Dane's back and did not look up as they climbed the last flight of steps.

"You talk to your dog?" Wescott was leaning casually against the balustrade. Apparently, he'd been observing her the whole time.

"He doesn't try to set any rules for me, and he doesn't criticize me in front of my guests. I like that in a dog." Rufus was standing between her and Wescott with his ears pricked up.

A single lamp on the wall cast a feeble light across the gallery, where Jane had hung an engraving of Rosewood Hall and various landscape paintings. Wescott had doffed his frock coat, and his dark hair fell to the open collar of his shirt. He clearly had little regard for the current convention that dictated a gentleman should wear his hair short.

"I did not criticize you, Jane. My responsibility is to protect you, and because I know Hargrave and Rutland better than you, I recommend—again—that you keep your distance from them."

"Protect me?" She let out a short, dry laugh. "From what? I think you're more interested in preserving my good reputation. But part of our agreement was that we enjoy a spotless social standing, so there's no need to worry, *David*. I'll keep my end of the bargain." She emphasized his name; the familiarity of addressing him that way did not come easily to her.

"I do not doubt it. At the same time, you should not be too proud to accept advice when it comes from someone with more experience than you." He pushed himself up from the balustrade and looked down at her with a sardonic smile.

"How dare you? You are not my uncle! You're just—," she began, suddenly furious, then held her tongue.

"Your husband," he said, finishing her sentence gently.

She would have liked nothing more than to stamp her feet, but that would have been childish and would only have made her look ridiculous. She swallowed, wiped away a traitorous, desperate tear, and, with the little dignity she had left, said, "Good night."

"Jane, please."

But she went into her room without turning back.

Jane slept restlessly. From the adjoining room, she heard Wescott pacing back and forth before finally going to bed late. When Hettie woke her the next morning, Jane could tell from her maid's expression that something was not right.

"Good morning, ma'am. Your bath is ready." Hettie turned down the bedclothes, drew back the curtains, and pushed open the shutters.

Jane was wearing just a thin nightdress, and the fresh, cool air made her feel cold. She quickly pulled on her dressing gown. "What's the matter, Hettie? You look so cross."

"He's already left. A crying shame, too. I hardly even got a look at him. And he's left that strange valet of his behind," said the maid as she tied the curtains back.

Jane was wide awake in an instant. "Wescott's gone?"

"That's what I said. The sun was hardly up, and he had someone fetch his horse and off he rode. Poor man, hardly even got here and had to go again. It's much nicer having visitors in the house. These old walls are so gray and dreary and, I must say, horribly dull. Nobody visits and—" She chattered on and on while she straightened up the room.

"Enough!" Jane interrupted her harshly. "Did you talk to him? Did he leave me a message?"

"No. But he sat in the library for a little while. I think he wrote something."

Jane took a deep breath and closed her eyes for a moment. "Put out the gray riding dress with the black fasteners."

The riding dress was comfortable, and the skirt disguised a pair of breeches. She hurried down the stairs and went directly to the library, where on her desk she found a folded sheet of notepaper sealed with wax. *Jane,* it read in clear, flowing handwriting. She broke the seal and unfolded the paper with trembling fingers.

> *Dear Jane,*
>
> *Nothing could be further from my intentions than to aggrieve you. But I have made a promise, and that includes taking care of your well-being. If you will not take my advice, find out for yourself, but be warned! Men like Hargrave and Rutland wear no more than the mask of gentlemen.*
>
> *Blount will accompany you on your excursions. That is not a request, but a necessary precautionary measure that will not restrict your freedom in any way. He will be there to ensure your safety, no more.*
>
> *With regard to your cousin, I believe it is of the utmost importance that you visit him in Rosewood Hall and have him show you the promissory notes. We will discuss everything else on my return from London.*
> *David*

Jane read the letter through a second time, then screwed it up furiously into a ball and threw it onto the desk. Deep inside, though, she realized that Wescott was right. It had been him, after all, who helped her with the dying girl at Rosewood Hall. She smoothed out the letter and put it away in one of the small drawers, then went down to breakfast in the empty dining room. She had been looking forward to Wescott's company that day. He might well play her protector with a leaning toward arrogance, but his unpredictable style and his underlying humor held some attraction for her. Smiling to herself, she took a slice of toast. And he was among the best-looking men she had ever met.

After breakfast, she found Stuart in the hallway. "Have my horse saddled. Where is Blount?"

The young man looked at her in surprise. "Who?"

"My husband's valet. Is there someone else here by that name?" she replied impatiently.

"No, ma'am. I beg your pardon. I thought that he left with the master this morning." He turned slightly to one side, and the door to the kitchen area behind him opened.

Mr. Roche and Blount stepped into the hallway and bowed their heads politely. "Good morning, my lady," said the caretaker.

Blount waited. Despite his unassuming appearance, there was something forceful about the man, thought Jane, as she assessed her husband's former adjutant. "I will be going riding soon, Mr. Blount."

"Very good, my lady." The wiry man nodded again and disappeared through the back entrance.

In the library, Jane offered Mr. Roche a chair, but the caretaker preferred to stand. He turned his hat nervously in his hands. "My lady, I wanted to ask you about my authority here. Now that Mr. Coleman is indisposed, I mean. The lease is due, and the taxes have to be paid. I know you put more stock in Mr. Coleman, but I would gladly prove to you that Lord Henry's trust in us was thoroughly justified."

Jane sat at her desk and toyed with a paperweight shaped like an elephant. "To be honest, Mr. Roche, I would appreciate it most if you continue to manage the business side of the estate and present the books to Mr. Coleman for countersigning. In time, I am sure that we will find an allocation of duties that is acceptable to everyone. But I must say, I have been wondering what became of the large contingent of game at Mulberry Park. It seems to me that too few sales have been recorded, and not much of the game would have been consumed in my uncle's absence. Have there been many hunts here?"

Mr. Roche blinked in confusion and shuffled his feet restlessly. "Whenever Lord Hargrave's low on game for his hunting parties, Blythe helps him out. We've always had enough."

"Oh, yes?" Jane's forehead creased. "So Lord Hargrave buys my animals?"

The caretaker stared at his feet. "My lady, that's not quite how it is, I mean, not exactly."

"Then explain it to me!" Jane demanded sharply.

"Blythe is quick to anger. He's not a bad man, really he's not, but he's quick to let fly. He loves his wife and is very jealous. Three years back, there was a man who worked for Lord Hargrave, and he was always after Jacob's wife. No one could stand him. He worked in the stables and went around with the lord's valet, the same one Lord Hargrave has today." Mr. Roche cleared his throat. "Pat was the man's name. Not the valet, that's Jack. I'm not one to speak ill of others, my lady, but Pat was a scoundrel, a very nasty sort, and he found his fun in riling others up till they spat blood and bile. Jacob's wife is pretty. She's loyal, too, and would never go behind Jacob's back, but this Pat was after her for all he was worth. Something was bound to happen. Come May Day, everyone was out on the village square drinking beer and dancing, and one word led to another, and suddenly Jacob and Pat were at each other's throats. They were serious, ma'am. Deadly serious. I remember thinking that one or the other of 'em wouldn't be leaving the square alive. Normally, Pat would have finished our Jacob with one hand tied behind his back. He was a tough bugger and he had experience, but he'd had quite a bit to drink, and Jacob went at him like a man possessed."

Jane listened excitedly. "What happened?"

"Both were bleeding, but Jacob was on top and beating on Pat like a wild man. Then along came Lord Hargrave and split the two of them with his stick. He claimed that Jacob had beat up his man and had to sit in prison for it. Well, what were we to say? Jacob was known for his fits of anger. But then Lord Hargrave called for Jacob and made a proposal. Pat did not lay a charge against Jacob, and moved on shortly after. My guess is that Lord Hargrave paid him off. In return, Jacob was supposed to do him a favor from time to time." Mr. Roche took a deep breath and looked at Jane. "No one else knew about it. I only found out myself because I keep the books with the stock of game. Jacob confided in me. He was desperate. He didn't want to go to jail. He's the kind who'd die if someone locked him away. Always out in the woods, with the animals. That's no excuse, my lady, but that's how it was."

"You should have talked to my uncle, Mr. Roche. He would have settled the matter."

"We all liked your uncle, my lady, but he so seldom came out here, and a thing like that would have upset him. He wasn't too healthy, even then." Mr. Roche shook his head. "It wasn't right, but it was better that way. And no one was hurt by it."

Jane regarded the man, who repeatedly looked down at his feet. She sensed that what he'd told her was only part of the truth. "Why did your wife hire Becky Thomas?"

Surprised, Mr. Roche flinched at the question, and his eyes opened wide for a moment. But he quickly got himself under control and replied, "She was the only cook we could find on short notice."

"Do you know what I think? Fred or someone else in the Thomas clan got wind of Jacob's secret deal with Lord Hargrave and blackmailed you with it."

"What? No, no, it wasn't like that! My lady, please don't think that," Mr. Roche defended himself.

With a sigh, Jane set the paperweight back on the desk heavily. The unexpected noise startled the caretaker and confirmed her assumption that Roche was afraid. Not of her, no. He had never once showed any fear, not even before her uncle, as Floyd had once told her. The only name he feared was Thomas. The family pulled their strings here in the region, blackmailing people with their dirty little secrets.

"Let's leave it at that for today, Mr. Roche. Things can't go on like this, though."

"No." Embarrassed, the powerful man turned his hat in his hands.

"Lord Hargrave has profited from the gamekeeper's foolishness long enough. There will be no repercussions for Jacob."

"He will be grateful to hear that, my lady."

"I hope so. Leave me now."

When Mr. Roche was gone, Jane sank her face into her hands and tried to put the man's outrageous news into the scheme of things. *There is something wrong with the story,* she thought. *Something doesn't fit, or fits altogether too well. Who is Pat?* She looked up and, through the window, saw Blount waiting for her with the horses.

Perhaps he was exactly the right man to help her in this matter. She was not too proud to realize she needed help. *Too much pride equates to foolishness,* she thought as she stood. She took her riding crop from the table and swung it against her boots. "And I'm not foolish, my dear David."

22.

Wild gorse lined the path and grew among the rocks all along the stark coastal landscape. Ahead of them, a shepherd drove a flock of lambs with the help of his quick sheepdog. Jane called Rufus back to her—the Great Dane was trying to make friends with the growling sheepdog—and steered her horse toward the cliffs. A light wind carried the scent of the sea. Just off the beach, fishing boats bobbed on the choppy water, and a three-master was visible some distance farther out. Plymouth Harbor was not far away, and ships left from there almost daily, bound for France, America, or the colonies in the West Indies.

But Jane had not ridden this way only for the beautiful view. She secretly hoped to encounter Lord Hargrave. She could not simply show up unannounced at Bromfield Manor before three in the afternoon. Even out in the country, where the rules were observed more loosely, that would have been seen as unacceptable behavior and would have brought her into disrepute. She turned back to Blount, who rode in silence behind her. His riding outfit was plain but well cut, and the materials were of high quality. He sat on his horse as if he had spent a lifetime in the saddle.

"Mr. Blount," she called, and the man brought his powerful brown horse up, level with her own.

"My lady?" His pale eyes turned to her attentively, but remained vigilant of their surroundings.

"What do you know about the local situation?"

"The captain has apprised me of the most important factors, my lady."

Of course he has, thought Jane. He had ordered the man to watch over her. She considered for a moment, then decided that it would be best to explain the current state of affairs to Blount. At the least, she had nothing to lose. "Mr. Roche told me something about our gamekeeper."

"Blythe? Yes, the captain did indicate that something was not in order there."

"What? Did Blythe tell him about Hargrave blackmailing him?"

"Blackmail? No, my lady."

Jane nodded, satisfied. She would have been hurt to discover that Wescott knew about that and had kept it from her. She filled Blount in, and he whistled softly when she'd finished.

"What do you think of that? I don't know how I am to conduct myself now with respect to Lord Hargrave, but I refuse to accept such goings-on any longer. The man is stealing from me!"

Blount pushed his flat cap to the back of his head and turned his gaze to a point in the distance. "It is unacceptable. But Lord Hargrave is a powerful man."

She waited, but he said no more than that. "Would you advise me to confront him with the facts?"

Blount glanced sideways at her. "It is not my place to offer advice, my lady."

"To the devil with that! I asked your opinion! The captain has left you here as my protector."

"To keep you safe, my lady. Only to keep you safe. It is dangerous out here for a woman alone. That's true everywhere."

Impatient, she dug her boots rather too heavily into her mare's flanks, and the horse jerked its head up. "Do you know anything about Lord Hargrave that I don't? My husband made some insinuations about the reputations of Hargrave and Rutland. My God, man, don't make me drag every word out of you!"

Blount hesitated for a fraction of a second, then answered, "I'm sorry, my lady. I can only repeat what the captain said. In London, Hargrave and Rutland are well known for their excessive masked balls and similar events. There is a certain circle of gentlemen who enjoy a somewhat questionable reputation. For a respectable lady, moving in such company is not recommended."

"Aaarrgh!" Furiously, Jane struck her horse sharply with the riding crop to bring it up to a fast trot. "I will be paying a visit to Mrs. Sutton this afternoon!" Jane shouted and galloped off across the meadow.

Blount followed her effortlessly.

At precisely one minute past three, Jane's coach rolled up to the front entrance of Bromfield Manor. Hettie was about to open the door, but Blount, who had ridden with them on the coachman's seat, was faster and helped the two women climb out. He had swapped his riding jacket for the more respectable frock coat of a servant, and his manners were impeccable. His ever-vigilant eyes, however, did not escape Jane's attention. When they met Lord Hargrave's valet on the stairs, Blount's body tensed in a barely perceptible fashion, as if readying himself for an attack. *Perhaps war changes people that way,* thought Jane, but she paid more attention to Hargrave's valet than she had on her first visit.

Hettie reddened when she saw the slender man, who carried a traveling case in his hand. Well aware of his good looks, Lord Hargrave's valet bowed his head arrogantly. Then Hargrave's butler hurried down the steps, urging the valet to hurry up. "Stir your stumps, Jack! His lordship wants to be off in an hour. Beg pardon, good day, Lady Jane."

"I've come unannounced, but I do hope Mrs. Sutton will receive me?" said Jane with a charming smile.

The butler beckoned Jane to follow him into the home, while Blount stayed outside with the coach.

"Please follow me into the salon. It will only take a moment." The butler led them into a small, sunlit room with an elegant sofa and two armchairs. Hettie and Jane waited by the open French doors that looked out on to the courtyard.

"That's Nancy's Jack. He's not half-bad looking, is he?" Hettie peered out between the curtains, giggling.

"He seems quite conceited for a valet. People like that are devious, Hettie. He's the kind of man who causes trouble. Don't go getting involved with the likes of him!" Jane felt an instinctive aversion to Lord Hargrave's valet.

Hettie screwed up her nose. "Oh, a fellow like that's not for me. If I ever do get married, it will be to a man who's learned a trade and has his own little shop. A baker or a grocer . . ." She sighed. "So long as he's not a fisherman."

Jane smiled. "I'm going to have to keep an eye on you. I would be sorry to lose you anytime soon, Hettie."

"Oh, ma'am, I don't want to get married yet. But . . ." She looked farther out, where Lord Hargrave's coach was being brought around. "If the lord leaves, will you perhaps no longer be coming here? I mean, to visit his sister?"

Jane stroked the feathers in her artfully decorated hat. She had taken special care with her clothes for this afternoon's visit, though black was still the prevailing color of her wardrobe. "I hope that we'll be lucky, Hettie. But I'm surprised that Mrs. Sutton did not send me a message. We wanted to visit St. Austell together."

The door opened and Jane swung her expansive skirts around. The butler waved them out. "This way. Mrs. Sutton will see you. But she is not well."

The butler's announcement cautioned Jane to keep her visit as short as possible. "I'm very sorry to hear that."

Hettie disappeared into the domestic wing, and Jane was led into the same magnificent salon where she had visited the Hargraves and the Rutlands on her first visit. This time, however, Violet Sutton was lying on a chaise longue.

"Lady Jane," the butler proclaimed in a low voice before leaving again.

The curtains were half-closed, and the scent of lavender and rose oil hung in the air. Violet Sutton wore a pale-green dress, and against it she looked even paler than she had on Jane's last visit. She lifted one hand weakly. It was as if Violet found it difficult even to wave. "Lady Jane," she whispered in a flat voice and blinked tiredly.

On a table stood a samovar and small tea glasses. Beside the glasses stood an expensive-looking jewelry box. A little oil lamp gave off the sweet odor. "My dear, I'm so terribly sorry to find you not well!" Jane stood uncertainly by the table and did not know if she should even sit.

"Please, take a seat. I'm happy to have you to keep me company. It is always so dreadfully quiet here, you know? So quiet that it could make you think that everyone was gone, or dead." Violet's eyes were large and very dark when she looked at Jane.

Her pupils are unnaturally large, thought Jane, and then she saw Violet's arm. The sleeve of her dress had slid up, revealing the crook of her elbow. Jane could see old and new needle marks, and it suddenly occurred to her why Doctor Woodfall had come to visit this patient so late in the evening.

"Are you injecting morphine?" Jane asked gently.

Violet ran the tip of her tongue over her dry lips and turned slightly to lie flat on her back, her eyes looking up to the ceiling. "Mmm, it eases the pain and gives me pleasant dreams."

"Would you like to drink something?"

Violet slowly turned her head. "A glass of tea. Please, help yourself. The samovar was a gift from my brother. From Crimea. He was gone a long time, just like my husband. Sebastopol. Many good men died there. Too many. My Howard was among them. He was a good man."

Jane lifted the small silver pot from the samovar and tipped some tea into a glass. Then she filled the glass with hot water from the tap on the bulbous kettle. "Sugar?"

"Hmm." Violet's eyes were closed, and Jane saw a single, heavy tear appear from beneath her eyelash and roll down her cheek.

Jane added a spoonful of sugar to the glass and handed it to Violet, who opened her hand uncertainly. When her weak fingers came into contact with the warm glass, some life seemed to return to her body, and Violet turned onto her side. She swallowed a little of the strong, sweet tea, and her eyes looked at Jane with more alertness.

"The tea comes from India. Devereaux brings it with him. Do you know Devereaux? An attractive man. If I were younger and beautiful . . . I was never beautiful . . ." A strangely raw laugh escaped Violet's throat.

Embarrassed, Jane drew a glass of tea for herself from the samovar before settling into an armchair beside the table.

"Are you expecting?" Violet suddenly asked.

The glass nearly fell out of Jane's hand. "Me? No!"

"How sad. I always wanted to have children. Always. But Howard went off to war, and my body . . . stayed empty."

Jane cleared her throat. "But you help many children, Mrs. Sutton. That's wonderful. Are you driving to London with your brother? I would regret—"

"What? What would you regret, Lady Jane?" Lord Hargrave's deep voice cut through the numbed atmosphere of the room like a blade.

Jane held the glass tightly between her trembling fingers and turned to face the lord of the manor, who had approached unnoticed from the other side of the salon. His dark frock coat was custom tailored, and his shoes were immaculate.

"Would you regret my leaving?" He leaned forward and reached for her hand to kiss her fingers. He actually touched her with his lips!

She immediately withdrew her hand and shot him a disapproving look. "Are you planning to leave your sister here alone?"

Lord Hargrave walked around her and helped himself to a glass of tea. His legs touched her skirt, but such unseemly proximity apparently meant nothing to him. On the contrary, he actually appeared to be enjoying her discomfort with the situation. With his glass in his hand, he leaned forward and stroked his morphine-intoxicated sister's hair. "Poor little Violet. Always had to fight for everything and never, ever won."

Violet nestled her cheek into her brother's hand. "Don't go, Robert. Don't leave me alone!" she murmured.

"But you're not alone. Look, Lady Jane has taken the time to visit, just for you. Isn't that right, my lady? You've come all the way here just to visit my sister!" His eyes flashed and his words dripped mockery.

Violet seemed undisturbed by his words, or did not perceive the undertone in them, for she smiled blissfully. Her veins, a bluish sheen beneath her thin skin, gave her such a morbid appearance that she looked almost repellant, Jane thought.

"To be honest, I had hoped to meet you here, Lord Hargrave."

"Is that a fact? To what do I owe the honor? Wasn't your husband just here on a visit? Why did you keep him all to yourself? That was not nice of you, Lady Jane, not nice at all!" He wagged a finger at her in playful threat, but his eyes were cold and devoid of any humor.

"I regret David's sudden departure far more, believe me," said Jane with a sugary smile, very aware of the open neckline of her dress.

Lord Hargrave's eyes wandered desirously over the swell of her firm breasts. "How may I be of service, my lady?"

Jane, in that moment, was deeply grateful for Blount's presence. Though the man was outside, she had the feeling that he would be there in an instant if she needed help. "It's about my gamekeeper, Jacob Blythe."

She paused, and Lord Hargrave's posture changed from one moment to the next. Feigned playfulness gave way to calculation. "The name doesn't ring a bell. Please jog my memory a little."

"A fistfight, three years ago. Your man's name was Pat. Jacob defended his wife's honor, and you separated the two brawlers. Must I go on?"

Hargrave set down his tea glass loudly on the table. Violet reached for his hand, but he pushed her aside roughly. "No. I remember. Your gamekeeper beat my man half to death. A bad sort, that one!"

Jane also put down her glass. She stood up. Hargrave had to take a step back to make room for her dress, and Jane, for once, was thankful for the voluminous crinoline so in vogue. "That is not true and you know it. Mr. Blythe was provoked by your man. But aside from that, I believe you have received adequate compensation for my gamekeeper's assumed guilt."

Jane stood to her full height. She set her jaw and held Hargrave's stare.

Hargrave looked at her for an agonizingly long moment. Finally, his lips stretched into a patronizing smile. "Lady Jane. I can only bow before such a display of female fortitude. I have always admired strong women." He reached one hand out to her.

Surprised, Jane shook the offered hand and felt Lord Hargrave's firm grip. Too firm, really. It felt like a warning.

"We are neighbors, and squabbling among neighbors is unseemly. For me, the matter is hereby settled." He let go of her hand.

"Good." She smiled. "I am happy to have this affair off the table."

Violet groaned and held her hands to her forehead. "My skull is exploding. Robert, are you still here? Help me."

"But of course, my angel." Lord Hargrave went to the table and opened the jewelry box. Inside, a silver-plated syringe and an ampoule lay on the red velvet. Hargrave looked at Jane, not Violet, as he removed the syringe. "I'm bringing your respite, Violet. It will soon be better."

Jane bumped into the armchair as she stepped aside. "Violet, I look forward to hearing from you. I'll be leaving now. Lord Hargrave, I wish you a pleasant journey."

"You seem apprehensive, but there's no need to be," said Lord Hargrave. "I assume you haven't been to London for quite some time. The Season is just starting. If you happen to visit the theater, you will meet many women who sweeten their lonely existences with such honeyed dreams. There is nothing remiss in it, my lady."

"One must decide for oneself where to look for happiness. I will not be looking for mine there." Her eyes fell on the syringe in Hargrave's hand as she said it. "Good day!"

Jane left the salon and went down the hallway and outside, where the fresh air made her feel like she'd been liberated. Her coach had rolled forward a short distance to make room for Lord Hargrave's coach, decorated with the family crest. Close by the coach, Jack was leaning against a stone balustrade in front of a flower bed smoking a cigar. Jane's coachman and Blount were standing by their horses, by all appearances doing no more than discussing harness and coachwork. Blount noticed Jane immediately and gave her an inconspicuous wink. Jane did not at first understand what he meant, but then Hettie suddenly appeared, running down the steps. She cried excitedly, "Ma'am, this will floor you! You won't believe what I . . ."

The maid pulled up when she saw Jack. She reddened and turned so that she had her back to Lord Hargrave's valet. She whispered in Jane's ear. "Jack has an injured hand, ma'am. He's missing part of his little finger."

It was too late. Jack must have suspected something, for he flicked his cigar away and looked in their direction. When Jane's eyes met his, a shudder ran down her spine. She saw Blount shake his head very slightly, as if to tell her to lie low.

"Time to go, Hettie. You can tell me all your gossip as we drive," said Jane, louder than necessary.

23.

Mary

Mary sat beside Fiona on one of the benches in the classroom and hardly dared to move. Miss Horn had been employed to replace Miss Fannigan, who resigned shortly after she and Mary had talked about Mr. Gaunt's clothes. Miss Horn was even faster to reach for the cane than the camel was. She also enjoyed taking a long wooden ruler and whacking it randomly on the tables if a book was not lying straight or if a pupil's hands were not properly placed beside the book when reading. Many of the children now had bruises on their hands, and little Tom even had a broken index finger from being hit.

"It's my birthday next week, Fiona," Mary whispered.

"I don't 'ave the foggiest when I was born." Fiona bit her lips with concentration as she copied the words from the blackboard into her notebook.

"I'll be eleven." Mary looked nervously toward the front of the room, but the teacher was busy with one of the younger girls. The poor thing had dropped her slate on the floor and broken it.

"Stand up, you useless creature," the teacher raged at the child. Miss Horn was a big, powerful middle-aged woman. "Now who's supposed to pay for that? Go and stand in the corner, and don't move a muscle!"

The girl cried and did as she was told.

Fiona looked at her friend. "Eleven? Damn, then they'll throw you out. 'ave they said anything?"

"No, but the camel examined me."

"You two, stand up!" Miss Horn ordered, and the ruler cracked onto the table in front of them. Her unsympathetic eyes scrutinized them from behind round spectacles. The woman's graying black hair was tied back severely at her neck, and around her white lace collar she wore a velvet band with a silver cross hanging from it. She made the children pray before every lesson and seemed to idolize the pastor who delivered the Sunday sermon in the big hall.

"You with the red hair, what did you just say?"

"Nothing, Miss 'orn," said Fiona.

"You were whispering. What about?" She jabbed Mary in the ribs with the ruler.

"None of your business!" Mary bit her lips, because she knew what was coming next. But she no longer cared. One way or the other, she wouldn't be there much longer.

"You cheeky little brat, you dare . . ." The ruler dropped onto the table, and the woman snatched the cane from her belt. Mary automatically stretched out her hands. The strokes were painful, but the uncertain future awaiting her was much worse.

Fiona took just as many strokes as Mary, but she was allowed to sit down again. Then the spiteful woman said to Mary, "No lunch and no dinner, and I'm going to speak to the master about you. Sit down."

During the lunch break, Fiona crept over to Mary in the corner behind the big oak. She fished a hard chunk of bread out of her pocket. " 'ere. That's all there was."

Mary looked gratefully at her friend and nibbled at the dry bread. "I'm frightened, Fiona. I'm so frightened!"

"We could take off, Mary, but I'll tell you, living on the streets is no picnic." Fiona crouched beside Mary and wrapped her arms around her bony knees. "If only Miss Fannigan 'adn't left. Perhaps she could've 'elped us get a position somewhere together."

"We could still ask the mistress. What have we got to lose, after all?"

The girls looked at each other and sighed.

"Nothing," said Mary.

But Fiona raised one finger. "Don't say that. Every girl 'as a treasure that men are willing to pay for. So far, they 'aven't taken us over to the men at night. We should be 'appy about that. It means they want to sell us to someplace better."

"Look, over there." Mary pointed to the entrance to the main building of the orphanage, where Miss Horn, Sister Susan, and Mr. Cooper huddled together, now and then turning and looking out into the courtyard. "Now the camel's turning them against us, the old toad! Why did Miss Fannigan have to leave?" Mary groaned.

"Without Mr. Gaunt, she couldn't put up with it 'ere anymore. Guess what I found over yonder? A place behind the stone pile where they burn rubbish. I'm going over again tonight. Cooper mooches round there sometimes, and 'e buried something there."

"Let me come with you, Fiona." The grim sheds of the workhouse beyond the wall were a source of irresistible fascination for Mary.

"No. You'll stick out like a sore thumb with your blond hair. I look like 'em over there, and I can act like 'em, too. Not you, Mary." Fiona lovingly stroked her friend's silky blond hair, which curled around her pretty face.

During the evening meal, Mary was forced to sit in a corner of the dining hall and was given just a bowl of thin milk to drink. Her stomach growled loudly, and the smell of the food made her punishment even worse. She was happy to return to her bed that evening.

Fiona waited until everyone else had fallen asleep. As silent as a cat, she slipped on her dress and kneeled beside Mary's bed, then whispered in her ear, "I'm going over. Make sure the window stays open. Got it?"

"Of course, but be careful, all right?" Mary crept out of her bed, which was in the corner beside a window, and helped her friend climb outside. Agile as a monkey, Fiona clambered down a drainpipe to the ground and was swallowed by the darkness. Mary waited awhile at the window, but saw and heard nothing more, and lay back down on her bed. She must have fallen asleep, for when she awoke, dawn was already breaking. She looked over to Fiona's bed immediately. Empty! She was wide awake in an instant and sprang to the window, which was still open. "Fiona, where are you?" she murmured to herself, and peered out into the morning twilight.

She could hear sounds from the kitchen and the laundry over at the workhouse, and a dog barked. The milk cart pulled up at the gate on its rounds. She heard the clattering of the milk cans. A maid came out of the master's house and collected two. Then there was silence again. Mary crawled back into her bed and cowered there fearfully, listening to every sound inside and outside of the building. Finally, Sister Susan pushed open the dormitory door.

"Wakey, wakey!" she shouted. A groaning and grumbling spread through the dormitory.

Mary was one of the first in the washroom that morning, and when she saw Sister Susan standing among the tubs with a look of triumph on her face, she knew that something terrible had happened. Mary took off her nightdress, climbed into a tub, and washed herself. When she had dried herself and pulled on her dress, she went to Sister Susan.

"Where's Fiona?"

The woman's top lip pulled back unpleasantly to reveal yellow teeth. "She's moved. She's in the small dorm now."

Mary began to shake, and her knees threatened to give way. "No, she can't. We belong together! We don't have anything else."

Sister Susan's repulsive grin broadened. "March and get dressed. Or do you want to miss breakfast?"

With tears in her eyes, Mary ran down the corridor and caught a glimpse through the open door of the small dormitory. On a bed in the first row, against the wall, she saw a mop of red hair. The slender figure of her friend lay curled up under a sheet.

"Fiona!" Mary cried. She took a step into the room but was grabbed roughly by Sister Susan and pushed back into the corridor.

"Disappear, unless you want to join her."

There was nothing she could do for Fiona. She could only try to avoid attracting attention and getting locked up herself. That way, at least, she could be there when Fiona came back. Her friend was not there for breakfast, nor did she join Mary in the classroom or for lunch. Mary felt as if the atmosphere inside the orphanage had changed. It had never been a pleasant place, but now a menacing cloud hovered over everyone. Alone, Mary crouched with an apple behind the oak, but finally stuffed the piece of fruit into her pocket, crept behind the bush, and peeked through the wall.

Until a few moments earlier, it had been drizzling. Now, however, the dark clouds had parted and a few rays of sunlight broke through. It was no longer cold, even at night, and everywhere the plants were sprouting new growth and flowers. *If they catch me, I'll say I wanted to pick the flowers there*, Mary thought as she squeezed through the opening in the wall. She had only ever seen the workhouse yard from inside the workshops, when she'd been sent over to work. She screwed up her nose. It smelled awful there, reeking of moldy food scraps, old rope, manure. Or was that the cesspit?

Mary ducked behind a pile of wood and crept toward a pile of stones in the other corner. Fiona had mentioned that. Overgrown bushes and weeds grew everywhere. She heard the rough dialect of the London laborers and the crack of hammers on stone and sheet metal. From the main building came the crying of a child, but that was quickly silenced. The ground was covered in shards of stone and splinters of wood, and in a careless moment Mary stabbed her hand on a splinter. The pain was sudden and sharp, but she suppressed a cry and crept on as far as a dark patch in the grass. It smelled of ash and bones. At the wall of a shed stood a bucket of kitchen waste, and in front of the shed lay a dog, growling and tearing at the gristle of a pig bone. It growled louder as Mary moved closer.

She changed course, creeping back to the wall and from there farther along to the ash pile. She looked around and discovered a shovel leaning against a shed wall. Old boards, a ruined wooden barrel, and a pile of crates stood beside it. But there was no sign of anything that belonged to Mr. Gaunt. If the ground over here had been dug up, she could see no sign of it. And as long as the dog was lying there, she couldn't look closer. Cautiously, she went to the stack of crates. They were nailed shut. Her hand burned from the splinter, but she did not let that dissuade her. She looked around for something she could use to open the crates, but found nothing. From the yard, this corner was out of sight, so Mary gathered her courage and pulled down the top crate, which was not heavy. She tugged at the boards nailed shut on top until one of them came loose and she could twist it aside.

She caught her breath when she saw the leather cover of a book inside. A book! Who would leave a valuable book lying around outside like this? She had no time to see what kind of book it was, for just then the dog howled.

"Away, you filthy mongrel! Aha, what do we 'ave 'ere?" The bulky form of Mr. Cooper moved around the crates, and his heavy hand grabbed hold of Mary and pulled her close to him effortlessly. She had never stood this near to him before. He stank of tobacco and gin, and dark slime oozed from one corner of his mouth. The former boxer spat out a plug of tobacco and wiped his mouth with the back of his hand.

The scar on his forehead darkened, and his deep-set eyes squinted at her unpleasantly. "What are you doing sniffing round 'ere? Don't 'ave enough work to do?"

Mary was paralyzed with fear. She could not move. Cooper's hand gripped her arm like a vise. He pushed his other hand through her blond curls. "Pretty thing. And so grown up, aren't you?"

He grinned, revealing an incomplete row of brown teeth. His breath was so nauseating that Mary felt ill. Or perhaps it was fear. Her stomach rebelled, and she vomited on Cooper's jacket.

He let go of her instantly and punched her in the face. "You little shite! Look at this mess! You'll pay for this."

"Pat? Pat, is that you?" It was Sister Susan, calling from the other side of the wall.

"Yes! Blast it, come 'ere and get this little rat. She's been sniffin' round my things," Cooper bawled.

It wasn't long before Sister Susan came running around the shed. She spotted the crates, then she looked at Cooper, but he was so furious that he only had eyes for his soiled suit.

Mary was curled on the ground, crying in misery. "I'm sorry! I didn't mean it! The flowers . . ."

Sister Susan looked at her suspiciously. "Flowers? There are no flowers here. You're just as bad as the redhead, but she got what was coming to her."

Cooper pulled off his jacket and shook it. "Gawd, that stinks."

"Give it here, I'll get it clean." Susan jerked the jacket out of his hand.

"You'll get more for the blond 'ere than you did for the redhead, I'm sure o' that. Then I get 'er. She owes me that." He reached out his hand for Mary, but Susan pulled her away.

"Not her! The master sold her today."

24.

The discovery that Lord Hargrave's valet had an injury to his hand that matched exactly with what Sadie had reported from Fearnham might, of course, mean nothing. Jane was well aware of that, though her mind was in turmoil, inferring the most absurd connections. Besides, Jack was considerably younger than the man Sadie had described. Jane swore Hettie to silence, which was not easy for the maid, but it was better that way. And Jane herself would not bring it up with Lord Hargrave. The man was unpredictable and not one to have anyone tell him how to run his affairs. Jane had sensed that very clearly from him. She was also uncertain as to whether he would really let the affair with Blythe rest. But that could wait. Now that he had returned to London, he would not be back in Cornwall for some time.

The London Season was a must for any self-respecting member of high society. For Jane, too, there were commitments to fulfill, whether she wanted to or not. The main part of the social season began each year after Easter in the city on the Thames. One could ignore the Derby, but Ascot was a sacred obligation, followed by the Henley Regatta. And there were numerous important balls and dinners to which she was invited. Lady Alison was throwing a party that Jane was looking forward to, but mainly because it was an opportunity to see her friend again. This year, she would not attend the event alone; Wescott would be at her side. The thought of her husband being there left her feeling ambivalent.

Blount had diplomatically suggested she inform Wescott about Hargrave's valet, and then do nothing more. When she tried to sound Blount out about exactly what Wescott did in London, Blount prevaricated, and she gave up trying to ask the man anything else.

April drew to a close with warmer days. The sun was in the sky longer, and the heavy, gunmetal rain clouds had, for now, disappeared. In Cornwall, one could always count on wind and rain, but the days when the weather was good made up for the weeks of gray drabness.

Floyd, using a walking stick, emerged from the dining room, which was to be thoroughly cleaned and freshly carpeted during her upcoming absence. Jane wanted light colors and fresh, airy materials to drive out the oppressive atmosphere of the house.

"I'm leaving you behind only with great reluctance, Floyd, but I will sleep easier knowing you are here while I'm gone." She looked warmly at her loyal butler, who was recovering well.

He would probably favor his injured leg for quite a while, but even that would settle with time. Doctor Woodfall had done good work.

"Thank you, my lady. I won't be alone here." Rufus had positioned himself between them, and the butler scratched the Great Dane's back.

Jane sighed and nodded. "I'm not allowed to be selfish, am I? I would prefer to take him with me, but he's used to living on the land and wouldn't have any fun in a dirty city."

She stroked Rufus's silky fur. "I believe you will have an easier time of it with Mr. Roche now, but if you have any difficulties, let me know immediately."

"Very good, my lady. And are you determined to stop by Rosewood Hall?" Floyd was immaculately dressed. Apart from the walking stick and pale patches on his cheeks, he was the epitome of a perfect butler.

"It is on my way. I am not in any hurry to visit my cousin, but it has to be done, unfortunately . . ." She waved to Hettie, who was hurrying down the stairs carrying three hatboxes. "In the coach, then the rest in the wagon and we can go. I don't want to have to spend the night in Newbridge."

She planned to visit the orphanage in Newbridge on her way. The visit to St. Austell with Violet Sutton had proved fruitless, though only in terms of her investigation. The orphanage was run by a friendly older couple and seemed to be a godsend for the area. The children had been happy and laughing and free to move around the buildings and yard without fear. Poverty was still the rule there, but it seemed that no one suffered for a lack of food, and the children were clean. But Violet was moody, swinging between hysterical, disconsolate, and waspish. After that visit, Jane had sworn to never to go anywhere again with the woman. When, back in the carriage, Violet produced the box with the syringe and ampoules, it was clear to Jane just how dependent on the opiate she had become. She felt sympathy and loathing for the woman, in equal measure.

Floyd nodded understandingly. Jane had spoken to him about the problem of the promissory notes that her cousin had uncovered among her uncle's assets. Lord Henry had never mentioned them to Floyd. It could be assumed that, for Lord Henry, the matter was closed and no longer even worth mentioning.

"His lordship would never have allowed things to come this far. I hope you are able to reach an amicable agreement with your cousin." The fact that Floyd never referred to Matthew as the new lord made it clear how little respect he had for Lord Henry's avaricious son.

Mrs. Roche entered the hallway and stood slightly apart, waiting.

Jane was aware of being observed by the housekeeper when she shook Floyd's hand. The familiar gesture demonstrated both respect and appreciation, and set the butler apart from the rest of the staff.

"I wish you a pleasant journey, my lady," said Floyd, and his voice shook slightly. "Let me know in advance of your return, and I shall ensure that everything is prepared."

It would not have befitted him to ask how long she would be away, but Jane said, "Three months in London is more than enough, Floyd. Until then."

As Jane went out, she nodded to Mrs. Roche and was surprised to find the entire domestic staff lined up in the courtyard. When she took her place beside Hettie in the coach, she waved a final time from the window.

"Mrs. Roche has really shaped up, don't you think, ma'am?" Hettie said, sitting back.

"And not without reason. She and her husband have profited from Blythe's lapse themselves, or do you think that all the game that has disappeared in the last three years has gone to Hargrave?"

Rufus ran behind the coach barking, but gave up at the gate. Blount, who was accompanying them on horseback, made sure that the Great Dane returned to the house. Jane looked back sadly at her dog as the coach rolled alongside the stone walls that bordered the fields and meadows of Mulberry Park. Before the path led off into the woods, she saw a figure standing alone on a hilltop. The man doffed his hat and stood his ground until she could no longer see him.

"Blythe," Jane murmured, and leaned back against the upholstered seat.

The closer they got to Newbridge, the busier the streets became. The tiny village was not far from Callington, a small town on one of the main traffic routes that led from the north coast to the south. Plymouth, with its important harbor, was only eight miles away, and to the east began the broad, uninhabited moorlands of Dartmoor. The region was notorious for its inhospitable climate and treacherous bogs, where those unfamiliar with the area could be easily lost. Ten years earlier, a prison originally built for prisoners from the Napoleonic wars had been reopened as a convict jail in Princetown, in the moor itself.

Jane was glad that she did not have to cross the notorious moor, because there was another hamlet, also called Newbridge, there.

The orphanage, which Violet Sutton had described as desolate and run-down, lay outside the village, surrounded by bleak fields and heavily thinned forests. Violet had mentioned that the women on the committee did not go out of their way to visit the place because the director was a most unpleasant patron. For Jane, that was just one more reason to see for herself the place that was supposed to be a refuge for needy children.

Along the way, Jane had asked the driver to stop and had bought several baskets of fruit and sweets for the children. The wagon carrying most of her luggage had taken the direct route to London. It had been mild the whole day, but now a thunderstorm was brewing, and the first raindrops spattered against the coach windows.

They could make out the vague outlines of several buildings behind a wall interrupted only by a gatehouse. A sign rattled beneath a cast-iron arch spanning the gateposts. Blount, who had pulled on his waxed cloak, leaned down from his horse and shouted toward the gatehouse, "Hey! Anyone here?"

Hettie deciphered the sign and whispered, "It's an orphanage and a workhouse."

"Why are you whispering?" asked Jane, but the sight of the forbidding walls and desolate buildings made her uneasy as well.

A door creaked open, and the gatekeeper slowly emerged from his cabin. "Who are you and what do you want?" Gray, lank hair fell from beneath the sleepy old man's cap. He was chewing a wad of tobacco.

"Open up. Lady Allen wishes to speak to the director of this facility," Blount snapped at the gatekeeper in an imperious tone.

The man spat and shuffled forward to take a closer look at the coach. "Another o' them fine crates! Like I care. Drive on through. The master's house is down and right. You can't miss it."

Fat raindrops rattled against the roof of the coach, and they heard the coachman swear. Neither the roadway nor the yard in front of the buildings was sealed, and both had been transformed into a sea of mud. As far as Jane could make out through the streaming rain, behind the walls was a complex of barrack-like buildings, perhaps workhalls. She could hear the sound of hammers beating on rocks. Directly in front of her rose two conjoined buildings, the one on the right apparently of more recent construction. A sign hung over the entrance, and Blount swung the door knocker vigorously.

He spoke a few words with a servant girl who appeared, then returned to the coach and helped Jane and Hettie climb down.

"This way, my lady!" He guided her around puddles to the entrance.

In an astonishingly well-appointed hallway stood two chairs beside a table with a vase of flowers. It smelled of bread, and from a distant part of the building came the sound of singing. Jane allowed a servant to take her cloak and was about to hand the woman her calling card when a man of average height and appearance came toward her, his head slightly bowed.

His bearing was humble, but his humility was for show. Jane could see that his eyes were alert and calculating. "Lady Allen! What an honor to welcome such a prominent visitor within our modest walls. If we had known you were coming . . . Ledford is my name. I run this institute. If you please." He gestured invitingly.

The maid waited off to one side in a passage from which the smell of bread wafted.

"Paula will serve your butler and maid tea in the kitchen," Mr. Ledford directed. Then he led Jane through modest but comfortably furnished rooms into a small reception chamber.

A blond woman of around thirty rose to her feet as they entered.

"My wife, Virginia. Ginny, may I introduce Lady Allen?" said Ledford. He offered Jane an armchair that stood between a sofa and two chairs.

"The pleasure is mine, Mrs. Ledford. I don't want to keep you long." Jane sat politely and shook her head as the mistress reached for a teapot. "I'm just passing through on my way to London. I'm mostly here in place of my friend Mrs. Sutton."

She had, in fact, talked to Violet about visiting Newbridge, and the ailing woman had welcomed the plan. She herself felt in no condition to follow her brother to London.

Mrs. Ledford's lips were thin, and her smile did not make it to her eyes. "So you are one of the women on the committee?"

"Well, I've only just moved into my estate in Cornwall, actually, and Violet has been so gracious as to familiarize me with her work," Jane explained, noting a vitrine with silverware and good porcelain, Persian carpets, and heavy, brocade curtains. If things were this good for the directors of the orphanage, one could only hope that the children also benefited from such affluence.

Mr. Ledford sat opposite her on one of the chairs and followed her glance. "Then you are here to represent the committee, would you say? The official visit was cancelled, unfortunately."

"Was it? Well, I've brought the children fruit and some other things, and I would be glad to form an impression for myself. Perhaps I might visit a classroom? I heard singing, and very lovely, too," said Jane, smiling endearingly. Seeing reluctance on the faces of the master and his wife, she added, "Of course, I am well aware that maintaining such a home is not easy, and that perhaps an endowment of some sort might be in order, for renovations or an extension?"

Her host's negative expression changed instantly, and the couple exchanged a knowing look. Mr. Ledford wore his hair combed over his scalp and had sideburns all the way to his chin. His lips curled, and his entire expression transformed into one of grateful submissiveness.

"My most distinguished Lady Allen, we find ourselves deeply in your debt, and will naturally show you whatever you would like to see. The singing of the children is truly enchanting, I can only agree with you. They are just finishing the final hour of the day. If you like, we will pay a quick visit to the classroom."

"I would love to." Jane stood, then hesitated. "There was something else . . ."

Mrs. Ledford, who had also risen to her feet, nodded encouragingly. "Yes, my lady?"

"Do you have a teacher here by the name of Peter Gaunt?"

Every trace of courtesy vanished from Mrs. Ledford's face, and an icy silence descended on the room for several seconds. "Why do you ask?" the mistress finally said.

"Why don't you simply answer my question? I have something that belongs to him," Jane replied frostily.

Mrs. Ledford was about to reply when her husband interrupted her. "Mr. Gaunt left us of his own free will. We were sad to lose him. He was very popular here. But what is it they say? A rolling stone gathers no moss."

"He's gone off to America to make his fortune in a better world! Ha! As if it's any better over there," Mrs. Ledford snarled.

Jane had to make an effort to contain her excitement. Finally, she was on to something. "Well, who can really say? Apparently, there are some who have made a fortune there. Perhaps he wants to prospect for gold." She began to move toward the door, and her host accompanied her into the corridor.

"Hettie!" Jane called, ignoring Mrs. Ledford's icy glare. "My maid loves children so very much, just like me. She wanted to be a teacher."

"Oh, really?" said Mrs. Ledford. She could hardly have sounded less interested.

"I'm sad to say we haven't been blessed with children of our own," said Mr. Ledford, and gave his wife a stern look. "So we dedicate our lives to the well-being of orphans, and there are so many of them. Though you may not believe it, poverty in our country is widespread. This way, if you please. We have to go outside for a moment, but we will be under cover."

Hettie had come out of the kitchen and followed the small group down a long corridor and out into a small garden surrounded by high walls. From there, they passed through a narrow doorway into a large courtyard filled with huge puddles.

"The children's courtyard. Some gravel would certainly help it drain, but there is always something more pressing to be done. The dormitory roof has a leak, the bathrooms have to be replaced, and now that we have over two hundred children the bathrooms are too small anyway. And there are always more children coming. Over there is the poorhouse. It isn't large, but it's a haven for the most needy." Mr. Ledford spoke quickly and without emotion. "Many women exploit us shamelessly."

"Ned, leave off . . . ," Mrs. Ledford said, trying to slow down her husband's monologue.

"Why should I? It's the truth. They come looking for a bed for the night and say thank-you by leaving their children behind. Ah, do you hear?"

They were standing beneath the eaves of a long building that looked like a row of schoolrooms. Through the rain, Jane could see a rectangular yard with a huge, ancient oak tree at the far end. Behind the wall lay the barracks of the poorhouse, from where she'd heard stone breaking.

From the ground-floor windows came the sound of the polyphonic singing from innumerable young mouths, the last verse of a chorale. When it was over, there was silence, followed by the children shuffling from the classroom and out into the courtyard. Because it was raining, the children—girls between four and ten years of age, all in thin dresses—huddled along the wall, anxious not to get too close to the master and his entourage. *An aura of fear reigns here,* thought Jane.

At the other end of the school building, another door opened to release the boys into the courtyard. A grim-looking man walked out with them and took up a post by the wall from where he watched the children, his arms crossed over his chest.

"That is Mr. Cooper, our custodian. He also assists with the monitoring and disciplines the children for misconduct." Mr. Ledford looked at Jane. "Without discipline, it is not possible to keep a horde of neglected children under control, my lady."

"Please excuse me," said Mrs. Ledford. "Sister Susan!" She approached a tough-looking woman with a coarse face who was just coming out of the girls' section.

"Our able nurse and surrogate mother. She looks after the littlest children and takes care of any first aid that might be required," said Mr. Ledford.

Jane observed the girls. They were standing together in small groups in front of the house and seemed unsure of what was expected of them. "Would it be all right if we distributed the baskets I've brought? It strikes me as a nice reward for the end of the lesson. Hettie, run to Blount and fetch the things."

"Yes, ma'am," Hettie said and hurried off.

A girl with flame-red hair caught Jane's eye. She was leaning listlessly against a pillar, staring out into the rain. The girl seemed deeply sad, lost even. *Like a bird whose owner has clipped its wings and slammed the door of the cage,* thought Jane.

"Do you know the names and backgrounds of the children who come here?" she asked, unable to take her eyes off the lonely looking girl.

"Not all of them, my lady," the director explained. "If they don't have a name, we have to give them one. Sometimes we name them after the place they were found. We've had a Mary Field, a Mary Wood, and . . ."

"Mary? So Mary is quite a common name here?" Jane asked.

"Yes, indeed."

"Which of the girls is a Mary, then?" she asked, as innocently as she could. Whatever Mr. Gaunt had to do with the matter, she didn't want her questions to put any of the children in harm's way.

Ledford's brow creased. "The little one back there and—" He paused.

Jane had not missed the reaction of the red-haired girl at the mention of the name Mary. She had turned her head slightly, not too far, but as if the name meant something to her. There was something very wrong there, Jane realized. She could sense it.

Behind them, the door squeaked and Mr. Ledford's maid called out to him. "One moment, if you please," the director excused himself. He disappeared through the door.

As if she had been waiting for this moment, the red-haired girl pushed herself away from the pole and strolled close to Jane, as inconspicuously as possible. She looked all around nervously, and then motioned secretly to attract Jane's attention. "Lady!" she whispered.

Jane was about to take a step forward, but the girl hissed, "No! Stay there. I . . . I know a Mary."

Surprised, Jane whispered back, "Yes, but . . ."

"I always knew she was different. But you're too late. She's gone away. To London." The redhead shuffled her feet in the slurry.

Mrs. Ledford finished her talk with Sister Susan and turned back toward Jane.

"Later," the girl whispered, and wandered away.

25.

While the fruit and sweets were being distributed, Jane tried to catch a glimpse of the red-haired girl, but she was nowhere to be seen. It was almost as if the girl had never existed. Jane had the director show her one of the dormitories, and found the conditions inside almost unbearable; the faces of the children were pale and forlorn. In the stairway, she stopped in her tracks. An unpleasant odor was spreading through the building from the basement.

Jane pressed a handkerchief to her mouth. "What is that?"

Mr. Ledford's expression did not change. "The wash, my lady. We also do the laundry for the poorhouse."

Hettie, too, had turned pale and moved on quickly. Jane followed her and took a deep breath as she passed through the main entrance into the yard. The rain had stopped, but the orphanage did not leave a better impression for being more visible, and there was neither sight nor sound of the children. Jane had seen how their eyes lit up at the unaccustomed sweets and fruit.

Blount exited the Ledfords' house and went to his horse, which was waiting patiently alongside the coach. The coachman had tied a nose bag to each of the horses and now removed them.

Mr. and Mrs. Ledford stood side by side on the landing in front of the entrance and smiled pleasantly at Jane. "Were we able to show you everything you wanted to see, my lady? There is work to be done left and right, but . . ." Mr. Ledford shrugged and sighed dramatically. "We are grateful for any assistance in furthering our good work."

They were waiting for a donation. "I will have the money transferred from my bank as soon as I arrive in London," said Jane. She looked up to the windows of the dormitory above, and saw that the children were pressing their faces to the glass and waving to her.

"That is very good of you, most generous, my lady," Mr. Ledford kowtowed.

Jane lifted the hem of her skirt to prevent it from dragging in the mud. "Oh, one thing. The red-haired girl I saw earlier in the yard. What was her name?"

The director and his wife looked at each other and said, almost as one, "Which girl?"

"A very thin girl, maybe eleven, with unmistakable red hair. She reminded me very much of the daughter of a friend. The same hair." Jane raised her eyebrows, waiting for an answer.

"I really couldn't say who you mean. We have only a few older girls, and none of them have red hair, my lady." The director's tone made it clear that he considered the topic at an end.

"Ah, well, I guess I was mistaken. Oh, there was one other thing." Jane looked back up to the orphanage windows. "Have you found a high-society placement in London lately? For a girl? I'm on my way *to* London, you see, and my friends there are often in search of maids. I could perhaps help in finding positions."

"We did place a girl in Norfolk not long ago. Not a high-society position, but a good house, for a businessman. Anything else, my lady?"

Her questions had been no more than fishing, and Jane gave up. Mr. and Mrs. Ledford had been playing this game longer than she had and would not disclose anything they did not want to.

"I shall inform the committee that you are planning extensive renovations." Jane's words were an indirect threat that she would retain control over how her money was spent, but that did not shake the Ledfords.

"We are looking forward to hearing from you and from the other women. Many things will have changed here by the next time you visit," Mrs. Ledford assured her.

Just before stepping into the coach, Jane turned up to the windows one last time. A movement behind one of the tiny windows in the attic caught her eye. A ray of sunlight broke through the clouds, and for a second she saw red hair and a pale face. Had someone locked the girl in the attic to prevent her from speaking to Jane? Or was her imagination playing tricks on her? A lot had happened in recent weeks. Disappointed, she sank back into the seat.

The coach wheels churned through the mud and finally rattled out onto the cobblestones in front of the gate. As if she had been waiting to escape the oppressive walls of the institute, Hettie said, "Phew. Ma'am, that certainly was a strange bunch. The master and mistress weren't too bad, but the sister and that custodian were downright terrifying. Those poor children!"

"Hmm. Mr. Cooper . . . he looked rather like the man we saw in Bodmin, but I'm sure it wasn't him." Jane looked out the window and waved Blount over to her.

"My lady?" Blount leaned down effortlessly to her while his horse continued at its quick pace alongside the coach.

"Did you notice anything untoward?" She hoped that this capable man had been able to look around while she had been visiting the buildings with the Ledfords.

Blount's pale eyes flashed. "Yes, I think you could say that. I spent quite some time talking to the maid. A friendly girl. She told me that another coach arrived just yesterday to pick up one of the girls."

"Which girl? Come on, man, enough suspense."

"Mary. Her name was Mary. A blond girl, eleven years old. Once the girls reach eleven, they have to leave the orphanage and find work."

Jane inhaled sharply. "My God, we missed her by a day. And she is on her way to Norfolk?"

"No, my lady. The coach was on its way to London."

The road narrowed and Blount let his horse fall back. He was only able to draw alongside again a few minutes later. "The maid said the Ledfords always make a great secret about who a new employer is. Apparently, that's the usual arrangement if a high-society position is involved." He tapped his hat with his fingers. "It will be dark soon. I'll take care of lodgings for the night, my lady," he said, and galloped ahead.

"Did you hear that, Hettie? A high-society position in London," said Jane pensively.

"Do you think that's our Mary, ma'am? And that she might end up in the same place as her friend?"

Jane hadn't wanted to say it out loud, but that was exactly what she was thinking. She sighed unhappily. "I'm afraid it may be. They did admit Mr. Gaunt had been a teacher there. But we can't be sure it's her. It could also be that he had a position somewhere else and gave the book to the girl there. Anything's possible."

"But the Ledfords' orphanage was the worst we've seen, by far. That Mr. Cooper was plain fearsome! No, they had something to hide," said Hettie with absolute conviction.

Jane smiled. "Orphanages are never nice places, Hettie, but I agree with you. Their reception room was certainly very nice for such a poor home, and then there was the girl with red hair."

Jane did not have a chance to give voice to any more thoughts. Without warning, the coach was knocked off course by something and bounced and swerved wildly for a moment. Jane and Hettie were thrown sideways. Glass shattered, the coachman bellowed, the horses whinnied frantically but stopped, and Jane found herself underneath her maid, lying on the street through the half-open door of the carriage.

"Hettie! My God, you're heavy!" Jane couldn't move under the weight of her maid, and Hettie's petticoats were covering her face.

But the maid did not move. She simply lay on top of Jane, motionless as a sack. "Rogers! Blount! Help us, for God's sake," Jane shouted. She could feel a strange warm wetness on her cheek and a growing pain in her arm.

Suddenly, someone jerked open the door on the other side of the coach, above her, and the red glow of the setting sun fell through the opening. Jane managed to push Hettie's body a little to one side and found herself squinting up into the unexpected brightness. "What the devil is going on? Help me!" Jane seethed.

The outline of a man appeared in the opening. With the light behind him, Jane could not see his face. He simply stood and looked down at her.

"Why are you just standing there? Help us!" she shouted.

Hettie began to move, and her skirts fell back over Jane's face. When Jane managed to free herself from the material again, the silhouette above her had disappeared. *Like a ghost,* thought Jane. Disconcerted, she peered up at the red sky.

Hettie floundered around and kicked her feet, which were up in the air. "What was that? Did we hit a pothole?"

Moments later, the coachman, Rogers, groaned and appeared at the door, and then Blount finally returned from his search for a place to spend the night, and the two men freed the women from their predicament. The coach was tipped half onto one side, a wheel missing.

"Ma'am, you're bleeding," cried Hettie, who, apart from fainting, was unhurt.

Hettie and Blount sat Jane down on a case that had fallen from the roof, and Blount examined her face. "Some small cuts from the window glass. Just scratches. When we get to the guesthouse, we should send for a doctor. My God, Rogers, how could this happen?"

The coachman rubbed the back of his head. His weathered, honest face seemed perplexed. "Ma'am, I don't know." He shook his head. "I checked the wheels, the belts, the harness, everything. Everything was in top shape this morning. All I did was adjust the brakes. A little pothole should not have made a wheel come off like that. And then I took a blow on the head! At least, that's what it feels like. I don't understand it."

"Nonsense," Blount snapped at the coachman, but Jane interrupted him.

"No, unfortunately, it does make sense. This was no accident." Jane told them about the stranger she saw, then felt a dull, throbbing pain in her shoulder.

"Damn it, this should not have happened!" Blount swore. "He waited until I'd ridden ahead."

Jane looked up and down the road. There was only one lane, and bushes and trees lined both sides. Someone could disappear easily into any small copse or thicket. A little farther back the moorlands began, and if you knew your way around them, no one would find you there.

Hettie had taken a linen cloth from one of their travel bags to clean Jane's wounds. "The bleeding has stopped, thank heavens. Do we have any alcohol?"

"Rogers?" Blount barked the question, and the coachman fished a flask from beneath the driver's seat.

The strong alcohol burned when it made contact with the cuts, and Jane winced. When she tried to move her left arm, a sharp pain shot through it. "Hettie, you're too heavy. You've crushed my shoulder."

Hettie's big round eyes filled with tears. "Ma'am, I'm so sorry, I didn't mean to!"

"I know that, but from now on, no more sweets," said Jane, trying to smile through gritted teeth.

"No, ma'am," Hettie murmured.

"Do we go for help? Is the guesthouse in a village?" Rogers asked, and took a deep swig from the liquor flask when Hettie handed it back to him.

Blount shook his head, looked at the half-tipped coach, and said, "We'll put the wheel back on provisionally. It will hold as far as the guesthouse. We can't leave the women here alone. Do you have any sort of weapon?"

"Just a stick," the coachman replied sheepishly.

"I think someone's hackles are up at the questions I'm asking, and that we're getting closer to Mary," said Jane, observing the dark expression on Blount's face.

"Then you also know that the people we're dealing with won't shy away from anything, my lady."

Jane sighed and rubbed her arm gingerly. "And if it was really no more than an accident?"

Blount snorted scornfully, shrugged off his jacket, and rolled up his sleeves. "The captain will tell you soon enough what he thinks of that."

Ignoring the remark, Jane held her sore arm out to Hettie. "It's like an elephant fell on it."

"Oh." Hettie rummaged unhappily through a travel bag for medicine. "Laudanum for the pain, ma'am?" she asked.

"And turn myself into a hysterical wreck like Violet Sutton?" Jane snapped back.

26.

London, May 1860

Hettie could not get enough of the hustle and bustle of London. There were street vendors who sold barrels of herring, while others sold costume jewelry and lace; bootblacks; an Italian harpist; a street theater doing their best with *Punch and Judy*—the maid was thrilled by all of it. If Jane did not keep a tight rein on her, she would have wasted every penny she had on useless trinkets and slick con men.

"Oh, look, ma'am!" she cried.

But Jane kept on walking and pushed open the gate to the London townhouse on Seymour Street. They had been there only for three days, so Jane did not think any worse of her young maid for all her effusive delight. Hettie would be longing to return to the country soon enough. Certainly, she would once the weather grew warmer and the stink of the sewers lay over the city like a putrid blanket.

It was only a few steps from the gate to the front door, but that was enough space for a lovely front garden with a magnificent weeping willow, and the house was freestanding. It was two stories, and was roomier than it looked from the outside. From what Wescott had implied about the place, Jane had expected something decidedly more modest and was pleasantly surprised at what she found. The windows were large and the rooms well lit, the grounds were neatly trimmed and cultivated, and there was a conservatory and a terrace that led out to a garden and pond behind. Seymour Street led off Portman Square, and in good weather it was an easy stroll to Hyde Park or Grosvenor Square, where some of London's grandest homes stood, among them Lady Alison's and the house of the Pembrokes.

Jane swung the door knocker, and the door opened a moment later. Levi, a taciturn older man with immaculate manners and an eastern European accent, greeted her. Jane could only guess at the man's origins, but she imagined he came from somewhere in the Caucasus. He also played violin extremely well, as Jane had discovered one evening. His son, Josiah, was also part of the household, a slender young boy with large, intelligent eyes. Blount played the role of butler and caretaker, but during his absence, Levi seemed to have taken over those duties.

"Is Mr. Wescott home?" Jane asked as she handed Levi her umbrella.

"No, my lady. But he wanted me to inform you that he would like you to dress for dinner this evening. The coach has been ordered for eight o'clock," said Levi in his silky voice.

"Where have we been invited?" Jane asked.

"To the Duke of Rutland."

"Thank you." Surprised, Jane climbed the stairs.

Hettie came up behind her, slightly out of breath. "Ma'am! Are you going out to the Rutlands' this evening?"

"Yes, it would appear I am." Jane was not happy at the way Wescott was using her. But social obligations were part of their agreement. She had already sent a message to Alison to tell her she was in the city. With a little luck, Alison would be present that evening. And with a little less luck, she would also see Violet and Hargrave.

"Then we should find an especially beautiful dress for you. Black?" asked Hettie doubtfully, and when Jane shook her head, her maid beamed. Eagerly, she helped her mistress out of the jacket she was wearing and carried it into the dressing room. From there, a door opened into a luxurious bathroom.

Jane's bedroom was not particularly large, but decorated in warm ocher tones. A double door led into Wescott's bedroom next door, but the door was locked with the key on Wescott's side, and Jane had not yet caught a glimpse of the interior. Her husband had only greeted her briefly on their arrival and had been out constantly ever since. Late at night, she sometimes heard noises coming from his room, but when she came down for breakfast he was already long gone.

Just before eight, Jane gave herself a final check in the mirror. "Hettie, you're a treasure!"

Her hair had been pinned up artfully. A single lock of chestnut hair curled at her neck, around which she wore an emerald necklace. The color of the precious stones matched that of her elegant dress and made Jane's complexion glow.

"You look beautiful, my lady! I would love to see you dancing in this dress." The girl twirled dreamily on the spot.

"It won't come to that this evening. We will have dinner, and after that I will have to put up with boring conversations. Have you put out the cape with the fur collar?"

Hettie ran into the next room and returned carrying the sumptuous cape, which would create precisely the right impression on such an evening.

If Jane had been thinking that Wescott would meet her at the door to her room, she was disappointed. Well, she was perfectly capable of going down alone.

Levi was waiting for her in the hall. He opened the door and walked with her as far as the gate. "I wish you a pleasant evening, my lady."

The coach was already waiting in the street. Few houses in London had their own stables, and consequently most of the upper class relied on rented coaches. Jane had traveled by coach to Rosewood Hall and from there to the train station in Salisbury. In Salisbury, she had sent Rogers back to Cornwall. The train trip to London was shorter and more comfortable.

The moment Levi swung open the squeaky front gate, the coach door opened and Wescott jumped down to the sidewalk. "I would have come earlier, but it was simply not possible. After you, Jane." He reached out one hand and helped her climb into the interior, then gave the coachman a signal to go.

When he sat opposite her, she realized that he was wearing a dinner jacket. "You've already changed?"

The suspicion came to her that he perhaps had a lover and was spending his time there. The notion did not sit well with her, though given the nature of their agreement, she knew she had no right to be angry.

He seemed a little tired and swept the hair out of his face. "I was at the club. It is, in fact, the true home of many men, as you no doubt know."

"My experience in this field is rather limited, but if you say so, then I guess that's how it is," she replied archly.

"Jane." There was warmth and a certain sadness in his tone. He leaned forward and reached for her hand.

Jane flinched instinctively, and Wescott looked at her, taken aback. "Oh, it's nothing," she quickly reassured him. "The accident. Hettie was thrown on top of me, and I managed to twist my arm."

"I didn't know."

"Does it matter?" she asked and took her hand back. "I'm here, as you wanted me to be."

His dark eyes looked at her earnestly, and a crease formed between them. "Why do you say that?"

"Why should it bother you? Since I arrived, I've seen you but once, and then only briefly. In three days, all I've heard from you is an order to accompany you to the Rutlands'."

"It was no order, Jane. You could have refused." He leaned back on the seat and stretched his long legs out beside hers.

"I am holding to our agreement. If I find myself indisposed, I will let you know." The coach felt far too small for her, and the air inside oppressive, but that was because of the corset, which Hettie had laced far too tightly.

"You look exceptionally beautiful, Jane."

She shot him an irritated look from beneath lowered eyelids. "I can hardly breathe, but thank you. If I look like I'm going to faint, feel free to administer smelling salts." She shook the bag she carried.

Wescott looked at her in surprise, then laughed so sincerely that Jane could only smile. Finally, he leaned forward again and pressed a kiss to her cheek. "This could be an amusing evening after all. Oh, you didn't tell me how the visit to your cousin went."

"We argued, as usual. Bridget was even more insufferable than ever. Matthew flapped the promissory notes in my face in triumph." She sighed. "They're real, as far as I can tell. My God, how I hate him for having them!"

"Were you able to see exactly where he keeps them?"

"In my uncle's desk. Ah! He actually sat at Uncle Henry's desk and acted like—" She broke off. What she had wanted to say suddenly felt preposterous.

"Like the Lord of Pembroke," said Wescott gently. "Jane, he possesses the title now, though he doesn't deserve it."

Again, she found herself crying. Crying *now*, just before they were due at the duke's house. "Sorry."

But before she could find a handkerchief in her purse, she found one pressed into her hand. "Shall I have the coachman drive us around the block?"

She nodded and wiped her eyes. The thought of Rosewood Hall and her cousin was unbearable. It had been her home, and her memories of happier days there had overwhelmed her the minute she set foot in the hallway. And Matthew couldn't wait to rub her nose in his newfound superiority, to humiliate her in every way he could.

"We grew up together! How can he do this to me?"

"The people close to us can hurt us most easily. It is contemptible, because it is simple. He knows his father loved you, and that is reason enough for him to hate you. Jealousy is an evil thing, Jane." He stroked her cheek gently and placed one finger under her chin, making her look him in the eye. "You are a decent person. He is not. And we've arrived."

A jolt ran through the carriage as it jerked to a stop. Jane slipped forward, against Wescott's shoulder. But she resisted her impulse to lean on him. Instead, she took a deep breath, cleared her throat, and put on a smile.

Berkeley Square was among the most prestigious addresses in London. Grand mansions designed by Robert Adams vied with each other for the attention of passersby. Close to the Rutlands' was number thirty-eight, one of the most magnificent homes. It belonged to the Countess of Jersey, a famous society lady and for many years a patroness of Almack's tea and dance club.

Wescott held out his arm for Jane to take and gave her an encouraging look. "Ready?"

"Always."

They followed a lighted path paved with pale marble to the columns at the entrance of the Rutlands' mansion. In the darkness, the formidable size of the place could only be guessed at. Music rang from brightly lit windows on the ground floor. A liveried servant led them into the main hall, which itself was big enough to house a major society ball. Pink marble, antique statues, and valuable tapestries caught Jane's eye.

"Are you sure this is just a dinner and not a party?" Jane whispered to Wescott.

"The duke and his wife love pomp and ceremony. You've met them, haven't you?"

Jane recalled the gaudily made-up woman she'd met at Hargrave's. "Hmm. Which club do you go to, by the way?"

"Beg pardon?" Wescott said in surprise.

"Which club? A wife ought to know that."

"Brooks's," he murmured.

"Who would have thought? That's the meeting place of the aristocrats. I've heard that the most eccentric wagers are made there. Don't you bump into your father?"

"No. He's a member of Boodle's. The conservatives are among friends there." As soon as he mentioned his father, his tone grew bitter.

"I would have thought you were more a Rag type," she said airily as she spotted another servant approaching them. The established Army and Navy Club was better known as the Rag.

"I keep up membership of several clubs, according to my needs, if you really must know."

"I really must."

The servant bowed to them and said, "This way, please."

They were led into a music room, where a string quartet was playing. There were a dozen guests in all, a manageable number, and to Jane's great joy she immediately spied the back of a petite woman with long blond hair. Alison and Thomas were there! The next moment, though, her delight was tempered somewhat when she saw Lord Hargrave and his sister and the chiseled features of Mr. Devereaux.

Into the fray, thought Jane. She raised her eyebrows expectantly as the Duke of Rutland and his flamboyantly dressed wife came toward them.

Florence Rutland behaved as if Jane were a best friend she hadn't seen in years. "My dear Lady Jane, how delightful to have you visit us!"

Jane and Florence exchanged compliments—superficial, empty phrases—then Jane moved on to the other guests. When she came to Violet, she was shocked at the gray shadows under her eyes, too dark even for powder to conceal. But before she could talk to Hargrave's sister at any length, Violet's brother joined them.

His dinner jacket was particularly elegant, tailored by one of the most expensive gentlemen's outfitters in London, Jane assumed, just like the duke's. The two men seemed to maintain a close connection, and Devereaux appeared to belong to the same charmed circle.

"You've met? Mr. Devereaux, Lady Jane," Lord Hargrave said, introducing his friend.

Devereaux took Jane's hand and insinuated a kiss. He eyed her appreciatively. "You lend the evening a special grace, my lady. I very much regret that I came too late several months ago."

Wescott, in conversation with Rutland, moved close beside his wife and brushed his hand lightly over her back. "I hope we won't have to get out the dueling pistols, Charles."

Devereaux laughed. "I'm a good loser, as you well know." His words sounded ambiguous, almost lewd.

Jane did not like the way the men were talking about her—and about things of which she knew nothing. Some past lover the two men had shared? Gambling debts?

"Please excuse me," she said brusquely, leaving Wescott and Devereaux to their conversation and joining her friend Alison, who was likewise looking for an opportunity to be with Jane.

Alison, as usual, looked stunning. Motherhood had given her a bright, lively charm. The two women embraced and Jane nearly burst into tears. "You look gorgeous, Ally. I've missed you so much and, my God, I have a lot to tell you. Can we escape this rabble for a few minutes?"

Looking concerned, Alison hooked her arm through Jane's. They took a few steps toward the musicians, and Alison said, "You look wonderful, Jane, but I must say rather strained. I only know what you've mentioned in your letters. Is it to do with your husband?"

Jane sighed, and briefly related the most important incidents of recent months. When she mentioned the accident with the coach, Alison clapped one hand to her mouth. "And you're well again, I hope?"

"It could be worse. The arm is coming along well. Look, I know that Mary is here in London. You have to help me, Ally. Couldn't you ask your servants? They must know something among them. I'll come visit you and bring my maid. They—"

That was as far as she got, for just then Florence Rutland joined them. "Dinner is served, ladies. My cook is determined to spoil us with a crab dish, some French recipe."

Florence had clearly gone to great effort in dressing for the evening. The gleaming violet of her dress was certainly all the rage just then, but clashed with her glittering diamond necklace, elaborate earrings, and colorful brooch. And she had added ornamental pins to her lavishly piled hair. With all her finery, she practically blinded anyone looking in her direction.

During the meal, Jane was seated between Rutland and Hargrave, with Wescott, Alison, Devereaux, and Florence across the table. The lofty gathering also included the up-and-coming politician and businessman Mr. Lock, with his shy young Prussian wife, and Kayman, a famous cricketer.

Once the six-course meal was finished, the guests strolled through the rooms on the ground floor, while the string quartet continued to play minuets and polkas in the music room. Bennet Kayman was an interesting young man who had spent a large part of his life in India.

His skin had the olive tone of one who had spent his life in southern climes.

Jane found herself beside the sportsman as they entered a salon hung with paintings and handicrafts from the Orient. A water pipe and a samovar stood on a table, but Jane was drawn to a depiction of an Indian wedding parade.

"I can almost smell the sand and the spices, and hear the bells on the elephants and the women singing," she said dreamily.

"Were you in India?" Kayman asked. He was only slightly taller than Jane and wore his blond hair cut short. His green eyes gazed at her.

"As a child. I spent my first few years there." She heard footsteps and saw Wescott enter the room.

"Devereaux was asking after you, Kayman," Wescott said firmly, and waited until the cricketer had left.

"A beautiful picture, isn't it, David?" Her husband seemed to be in a bad mood, but Jane ignored it.

"What was that all about?" He was standing close and glaring at her.

"I'm sorry, I don't follow you. Have I said something wrong?" If she had not known better, she would have said he was jealous.

"Enjoying yourself, are you?"

"Isn't that the point of social evenings like these? People come together to chat." She opened her fan and swished it through the air with deliberate slowness. "Mr. Kayman is very entertaining, and he was about to tell me about India before you came in. But perhaps you could continue in the same vein?"

His dark eyes sparkled in the low light of the salon, and Jane's heart beat a little faster. She could see the rise and fall of his chest while he considered her words. Finally, he smiled wryly, and Jane could not take her eyes off the lovely curve of his lips. *Sensual,* she thought. *My husband has sensual lips.* Wasn't that a strange irony? Here stood an attractive man who was her husband, and he was no more than a business partner.

"I would like to ask you to talk to Mr. Lock's wife. Perhaps you can find out whether they are planning to travel on the Continent."

"Why?"

"Jane, can't you just do it?" he said. He looked back to the door; outside it, the guests were strolling back and forth.

"I would at least like to understand what it is you do. What business are you pursuing? Or is it a secret? Is Mrs. Lock a spy?"

Wescott audibly drew a breath. "I am not allowed to discuss it with you, but it is, in fact, in the interests of national security. Lock is being groomed as a candidate for the office of prime minister, and his wife has been seen in reactionary circles a number of times. There is talk of secret dealings between Prussia and the Russians." He lowered his voice to a whisper. "The Russian bear suffered from its defeat in Crimea and is out for revenge."

"So it *is* espionage! Have you left the army to become an agent of Her Majesty, David? You don't wear your uniform anymore." She looked at him wide-eyed.

He shook his head. "Enough now. The less you know, the better."

She took his arm and they strolled into the brightly lit music room together. The moment they entered, Violet and Florence made a beeline for them. Wescott excused himself and wandered off toward Kayman and Lord Thomas.

"We were just talking about our activities with the orphanages," said Violet. "Wouldn't you be interested in joining a committee here in London, too?"

Florence nodded. "It would be wonderful. One can't party all the time, after all! The Season is such a strain. I don't know where my head is half the time. I have to pay a visit to the tailor tomorrow. We've been invited to the royal court, and then there's the regatta. My God! One really ought to do something for the poor children as well."

To mollify your conscience, thought Jane, and immediately chastened herself. For whatever reasons the women made their donations, the money was urgently needed. "Gladly. Listen, Violet, I stopped by Newbridge on the way to London. Things look much worse there than they do in the other orphanages. What do you know about the Ledfords?"

Violet's expression darkened. She thought for a moment, looking around, and winced when she saw her brother approaching. "Not much, Lady Jane. Nothing, really. They do what they can."

"Who does, my dear?" asked Lord Hargrave, joining them.

"The Ledfords in Newbridge. They manage an orphanage and workhouse. It's a deeply impoverished place, and the children seem extremely low-spirited," said Jane.

Lord Hargrave shot his sister a quick warning glance and said, "Well, that's what orphanages tend to be like. The children there haven't had much luck in their lives. They should be thankful that anyone looks after them at all."

"Is that how you see it?" Jane was feeling combative. She flapped open her fan and eyed Lord Hargrave.

"It's late, Robert, and I'd like to go home. I'm not feeling well." Violet did, in fact, look anything but healthy, but Jane knew the source of her problems.

"They're not all little angels, my lady, though women would have it so." Lord Hargrave took his sister's hand. "My sister's heart is far too soft for her own good, like most of your kind. But that is how nature arranged things."

"And you reproach us, as women, for that? Didn't you have a mother?" Jane, incensed, shot back.

Florence fluttered her eyelids nervously, and Violet scratched gently at her brother's arm, but Hargrave, seemingly unperturbed, replied, "You have misunderstood me, my lady. It is merely my conviction that everything has its counterbalance, and that it is nature's way."

"Then you are a Darwinist?" Jane was not about to simply give up. She sensed that she had gotten deeply under the man's skin, and she knew that in such moments, people were apt to give away things they normally kept under wraps. "The stronger defeats the weaker, and that is a God-given fact?"

Hargrave's eyes narrowed dangerously. "Yes, my lady. If you want to put it so bluntly. Yes, I am convinced that might is right, as they say. Or else there would be no strong and no weak, would there?"

"Ha! I reject that argument, it is absolutely—," said Jane, warming up, but a soft touch at her back interrupted her.

"Here you are, darling," said Wescott loudly and then, his mouth to her ear, whispered, "That will do!"

Hargrave, whose cheeks had gone bright red, relaxed. "Wescott, save me before I insult your charming wife beyond repair. You do lean toward hysteria, don't you, my dear? Violet here has a wonderful cure for that—"

"Ah, *there* is dear Mrs. Lock. Excuse me." *Retreat,* Jane thought, *is the wiser course.* She swallowed her wrath at Hargrave's self-importance.

At the mention of her name, Mrs. Lock turned her dainty head and smiled shyly at Jane. The woman was very young and had a boyish figure. She was unusually attractive, helped by her captivatingly large, dark eyes.

Her timidity may just be a means to getting what she wants, thought Jane. "My dear Mrs. Lock, how do you find it here in England? You must miss your homeland terribly. I'm sure I would."

Mrs. Lock stood with her hands folded primly in front of her. Her pale-pink dress made her look almost translucent. "You are so kind, my lady. I find my feet here, and also some who are like-minded." She spoke in broken English. Her accent was so strong, she was not easy to understand.

Jane raised her eyebrows. "Like-minded? In what way? A religious society?"

The young woman shook her head. "Oh, no. Foreign artists, like me. We meet once in the week. I was a singer."

"Wonderful! That is a talent not to be cast aside. We English love music. I will arrange a social evening soon and invite you. You could sing for us. What do you think?"

Mrs. Lock blushed. "You have not heard me sing yet."

"Let's chance it. I like to take risks." She smiled brightly at the woman, whom she found friendly. "Or are you planning a trip home in the next few weeks? I hope not before the end of the Season."

Surprised, and somewhat hesitant, Mrs. Lock replied, "No, no. I am look forward to your invitation, Lady Jane."

A short time later, the party began to break up. When Jane and Wescott were sitting opposite each other in their carriage, Jane snarled, "Rebuking me in front of Hargrave was uncalled for. You made me look ridiculous! I am not hysterical."

Wescott smiled thinly. "Conducting yourself as you did, you refute your own words."

"You're all the same. Smug, arrogant snobs. The moment a woman voices an opinion, she's hysterical!"

He grasped her hand. "Listen to me. I'll say this only once. I know Hargrave better than you do. He is not a man to provoke just for the fun of it. You would not like the kind of pleasures he pursues. Believe me, Jane."

"I am not his sister. He can't take the wind out of my sails with a dose of morphine."

"Oh, Jane, can't you just take my advice and show some restraint around him?" She felt moved by the urgency of his words.

"Humph."

"You're very stubborn."

"I know. It's my nature."

His face was hidden in the shadows, but she thought she saw him smile.

27.

Mary

"I don't want to go. No, please, please let Fiona come with me!" Mary cried.

But Mr. Ledford slapped her in the face. "Shut up! Do you want to wake the whole building? Ungrateful vermin. All these years we've dressed you, fed you, taught you how to read and write. Now you have the chance to go into a grand house in London, and what thanks do we get?"

It was dark. The clock tower at the church had struck ten, and a light drizzle had set in. The coach was standing at the gate, a lamp gleaming on the driver's seat where the coachman, wearing a long rain cape, squatted sullenly. "Can we finally be off? This rain won't be makin' the roads no better."

Mary cried and pressed her hands over her face. Her ear hurt and the dizziness set in. Even so, she looked up covertly between her fingers to the dormitory building. She knew they had shut Fiona away in the attic.

Late in the afternoon, Mary had managed to sneak safely into the room to visit her friend. Fiona was still lying there curled up like an embryo under a sheet. Mary stroked her friend's face, her pale forehead, and saw her split lips and the blue marks on her throat and skinny arms. "Fiona, wake up. It's me, Mary. Come on, you're not allowed to die."

Laboriously, as if returning from another world, Fiona had opened her eyes. Mary would never forget the look of infinite hopelessness and despair she saw there. Fiona—strong, clever, funny Fiona—was gone. In the green eyes of that maltreated creature, Mary saw a maimed and broken spirit. "I am already dead, Mary. I'm dead . . ."

"No! Don't say that," Mary sobbed, embracing her friend. Then she was grabbed harshly and jerked away.

"Who let you in here?" Sister Susan hissed at her, pushing her into the bathroom. "We're going to clean you up, then you're to put on the new clothes on this chair. You're being collected this evening, so don't go getting yourself filthy again."

Now Mary found herself sitting in the cramped coach beside a man who stank and looked at her in a way that made her skin crawl. But Mr. Ledford had impressed upon the man not to touch her, or he wouldn't get his money. The man was dozing now. Mary pulled her feet up onto the seat and wrapped her arms around her knees. The stinking man looked like Mr. Cooper, but younger. Mr. Ledford had called him Jed.

"Are you Mr. Cooper's brother?" They had been on the road for God knows how many hours, and Mary had become used to the sight of the grim-looking man.

"None o' your business," he growled, opening his eyes to slits.

"What's Jed mean? Is that short for something?"

"Jedidiah."

"I've never heard that name. Is it from the Bible?"

Jed grinned hatefully and showed the brown ruins of a row of teeth. "Samuel two, verse twelve, means 'beloved of Jesus.' And 'e sent by the 'and of Nathan the prophet; and 'e called 'is name Jedidiah, because of the Lord."

"Then you are a godly man." Mary could think of nothing else to say. She wanted to talk because her teeth were chattering in fear and the buzzing in her ear was growing unbearable.

"Do I look like a godly man?"

"I'm hungry." Mary's stomach growled as if on cue. It had been six hours since her last meager meal.

Jedidiah took a bottle from his coat pocket and held it out to Mary. " 'ere. Take a swig. Cures 'unger and thirst."

"Whisky? No, thank you." Mary huddled even deeper into her corner. "What about Fiona? Will she also go to work somewhere?"

"Who's Fiona?" Jed pulled the cork out of the bottle and took a long swig.

"My friend. She's got red hair. The master locked her up and she didn't do anything."

"The master don't do nothing without a reason. 'e's a sharp man. That's why I work for 'im." Jed contorted his ugly face into a grimace and wiped his throat with the back of his fist. "I'm 'is right-'and man, the 'and of God the just! Your friend got too curious. The master can't let that go unpunished."

"Will he kill her?" Mary whispered, her eyes wide with fear.

The coach swayed on the stony road, and Mary had to hold on tight to stop herself from sliding off the seat.

"There are better ways to get rid of someone. She'll be rode down to Plymouth tomorrow. There's a ship sailing from there to Australia. There she'll be of some use at least and can work for the empire." He laughed venomously.

"No! You can't let her. Fiona never wanted to leave England. Anything but that, please, anything but that," Mary sobbed. Her ear was hurting terribly.

"Stop sniveling and shut your mouth," Jedidiah ordered.

At midday two days later, the coach trundled past a large park. Mary pressed her face to the window, amazed at the colorful parade of strollers, newspaper boys, heavily laden carts, elegant riders, carriages, nannies with their charges, and the many, many street vendors. On one corner stood a singer, and just past him a soup salesman was plying his wares in a loud voice. But despite all the hubbub, there was no sense of the confinement of a city. A glass dome loomed among the trees.

"What is that?" asked Mary reverently.

"One o' the prince consort's notions. Now listen to me. We'll be there in a minute. Not a word from you except to answer what you're asked. Don't say a word about your little friend unless you want trouble. We 'ave our eyes and ears everywhere. Anyone who tries to betray us gets what they deserved."

"Polly!" Mary blurted.

Jed leaned forward in alarm and grabbed hold of Mary's wrist. "That little shite gave us no end of trouble."

Fighting the acrid smell of the man, Mary dared a final question. "Where is Polly now?"

The pressure on her wrist was so great that she cried out in pain. "Feedin' worms. Like you will be if you don't do what you're told."

The coach slowed down and rolled through a huge, decorative gate. Stone spheres were set atop the gateposts, and as the coach rolled along a carefully raked gravel driveway, the sounds of the city slowly faded behind them. But Mary did not look at the beauty of the estate or the impressive house. All she could do was stare at her wrist, which was turning blue now that Jed had released her.

"Dead," she whispered in a hoarse, breaking voice. Polly was dead. Now she knew for certain what she had feared all along. She was certain that Jedidiah, this vile man with the biblical name, was not lying. Perhaps he himself had killed Polly. She fought back the tears that sprang to her eyes, afraid she would not be able to see what Jed did next.

Polly, the friend she'd loved the most, was dead. Her brother had abandoned her, and Mr. Gaunt had disappeared, just like Miss Fannigan and now Fiona. Maybe she brought bad luck to everyone she loved. Maybe this was her punishment for the baby's death. She was supposed to save her. That was her job, and she had failed. Her mother had entrusted the tiny, helpless thing to her care, had counted on her.

"You, girl! Get out. Or do you fancy yourself the Queen of England?" A woman's sharp voice cut through Mary's grief-stricken thoughts. She climbed quickly out of the carriage and found herself at the rear entrance of a manor house that was huge and splendid, like the houses she had seen in fairy tales.

Jedidiah was standing in front of a pretty woman whose age Mary found hard to judge. Her tightly coiffed hair and the black dress she wore probably made her look older than she really was. A band of keys hung at her belt. She plucked at Mary's wrinkled old dress with her thin fingers.

"I hope she has other clothes?"

Jed shrugged and dropped the linen sack containing Mary's belongings beside her on the ground. "Buggered if I know. She's not been touched. I want my money, as agreed, then I'll vanish."

"She stinks to high heaven!" The woman waved a snow-white handkerchief in front of her nose and took a bundle of banknotes from the pocket of her skirt. "Here. Woe betide you if you've been at her. She'll go to Lulu and you, well, you know what will happen to you."

"No, ma'am, I 'aven't laid a finger on her, word of 'onor," Jedidiah assured her hurriedly. He seemed very afraid of the woman.

"As if you had any!" She turned, and her intense, dark eyes fell on Mary. Something dangerous seemed to smolder in them. "Your hair is perfect. And you're pretty. What's your name?"

"Mary, ma'am," whispered Mary. She squeezed the little wooden figure her brother had carved for her.

"I am Mrs. Avery, and from now on I will be your mistress. If you do what you're told and don't ask questions, we'll get along just fine. Many things will be new for you, and there will be a lot that you don't know, but I'll tell you more about that later. What do you have there?"

She held out one hand imperiously. Mary hesitantly acceded to her request and laid the little cat in her hand.

"My brother gave it to me," Mary murmured.

For a long moment, Mrs. Avery held the cat between two fingers, then let it drop back into Mary's hands. "Go inside over there. Jenny is waiting for you by the door and will show you to your quarters."

With the little wooden figure wrapped in her fist, Mary crossed the gravel path, marveling at the walls of light-colored stone and the lawn that looked as if it had just been mowed. Flower and herb beds began just beyond a boxwood hedge, and a servant girl—Jenny—sat on a bench by the wall of the house, peeling potatoes. She was wearing a clean, light-gray dress, a white apron, and a bonnet with a starched-lace trim. She screwed up her nose when Mary stopped in front of her.

"You reek. First thing we'll get you washed and deloused, then we'll find you some suitable clothes."

A clear growl came from Mary's stomach. "Sorry," she whispered, not daring to look at Jenny.

"Didn't they give you anything to eat along the way?" With her head held high, Jenny led Mary along a wide corridor, from which various doors led into kitchens and pantries. The smell of bread and roast meat filled the air.

"Wait here," Jenny ordered. She ducked into a kitchen and returned with a piece of bread and a slice of meat. "Here. Eat up before anyone sees you."

Mary wolfed down the soft bread, then pushed the meat into her mouth in one piece. There was still juice from the roasting pan on the meat, and Mary licked it from her fingers.

"Didn't you get enough to eat in the orphanage, then?" Jenny ignored the servants and kitchen hands they passed as they walked along. The place seemed to be swarming with staff. "You did come from an orphanage, didn't you?"

"Newbridge," said Mary. She could hardly keep up with Jenny.

"Really? Never heard of it. Where is that?" She pushed open a door onto a narrow stairway. Before Mary could answer, Jenny went on. "We're in the domestic wing. These steps lead up to our quarters on the third floor, and there are passages on every floor that lead into the manorial rooms. You're only allowed to enter those with me. Behave so as to draw as little attention to yourself as possible. Don't say a word. Do your work quickly and with no noise. One never knows how the master will react, and you do *not* want to attract his ire, most definitely not! Remember that."

"Yes, Jenny."

"Good. Here's the bathroom. Get undressed. Someone will come to you in a minute."

Another maid entered the bathroom and took charge of cleaning Mary, under the strict eye of Mrs. Avery. Mary subjected herself to the cleaning procedure without a murmur of complaint, although she felt humiliated at being treated like a piece of merchandise. Mrs. Avery was more selective in her language and had better manners, but she was as cold and heartless as Sister Susan.

"Wouldn't we do better to cut off her hair? It's easier that way," the girl suggested. She, too, wore clean clothes, but of a simpler cut than Jenny's.

"No. Her hair is exactly as it should be. Do what you're told. And here, use more powder!" Mrs. Avery pressed the delousing powder into the maid's hand, and the painful combing began anew.

Mary shared a room with two kitchen maids. Both of them came from the north, and they assigned her the bed beneath the drafty window. Because the weather was growing warmer, Mary didn't mind. She lay on her bed that night and gazed into London's dark night sky. Only now and then did a star appear through a break in the clouds. Mary murmured her nightly prayer and fell into a deep, dreamless sleep.

At five thirty the next morning, someone shook her by the shoulder. "Hey, get up!" The strain of the recent days still sat deep in Mary's bones. As if in a trance, she followed the girl to the bathroom, washed herself, then pulled on the dress she'd been given the previous evening. Before she went downstairs, she pocketed her wooden talisman. Jenny was waiting for her in the stairwell. There seemed to be a servant in the house for every task. Jenny, who Mary classed as friendly, was responsible for the master's chamber.

"You're to come to the second floor with me. Sweep the steps, mop them, take hot water to the master's rooms, and sweep the carpets. At a quarter past eight, everyone meets in the dining room beside the kitchen. The butler, Mr. Drew, delivers the morning prayer; after that we eat breakfast, and after that we go to work in the master's rooms."

After the unaccustomed hard work, Mary almost fell asleep at breakfast. But the food was surprisingly good and substantial, and she ate two portions of porridge, bread with marmalade, and cheese. At the end of the meal, she popped a boiled egg into her pocket. You never knew . . .

But as she was leaving the room, Mrs. Avery grabbed her by the arm and dragged her into her office. Although the butler was usually the head of the domestic staff, in this household the staff seemed to have the greatest respect for—or perhaps fear of—Mrs. Avery.

"What do you have in your pocket?" the housekeeper asked sharply.

"Nothing, ma'am," Mary stammered in embarrassment, placing one hand on the egg.

Mrs. Avery moved directly in front of Mary and narrowed her eyes. "Don't lie to me!"

This woman is not like Sister Susan, thought Mary, taking out the egg. *This woman is much worse. She has no cane because she doesn't need one.* Mary could sense what the woman was capable of if Mary went against her will.

A scornful smile spread across Mrs. Avery's attractive face. "An egg? You're stealing an egg? Wasn't there enough to eat this morning? No one here has ever complained that they didn't have enough to eat. No one has ever left my table hungry! There is no reason to steal anything. Remember that."

"Yes, ma'am, I . . . it's just . . . ," stammered Mary helplessly. "You never know the next time you'll get something."

Mrs. Avery's large dark eyes stared at her balefully for a long moment. "You've been through a lot, haven't you, Mary?" she said mildly. "So that you never forget that you are no longer an orphan but a member of the domestic staff of one of England's most eminent houses, I am going to teach you a lesson."

Mary lifted her eyes and looked at Mrs. Avery in apprehension, but saw neither a cane nor a hand poised to strike.

"Give me that wooden figure."

"What?"

"Are you deaf, girl? The wooden figure you had with you yesterday. I dare say you've got it tucked away in your skirt." Mrs. Avery smiled sympathetically and held out her hand.

Reluctantly, Mary retrieved the small wooden cat from the pocket of her skirt. "I don't understand—"

"But you soon will. A lesson teaches you something." Mrs. Avery took the cat and looked at it. "Very pretty. Who made it?"

"My brother, ma'am." Mary watched in stunned disbelief as Mrs. Avery went to the oven, opened the door, and threw the wooden cat into the flames. "No! Why? I'm never going to do it again," Mary cried.

"When you make a mistake, you will be punished for it. I'm glad you will never again steal from our table. I see we understand each other now. Go and get to work. Jenny is waiting for you," the housekeeper said in a friendly tone.

Her friendliness is like a knife that cuts you to pieces the minute you make a mistake, Mary thought, and quickly left the room.

Jenny was waiting for her on the first floor. "Oh my, did she nab you? What did you do?"

Sniffling, Mary wiped her eyes. "It was just an egg. I put it in my pocket. Why is that so bad? They've got enough eggs here!"

"That's not the point. You have to follow the rules. Just think if everyone here simply took what he wanted."

"I see that, but she burned my carving. It was all I had left of my brother."

"Be glad that's all she did. She can be quite horrible, our Mrs. Avery. Mr. Drew tends to lash out with his cane. Not her, though. Watch out around her, Mary! She's got a soft spot for the master and would do simply anything for him." Jenny led her from the domestic wing into the manorial rooms.

"Oh!" Mary stopped in her tracks. She had never seen such a magnificent place in her life.

A wide corridor stretched before her. Doors opened into rooms on both sides, and at the end of the corridor, two curving staircases rose to a gallery. From the hallway on the ground floor, she could hear the rattling of crockery. An enormous crystal chandelier hung from the domed ceiling, while in alcoves and corners she saw paintings, wall hangings, statues of white marble, ebony elephants with real tusks, and sinister-looking figures with many arms and gaping mouths. Everything had an exotic feel to it, and the paintings depicted foreign landscapes.

"You'll get used to it. Come on!" Jenny showed her where the linen closet was. Mary took fresh bedding, and Jenny led her into the first bedroom.

The room was dim, but Mary could make out deep-red silk wallpaper, golden candelabras, soft carpets, cushions, a divan, and a four-poster bed. She looked around the room wide-eyed. A heavy, sweet smell hung in the air. When a small figure stepped out of one corner, Mary shrieked.

The man was barely as tall as Mary herself. His skin was dark and he wore a turban. In his belt, he carried a dagger.

"Ignore him," Jenny whispered in her ear. "His name is Ramu. He's the master's personal servant. The master spends a lot of time in the colonies. He brought Ramu back from there. He belongs to a cult, I've heard, and he can kill people with a scarf."

"What?" Mary looked anxiously at the small Indian man, who took no notice of her and went about his own business.

When Mary went to open the curtains, Jenny hissed, "Hands off! They stay as they are. Come here and help me change the bedding. We do it every morning."

"Fresh sheets every morning?" Mary could not hide her amazement at so much extravagant luxury.

While she helped Jenny and learned how to pull the sheet so tight that not the slightest wrinkle could be seen, she kept looking across at Ramu. As a young child, she had lived in the London docks area and had seen some exotic-looking people, but she had never seen an Indian like Ramu. He was cleaning a water pipe, and sometimes his eyes glowed in the room's dim light.

"Jenny, that isn't true, is it? About the scarf?" Mary whispered.

"It is. Now hush. He's got ears like a rabbit. Take the old bedding and let's go," said Jenny.

Mary picked up the pile of fine bed linen and was about to follow Jenny when the door was pushed open and a tall, brown-haired man entered. Jenny instantly bowed, so Mary did the same and waited with her eyes lowered.

"You. Come here," the man ordered.

"Go! That's the master!" said Jenny quickly.

Mary held the pile of wash tightly and took a step toward the master of the house. He wore a velvet jacket with a golden crest on the breast pocket. Mary had never seen such a handsome man before.

"Put down the washing. I want to see you. You're new." He approached her, and Mary hurriedly pushed the washing into Jenny's arms. Jenny immediately stepped back out of sight.

The man exuded the smell of soap and something spicy that Mary did not recognize. He walked around her, raised her chin briefly, and held her blond curls between his fingers. Finally, he smiled at her benevolently and stepped away again.

"Ramu, I have a problem with . . ." He paused and cast a warning glance toward the two maids.

Mary stood as if paralyzed, but Jenny hissed at her, "Come on!"

Two days after her initial encounter with the master of the house, she saw him speaking confidentially with Mrs. Avery outside his bedroom. Mary was hidden from view by a statue of a Hindu goddess.

"Have you noticed our new arrival, sir?"

"The little blond? Of course. What would I do without you, Mrs. Avery?" The master smiled at his housekeeper appreciatively.

Mrs. Avery blushed and touched her hair. It was an unexpectedly feminine gesture that Mary would not have expected from the stern woman. But she could see that Mrs. Avery not only idolized the master, she was in love with him. Did he realize that? He probably thought it was impossible. Socially speaking, the housekeeper was far below him, after all.

"In two weeks, after the regatta, I'll be holding a small, private function. Take care of everything necessary by then."

"With pleasure, sir." Mrs. Avery curtsied, then walked past Mary without noticing her.

28.

The London Season was one continuous party. It was easy to lose track of all the invitations if one didn't pay attention. Jane was pondering what was next on the agenda when Alison greeted her.

"At last, a moment to ourselves! I've just been for a stroll. Come on. I want to show you our conservatory."

Lady Alison hooked her friend's arm in hers and pulled her along through the bright, tastefully decorated rooms of her London townhouse. Every piece of furniture and every painting pointed to the long and honorable tradition of the two families united by the marriage of Thomas and Alison. Alison was actually listed as a successor to the throne. As the eighty-fifth in line, her chances of ever ascending to the crown were certainly slim, but the connection to the royal family brought her and her husband many advantages and made them highly desirable company in society circles.

Jane felt a pang at the sight of a collection of blooming orchids. She thought of her uncle, who had loved orchids very much. "They're beautiful, Ally," she said, her voice heavy with emotion.

Her friend squeezed her arm. "I can well imagine what you're thinking about right now, but don't be sad, Jane. That would be the last thing your uncle would want."

"You're right. He always looked on the bright side. Unfortunately, when it came to his son, too."

They strolled slowly among the planters and shelves. Every plant had a small sign stating its name and origin. Jane stopped at a strangely formed yellow bulb that looked as if it was rolled together from a single leaf. "A cobra lily from China. How exotic."

Alison smiled absently. "Oh, the gardener buys all of these fancy plants and is very proud of them. I don't really care. I like roses and violets and prefer to be outside in the garden. But Thomas says expensive plants are as important to a good reputation as artists, but the plants are easier to look after."

Being a patron for aspiring young artists was considered good form among society's wealthy aristocrats. While Jane enjoyed visiting the art galleries and loved the Sunday exhibitions put on by the Royal Academy, she certainly didn't feel the need to commit herself to any one artist. She bought pictures she liked if they were not exorbitantly priced, but was not foolhardy enough to describe herself as an art expert.

With a smile, Jane replied, "No doubt he's absolutely right. Tell me, did you ever manage to find out anything about the orphan girl I mentioned?"

Alison's blond curls shimmered golden in the afternoon sunlight falling through the glass roof. "The girl, yes, of course. I prompted my cook, Bertha, to ask around. She said that there are a number of houses that prefer to take orphaned children as domestics, mostly because they're young and malleable and apparently less likely to run away. Whether that's true or not, I couldn't say. I've heard the opposite said as well. Florence, for instance, says that there were two very young girls with her who found themselves pregnant and ran away. One of them was seen"—she cleared her throat self-consciously before continuing—"in a brothel."

"The poor girl. Isn't that so unjust, Ally? Some louse gets a young thing like that pregnant and then gets off scot-free, but the girl lands in the gutter," Jane protested.

Alison looked at her in consternation. "Well, that's something she should have thought about ahead of time. They're just as much to blame if they go leading the chaps on."

"Not all of them do that, Ally. And what if they're forced?"

"You can speak your mind to me, Jane, but watch out or you'll find yourself with a bad name." Alison took a breath and continued. "What I wanted to say was that Bertha said that Lord Hargrave is known for being picky about having pretty young maids in his household. And besides, his parties are notorious—for the domestic staff, too. Imagine, once a week they hire a pianist or a violinist for the staff, and they have dancing and a special meal in the kitchens!"

"That's not something I would have expected of him," Jane said with surprise.

"I'm sure he has his reasons. Bertha also said that he's famous for his moods, and that if he weren't so generous with his salaries, his staff would leave as fast as they came."

"What about a Mary?"

"There are two girls there by that name. It's a common name, after all. We're invited to his place next week. Get your Hettie to ask around. I think that would be the smartest thing to do." Alison sighed. Something else seemed to be weighing on her. "Jane . . . this is hard for me to say, but I think you should hear it. Thomas says it's none of your business, and that actually bothers me a lot, you know, because he might have similar secrets."

"What in heaven's name are you talking about?"

"I can't help but feel that you decided too fast to marry Wescott. Then again, the circumstances were extraordinary, and I know you wanted to avoid Matthew's guardianship, which turns out to have been exactly the right decision."

"Ally, get to the point."

"I love you very much, Jane. I just don't want to see you hurt." Alison's blue eyes shimmered with tears. "I've seen Wescott with another woman three times now, and they seemed very familiar with each other."

Jane had to take a deep breath. She swallowed twice before replying. "Well, that's his right, I suppose. We . . . we have an agreement, Ally."

"Oh. I didn't know. I mean . . . can you tell me?" Alison wiped her eyes and looked intently at Jane. "Don't, if you don't want to."

Jane grinned. "I know you. If I didn't tell you, you'd keep probing until you found out everything. Remember that last evening in Rosewood Hall? When I told you I wanted to keep my freedom?"

Her friend nodded.

"Wescott overheard us and made me an offer—to marry me, but to let me keep it. My freedom. I owe him no explanations, and he owes me none."

"If I found out that Thomas had a lover, I'd turn into a right fury. We share a bed, after all. No, I could not stand that!"

Jane looked at her friend in silence.

"Do you not share a bed?" Alison asked.

Jane shook her head. She turned away and looked at an orchid. "It's better like this. Besides, he has no interest in me. Not that kind of interest."

"Oh. Well, fine, that's up to you. At any rate, the woman he was with was very beautiful, at least from what I could see through her veil. A little fancy, perhaps. Not as vulgar as Florence Rutland, but in that direction."

"Really, Ally, that's enough. I'm not interested, full stop. His interest in that woman could very well be professional." Jane looked around, but they were alone in the conservatory. "He keeps his work very much to himself, but it is very possible that he's involved in secret missions for the crown."

"Hmm. You know, I could probably tickle something out of Thomas about that. He's very good friends with one of the secretaries of our prime minister, Lord Palmerston." After a brief pause, she added, "Like I said, it all seemed rather familiar."

"The stench!" Jane pressed a handkerchief over her mouth and nose and could not bring herself to believe that Violet Sutton actually walked through the streets of Lambeth as if she were at home. She almost seemed to enjoy stumbling through the mud in her boots.

"It's up ahead," the widow said. She was bubbling over with energy that morning. Still, Jane feared the condition would not last very long, and it was impossible for the coach to follow them through the narrow alleys. Lambeth lay on the other side of the Thames, where run-down shacks and buildings formed slums that housed mostly dock workers and laborers from the glass and textile factories, surviving as best they could. The railway line did, indeed, go as far as Lambeth, but that had changed nothing for the poorest of the poor in the slums along the Thames. As they always had, the low-lying marshlands flooded in spring and autumn, leaving behind sodden shanties rife with cholera, fever, rheumatism, and dysentery.

"Why don't they dig up the mud left by the river and get rid of it? Then it wouldn't stink so much," Jane complained. Behind them trudged Hettie and an armed servant of Hargrave's.

Some distance away was a windmill, and from the river came the cries of boatbuilders, mariners, fishermen, and vendors touting their wares. In every dark corner crouched a picture of misery with outstretched hands. *And the few not begging are too weak or already dead,* Jane thought, regretting that she had said nothing to Blount about this particular outing. She felt safe in his presence. The unassuming man knew how to deal with all kinds of people. Since her conversation with Alison, she had pushed Wescott—and his valet—out of her mind, which had not been difficult: she had not seen her husband for two days.

In front of a two-story building stood a sleazy-looking man who eyed her and her companions with disdain. A red lamp hung over the entrance.

"A brothel. It isn't right, is it? The poor children have to live in this filth, and if they make a slip, the girls soon find out where they'll wind up," said Violet. She tugged on the string hanging from a doorbell dangling over the narrow entrance of the building next door.

Although the orphanage was no more than a stable with triple bunks and a dining room, Jane found it far more comfortable inside than out in the lane among the shady-looking ruffians who seemed to be hanging around waiting for an opportunity to rob them or cut their throats. Did Violet think of herself as some sort of saint to whom nothing could happen? Jane feared as much.

The place was run by an aging missionary and his daughter. In one room, children sang spirituals, and a few youngsters were playing with blocks and dolls in a corridor. Their little bodies looked underdeveloped and rickety. They were even paler and more wretched than the orphans out in the country, who at least got more sun and better air. On their way there, Violet had told Jane about orphan girls who became pregnant and whose deformed bones caused life-threatening complications when they later gave birth. Just recently, a wave of Irish immigrants had caused a widespread diphtheria outbreak, and now many of the orphans were of Irish heritage.

"How nice to see you again, Mrs. Sutton. You are a gift from the Lord himself!" The old missionary greeted his visitors and led them into a small living room.

"I'm not going anywhere, ma'am. I'm staying here with you," whispered Hettie firmly, positioning herself beside Jane's chair.

Violet's servant waited in the hallway while the missionary's daughter, a pale woman in her midforties, brought in a pot of tea. Jane thanked her but declined, and Violet did the same.

"As well as providing for the orphans, we have now become a branch of the society to protect young girls under fifteen years of age who have slipped into prostitution," the missionary declared proudly. His skin was marked by deep creases, and a snow-white beard covered his cheeks and chin. But his eyes were alert and filled with genuine sympathy for his charges.

His daughter was obviously devoted to him and sat quietly beside her father.

"Such girls—," Jane began, then faltered. "Where do they tend to come from?"

"Poverty is at its worst out in the country, and many girls are tempted to the city with promises of work and better earnings, but quickly find themselves in a brothel. Sometimes they are with child, and the shame of going home with a baby born out of wedlock is simply too much for them, and more often than not there are enough hungry mouths at home already. A nip of whisky, a few pretty words, and there's no turning back." The missionary seemed in his element. "And then there are the girls who have actually found a decent position in a good house. Then one night they get caught by scouts or compromised or simply lured into a brothel. Now I had one very sad case a few months back. A pretty girl, that one. Very young."

The missionary scratched his head thoughtfully and finally turned to his daughter. "What was her name again?"

"Polly? The one who came in from Hyde Park."

"That's the one. Imagine this: the girl was so afraid of her former employer—who was also her torturer, apparently—that she wouldn't even say his name. She was terribly traumatized. All she did was talk about her friend Mary. She had to warn Mary."

Jane froze on her chair. "Polly? Was she a petite blond girl, perhaps twelve at the most?"

"Yes. How do you know that?"

"Wasn't there something in the newspaper? But please go on. I might be mistaken."

Hettie had begun to breathe faster, and Jane gave her a warning pinch on the leg, beneath her skirt.

The old man's brow furrowed. "There was nothing about Polly in the papers here. Be that as it may, she was a runaway. I wanted to help her, but she was so terribly frightened. She kept saying that she was being followed. She was looking around the whole time, talking about a dark-skinned man who wanted to throttle her with a scarf."

Violet let out a kind of strangled cry, and in her mind's eye, Jane saw images of Indian assassins. Her nanny in India had told her about the infamous Thugs, who were said to have used their scarves to murder thousands of travelers.

"Poor child. Very sad. We made such an effort with her," the daughter said. "She must have been very badly hurt in both her soul and her body. Perhaps we should have sent her away from here immediately, somewhere out in the country. She would certainly have felt safer out there. But our means are limited."

Jane reached for her purse automatically. "That's why we are here. But please, go on. Tell me what happened to Polly."

"She was with us for two nights, and on the second night, she disappeared. She climbed out the window and ran away. It was a cold night with the snow piling up, and all she had on was a thin dress." The missionary shook his head sadly. "I felt very sorry for her. And you say you know where the girl is?"

Jane sensed Violet's eager stare. "I fear she is dead, and buried now in a village cemetery in Wiltshire."

"You don't mean the girl from Rosewood Hall? Much has been spoken about her," said Violet in all innocence.

"Ah! I've read about it myself. You're Lady Jane! But, of course, you found the girl. The Lord's blessing be on you!" the missionary exclaimed. "Did she tell you who had tortured her or where she came from?"

"No. She was barely alive when I found her on the grounds that night. She died before she could say anything. But she mentioned a Mary, and that set me wondering. How terribly sad." Jane took a handkerchief and pressed it to her nose and eyes. "I would like to leave, Violet, if you don't mind."

"No, no, of course. Painful memories. And it was your uncle's last ball, wasn't it?" Violet remarked, withdrawing her purse as well.

Just let me out of here was all Jane could think. Suddenly, it was as if danger lurked in every doorway and behind every shack. She knew she was in over her head, but her instincts had never let her down before.

29.

Only a few minutes had passed, but in the time since they'd left the orphanage, the sky had clouded over and the narrow alleys were already nearly dark. Stinking fumes poured from chimneys and windows, and it was starting to rain.

"That's all we need," Hettie groaned as she raised her umbrella to at least protect her mistress from the unwelcome weather.

In front of them, beneath an umbrella, were the feet of Violet and Hargrave's servant, whom Jane and Hettie walked behind like sheep, and then even those vanished a moment later around the corner of a house. Jane tried to catch up to them, but two pairs of boots abruptly blocked her path. She stopped, pushing Hettie with her umbrella to one side. "What the devil . . . ?"

But it was not Hargrave's servant standing there in the narrow alley in the pouring rain staring grimly at her. The two men were strangers, and their intentions were clearly not benign. Jane had no idea of where she and Hettie were, and called out, "Violet! Where are you?"

At that, the taller of the two men sent his companion away with a nod. "My lady," he said.

The man took a step toward her as he drew a knife. "Your purse, if you please. And I have a message for you."

The glinting knife sliced toward Jane's throat. But Hettie had folded her umbrella and now swung it with all her might at the assassin's extended arm. The man, however, had more experience in a fight, and he quickly recovered from the unexpected attack and lashed out at Hettie with the knife. She screamed and pressed her hand to her side. Jane ducked and tried to dodge to one side, but her skirt caught on a nail jutting from a post. Her eyes had adjusted almost immediately to the dim light of the alley, and she saw the blade coming toward her. Desperately, she tugged at her skirt, seeing death before her eyes. Then she heard a dull thud that was followed by a horrible hissing sound, and her assailant toppled into the mud like a felled tree. As if from nowhere, Blount was standing in front of her. He cut her skirt free from the nail and said, "Come with me."

Hettie was crying and holding her side. Blood was seeping between her fingers, and Jane took hold of the brave girl's arm. "We have to get away from here. Everything will be all right, Hettie."

"Yes, ma'am," her maid whispered, reeling through the mud with Jane.

Finally, they reached the end of the dark alley. At the corner of the building, Jane nearly tripped over the body of the knife wielder's accomplice. The rain grew heavier, and a thunderstorm announced itself with a flash of lightning. The road was utterly deserted, the shutters closed over the windows. No one cared what was going on out on the street. At least, it felt that way to Jane. She was sure that the rats would crawl out of their holes and steal anything of any use from the dead men.

Blount stopped and pointed at the body on the ground. The man lay on his back, his eyes gazing up sightlessly. A deep cut crossed his throat. No sound would ever come from his mouth again. "I got here in the nick of time. My lady, never drive to such a place alone again."

"I could never have guessed this would happen. I only came here to visit an orphanage with Mrs. Sutton," said Jane in meek defense and cast a furtive glance at the body on the ground. "Did you do that?"

Blount ignored the question. "Hettie needs medical attention. I know someone, not far from here. Someone discreet."

"Where is Mrs. Sutton?" Jane looked around for the coach they had arrived in, but could not see it anywhere. There was no sign of either Mrs. Sutton or her servant. "Was she also robbed? Did you see her, Blount?"

Wescott's valet inspected Hettie's wound. "Your ribs took most of it. You were lucky, Hettie." To Jane, he said, "If you mean the hysterical woman running through the alley screaming . . . she jumped into a carriage with her servant and hightailed it."

"Wonderful! Now we have no transport. Where are we going to find something around here?" Jane looked down at her clothes and smiled sadly. "Who would take us anywhere like this anyway?"

Her dress was torn, wet, and soiled with mud, filth, and Hettie's blood. It was pouring relentlessly, and the rain was running from the ruins of her hat to the loose strands of hair, over her face, and down the collar of her dress. As the material soaked up the water, it grew heavier and heavier and, along with the bulky crinoline, increasingly unbearable. *It's like having a millstone tied around my body,* thought Jane, who was finding it hard to maintain a dignified posture.

"How did you get here?" she asked Blount, who just pointed along the road.

"Come on," he said. "There's a hansom cab waiting up ahead." He moved off toward a vague outline at the end of the street, leaving Jane and Hettie no choice but to follow.

"Hettie, can you manage it?" Jane put one arm around her maid to support her.

"Hmm, yes," the injured girl groaned, and set one foot in front of the other resolutely.

The hansom cab had just finished a tour to Battersea Park and was happy to find a customer for a drive to Belgravia. Because the hansom sat only two, Blount climbed up on the back beside the driver.

Hettie pressed close to Jane, who took her hand, alternately squeezing and stroking it. "You'll be fine again soon, Hettie. I owe you my life, truly. You took your umbrella and stopped that treacherous assassin from—"

"Don't say it, ma'am. It was too terrible! I don't want to think about what might have happened."

"I'll double your pay, Hettie, but it stays our secret."

"Oh, no, ma'am, I don't want that," Hettie protested.

"Shush, not another word. It's the least I can do."

Lambeth was on the southeast bank of the Thames, and so they only had to cross a bridge to get to Pimlico or fashionable Belgravia Square, both in Westminster. The cab pulled up in front of a heavy gate on a side street off the square. The gate revealed little of the house on the other side, and the dense foliage of old chestnut trees concealed all but patches of a light-colored facade with oriel windows. Neither name nor crest gave any indication of who lived there. Blount paid the coachman, stepped over to the gate, and rang the bell. A few moments later, a servant bade them enter. He seemed to know Blount well, for he asked no questions and simply led the three of them to the main entrance.

Stepping into the hall was like entering another world. Confronted by the unusually beautiful interior, for a moment Jane forgot her bedraggled appearance and the circumstances of their arrival. Beauty seemed to be the single principle that ruled the place, a principle to which everything else took second place. Architecture, paintings, carpets, busts, and lamps were all carefully harmonized, forming an intoxicating blend of colors and shapes, which seduced a visitor. *Most fascinating of all,* Jane mused, *is that one feels at home here, even protected. How extraordinary!* Who lived there?

A pleasant scent of exotic flowers and sandalwood hung in the air, and Jane suddenly felt even dirtier than she actually was.

"Blount, would you tell me where we are?" she asked softly, but the servant, who had left them alone, returned at that moment.

"This way, please." He led them into a small salon with a divan and a folding screen. "A messenger has been sent to fetch the doctor."

"The doctor?" On a table, Jane spied bandages and a number of medical instruments. "Is this a private practice?"

Blount, who had followed them, replied, "No, my lady. This is the house of Madame La Roche. She is a friend of the captain's and absolutely trustworthy. I believe it is for the best to keep you out of a police investigation, my lady."

"The two dead men . . . were they both dead? My God, what did we get ourselves into? Hettie?" She turned to her maid, who had slumped onto the divan with a light sigh. "A brandy would probably be . . ."

Blount crossed to a sideboard and returned with a glass of amber-colored liquid. He handed it to Jane, and Jane pushed it into Hettie's free hand.

"Drink some," she ordered.

Hettie obeyed, but did not regain any of her color. Just then, the door opened and an elegant, dark-haired woman entered.

It was only when the light fell directly on the woman's beautiful, expressive face that Jane saw the network of fine lines that signified an eventful life of more than five decades. Relief filled Jane and, as if her hostess had read her mind, the elegant woman's lips curled into a slightly mocking smile.

"Blount, my dear, what have you brought me?" Her voice was deep and smoky and marked by a foreign accent.

More Russian than French, Jane suspected, despite her name.

"Now leave us women alone so I can tend to the wound."

Blount nodded and exited the room.

"Madame, pardon our barging in like this. It was not my intention—," Jane began, then faltered. She was standing beside Hettie and stroking her shoulder.

"There will be time for formalities later. Better help me get her undressed. She has lost a lot of blood."

In silence, they freed Hettie from her jacket, her top, and the laced bodice underneath, the heavy material of which had protected her somewhat from the blade of the knife. The maid leaned on her side against the raised end of the divan and kept her eyes closed the whole time.

"The blade cut through the material, but did not penetrate her ribs. She was lucky. We'll clean this up, I'll make two tiny stitches, and in a few days she'll have forgotten all about it," Madame La Roche declared. She clearly had some medical experience.

Hettie's eyelids fluttered. "Stitches? I don't want any needles in my skin, thank you!"

"Oh, no, you've misheard." Jane watched Madame La Roche dribble a few drops of liquid from a tiny bottle onto a handkerchief.

"Chloroform?" Jane asked. She had heard of this new sedative, but had never seen it administered. A Scottish professor had discovered it and, in a single stroke, elevated surgery above the work of a slaughterman. And when Queen Victoria allowed chloroform to be administered during the birth of her eighth child, the substance became firmly established.

Madame La Roche nodded and held the cloth under Hettie's nose. "Breathe in, slowly now."

Jane stroked her maid's forehead and hair and watched as her eyelids grew heavier. When Hettie was breathing easily and her limbs were relaxed, Madame La Roche said, "Quickly, now. Before she wakes again."

Jane watched with respect as Madame La Roche deftly cleaned, stitched, and bandaged Hettie's wound. Jane handed her what she needed without being asked. Finally, both women washed their hands with soap and water, then Madame La Roche tugged on a bell pull beside the door and an elderly woman in the black dress of a housekeeper appeared. The two women spoke together softly in Russian for a moment.

Madame La Roche indicated to Jane to follow her into a small living room. The room was more plainly decorated and intimate. A number of gilded icons hung above the fireplace, and on a round table there stood a samovar, a tiered dish with pastries and cookies, and a large silver bowl with a lid.

"Please, sit down. Olga will take care of your maid." Madame La Roche poured tea into dark-blue cups with golden rims.

Jane raised her cup, then set it down again. She had a hundred questions she wanted to ask.

"Drink your tea. It's strong and will do you good. Then eat some blini." She raised the lid on the silver bowl and removed two small pancakes, which she arranged on a plate with sour cream and a piece of smoked fish. "You were lucky that Blount followed you. Someone wanted to kill you, my lady." Madame La Roche took an almond ring and dunked it in her tea.

"But—"

"You don't trust your husband, and that is not good. David is an honest person, a man of character. If he gives you a piece of counsel, you would do well to follow it."

Jane set down her teacup and saucer fiercely and was about to square her shoulders when she caught sight of her own dirty dress. Her concern for Hettie had caused her to forget her own soiled state.

"Would you like to change? I'd be happy to let you borrow a dress. I would hazard a guess that we are about the same size," Madame La Roche proposed, unconcerned by Jane's show of affront.

"No! I am not feeling especially comfortable, I admit, but I would like to ask you where you know my husband from. And why you feel you have the right to give me advice. Were you in Crimea with him? Did you learn to sew from Florence Nightingale? We have not been properly introduced, Madame!"

Madame La Roche's full lips widened into an eloquent smile, and her dark, now-earnest eyes rested on Jane's. "I take it you haven't opened your uncle's letter?"

"I . . . no!" Jane almost shouted in surprise, suddenly recalling the sealed document her uncle had given her shortly before his death.

"I am mentioned as a reference in it. As a reference with regard to your husband, my lady." Madame La Roche looked at her in silence. "You don't know, do you?"

"What?"

Madame La Roche looked up to the ceiling and drew a deep breath. "It was a long time ago, but I had a relationship with Lord Pembroke for many years."

"Excuse me? But when? I mean, I don't remember him ever mentioning a woman."

The Russian woman looked her in the eye. "There are women with whom one is not seen in polite society."

"Oh" was all Jane could think of to say. She searched her memory for any hint that her uncle had had a secret love life. She realized that he must have been exceedingly discreet. Apart from his regular trips to London, there was nothing that even suggested what Madame La Roche was telling her. And even for those London trips, he had always had an explanation. "Well, it seems I didn't know my uncle as well as I thought."

"You have no reason to feel hurt, my lady. We had an arrangement that suited us both. I was only ever the consort of one man."

"Then you must have had generous patrons, or still do," said Jane, looking around the room.

Madame La Roche laughed a deep, sparkling laugh. "A woman must be able to manage her money as much as her beauty. There was only one man I would have married, but we were both too young, and his parents would never have agreed to him marrying a Russian companion with a dubious background."

"My uncle?"

"Oh, no, that was much later. My lady, I was the best friend of David's mother, Larisa, the daughter of Prince Turenin. My mother was the princess's lady-in-waiting. Larisa and I grew up as sisters. Her family went on an extended tour of Europe that took us through London and Paris. It was there that Larisa met St. Amand. Larisa was a girl of unearthly beauty, and the duke had been a widower for a year. He was captivated by her instantly. She could have had any man she wanted. If she had been stronger and believed in herself more, she might have been another Lady Ellenborough."

The scandalous life of the fiery and travel-besotted Lady Ellenborough, who'd had four husbands and finally found the love of her life, an Arab sheikh twenty years her junior, had stirred the soul of stiff and stodgy English society. Mesmerized, Jane drank her tea, bit into a blin—which tasted surprisingly good—and had all but forgotten the dramatic circumstances that had brought them to Madame La Roche's house.

She sat up abruptly. "The police! Mrs. Sutton! Don't I have to lodge a report?"

"No, my dear. It is always better to keep the police out of such matters. The less notice taken, the better. Send Mrs. Sutton a note to say that you are well. Most likely, she simply ran off in a panic and left you in the lurch." She stood and pulled on a cord.

Olga came in and Jane wrote a few soothing lines to Violet, whom she couldn't help but feel sorry for. "She's probably afraid of her brother," said Jane, giving voice to her thoughts as she folded the letter and passed it to Olga. "How is Hettie?"

"She sleeps, madam. She is sleeping well," the woman answered with a heavy Russian accent before departing again.

"My Olga is a loyal soul. Loyalty is not something you can buy—or at least sincere loyalty cannot be bought, and I cherish sincere people."

"What do you think of Lord Hargrave?"

Madame La Roche made a dismissive gesture. "A passionate man, very power-conscious, and with certain inclinations, as far as I've heard. It could cost him his office one day, but the elegant gentlemen of society do stick together, don't they? Do the English have the expression 'a crow does not peck out another's eye'?"

Jane bit her lip and, in a cautious tone, said, "I barely dare to say it aloud, but I suspect Lord Hargrave may be employing orphaned girls and abusing them, or even killing them."

Madame La Roche raised her eyebrows in astonishment. "Really? I know about his dissolute parties, and I like to imagine I am well informed, but rumors of that nature are not something I have come across before. Do you have proof?"

"Not directly. But the assault today leads me to think I am on the right track. Everything is connected to the girl who died at Rosewood Hall. Has David talked to you about that?"

Jane's hostess nodded thoughtfully. "Yes. He is investigating the matter, my lady."

"He's what?" Jane said, flaring up, at once disappointed and angry.

"I should not have mentioned it. He is worried about you, my lady. You will have to take my word for that. He would not be able to bear it if something happened to you. You saw for yourself the danger you were in today."

"Perhaps it would not have come so far if he had told me how things stand."

"So you would have done as he said and stayed home?" The question sounded like a rhetorical challenge. Jane thought it over, and Madame La Roche said, "I didn't think so."

The door swung open silently, and Olga said something in Russian to her mistress. Madame La Roche thanked her and stood. "Your maid is awake. She should go home now and spend a few days in bed. Talk to David about what you found out today. And if the police do happen to turn up on your doorstep, you don't know anything. Act nervous and hysterical." She smiled and stroked Jane's arm. "Although I know you are far from that."

"One more thing, madame. My uncle and David were well known to each other, weren't they?"

"Yes, absolutely."

"Did they discuss our marriage? It is vital for me to know that."

Madame La Roche's dark eyes softened. "Not in my presence."

"Thank you. One last question. Your name doesn't sound Russian . . . ?"

The sparkling, smoky laugh rang out again. "Blanche La Roche. Who wants a courtesan with a name like Uljana Achmatova?"

30.

As they stepped through the door into the townhouse, the master of the home himself appeared in the hallway, his expression dour. He was wearing a dinner jacket and had come either directly from one of his clubs or was on his way out to one.

"Jane!" It was hard to tell whether he was angry, worried, or simply annoyed at the disruption to his daily routine.

"Don't let us hold you up. We'll cope by ourselves." Jane had one arm slung around Hettie's hips and, with Blount's help, set about getting her upstairs.

The patch of blood on Hettie's dress and the dreadful state of both women's clothes must have been a terrifying sight. Levi, who had opened the door for them, was terribly shaken and running around like a startled chicken.

"Levi, you and Blount take the girl upstairs. Jane, you come with me," Wescott ordered, taking her by the arm.

She could see that his scar had reddened and a vein on his forehead was throbbing. Her husband was more furious than she had ever seen him before. However, as they had barely spent any time together, she could not really say what kind of emotional outbursts he was capable of. Right now, though, she decided it would be wiser to not object.

His hand was wrapped around her wrist, not too tightly, but with enough pressure to add emphasis. He laid his other hand on the small of her back and pushed her ahead of him into a small salon that served as a reception room. After closing the door behind him, he stood in front of her and looked her up and down thoroughly. "Are you injured?"

"No. But Hettie is."

He raised one hand for silence. "You acted irresponsibly, Jane. I'm terribly disappointed in you. Why the devil didn't you tell Blount where you were going? If I hadn't told him to follow you at all times, you would be dead now. You'd be lying in the gutter of a slum with a knife in your ribs!"

"How do you even know about it? We only just got back." Jane was trying to retain as much dignity as she could.

"Blount sent me a message while you were at Blanche's house. He is more level-headed than you!" he barked.

"Don't you dare take that tone with me. I am not a child for you to order around!" Jane said, her voice hot.

"Then don't behave like one!" He took a step toward her, and Jane retreated. Was he going to hit her?

Instead, he stroked her hair, then turned away and went to the fireplace. He leaned against the mantelpiece. "Jane, I'm worried about you. Is that so hard to understand?"

Relieved, she exhaled and held his gaze. "I do find it difficult to believe. You expect me to ask no questions about what you do. You expect me to trust you blindly, although you are very obviously harboring a bevy of secrets, one of those being Blanche La Roche, or, no, I mean Uljana Achmatova. Who, by the way, was my uncle's lover. I didn't know that, but you did. Was she your lover, too? She is a strikingly beautiful and well-educated woman. It would not surprise me to find out she had tutored you. But"—she raised her hand and turned around—"that's none of my business."

She went to the door, but before she turned the handle she looked back one more time to where he stood. "There is one thing that certainly interests me. Was this marriage planned? Did you have some sort of arrangement with my uncle, and that's why you seized upon my stupid, childish proposal? Were you having a secret laugh at the naïve lass who wanted to hold on to her freedom?"

Wescott did not reply. He was still leaning on the mantelpiece, unmoving. But there was something in the way he looked at her that she found confusing. He no longer seemed angry, just tired. "You should take a bath, Jane. Lambeth is a diseased hole. We can talk over dinner."

"Please don't let me hold you back from your other obligations," she said archly, then pulled the door open and stalked out.

She did not go directly to her bedroom, though. Instead she climbed one floor higher, to Hettie's room. Hettie was lying on her bed, pale faced. She made as if to get out of bed as soon as Jane entered.

"Don't get up, Hettie. You need to stay in bed. You've been through enough today. I'll have dinner brought up for you, and then you'll need to stay in bed tomorrow. That's an order!" She took Hettie's hand lovingly and squeezed it.

"Thank you, ma'am. But who will help you change?" She tried to get up again, but Jane restrained her gently.

"Let me worry about that." She filled a glass with water from a pitcher on the nightstand and handed it to her maid. "Drink this. And try to sleep."

"Yes, ma'am." Obediently, Hettie emptied the glass and sank back onto the pillow.

Jane pulled the curtains over the small window and opened the hatch of the heater. It looked as if it had been some time since there had been a fire in it.

"I'll send someone up to get a fire going. Then I'll free myself from these rags. Could this be patched, I wonder?" With a grin, she picked at the shredded material, which could clearly only serve as a washrag, at best.

Hettie giggled and held her side in pain. "I can try, ma'am."

When Jane entered her own room, the young servant girl who also helped out in the kitchen was waiting for her. The girl curtsied shyly. "The master said you would be needing my help, ma'am."

"Thank you. That's very nice of you." *How level-headed of my husband,* Jane thought cynically, but accepted the girl's help. Getting out of her corset by herself was practically impossible.

Some time later, she was sitting in the bathtub, and while the rose-scented soap displaced the stink of the Lambeth alleys, she ran through the events of the day again in her mind. *Polly,* she thought. The young girl had a name, and she had been abused in some high-society house. Had her emaciated body shown any sign of pregnancy? No, at least nothing visible. Was she even old enough? The girl had been so young, and must have experienced terrors of which she had no conception. And now it seemed a similar fate threatened Mary. Jane only had to find out where Polly had been. A foreign man with a scarf. Perhaps Wescott knew of a gentlemen with exotic tastes and servants. For Mary's sake, Jane determined to keep her annoyance at her husband's behavior in check.

She had just taken her place at the dinner table when Levi appeared carrying a silver tray on which lay a letter addressed to her.

"Thank you," said Jane, and took the letter. Wescott was sitting opposite her, and she held the letter in the air. "May I?"

"Of course." He leaned back and sipped his wine.

Jane quickly scanned the lines Violet Sutton had penned. The woman apologized extravagantly for her panic-stricken flight and begged Jane for forgiveness. She invoked her nervous constitution and said that she wanted to come by in the next few days with a gift. "Mrs.

Sutton excuses herself, but doesn't really mention the incident. I don't think she knows about the dead men."

"Dead *man*. Only one of those cutthroats died. The police were there but found out nothing from any of the residents. No one saw or heard a thing. That's typical for people who live in the slums. Police mean trouble, and they've got enough trouble in their lives already," said Wescott, setting down his glass.

"Did Blount tell you everything? I mean, did he mention the orphanage run by the missionary in Lambeth? And Polly?"

"So that was the name of the girl at Rosewood. Polly," he said and smiled sadly. "Polly and Mary. Did you find out anything else?"

His sympathy affected her and, full of hope, she said, "I fear that Mary is heading down the same path as Polly, and that she will suffer the same fate. Everything points to it. Both came from Newbridge, and both were supposed to be taking up a position in London. Ledford lied! He told me that Mary went to Norfolk. Why? He's got something to hide. He knows that the girls he sends here are in danger."

For the first course, Levi served an artichoke soup. It was very tasty, but Jane managed to swallow only two spoonfuls. "What if it really is Hargrave ordering girls from Newbridge? There was another girl who died quite close to Mulberry Park, not so long ago. No one misses the poor things."

"And what do you think Hargrave is doing with these girls?"

"He's abusing them! He's exploiting their innocence. I don't need to have Madame La Roche's experience to know that some men will pay a lot of money for a girl's virginity." She reddened slightly as she said it, and was immediately annoyed at herself for doing so.

"I would not have married you if you had Blanche La Roche's experience, Jane," said Wescott. He leaned forward and set his spoon aside. "But that is beside the point. No, I don't know Hargrave particularly well, at least not as well as his bosom friend Rutland does. They're a notorious team, those two. Still . . . I doubt either of them would be capable of murdering a young girl for the sake of satisfying their own lust."

Jane lowered her eyes. She took a sip of wine and looked up again at Wescott. "Why not?"

He seemed more relaxed than he had when she and Hettie first returned. He had exchanged his dinner jacket for a house jacket and stretched out his long legs under the table. "I've been through a lot. During the war. Let's say that I've picked up a certain feeling for people, and Hargrave and Rutland are certainly a pair of libertines. They love debauched parties and amusing themselves with women, including women you pay for. But children? No, I don't know about that. There are—how can I put it?—there are certain taboos, in the clubs, too, among initiates. Taboos that cannot be broken or there will be consequences, even in the highest circles."

"Well, they're not going to announce it in the papers, are they? They meet in secret," said Jane.

Wescott sighed. "There's no such thing as a secret, unless those keeping the secret are dead."

"Is that true?"

Wescott grinned. "It's true. A secret stops being a secret the moment you share it with someone else. Every confidant is a threat, every servant a risk."

"Oh, I just remembered. Polly was deathly scared of a dark-skinned man who wanted to strangle her with a scarf. What do you suppose that means? It sounds to me like one of the Thugs."

"A Thug? Why?" Every trace of humor vanished from Wescott's face.

"I thought of my childhood in India. My nanny there told me stories about gods with many arms and secret societies. She always warned me about the Thugs, the killers with the yellow scarves, who silently murdered entire groups of travelers. And Henry Sleeman published his memoir just a few years ago. Even Queen Victoria has read *Confessions of a Thug*," said Jane.

"Then you also know that Sleeman eradicated the Thug cult. And the whole story's been blown out of proportion in any case," he said, but his words lacked conviction.

Jane raised her eyebrows. "Do you seriously believe they wiped out all of the Thugs? With all due respect to our empire and its army, I find that highly unlikely."

"Jane, I simply don't want you talking about such things. It is too dangerous," Wescott said indignantly.

Jane let out a dry laugh. "Rubbish. Why should I keep my mouth shut about Indian assassins? We're alone here, and I lived in India, didn't I? My parents spent many years there."

"You don't want to understand, do you? I'm not just talking about the Thugs. I mean all of it, including talking about people like Hargrave and Rutland. This is no topic of conversation for a respectable woman."

"Aha!" Jane sniffed.

"By poking around and asking questions, you put yourself in harm's way, and you hear and see things you shouldn't hear or see. That's what I mean!"

"David, I don't want to spend my life at tea parties prattling mindlessly about dreary balls and things like that, nor do I want to fill my days redecorating my home and paying formal visits to superficial people I don't particularly like. Polly died in my arms and begged me to save her friend. Now I've picked up Mary's scent! I feel—I *know*—that she is somewhere here in London, perhaps very close to where we sit! I will not ignore Polly's dying wish! That orphan girl, that poor, tortured waif . . . she gave my life a purpose. I can help. Don't you see that?"

His expression remained inscrutable. "What's your plan, Jane? Do you want to visit every respectable house in London and ask about Mary and an Indian servant?"

"Laugh all you want, but yes, why not? Alison has outstanding contacts, as you know. Oh, I almost forgot. Hargrave's masked ball is in four days. That would be a good opportunity. His house is on Park Lane. I believe we can rule out Rutland. What do you think?"

"You won't give up."

"No."

Levi brought in the next course, and they sat silent until he had closed the door behind him again. Jane prodded disinterestedly at her fish, and rolled peas from one side of her plate to the other. Finally, she dropped the fork on her plate with a clang.

"Why should I trust you when you won't come so much as a step in my direction?"

"In what way?"

"Madame La Roche said that you've been investigating."

"Did she now? She talks too much sometimes. You shouldn't believe everything—"

"Oh, stop sidestepping! She knew exactly what she was saying. I'm sick of it all!" Jane threw her napkin on the table and was about to stand up when Wescott shook his head.

"Jane, please. Stay. There is, in fact, a great deal that I can't tell you and don't want to tell you. My past is like a dark shadow that still holds me in its claws. But beyond that, my current work demands absolute confidentiality with respect to my employers. But I want to help you. You just have to let me do it my way."

"Hmm."

"I've been making some inquiries into Ledford. He's got a past. He used to run an orphanage in Manchester but had to give it up after some improprieties with donated funds. Convicts are still being transported to the colonies. Children, too. It seems that Ledford is secretly sending far more than the officially listed number of children to Australia and America. I don't yet know how or with whom he's in league, but I'm working on it. We cannot do anything without proof, and I fear he has an influential employer. But it isn't Hargrave. That much is certain."

"My God! So Ledford is selling children to the colonies? That's what you mean, isn't it?"

"Yes, unfortunately. And there's no promised land waiting for them there."

Jane's eyes filled with tears. "Why? What more do they have to bear? No one deserves to suffer like that."

"Don't cry, Jane. We will get him, but we can't afford to scare them off. I want whoever's paying him, not the small fry. Ledford's just a nasty little rat, a cog in a machine."

Jane dabbed at her eyes and nose and said, "What about that teacher, Peter Gaunt? Can you find out if he actually sailed off for America? And Miss Fannigan?"

"I've got someone checking the passenger lists of all the ships that sailed from Plymouth in that period. It will take some time, though. If Gaunt's name doesn't appear on the lists, then we have a reason to question Ledford."

"Why didn't you tell me about this earlier?"

"I would have told you as soon as I had a result."

"Is that how you always do things?"

"I've never had cause to do them any other way."

They finished the meal in silence. Neither ate dessert, and Wescott escorted Jane up to her bedroom.

"Good night, David."

They were standing opposite each other in the dim light of the corridor. Down below, Levi and little Josiah scurried back and forth, clearing up. *A normal household. But we are not a normal couple,* thought Jane with a pang of regret.

Very gently, David touched her cheek with his fingers. "Our marriage was not something arranged with your uncle, Jane. I married you because I wanted to. Good night."

31.

Mary

Mary had grown used to the daily routine and quickly proved so adept at her work that Jenny praised her and Mrs. Avery left her in peace. The food was so good and plentiful that her perpetual hunger began to fade, and Mary's body gradually took on more feminine curves. She was eleven years old, and her monthly bleeding would start soon. She knew that from Polly. As Mary climbed out of the washtub and dried herself that morning, Mrs. Avery entered and stood in front of her with a stern look on her face.

"Either you're not working enough or you're eating too much. You're getting too fat. The master doesn't like that. From today, no more sweets for you."

"Yes, ma'am," Mary murmured, disappointed. She loved the pastries and candied fruit that were prepared in the kitchens along with all the other delicacies.

"You'll be working in the laundry today. One of the girls is sick, though I think she's gone and got herself pregnant. You're not there yet, are you? Or are you?" Mrs. Avery eyed her suspiciously.

"What do you mean?"

"I mean, have you got your monthlies! Idiot child."

Mary shook her head, ashamed.

"Well, get on then. Hurry!" Mrs. Avery adopted her usual haughty posture and strode away.

Mary took less than usual at breakfast, which the cook noticed. "What's the matter with you, then? You normally eat twice as much. Don't you like the food anymore?"

"Oh, yes, it's wonderful, but Mrs. Avery said I'm getting too fat," Mary explained sadly.

The other servants laughed, and the cook patted her cheek. "Don't take it too hard. Then we'll just have to let out your dress a little. You were such a skinny thing, and there's still not much meat on your bones."

The cook was a short, plump woman with a friendly face. She maintained a strict rule over her kitchen kingdom, but her heart was big.

Mary smiled sweetly, but could not bring herself to eat more, and headed off for the laundry. The wash was boiled, rinsed, and wrung through a mangle in a room at the end of the long corridor that led to the backyard. Lines had been strung up in the yard and were used mainly to hang the servants' clothes, the towels, and sheets. An additional large room was equipped with roll-out drying cabinets and ironing tables. This was where the laundry for the master and his guests was dried.

Laundry girls ran back and forth, carrying baskets of dirty wash, folding and smoothing towels, ironing linen. Maids in light-blue dresses and white aprons ironed underskirts and embroidered handkerchiefs. Hot steam from the irons and the vats drifted through the passages and rooms, making everyone who worked there sweat profusely. After two unrelieved hours of stirring laundry in one of the vats, Mary was exhausted and went out to the yard where there was a water pump. She leaned down and held her face under the cool stream of water and was about to straighten up when someone suddenly grabbed hold of her and pushed her face into the basin beneath the pump.

Mary fought desperately to free herself from the grip of her unseen assailant. She lashed out wildly, splashing and swallowing water until she thought her lungs would explode. Just before she thought she would drown, she was jerked back and thrown to the ground.

"You miserable little bitch! Look at me," snarled a familiar voice that struck fear all the way into her bones.

Mary choked and spat water. She had to prop herself up on both trembling arms to look at the man. Through a curtain of her own blond hair, she recognized the face of Jedidiah, contorted with hate. He looked even seedier than the last time she had seen him, and one hand was wrapped in a bandage.

"I'd drown you like a dog. You and your girlfriend, Polly. That was 'er name, right? You and 'er 'ave given us nothin' but trouble, and it started with 'er. All 'cause they didn't keep an eye on 'er. She got away, and now we got this blasted nosy lady on our backs. Nothin' but trouble!" He kicked furiously at Mary, who curled into a ball and wrapped her arms around her head protectively.

"What the devil is going on here?" snapped the sharp voice of Mrs. Avery. "Jedidiah! Leave her alone!"

Terrified, Mary pushed herself backward over the sand until she felt the stone basin below the pump at her back.

"Look at this, ma'am!" Jedidiah held up his bandaged hand reproachfully.

"Shut up, you stupid fool!" Mrs. Avery barked. She dragged the burly man across the yard with her, away from Mary. Behind a plane tree, she berated him.

Carefully, Mary climbed to her feet and wiped the hair out of her face. Moving between the lines of washing, she approached the pair as closely as she dared. When she could hear their voices clearly, she stopped.

"I want to talk to the master! I need more money. I can't stay 'ere. I 'ave to disappear. She 'ad a bodyguard we didn't see. 'e came out of nowhere like a damn cat and sliced Eddie's throat like a pie! A devil 'e was! I ain't never seen no one like 'im," Jedidiah whined, with real fear in his voice.

Who was he talking about? Who could frighten a paragon of wickedness like Jedidiah?

"Be quiet, Jed, and wait here. I'll go to the master and ask him what's to be done. Were you recognized?"

"No, no, I don't think so. There were no one else around, in any case. The lady didn't get a clear look at me, that's certain. Only 'er maid looked right at me when she bashed my arm. I got 'er with the knife."

"Then let's hope she's dead, or we've got something else to take care of. No witnesses, you know that. What's got into you? Are you getting too old for this kind of work?"

Mary heard the murderer groan in pain.

"And he got you, too? That never would have happened before. Wait here." Mrs. Avery's shoes crunched on the gravel.

Quickly, Mary dodged back between the lines of washing and dropped at the wall of the house as if she had collapsed there.

"Mary! Get up. Not a word to anyone." Mrs. Avery grabbed hold of her arm and dragged her to her feet. She glared balefully at Mary. "If you breathe so much as a syllable about this to a soul, I'll take you to court as a thief. And you know what that means."

Mary nodded, but said nothing. She had to summon all her courage not to cry. Punishment was drastic and designed to deter. She'd heard that a fifteen-year-old lad was sentenced to seven years of hard labor in the colonies for the theft of a pocket handkerchief. Some judges were more lenient and would sentence you to only a year in prison, but even the thought of that—of ending up in Brixton's notorious women's prison—made Mary's heart race with fear.

Polly had been here. Jedidiah let the cat out of the bag, even if he didn't mean to. Someone had to know about her. But whom could Mary trust? Everyone feared Mrs. Avery and could betray Mary to her. She did not want to think about what would happen to her then. Maybe the only choice was to run away, like Polly.

"You listen to me, girl," said Mrs. Avery, shaking her roughly by the shoulders. "I know what you're thinking. Don't even try it. We'll find you just like we've found every other one who tried to run away from us."

"Polly got away," Mary whispered.

"And where's your precious Polly now?" asked Mrs. Avery, almost gently.

Mary said nothing.

"You see? Go and change and come straight back down!"

Mary did as she was told, then spent the rest of the day working in the laundry. She spoke to no one. But she was determined not to spend a single day more in that house. After everyone had gone to bed and the domestic wing was quiet, Mary climbed out of bed as silently as she could. The floorboards creaked a little underfoot, and the two kitchen hands she shared the room with turned in their beds but went on snoring. Their working day was long and hard, and once they fell asleep they were not quick to wake up again.

Carefully, Mary pulled out her bundle of clothes from beneath her bed. She took her boots and opened the door. The hall was dark and quiet. Mary padded down the corridor, flinching at every sound. Finally, she reached the stairs. Getting down the stairs unobserved seemed to Mary to be the most dangerous part of her flight, for the master and his guests needed their domestic staff even at night, and someone could be called for at any moment. But Mary was lucky. She kept her bundle of clothes pressed close and made it to the ground floor, where she very cautiously opened the door to the kitchen and laundry wing. The quarters and offices of the butler and Mrs. Avery were down there. Although the butler was ostensibly in charge of the domestic staff, it was Mrs. Avery who seemed to rule over the servants—no doubt her role was rooted in the special position of trust she enjoyed with the master.

A light was burning in the kitchen, and Mary swallowed. If she failed here, she would have to go back upstairs, and she doubted her luck would hold out twice. Slowly, she crept closer, silent on her bare feet. The light was shining through the kitchen window from the outside. It was the lantern in the yard, which they kept alight through the night. No doubt there was also a guard patrolling outside, but he couldn't be everywhere at once. She had no fear of the dogs. They knew her and would not bother her.

She banged her toes against a wooden crate standing in the dark corridor, and swallowed a cry. She'd probably picked up a splinter from it. In her ears, the buzzing began. *No,* thought Mary. *Not now!* She could not afford a dizzy spell now. Her ear still hurt from time to time, and she would become giddy. She stopped, leaned against the wall, pressed her hands to her ears, and breathed in and out several times.

She had no idea what she was supposed to do once she got outside, or to whom she could turn, but she knew she had to get away from there or she would die inside these walls. Polly had known it. And she had fled. Maybe Mary would be able to find her brother. She just had to make sure she didn't get caught by the police. That's what she was most afraid of. She didn't want to go back to a workhouse.

There was only one door between her and the yard. She pressed down on the door handle and groaned. Locked! And the key had to be with the butler or Mrs. Avery.

Thinking feverishly, Mary ran into the large servants' kitchen, which was dimly lit by the lantern outside. The windows were not barred. She quickly climbed onto a table and, on the stone windowsill, found enough room to kneel and turn the lever that held the window closed. She threw down her bundle of clothes and jumped after it.

For a long moment, she crouched in the shadow of the wall and listened for noises in the night. Far off, she heard a church clock strike the hour, and the clop of horse hooves on the cobbled street. The grass growing between the stones was wet and the air cool. Mary was still wearing her nightdress and wanted desperately to change into something warmer.

The single lantern lit the rear courtyard of the house only sparsely, and the cloths and towels still hanging on the washing lines fluttered in the darkness as if a ghostly hand were shaking them. One side of the yard opened onto the garden that then led into the grounds behind the next wing of the house. The massive branches of the plane trees swayed and rustled in the wind. It sounded as if the leaves were whispering to one another. Mary ran toward the tree but pulled up short, for now she heard real voices, human voices. Or rather, she heard someone whispering in a language she did not know, while the other person made gurgling sounds and uttered a curse that quickly faded.

That can't be good, thought Mary. Her heart was pounding in her throat. As quickly as she could, she squeezed into the bushes along the wall behind the washing lines. Her heart was so loud in her ears that she thought anyone could hear it beating. She peered out through the bushes, and what she saw made her blood run cold. At the base of the plane tree kneeled Jedidiah. Behind him stood Ramu, the master's Indian servant, strangling Jedidiah with his yellow scarf. She had no sympathy for the terrible Jedidiah, but compared to Ramu, the powerfully built man seemed practically harmless.

Ramu's eyes glinted in the darkness, just like his teeth, for he grinned evilly as he completed his deft and seemingly effortless handiwork. Finally, Jedidiah's limbs fell slack, and with a dexterous flick, Ramu whipped the scarf from the man's neck and slung it around his own. Then he turned and, as quick as a tiger, leaped toward Mary's hiding place and hauled her out of the bushes.

Mary was frozen with fear. In front of her stood Death personified. Her heart was racing and she gasped for air. Breathing suddenly grew difficult, and the buzzing in her head became so intense that she crushed her hands to her ears and felt her senses slipping away. *Thank you, God,* she thought. *Thank you for sparing me from seeing this devil murder me.* But the thought was not followed by any pain, just darkness. She dreamed of Polly, of how she must have run from the murderous man, must have torn the scarf from around her neck and wandered lost through the streets of London. Then she saw Fiona at the railing of a ship. Her red hair was blowing in the wind, and Mary waved to her, but Fiona's face was strangely pale as she opened her mouth into a silent scream.

Then came the pain. "Will you stop shrieking!"

Someone slapped her face. She had not been throttled, only slapped by Mrs. Avery, and she was no longer outside in the yard. She was in a dark room. A candle stood on a footstool, and in the candlelight Mary could see that she was lying on a narrow cot.

"Wake up!" Mrs. Avery hissed, shaking her anew.

Mary's head hurt. Her ear, too. She whimpered and pulled her legs up and wrapped her arms around them.

"You've only yourself to blame. I did warn you, after all. Hold your tongue for the next few days and nothing will happen to you. If you scream or try to open that door, I'll send in Ramu."

Mary's eyes widened in horror. "No, ma'am, not that dreadful man! He's a demon from hell!"

Mrs. Avery twisted her mouth. "You're not far off there, girl. Ramu is the devil's right hand."

"No! I'll do anything you want," Mary sobbed.

"Good girl. Why didn't we do it like this straightaway? We could have saved ourselves a lot of grief. Can you read? I'll bring you a book to fill the time until the party."

"A party?" Mary asked.

"A special party that the master is hosting. As his blond angel, you will be its climax. That's why you're here."

That did not sound like anything good at all. She had to get away!

32.

"Be prudent, Jane. With whomever you speak. We still don't know who is pulling the strings in this trade in children," Wescott whispered into her ear.

Her hand lay on his arm as he led her through the elaborately decorated hall of Hargrave's townhouse. Only a few days had passed since the attack in Lambeth, but functions had followed one after another in the brief time between. They had gone to a Lords & Commons cricket match together and attended a Private View Day at the Royal Academy. Jane was especially fond of art exhibitions when there were young artists who did unusual and surprising work.

On both occasions, she had spoken with Mrs. Lock, and discovered that the young Prussian's reserve was a facade. Behind it lay a passionate woman who took an active part in political events. Just the kind of woman to throw herself into a revolutionary cause, Wescott believed. He was grateful to Jane for the information.

Hargrave's townhouse was in Park Lane, directly opposite Hyde Park. Although not one of the largest houses, it was impressive in its luxurious appointments. The servants were selected for their good looks as much as anything else, but as much as Jane looked, she saw no sign of an Indian among the staff.

"No Indians . . . ," she murmured and smiled at the other guests.

Unfortunately, Alison was not there. Her children were in bed with some minor malady or other, and because with small children one could never be sure whether the fever had really gone down, Alison—who had no faith in doctors—had stayed home.

All of the guests still held their masks in front of their faces, which gave the whole affair a frivolous and secretive air. The women's dresses were very fancy and designed to show off their bodies, and the men wore formal dress. At midnight, the masks would come down, but Jane did not want to stay that long.

"And no yellow scarves? Jane, not a word about that. Ah, there's our host. And I see Violet up ahead. She looks particularly nervous. Perhaps you should go to her."

"Lady Jane and Captain Wescott! What a pleasure to see you again!" Lord Hargrave greeted them. He was holding the stick of his mask in one hand and seemed in high spirits. He seemed to know nothing about Violet's hasty departure from Lambeth. Violet, ashamed of her cowardly behavior, had implored Jane to be discreet about the incident.

"Your wife only gets more beautiful, if you will allow me the observation," said Hargrave flatteringly, and let his gaze linger on Jane's décolletage for a long moment.

Jane was wearing a black-and-red dress, and instead of a necklace she wore a black velvet band with a tear-shaped ruby pendant. Were Hargrave's compliments just a pretense? Did he really prefer the delicate bodies of young girls, children? He had a reputation as a ladies' man, and even Madame La Roche had doubted that Hargrave would pursue inclinations of that sort.

She waved to Violet. "A most enchanting party, Lord Hargrave. Please excuse me. Your sister . . ."

"Of course. But you must save a dance for me, my lady," Hargrave said.

Wescott remained silent, but she felt his eyes on her back.

"Violet!" Jane called, and the two women kissed each other on the cheek.

It wasn't that Jane was especially overjoyed to see Hargrave's sister, but she felt sorry for the woman. Violet's hands were shaking as she touched Jane's and whispered, "I am so grateful to you for not saying anything to my brother. He would punish me by taking away my syringe." Violet was wearing a green dress with black lace that did her no favors. It made her look wan and ill.

She pulled Jane with her into one of three salons that were decorated with valuable furniture and paintings. All the rooms on the ground floor had been opened up for guests to visit. Blue-liveried servants stood ready to cater to the visitors' every need. In the large ballroom, a ten-piece orchestra struck up a dance number, and there was a relaxed buzz of voices from the guests, who were clearly enjoying themselves.

Jane decided to exploit her position. Violet, to some extent at least, was now in her debt. "Violet, I don't have much experience in these things, but I've heard a lot of rumors of, let's say, indulgent parties where the usual conventions are not necessarily observed . . ."

Jane fluttered her fan coquettishly, and Violet looked at her doubtfully. "Are you sure that's something you want?"

"My life is so terribly dull. One can't just go visiting orphanages, although that's a wonderful thing, naturally, but . . ." She took Violet's hand. "Do you know what I mean? A little adventure where one could remain anonymous might be rather charming."

"Anonymous?"

Jane held her mask playfully in front of her face. "When we all have masks on, one never knows whom one will bump into."

"Florence Rutland is the true master in such affairs." Violet paused and thought for a moment. "I have seen and experienced everything, and I must dissuade you, my lady. My brother is a philanderer, and he has his eye on you. You should know that he has asked me to take you up to the first floor after midnight. A different kind of party will take place up there. Unfettered, my lady. Decadent."

Jane let out an affected giggle.

But Violet took her by the arm. "Don't do it. You are not the kind of woman to come through those kinds of games unscathed. You will feel dirty and shabby and hate yourself for it."

"Who will be there?"

Violet looked around, but no one was close enough to overhear her. "My brother, Rutland, Devereaux, and Kayman. Of the women, Mrs. Lock is one of the favorites."

"Mrs. Lock?" Jane could not contain her surprise.

Violet laughed dryly. "Not what you'd expect of our shy Prussian, is it? My brother took one look at her and knew immediately that it was all a masquerade. With you, he wasn't so sure. It would certainly please him, but I warn you, Lady Jane. Don't do it. Robert is a devil. He enjoys toying with people, manipulating them." Unconsciously, Violet stroked the pincushioned crook of her elbow.

"Thank you for your candor, Violet," Jane said. No word of children, which didn't necessarily mean anything, but Jane was certain that Hargrave's sister would have mentioned it. Violet loved children and could certainly not have borne the knowledge that they were being abused.

When she looked up, she saw Wescott standing in the doorway. "Excuse me, Violet. I believe my husband would like to dance."

Violet Sutton smiled sadly and reached for her pearl-studded handbag.

With one hand outstretched, Jane went to Wescott. "You wanted to dance with me?"

He hesitated for a split second. "Yes, I did."

The orchestra played a waltz, and Wescott led her effortlessly among the dancing couples. For a few moments, Jane let the music carry her away and enjoyed the motion and the closeness to her husband, who seemed to her like an island of safety in a sea of depravity and lies.

"I talked to Violet," Jane began, catching Wescott's brooding eye.

"I sense nothing good." His hand was firmly placed on her waist, and he directed her safely past a collision with Florence Rutland, who was dancing with Devereaux.

Jane briefed him on what she had learned from Violet, and watched as Wescott's expression darkened with every word.

"Are you serious?" he growled.

"I did not breathe a word about Thugs or orphans."

"Worse!" He pulled her so close that she could feel his thigh against her leg.

"But what I've discovered basically absolves Hargrave, doesn't it? You could at least admit that I've acted rather cleverly."

"I don't know what to say to that, but 'clever' is not the first word that springs to mind." He relaxed his grip and let his hand glide down the deeply cut back of her dress.

"Does Mr. Lock know what his wife is up to, I wonder?" Jane mused.

"I doubt it. At the very least, he can forget his candidacy for prime minister if she compromises him." He looked at her suddenly with an appreciative smile. "Actually, Jane, that was very clever of you. Lock can be blackmailed through his wife. I suspect that may have been engineered by Hargrave. What could be better than a prime minister one can extort with a dirty little secret?"

"Ha!" Jane smiled triumphantly as they whirled over the parquetry of the dance floor.

When the music fell silent, she was slightly out of breath. She fanned a little fresh air over her face to recover.

Wescott offered her his arm. "Let's have a drink, Jane."

In keeping with the rules of the party, they both held their masks over their faces.

"I'd like to step outside for a moment, David. You could cut the air in here with a knife," Jane said. She looked longingly toward the doors that opened onto the terrace.

Wescott accompanied her outside. The terrace had been decorated with colorful lamps and garlands of flowers. One could not see how big the garden was, but it smelled of freshly cut grass, and the crowns of leaves on the ancient trees rustled softly in the cool night air. They were not alone out here, as evidenced by the muffled sounds of laughter and the murmur of voices not far away.

Jane sighed and thought of the last party they had celebrated at Rosewood Hall. "I still miss my uncle. Perhaps it would be easier if Matthew weren't so . . ."

Her voice failed her. It was too painful to think about her unpleasant cousin, whose demands were still hanging over her head.

"He won't get away with it, Jane. I promise you," Wescott said firmly.

"But how can we stop him from taking Mulberry Park away? His demands are enormous."

"There's a way. Believe me." He was standing very close to her and looking at her steadfastly in a way that she found unsettling.

"I would love that, of course, but . . ."

He reached one hand out to her, but a voice behind them held him back.

"Oh, excuse me, I didn't mean to interrupt such youthful bliss." Charles Devereaux lowered his mask and stepped up to join them. He put on his most charming smile and bowed before Jane. "But I would very much like to ask you to dance, Lady Jane, if you will allow me."

"Wescott! Here you are. A word, if you please." The Duke of Argyll approached. The duke, an influential parliamentarian who also threw one of the most important garden parties of the Season in Chiswick, was a man used to immediate attention.

Jane folded her fan and laid her hand on Devereaux's arm, following him back into the party. "My pleasure, although I'm desperate for something to drink."

"Well, we wouldn't want to let you die of thirst, my lady." Devereaux's gray eyes remained fixed on hers longer than they should have, and Jane raised her mask.

"Where is Lady Alison? When I first met you, she appeared as if on command. I do believe you wanted to get away from me," he said with a smile.

"Oh, no. Really." Jane laughed and waved to a woman in a white dress without knowing who was behind the mask.

"You know the Duchess of Cleveland?" Devereaux nodded to the woman as well, who blew him a kiss. The beautiful young woman was a rich heiress, making her one of the most sought-after women of the Season.

"Oh, is that her? I must have confused her with someone else," Jane replied, angry at herself, but mainly at Devereaux, who seemed not to miss a thing. "Why don't you propose to her?"

Devereaux flinched, then laughed heartily and looked at Jane. "Do you think she would turn me down, like you?"

"I didn't turn you down. I only asked for some time to think."

"Isn't that the same thing?"

"For me, yes, but it doesn't always have to be like that."

Devereaux smiled. "You're a quick-witted woman, Lady Jane, and you like to play with fire. Have you ever burned your fingers?"

He took her hand and lifted it to his lips, and she felt the tip of his tongue touch her skin. That was going too far! Jane, outraged, inhaled sharply, but Devereaux spoke first, a whisper in her ear.

"When the masks come down at midnight, my lady, the barriers come down with them. Fantasies you've never dared to dream will be within reach. Are you happy?"

His final question came so unexpectedly that Jane stared at him agape. "I'm thirsty."

"Of course. How could I forget that? But you will have to forgive me. I regret deeply that your choice did not fall in my favor. You could have accompanied me to India. Didn't you grow up there?" He waved a servant over and took two glasses of champagne from a tray.

Jane would have preferred water, but she took a swallow of the cool, bubbly liquid and decided to enjoy this unusual evening. "Yes. Sadly, my parents died there. But I have many memories of the land. The colors and smells, and the stories that my Indian nanny told me."

They were standing by a marble pillar close to the dance floor. Jane noticed they were being observed by several pairs of masked eyes. Jealous debutantes or yearning wives?

Devereaux seemed unimpressed and kept his entire attention on Jane. "Beneath all of its exotic colors, India is a dark continent, a land full of tragic legends and traditions. Have you ever heard of the custom of burning widows? We English will never manage to quash that particular tradition, let alone drive out their gods. They have cruel gods and secret societies we only think we've done away with."

"Are you talking about the Thugs?"

Devereaux frowned. "A gruesome story. They are said to have murdered more than a million people. Unbelievable, isn't it?"

Jane felt the fine hairs on the back of her neck rise. There was something in the way he talked about the Thugs, a kind of cynical appreciation. "Have you ever seen one?"

His eyes narrowed. "No, my lady. And I can assure you that no one would survive such an encounter."

The orchestra launched into the first bars of a mazurka, and Jane drank the last of her champagne. Devereaux watched her finish her champagne, took the glass from her hand, and led her onto the dance floor. He was an elegant dancer and led her effortlessly through the complicated forms of the dance, which involved jumps and fast turns and quickened her breathing. She was relieved when the music died and she could put a little distance between herself and Devereaux again. There was something demanding in the way the man conducted himself that repelled her.

Just like that evening at Rosewood Hall, thought Jane as she scanned the crowd of guests. When she saw Wescott, she gave him a sign.

"You mean to leave me in the lurch again, I see," Devereaux complained jokingly. Then he leaned close to her and whispered, "You are curious and courageous. Pain can be sweet, my lady."

Then he drifted away into the crowd.

When Wescott reached her, she was fanning her face energetically. "I want to leave. Right now."

"Did he come too close?" Wescott asked, and his eyes were grim as he followed the slim departing figure of the businessman.

"No, but I've had enough of this company for today."

"Good. Wait out in the hall for me. I have to talk to Argyll for another minute."

When they were sitting outside in the carriage, Jane sighed. "One should never overestimate one's abilities," she muttered.

Wescott smiled and pointed out the window at the mansion they were passing. "That's Charles Devereaux's place. He must really have earned a fortune in India." They were driving alongside a high wall, the top of which bristled with sharpened iron spikes. They could see the outline of a huge, many-winged edifice behind the trees. Only someone with enormous wealth at his disposal could afford an estate like that in the heart of London.

"He proposed to me, the night I met you," said Jane, without taking her eyes off the magnificent gate adorned with a crest. *Pretentious for someone with no title,* she thought. Wescott said nothing, and Jane added, "I am glad I did not accept."

Then she told Wescott about their conversation, but her husband only said, "That doesn't necessarily mean anything. Someone like Devereaux has no need to muddy his fingers."

33.

The following morning, Jane was surprised to receive a letter from Cornwall. Floyd had written, and his news was completely unexpected.

"Listen to this," Jane said to Wescott, who was sitting with her at the breakfast table. That, too, was unexpected, but Jane was silently pleased that he was there.

Wescott, who had also received a letter, put his aside and refilled his cup with tea, which he drank black.

"Floyd is well. He can get around without a stick, Rufus is chasing the ducks, and, ah, here, this is incredible!"

> My lady, we were all quite speechless, but Fred Thomas, the miller's brother, kept a girl locked up for several weeks in his hut in the woods and was having his way with her. It seems the girl finally managed to escape. She came from Foxhole, not far from St. Austell. She has several brothers and uncles in her family, and they took Fred to task, to put it mildly. What was left of him was hauled off to Bodmin, where he's to face court. After his arrest, he admitted to holding that girl from St. Winnow captive,

*and also to her murder. Indeed, he claims that he did not
mean to kill her, but that won't change anything. It is
the rope for him.*

Jane looked up. "Isn't that terrible? I would not have believed it
possible."

"It certainly is food for thought. But the Thomas clan apparently
has a number of black sheep. Does he mention your former cook?"

"No. He's checked the books and found a few small peccadillos,
but he says that, by and large, he's satisfied with Mr. and Mrs. Roche.
The gamekeeper seems to be making an extra effort. Sales of partridges
and pheasants to hunting clubs in the region have brought in a good
profit." She set the letter on the table and looked at Wescott, who was
eyeing his own missive thoughtfully.

"You remember I told you someone was making some inquiries for
me?" Wescott drummed his fingers on the paper. "The teacher, Gaunt.
His name isn't on any passenger lists. I've had all of them checked,
including those of ships still in port. Nothing."

"Which can only mean that Mr. Ledford was lying. And Miss
Fannigan?"

"Her name turned up in an agency that found a position for her as
a private teacher in Glasgow."

Jane sighed with relief. "Then she's still alive."

"Do you fear that Mr. Gaunt is dead?"

"Yes, as terrible as it sounds. I'm certain something is rotten there.
Why would Ledford go to such trouble to lie about Gaunt? Why come
up with a complicated story about migrating to America? I'll tell you
why: because he's got something to hide! You haven't seen Cooper, the
custodian at Newbridge. A brutal man. I wouldn't put anything past
him. The children seemed extremely intimidated by him, and the red-
haired girl wanted to tell me something, but they locked her up. I'm
sure of it. Can't the place be searched?"

"With a little pressure from above . . ." He grinned. "This is where my long sojourns in the clubs might pay off. No doubt a search and provisional detainment of Ledford can be arranged. Sometimes an arrest can work wonders. People start talking like a waterfall. It all depends on what kind of stuff Ledford's made of."

"Didn't you say that he'd already lost one post in Manchester? It occurs to me that he could not afford a second misconduct charge."

"Let's just hope that his fear of prison is greater than his fear of his patron. He is still a mystery, and therefore untouchable. The trade in children is almost impossible to get under control." Wescott wiped a hand over his cheek. His scar was barely visible this morning.

"There's no real duty to school the children, and the Poor Law Union has no laws that allow strong action to be taken against child labor," said Jane.

"It's the poverty. As long as people are hungry and have no work, they will continue to trade their children for cash. No one can stop it. We can investigate this or that orphanage when it's obvious that morals are being ignored and laws broken, but what about the children living on the streets? Not to mention the brothels."

"Are you trying to say that doing anything at all is pointless?" Jane glared at him, ready for a fight.

"No," Wescott replied gently. "I just don't want you getting your hopes up too high when it comes to making changes to the system. Ledford is just one of many."

"But you yourself talked about his patron, right? If we can find him, then many children will be better off."

Wescott hesitated. "The churches and other charitable organizations have been organizing the transport of children to the empire's colonies for more than a hundred years. British children for British colonies."

"The Children's Friend Society. Although not everything they do is really for the benefit of the children. I know, it's in the papers all the time. But then it comes down to the conditions they're sailing into.

Wasn't it just recently that they sent a commissioner to Canada to check on how the children there are provided for?"

"Some of what he found was good, but many families treat the children like slaves, and that's apart from the cases of rape." Wescott laid his hand on the letter in front of him. "We can't affect what happens over there. We can only act here, where people like Ledford are manifestly exploiting the situation for themselves. It's not only orphans being sent abroad. Ledford has also been giving false promises to mothers who spend the night in the workhouse and leave their children in his care."

"They believe their children are better off in the orphanage, and if they come back to collect them . . . ," Jane mused.

Wescott continued the thought, ". . . then Ledford tells them a sad tale of sickness and death. He gets paid for every child, that much is certain, but what I don't yet know is who is buying them from him."

"Gaunt found that out and they silenced him," speculated Jane.

"It would seem so. But without proof, we can't keep Ledford locked up for very long. We are so close to him, Jane! Damn it!"

"Would you have even latched on to Ledford without me sniffing around?" Jane asked with a sweet smile.

"I doubt it, although I was already looking into the case of the girl at Rosewood Hall."

"Feel free to admit that my inquiries bore fruit. My little excursions with Violet were not in vain."

"What do you want to hear, Jane? We have neither Ledford nor Mary."

"Not yet, not yet . . ." Because he was not prepared to admit that she had a good detective's nose and investigative talent, she stood up. "I have a few things to take care of. First, I'm off to visit Alison. I don't think Blount will be needed to escort me *there*."

• • •

Lady Alison, wearing a scented, rose-colored day dress, embraced Jane fondly, kissing her cheek.

"Darling! So lovely to see you! There's so much to tell." Alison grasped Jane's hand and led her into a prettily decorated salon with huge, blooming planters and a Madagascar palm. On a table stood fruit, tea, and cakes.

"Sit, sit! Try some of the almond cake. Bertha made it, oh, and there I am already on the subject," said Alison animatedly.

"Are the children all right?" Jane inquired.

"In the clear, thank God. The doctor was afraid they had scarlet fever, but it was only a slight temperature. Scarlet fever! My cousin's son died of scarlet fever just last year. I thought I would lose my mind when the doctor said that. Callous man. He should be sure of his diagnosis before he scares a mother half to death." Alison sent a young maid out of the room and sank onto an armchair. "I would have sent you a message if you weren't already on your way."

"You have my undivided attention. And if you don't tell me what's going on this instant . . . ," Jane said in mock threat, taking a piece of almond cake.

"Well, you asked me about Mary, the orphan girl?"

Jane nodded.

"And I knew from Bertha that two girls named Mary work for Hargrave." Alison let a pregnant pause settle.

"Ally!"

"I want to savor the moment, it's so exciting. Listen, Hargrave's two Marys are over twenty and full of life. A new kitchen maid was also taken on, but she's from Leeds and has a family."

Disappointed, Jane bit into the moist cake.

"But my dear Bertha has a niece who works for Mr. Devereaux."

Jane set the cake aside instantly and stared at her friend. "And?"

"Bertha's niece, Jenny, is on good terms with the cook, who is the only other nice person there. Jenny says the only reason the cook stays is because Devereaux pays so well. The head of housekeeping is supposed to be a real witch and everyone's afraid of her. I'm sorry, I'm rambling! In any case, Jenny told Bertha about a girl named Mary who worked there until recently. Jenny said that Mary actually did her work very well and was also very pretty. Long, blond hair."

"That has to be her," Jane whispered. *"Until recently?"*

"Mary was not very happy there and talked to Jenny about a friend of hers who she missed very much and who might have run away from a similar job. However that may be, one morning Mary simply didn't show up for work, and no one knows what happened to her. When Jenny asked the housekeeper about her, the woman turned especially nasty and said Jenny should keep her nose in her own business." Alison poured tea into two gilded porcelain cups.

"Too late again! I was on her trail, and now she's disappeared."

But Alison smiled impishly. "I haven't finished my story yet. Jenny was cleaning up in the master's rooms when she discovered a locked door that she thinks leads to a hidden suite of rooms. She says that strange things go on in the house, and she's afraid of the master's Indian servant . . ."

"Devereaux has an Indian servant?" Jane cried aloud.

"No need to shout about it. Yes. On his last trip to India, he brought back a spooky man with a turban. Thomas has actually seen him once, and found the man inordinately proud. Personally, I'm not in favor of bringing back locals as souvenirs. Not good form, definitely."

"Ally, do you know what this means? Oh, I can't believe it. Not Devereaux!"

"What? Jane, what else do you know?"

Jane thought feverishly. What could she do? "It's something I might have expected of Hargrave, but not Devereaux," she thought aloud.

"You like him, don't you? Well, I must say, he's a charming man. And incredibly rich, as Thomas likes to point out. Thomas says he would have done better to start with the East India Company, then we could also afford a palace on Park Lane, like Devereaux."

"Ally, that's not what's important." She knew she could not tell her friend everything. Alison would tell Thomas, and if he then went to a club and ran into . . . no, that could not be allowed.

"Not important? Devereaux doesn't have a title, but there's a rumor going around that he's to be ennobled at the next Royal Audience at Ascot. Only because he's rich and has supposedly set up important business relationships for the empire. Something about a monopoly on tea or something, I don't know. But I do know that if you have enough money, you can buy anything." Alison paused. "Somehow I don't think that's right. I mean, where will it lead if any old upstart can become a peer just because he's done a few lucrative business deals? He's not the Bayard of India, is he?"

"Bayard of India" was the honorable epithet earned by General James Outram for his military and diplomatic successes in Gujarat and Hyderabad. Jane loved her friend, but Alison had a tendency to open her mouth before thinking things through. She would heedlessly blather away about whatever was in her head at the moment. But perhaps Jane was doing Alison an injustice. She herself had seen too much misery in recent months, and had been forced to face the hopelessness of many people. And she had discovered that she felt it was her duty to help wherever she could.

"Ally, can I talk to Bertha?"

"Why?" Alison looked at her with large, blue eyes. "I've told you everything."

"Even so. I promise, I'm not trying to steal her away from you, if that's what you're afraid of." Jane grinned.

Lady Alison sighed and reached for a silver bell that stood on the table. "You have no idea what it means to have an excellent cook. I honestly fear that you waste far too much time on orphans and such. It's not that I don't admire you for it, but as a wife, one has to worry about having a presentable home. Then one's husband has no need to look elsewhere."

The maid entered and Alison said, "Tell Bertha that she's to come here."

Jane frowned. "Elsewhere? Have you seen Wescott with another woman *again*?"

"Not me. But Thomas has. Oh, Jane." Alison took Jane's hand in hers. "I want to see you happy, and I don't think you are. It doesn't matter how many girls you rescue or meals you distribute or schools you pay for."

Jane squeezed Alison's hand. "You mean well, I know. But right now, it's about Mary."

The door opened, and a plump woman stepped tentatively into the room. Her pale-blue dress was clean, but the white apron over it was covered in spots of grease. "Pardon, ma'am, but I'm in the middle of the roast for this evening. I don't want to get anything mucky."

"It's all right, Bertha. Lady Jane would just like to talk to you for a minute."

Jane stood up and went to Bertha, whose hair was covered by a white bonnet. "Bertha, it's about Jenny and the girl who's disappeared."

"Yes, ma'am?"

"Would it be possible for me to speak with Jenny without anyone from Mr. Devereaux's household finding out?"

Bertha's eyes widened. "I should think so, ma'am. Tomorrow's Thursday, and some of us go to the Red Hen. I see her there sometimes and could introduce you."

"Very good. Then let's do that," said Jane, a plan taking shape before her eyes.

34.

Mary

Mary had searched every inch of her prison, but there was no way out. She did not even know where in the house she was locked up. It was strangely quiet. She heard no sounds from the courtyard or the kitchen, and there were never any servants in the vicinity. She heard no whispers in the corridor or from any surrounding rooms. The only sound was the occasional rattling of Mrs. Avery's bundle of keys.

Like just then. Alarmed, Mary crouched on the bed, which was pushed against the wall in one corner. A narrow ray of light angled down from an unreachable height, and when the sunlight shone through, a pretty floral pattern appeared on the floor. The high window itself was barred. The walls of the cell were clad in wooden paneling, but she could find no point where the panels were even slightly loose. She had hoped to find a secret door, but if there was one, it was well hidden.

The floor was stone, the footstool and bed made of solid wood with turned legs. There was no furniture like that in the servants' quarters, and Mary suspected she had been locked up in the master's section of the huge house. Since she'd arrived at the house, she'd managed not much more than a glance at the extensive property, and she had no idea of the floor plan. She and Jenny had only ever been on the main floor, but this room seemed higher. Perhaps there was a tower?

The key was inserted into the lock and turned without a sound. The door opened just as silently. No squeak or creak betrayed someone entering. That made the room even more threatening, for Mary imagined that someone could surprise her in her sleep. But try as she might to stay awake, at some point every night, her eyes closed and she slept.

Mrs. Avery greeted her with a false smile. "It will soon be over, Mary. The party will take place tomorrow evening, and if you do your job well, you'll be rewarded. If not, well, we'll see."

"What kind of party? What am I supposed to do? I can't sing or dance!" said Mary as she watched Mrs. Avery withdraw the chamber pot from under the bed. A task that undignified was far below the level of the housekeeper, and the simple fact that she lowered herself to it could only signify that no one else in the household knew about this prison. The dark-haired woman screwed up her nose and set the pot outside the door.

"You don't have to. You have a God-given gift that makes you special." Mrs. Avery looked at her, biding her time.

While Mary continued to clasp her knees, her long blond hair hung like a curtain around her slender body. The meals served to her there in the room had been meager, and the delicate curves that the good food of the servants' kitchen had brought out were starting to disappear. "My hair?" Mary murmured, wishing she had a knife to cut it all off.

"No, girl. Your hair is just a bonus. You really haven't worked it out, have you? Your maidenhead." Mrs. Avery's eyes were fixed on her, and there was something cold and appraising in her gaze. "There are men who will pay a fortune for that. And many girls have no idea at all what they're giving away when they let the next lad who comes along have his way with them."

Mary's lips began to quiver. "I don't want that! I don't want to!" she sobbed.

"Why do you think we paid so much money for an uneducated orphan girl? Pull yourself together. If you try to fight, it will only be worse." The ruthless housekeeper stepped up to the bed and grabbed Mary's arm. "Come on, stand up!"

Mary reluctantly obeyed. She stood on the cold tiles with her head down and let herself be examined like a piece of meat. Mrs. Avery ran her hands over Mary's tiny breasts, her ribs, and protruding hipbones. "Excellent. That's what the master likes. This evening, we'll wash you and curl your hair. Tomorrow you'll look just like an angel."

As soon as the housekeeper disappeared and the door clicked shut, Mary crouched back on her bed and cried. What had she been thinking? Of course that's what they wanted from her. Poor Polly. What had she gone through? Had she also been here, counting the hours, staring at the strip of light over her head? And once Mary lost her innocence, what then? Would they kill her? Would Ramu come and twist his scarf around her neck? Mary jumped to her feet. She still had a night and a day to get out of there.

She crawled under the bed, where she had first checked the wall for hidden passages. Slowly, she ran her fingers over every inch of the paneling, following the grain to see if a small gap formed anywhere, anything that might indicate a secret door. The bed was heavy, but still she managed to haul it a few inches from the wall. Her fingers slid across the polished wood again and stopped where the wood suddenly felt uneven. Nervous, Mary dragged the bed a little farther out. The last rays of daylight shone weakly into her prison through the high slit window and illuminated what the bed had previously kept hidden.

Someone, very awkwardly, had scratched something into the wood: *Polly*, it read, and another letter that she could not recognize.

Mary cried out and pressed her hand to her mouth, then began to weep and beat her hands against the wood. Exhausted, she squatted between the bed and the wall and stroked the clumsy letter that her friend had left behind during her ordeal. *What did they do to you? Did they come for you here, then bring you back afterward?*

For some minutes, Mary could not stop herself from sobbing. Then she wiped her face and shoved the bed back where it had been. Now she knew with terrible certainty that her friend had been there. And she had proof! Excitedly, she paced around the narrow room. She could prove to someone from the outside that her friend had been locked up in there. They would have to believe her then! Mrs. Avery could not be allowed to find out about the inscription, not for anything. And somehow, Polly had managed to escape. But how? Polly had been somewhat taller and stronger than Mary. Still, she could not have reached the window. Maybe she had escaped during the party?

Mary heard the jangle of the keys and leaped back onto the bed. Mrs. Avery put the chamber pot inside the door and brought fresh water and an apple. Dinner.

"That won't fill me up!" Mary complained.

But the door was closed again without a word. Mary greedily ate the apple and looked around again in the dying light. Blast it, there was no way out!

Mary did not know how much time passed before Mrs. Avery came to fetch her to take a bath, but it was already dark. In the hated woman's iron grip, she padded barefoot along a dark corridor and, after several yards, was pushed into a small bathroom where a tub of hot water stood waiting. Soap and towels lay on a bench.

"Wash! I'm going to get the ribbons, then I'll be back."

Mary heard the click as the door was locked from outside. She looked around. The window in this room was somewhat larger, and Mary immediately dragged the bench and a small stool to the wall, climbed up, and looked out. What she saw was not encouraging. Far below was a lit path, where a watchman strolled past just then. Jumping from that height was impossible. The wall was smooth and there was no drainpipe that she might be able to climb down. She would probably be too weak to hold on anyway.

Disappointed, she pulled off her dress and climbed into the tub. The hot water caressed her body, and the soapy foam smelled of violets. The unaccustomed luxury, meted out only because she would soon be led like a sacrificial lamb to the slaughter, gave her a sense of bitter well-being that made her feel sick. As soon as she stepped out of the water and dried herself, she looked at her own body with repulsion. Ledford had sold her. If she ever got out of there alive, she would find him and take revenge.

She only had to survive. Then she could find her brother. He would help her avenge what was being done to her. Oh, yes, Tim would be sure to help. Tim, whose cat Mrs. Avery had thrown in the fire. Just then, the door was opened and her tormentor entered with a basket of hair ribbons.

When she saw the look on Mary's face, which reflected all the hate the girl felt, Mrs. Avery said to her bluntly, "If a pair of scissors lay here, I wager you'd stab me to death."

Mary's lips were white with fury. "You have no idea . . . ," she hissed.

"I think I probably do. I've been on this world somewhat longer than you, after all. Girls like you come and go. But the master holds on to me because he needs me." She stood directly in front of Mary and clamped her chin roughly between her fingers. "You're a pretty little virgin, but when he's done with you, he'll toss you aside like a filthy rag. But he places great store in me because I understand him. I know about his secret passions; I know his tastes. And I would do anything for him."

The housekeeper's eyes flashed intensely, and Mary saw a touch of insanity in them. Mrs. Avery was mad with love for a man she would never be able to have, a man who exploited her dependence.

"But he doesn't want you, does he?" Mary said. "All he sees is his housekeeper. You'll never be anything but a servant, you—"

Mary didn't get any further, because Mrs. Avery slapped her across the face. Mary screamed as she felt the pain shoot into her ear.

"Sit down!" Mrs. Avery shoved Mary onto the stool brutally and set about combing her hair and tying strands with the ribbons.

When she was finished, she smiled with satisfaction. "Very nice. Tomorrow morning, your hair will be dry, and we'll take the ribbons out. Then we'll find a dress for you, and you can eat whatever you like."

Mary reached for her thin slip and pulled it over her head. "What happened to Jedidiah?"

"What do you think happened?" Mrs. Avery grasped Mary's wrist and dragged her along behind her. Out in the corridor, she suddenly stopped. The muffled sounds of music could be heard, then laughter and the clack of a dice cup on a table.

Mary saw a thin strip of light at the end of the corridor and knew that the doorway must lead into the master's rooms. The wing she was in seemed uninhabited. "Where's he buried, I mean?"

"Buried? Well, now, that would have been far too honorable an end for a scrimshank like him. The Thames is good enough for his sort, girl. Back inside with you!" Mrs. Avery pushed Mary back into her cell and locked the door.

The hot bath had made Mary tired, but in the middle of the night she awoke from a nightmare and stared anxiously into the darkness. Was that a flash of white by the door? Were those the eyes of Ramu, standing there motionlessly, looking at her? Was he just waiting for his chance to sling his cloth around her neck? Her breathing quickened, and drops of sweat trickled down her neck and body. Finally, she summoned her courage and whispered, "Is someone there?"

She waited for minutes that felt like hours, but there was no sound save her own rattling breath and the call of an owl in the trees outside. Mary reached her hand up to the ribbons that were tied so tightly that her scalp hurt. Old cloth cut into strips was rolled into the hair to curl it. As if through a fog, Mary remembered her mother doing the same thing many years before.

Her mother had been a loving woman, a decent woman. She had toiled hard to get her children through. Mary remembered the woman's rough, overworked hands on her cheeks, and how she'd kiss Mary tenderly on her forehead and eyelids while she hummed an old song and did the girl's hair.

"Baby was sleeping, its mother was weeping, for her husband was far on the wild raging sea . . . ," Mary began to sing, and her hands pulled at the annoying ribbons. One after another, she took them out of her damp hair. She wound individual strands around her fingers and tore at them until they came out of her scalp and curled in her lap like threads of golden silk.

"The baby still slumbered, and smiled in her face as she bended her knee . . . ," Mary sang softly, still tearing at her hair, harder now, tugging the ribbons out forcefully, and when they caught, she jerked harder. She didn't feel the pain, nor did she notice the bloody skin that clung to the roots of the hair.

"O blest be that warning . . . for I know that the angels are whispering with thee . . ."

One strand of hair after another sank into her lap or fell on the bed and the floor, where the silver moonlight bathed the fallen blond locks in a ghostly white. When the pain finally came through and she could no longer bear it, Mary stopped and stared tearfully at her hands, sticky with blood and hair.

Whatever happened, she was no angel anymore.

35.

"Finished! You can try it on." Hettie pulled the needle out of the material, bit through the thread, and held the dress out to Jane.

"Wonderful!" Jane lifted the garment in the air, inspecting it. At first glance, it looked like a skirt. "Very good. This will do nicely. Something I can actually move in."

She had already taken off her petticoats and now slipped into the culottes, which were similar to her riding breeches but lighter and gave her even more freedom of movement. In addition, she would also wear a blouse and jacket and hide her hair beneath a coarse tweed cap. Hettie had bought the jacket and cap from a merchant in a part of the city where they normally never shopped.

"Where are your things, Hettie?" Jane asked, stretching her legs and trying out a crouch. "I wish we could wear clothes like this every day."

Her maid giggled. "That would cause a pretty scandal, ma'am. If anyone sees us, there'll be a scandal in any case."

She went into the adjoining room and came back with her own clothes. They looked similar to Jane's, although Hettie's more ample curves were harder to hide. But the unbecoming clothes had been cut for no other reason.

"Maybe we can hang a large bag over your shoulder. And you need to swing your hips less when you walk," said Jane critically when Hettie slipped into her clothes. Jane laid an old oiled-leather bag on her bed, opened the flap, and removed a hunting knife, a neat little dagger, and a pistol. She gave the dagger to Hettie.

"Stick this in your belt."

Hettie nodded doubtfully. "I don't know if I could stab anyone with it."

"You could if someone were threatening your life. You've already proved how brave you are, Hettie." Jane patted her maid on the shoulder. They had secretly been practicing how to use the knife.

For herself, Jane was relying on her years of experience with her uncle's hunting weapons. It was next to impossible to do any kind of shooting practice unnoticed here in the city, but it was a skill one never forgot, and she had always been an outstanding markswoman.

Down below, in the hallway, the large clock struck seven. It was already getting dark and there had been no rain that day, which favored her plans for the night.

"Dinner! Today of all days, he has to be home for dinner." Jane slipped out of the forbidden clothes and had Hettie lace her into a corset.

Hettie, still in her own culottes, bustled around arranging the skirts for Jane's evening dress. "What if Jenny doesn't keep her word? We'll find ourselves standing in front of a locked door and they'll arrest us as burglars. Or they'll set the dogs on us, or have us . . ."

"Enough! If Jenny really does leave us hanging—though I don't think she will—then we'll simply leave again the same way we came. And we'll take a bone for the dogs, of course. Better safe than sorry."

Jane was not as convinced of her plan as she sounded, but she had no choice. If she wanted to save Mary, it had to happen tonight.

Jenny had seen Mrs. Avery carrying food upstairs that was clearly not intended for the master, nor for herself or any other servant. And this evening, a party had been planned in Devereaux's house—a party where, as Jenny put it, something strange was afoot. The other servants whispered about immoral affairs that took place behind locked doors in a sealed-off section of the house. No one knew exactly what went on because on those occasions staff were hired in from outside, and only Mrs. Avery had access to the rooms, which were otherwise always locked.

At their meeting at the Red Hen, Jenny explained exactly where they would find a hidden gate in the wall. Jenny's boyfriend, a lad from the stables, would open it for them. The cook was also on Jenny's side, and had immediately declared herself ready to put bones out for the watchdogs. That would keep them distracted after midnight. The watchman had a weakness for liquor, and Jenny would leave a bottle for him on the windowsill in front of the kitchen. Jane had spiced the deal with a ten-pound note, and Jenny's eyes had lit up at the sight of it. Jane was sure that, coupled with the promise of a second such piece of paper, the chambermaid was motivated enough to suppress any loyalty or fears she might otherwise have.

As Jane, wearing an emerald-green dress, inspected herself in front of the mirror, she smiled encouragingly at Hettie, who was standing behind her. "Everything will work out, Hettie, believe me. Devereaux suspects nothing and thinks himself completely safe. That's our advantage. He would never dream that two women would have the audacity to enter his house."

"And if we tell the captain after all? He's going to be terribly angry with you when he finds out about this," Hettie said.

"He'll be angry either way, but if we tell him now, he'll prevent us from doing what we have to do to save Mary," Jane replied briskly, although, in truth, thinking about Wescott made her uncomfortable. It was not right to go behind his back like this, and she was certainly acting recklessly, but it was her duty to help that poor girl. Besides, at the mere thought of this dangerous nighttime adventure, she felt a boundless strength surge inside her. Her skin prickled with excitement. She felt alive.

She knew that she had to act as she was, but if anything happened, it should be her risk alone. It was crucial that Hettie not be put in serious danger. She would take steps to make sure that didn't happen.

Ten minutes later, she entered the dining room, where Wescott was already waiting. He wore a dinner jacket that fit perfectly and raised her hand to his lips.

"You look particularly lovely this evening, Jane." He looked at her intently. "Has something happened? Some news? You have a certain radiance."

"What? Oh, no. I'm just happy that Hettie is feeling better and that Ally's children are over the hump. Isn't it wonderful to have everyone well?"

"Hmm" was Wescott's only reply. He seemed unconvinced by her merry chatter.

In silence, Levi served smoked fish, but it seemed far too heavy for Jane's appetite. She ate only a little and sipped at her wine. "You're going out, I assume?" she said with a glance at his jacket.

"Yes, and it will be a late night. I'll probably sleep at the club," Wescott murmured between bites.

His hair was cut somewhat shorter, Jane noted. She had grown used to his wild mane, which matched the unpredictable, mysterious character she found more attractive than she wanted to admit. Since her visit to Ally, she had thought a great deal about her friend's words. Perhaps there was a spark of truth in them. But she was not like Ally and would never be happy in the role her friend accepted so easily. She had always known a traditional marriage would not make her happy. Her uncle had also seen that side of her and had allowed her all the freedom she wanted. Yet her eyes lingered on the delicious curve of Wescott's lips.

She caught herself, too often, imagining those lips touching hers and . . . she had some idea of what could come after that. But she also knew that it would bring unavoidable consequences. She slid her knife and fork onto her plate and reached for her water glass. And then there was another problem that Ally had pointed out. She could never fall in love with a man who was not true to her. Never!

"A penny for your thoughts, Jane," said Wescott, jerking her out of her inappropriate musings.

He had been watching her, she felt it, and she replied pertly, "They would only bore you. Men prefer to spend their time in clubs where they can have interesting conversations and amuse themselves together."

"I think you have the wrong impression of us, Jane." A faint smile played on his lips.

"What I've learned about men so far has taught me no different. How else can one explain the existence of so many clubs that allow only men to be members? It certainly points to a lack in domestic diversions."

Wescott laughed. "I would say it varies from case to case. And it depends upon what one expects from the other, wouldn't you say?"

"Very true. And because we expect nothing from each other, there is nothing more to be said on the matter. I'm not feeling well. Please excuse me. I'm going to go and lie down." She stood, and Wescott was instantly beside her to pull her chair back.

She felt his hand on her back. "I'm sorry to hear it," he said. "Just a passing upset, I hope?"

"A little rest, and I'll be back on my feet in the morning."

He took her arm. "Should I escort you upstairs?"

"Thank you, but don't trouble yourself. There are people waiting for you, I'm sure. I'll see you . . . well, whenever you get back. What's next on our list? Sion Hall, then Ascot?"

"Jane, what's the matter with you?" There was a tinge of sympathy in his eyes that made Jane feel ashamed.

She was being unfair and brusque, but just then was not the right time for a deep discussion of the state of their marriage. "It's just a small indisposition, that's all. Good night."

She freed herself from his hands and left the room. In the hallway, she met Levi, a tray piled high with crockery in his hands. He stopped and stood uncertainly. But Jane kept walking. She knew that if she stopped and spoke to him then, her voice would betray how close to tears she was.

When she reached the door to her room, she heard Wescott say, "Take the food back. I've lost my appetite."

He was angry. It wasn't long before she heard the clack of the front door closing.

Go then, thought Jane as she removed her jewelry. "Hettie!"

Her maid came from the adjoining room and immediately set to work unbuttoning the dress. "Was the captain upset? I heard the front door."

"Maybe. But the main thing is that he's gone and won't be back tonight, which means we can get ourselves ready without interruption, and the coach can wait for us closer to the house."

Half an hour before midnight, two odd-looking figures were standing at the corner of Seymour Street. From a distance, they looked like two young men, but their trousers had an unusual cut, and the jackets they wore could not entirely conceal the female figures beneath.

"Hettie, stop fidgeting and pull your tail in!" Jane whispered earnestly and waved to the coachman, who was about to drive right past them.

"Hey, you the gents who ordered a coach?" he called down from his seat, looking at them doubtfully. "Show me the cash up front!"

Jane beamed inwardly. If the coachman treated them with such disdain, then they certainly looked neither respectable nor particularly feminine. She produced a few coins from her trouser pocket and pressed them into the coachman's hand. "Park Lane, the corner of Upper Grosvenor Street," she said, speaking in as deep a voice as she could muster.

"That's a fine address for a couple of rowdies like you. If you've got something dishonest in mind . . ."

"We're helping with the horses at a party."

Hettie had already climbed into the coach, and Jane followed her.

The wagon rolled sedately through the quiet, nighttime city. There were few pubs in this part of London, and correspondingly few drunks. Despite this, shady characters could still be found here at night, and burglaries and violent crime were not uncommon.

It was easy to see when a party was going on in one of the wealthy estates by the presence of waiting coaches. Usually, the coachmen mingled and whiled away the time playing cards and drinking beer they brought with them. If there happened to be a pub close by, they would use the opportunity to pay it a visit and, often enough, the visiting lords and ladies had to wait for a drunken coachman to reappear before they could return home.

The coachman stopped his carriage at the agreed corner, which was just as quiet as the streets they'd ridden through, and the women climbed out.

"There's no party hereabouts!" the coachman yelled after them, but they waved him on and walked across to the wall opposite. The coachman shrugged and clucked his tongue, setting the coach rolling again in the hope of picking up another late-night fare. Jane straightened her jacket and oriented herself. Everything looked different in the dark, but she had memorized Jenny's description precisely.

"This way, Hettie," she whispered, and moved in the shadows of overhanging branches toward a narrow gate.

She said a silent prayer and pushed against the iron gate. It swung inward, and Jane sighed with relief.

36.

Her uncle had always compared Jane's eyes to a cat's. Even as a child, Jane had not been afraid of the dark and could easily find her way around at night. She had inherited the unusual skill from her mother, and just then Jane was infinitely grateful to her mother for passing it on.

"Give me your hand," she said, reaching behind her for Hettie. Her maid's soft hand instantly clasped hers.

"I can't see a blessed thing," Hettie complained, stumbling after her mistress, who weaved an unerring path through the bushes and trees.

Now and then, Jane stopped and listened, but heard no barking dogs, nor footsteps or voices. Light shone from a high floor in the home, and music drifted on the air. Jane looked up angrily. Up there, high society's most heartless were enjoying themselves at the expense of the rights and dignity of a young girl, simply because it was in their power to do so. She stepped on a twig that cracked beneath her boot, and stopped in shocked surprise. The sharp sound seemed to cut through the still of the night like a glass smashing on a rock, but nothing happened.

"Jenny seems to have kept her word," Hettie whispered.

"Yes, she has. Come on. The kitchen courtyard is just past that round box tree." Jane made her way between the geometrical forms of the hedge and stopped at a gravel path that gleamed whitely in the light from a lantern.

In one corner of the yard washing hung on lines, and behind them rose the hulking forms of huge trees in the darkness. The door to the kitchen was clear to see, flanked as it was by benches and stacked crates. A church clock not far away struck twelve. They were on time, and Jane could already see a pale outline behind one of the windows. That had to be Jenny. Good girl!

She turned and placed her hands on Hettie's shoulders. "You will wait out here for us, understood? That is vital. If you hear any unusual noise or you start to get scared, run back to the gate. From there, it's just five hundred yards to Grosvenor Square and Lady Alison's house. She will help you."

"No, ma'am. I'll stay here. I'm not about to run off," said Hettie.

"If you hear me yell, or you hear a shot, run to Lady Alison and fetch help. Promise me!" Jane squeezed the brave girl's shoulders.

"Yes, ma'am."

"All right." Jane did not have a clear conscience about roping Hettie into this plan with her, but she trusted her sense that the night stood under an auspicious star. Even if she were discovered, she did not think Devereaux would be able to harm her, because he had a soft spot for her. Whatever dark sides the man might have, his feelings for her were genuine. He'd made that extremely clear to her at their last meeting.

Jane stepped out of the protection of the hedge, jumped across the gravel path to the grass on the other side, which swallowed the sounds of her footfalls, and then moved silently across the cobblestoned courtyard to the kitchen door. Cautiously, she scratched as agreed on the kitchen door and waited breathless minutes until someone inside turned a key very slowly and then gingerly pulled open the door.

"Is that you, ma'am?" Jenny asked in a quaking voice.

"Yes. Were you expecting someone else?" Jane pushed inside past the girl, who closed the door.

They were standing in an enormous kitchen with a vaulted ceiling. "My God, you could cook for an army in here," said Jane in amazement.

"Psst! We have to be very quiet. The butler's room is at the end of the corridor. Sometimes he can't sleep at night and comes to get himself a glass of milk." Jenny looked pale and tense. She had twisted her hair into a long braid that fell all the way down her back.

"I'll follow you. Have you found out if Mary is here?"

Jenny went ahead without a lamp. "Stay close behind me and hold on to my shawl."

"I'll manage. Just go."

Jenny said nothing until they had made it inside a narrow stairwell and closed the door behind them. Only then did she say, "Mary has to be up there with them. One of the servants saw Mrs. Avery cleaning a chamber pot."

Jane clenched her teeth. "Then come on. We can't be too late."

They crept up the stairs to the first floor. When Jenny went to open the door into the master's quarters, Jane stopped her. "Here? Are you sure?"

"I work here, don't I? Come on. We have to go through here to get to the other side. We can only get into the other building from there. Look, if you don't trust me, we can drop the whole thing." Jenny looked at her in annoyance.

And if someone's offered you more and you're leading me into a trap? Jane wondered. No one knew where she was. It was true that Alison had some idea of what she was planning, but not in great detail. Alison thought that Jane would talk to the police and Wescott before doing anything. But Jane knew that they didn't have enough proof to move against Devereaux legally. And a single day lost could cost Mary her life.

Suddenly, they heard music and men's laughter. *Keep going,* Jane decided.

Although they were only passing through corridors, Devereaux's love of exotic opulence was evident all around, and Jane could only guess at how rich the man really was. She noted the gilded statues, fine carpets, and valuable weapons, while hoping they would not bump into the Indian servant. At every clatter of a chamber pot or squeak of a bed frame, the two women pressed breathlessly into a corner or hid behind drapes and waited until the corridor fell quiet again.

They moved across a gallery from which one could look down into a ballroom. A crystal chandelier was suspended from the center of a plaster rosette. At the end of the gallery, Jenny led her through a long passage with a vaulted ceiling along its length and then into a paneled salon. A narrow door was tucked away beside a bookshelf. The music had grown louder, and the men's voices were much closer now. Jenny pressed the door handle down carefully, but the door was locked.

"Blast it! We'll have to wait until they come out," Jenny whispered. She pointed to a bay window embrasure, where a bench was concealed behind a curtain.

The women had only just hidden themselves when they heard footsteps trotting down stairs behind the bookshelf, and the door flew open.

"I've got another bottle down here, Robert," Charles Devereaux called behind him as he crossed to a vitrine.

Jane excitedly took hold of Jenny's arm and felt the young woman's quaking. They heard the glass door of the vitrine close, then Devereaux's steps departing. But Jane did not hear the door beside the bookshelf close. Jane peeped from behind the curtains and saw that the door to the secret wing stood open. She was about to go to it when Jenny stopped her.

"I'm not going any further, ma'am. Give me my money!"

"As soon as I come back. Make sure the door stays open." Jane pushed free of her and dashed across the salon, silently thanking heaven for the culottes, which allowed her to take longer steps. She climbed the steps of the stone spiral staircase two at a time and prayed that no one would come down just then.

The music and voices grew louder. An icy shudder ran down her spine when she recognized Hargrave's laugh, and Devereaux said, "Sidney, you old rake, who would have thought? But wait, the night's just begun!"

"Charles, you're the best," Sidney Rutland bawled, and another man, whose voice Jane didn't recognize, laughed loudly.

Sweat pearled on Jane's forehead and ran down her neck. The passage ahead of her was lit by a single gas lamp. The ceilings were lower than on the floor below her, but she was not yet in the attic. On both sides of the passage, which was perhaps a hundred feet long, were doors. The party seemed to be going on in the rooms on the right. Jane estimated the distance between herself and a table that held a candelabra, and started moving again. The next chance to hide herself was at the end of the corridor behind a high glass cabinet.

But where should she look? If she opened the wrong door, all was lost. Jane looked around frantically, listening intently for any telltale sounds.

"Mrs. Avery!" The shout came from the room in the center of the corridor, the only one with a double door.

Jane dashed down the corridor and pressed against the wall behind the cabinet. Through a collection of Murano glass vases, she watched a woman emerge from the second door on the other side of the corridor and disappear immediately through the double doors. *Now or never,* thought Jane, and hurried back to the door through which the woman had appeared. There was no time now for caution, and she barged into the room without another thought. When she saw the girl standing by the wall inside, she let out a muffled cry, and the girl did the same. She stared back at Jane, wide-eyed.

"I don't want . . . ," the girl said, then faltered, tears springing to her eyes.

She had long blond hair that fell around her body from beneath a white veil suspended from a golden headband. Her skinny, girlish body was scantily clad in a white tunic. Her arms and legs were wrapped in gold ribbons, and a floral wreath hung at her chest. The girl, little more than a child, looked like a Roman sacrifice.

"Mary?" Jane managed to say as she reached out her arms to the poor girl.

Mary nodded, but did not move. She stood at the wall beneath the narrow window as if paralyzed. Jane took a step toward her, but the girl shrank away and threw her hands over her face.

"No! I don't want to!"

"Mary, I'm here to get you out. But we have to hurry before that woman comes back."

Something in her tone made the girl listen, and she lowered her hands. Then, trustingly, she held out her hand to Jane. It broke Jane's heart to see the gesture. She pulled the girl toward her, hugged her, and stroked her hair. The veil and headband fell to the floor, revealing ugly bald patches on her scalp. "My God!" said Jane. "Can you walk, Mary?"

The girl nodded bravely.

"Good. Then let's go!" Jane held Mary's hand in hers tightly, but the door swung open just then and Mrs. Avery entered.

"Well, this *is* a surprise. A visitor. May I ask with whom I have the pleasure—" She said no more, for Jane drew her pistol and aimed it at the astounded woman.

"Let us past!" she hissed fiercely, taking a step forward.

But Mrs. Avery grinned contemptuously, ducked before Jane could fire, and dashed back through the door. Jane's shot rang through the house. She hoped it would wake everyone in the building, and they would come to see what was going on. She pulled Mary behind her out into the corridor, but they did not get far. The double doors on the other side were jerked open, and Charles Devereaux stormed out in a fury.

"What the hell is going on out here?" At the sight of Jane, he pulled up in surprise, but the pistol leveled in his direction did not seem to impress him. He smiled. "You? So you've changed your mind after all and accepted my invitation?"

Very calmly, he reached around and pulled the doors closed behind him. Then he slowly took a step toward Jane, who kept the pistol trained on him.

"Don't come any closer!" she cried, and fired a shot over his head.

Devereaux barely flinched, but the amusement on his face disappeared. "Mrs. Avery, go and get Ramu."

Mary screamed and clung to Jane.

"Run, Mary! Down the stairs!" Jane shouted and fired again, this time in front of Devereaux's feet. He jumped back and banged into the door behind him.

The girl let out a strangled cry and ran. Jane momentarily turned to look after her, and that moment of inattention was enough for Devereaux. He threw himself on her and tore the pistol out of her hand. Then, with brutal strength, he grabbed hold of her and shoved her backward into the room from which she had freed Mary. Jane caught a glimpse of the double doors swinging open behind Devereaux, and Lord Hargrave coming out into the corridor.

"Charles? What the devil is going on?"

"Were those shots we heard?" Rutland joined Hargrave, but Devereaux closed the door behind him without responding, and Jane was alone with him in Mary's prison.

Jane's cap had fallen off, and her pinned hair came loose and tumbled over the shabby jacket she wore.

"Lady Jane. I must say, what an entrance!" Devereaux said, his voice full of admiration. "But why go to all this effort? All for the little orphan girl? You could have asked me."

"Really? And you would have handed Mary over, just like that?" Jane's words dripped with sarcasm.

Devereaux smiled thinly. "No. She knew too much. But you could have saved yourself a lot of trouble. I admit I find your appearance quite impressive, though."

"I guess that's the price I pay. Give me back my pistol and let me go, and we'll forget the whole thing," Jane demanded.

He threw back his head and laughed. "Oh, Lady Jane! Even if you wanted to, you could not. You'll set the police or your curious husband on me. But you've already done that, haven't you?" His eyes flashed dangerously. "The captain seems to have discovered a new field. He's been sticking his nose into things that are none of his business and confounding my interests left and right. That is something that I cannot stand."

Jane tried to hide her surprise. "Is that so? If you don't let me go, he'll come looking for you. He will hunt you until he finds you."

"I don't doubt it for a second, my lady. But he'll leave me in peace as long as I hold you. Which is why you will accompany me until I've reached safety."

There were shouts in the corridor outside, and a shot rang out. Someone banged a fist against the door.

"Sir, they're in the house!" Mrs. Avery screamed.

Devereaux turned around angrily and jerked the door open. "Who?"

A frantic Mrs. Avery was standing in front of him. She looked uncertainly to Jane. "I don't know. The police maybe, I don't know. You can hear them!"

Jane's heart leaped when she heard Wescott's voice shouting. "Where is she? Jane! Devereaux, I'll kill you! Jane!"

Devereaux did not hesitate. He grabbed Jane's arm and pulled her with him. He pushed Mrs. Avery aside heedlessly and ran to the other end of the corridor. "Ramu! Where is the man?"

Suddenly, the Indian was standing in front of them. He pointed into the darkness, and Jane saw another stairway. She feared Devereaux would escape if there was another secret exit. She fought against his grip with all her strength. The knife! How could she have forgotten the knife? As they stumbled down the stairs, she drew the knife from her belt and stabbed Devereaux's arm with all her strength. The man howled in fury and pain and let go of her. She desperately turned and ran back the way they'd come.

"David!" she cried as she ran back toward the commotion she now heard in the corridor. She saw Blount first. He ran past her, followed by Hargrave, who carried a knife. Behind them, she saw the dark form of Wescott.

Blount and Hargrave took no notice of her, and ran down the steps behind Devereaux and Ramu. Jane was still holding the knife in her hand when Wescott reached her. He looked her up and down, angry and relieved at the same time. "Are you planning to stab me?" he asked. He took the knife out of her hand and raised her chin with his fingers. "Are you hurt?"

She shook her head breathlessly.

"Wait here!" And with that, he followed the others down the dark stairway.

37.

Jane ran past a bewildered Rutland, standing in the doorway with his shirt open and a cigar in his hand. "What's all this then? Women were not invited!"

Mrs. Avery was nowhere to be seen, nor was Mary. Jane, fearing the worst, rushed back toward the room where she'd left Jenny. As she ran down the spiral staircase, tears came to her eyes. *It can't all have been in vain,* she thought.

"Mary! Jenny! Where are you?" she shouted desperately.

She pushed through the door and ran into the wood-paneled salon. It was empty. But then the curtain covering the embrasure moved, and Jenny cautiously peered out. "Is that you, ma'am?"

The noises coming from the gallery made it clear that everyone in the house was on their feet.

"Have you seen Mary?" Jane asked, looking around.

A pale face appeared from beneath Jenny's arm, and Jane sobbed with relief, ran to the two girls, and wrapped them both in her arms. Then she kneeled and took Mary's hand in hers. "Did they hurt you?"

Mary's big eyes widened, but she shook her head. "Not like they were going to." The girl bit her lips and began to cry.

"It's all right," Jane said. "It's all right. Everything will be good again. Shh." She stood and picked up Mary. Over the girl's head, she asked Jenny, "Did Mrs. Avery come past this way?"

Jenny nodded. "I've never seen her in such a state. Her room is downstairs."

"Who's here besides Wescott and Blount? The police?"

"I don't think so, ma'am. But there's another gentleman. That's him!" Jenny pointed behind Jane.

"Jane! My gosh, but you put a scare into us!" Thomas, Alison's husband, came into the salon, his pistol drawn.

Jane released Mary and pushed her to Jenny. "Take her downstairs, Jenny."

"I will, ma'am." Jenny smiled and grasped Mary's hand in hers.

Jane ran one hand through her hair and straightened her jacket. "Excuse the inappropriate attire, but the circumstances called for unusual steps to be taken. Did Ally give me away?"

Thomas, who towered a head and a half over her, frowned and put his gun away. "I practically had to drag it out of her. When Wescott pointed out what a nasty character Devereaux really was, she saw that it would be stupid not to put us in the know."

"And how did my husband—"

Just then, Wescott charged through the door, with Blount close behind. "Your husband, Jane, was setting plans in motion to have Devereaux's businesses searched. Then Levi sent me a message reporting your nocturnal outing. How could you be so foolish?" he snapped. He had blood on his cheek and wiped it impatiently away with the back of his hand.

"Don't yell at me!" Jane shot back. "If I had done nothing, Mary would now be the victim of rape. Or dead."

"You could have told me! I would have helped you!"

"Oh, yes? Would you have come here with me tonight? I doubt it. And where is Devereaux now?"

Wescott looked at Thomas. "Gone. The cur got away. He must have known he'd be raided sooner or later. He'll be out of the country before anyone can stop him. But at least he'll be gone, never to set foot on English soil again."

"My goodness, Hettie's still in the garden!" Jane said suddenly and turned to leave, but stopped. "What about Hargrave and Rutland?"

Thomas shrugged. "We've got nothing on them except being invited here by Devereaux. They're not about to tell us what took place here, and there are no witnesses. There are many men like them. Too many. Dubious morals, reprehensible behavior, but as long as they don't accost children under thirteen, you can't touch them."

"What if Mary's younger?"

"Did they molest her?" Thomas asked.

"She says no."

Just then, Lord Hargrave and the Duke of Rutland came down the stairs in the company of another man whom Jane recognized, the cricketer.

"Devereaux has escaped, Lady Jane," said Hargrave.

"I don't want to talk to you. To any of you." Jane turned her back on them.

Wescott tilted his head to one side as a sign to Hargrave, and the three men quickly disappeared into the gallery. The moment they disappeared from sight, a servant came running, calling, "Come quickly! Two women are fighting down below. One of them is Mrs. Avery."

"Hettie!" In a flash, Jane and the men followed the servant downstairs and outside, getting there just in time to see Hettie with the dagger held threateningly in her hand and Mrs. Avery backed up against the trunk of an enormous tree.

Wescott and Blount manhandled her into her own room in the domestic wing and locked the door. Jane was overcome by her maid's bravery and hugged her tightly.

"Hettie, you're amazing!"

Hettie's eyes lit up. "Oh, that was a lot of fun. The woman practically bowled me over, and she had a bag with her. It looked to me like she was trying to make a run for it, so I used this pointy little thing to stop her."

"Well done is all I can say!" said Thomas with a smile, and clapped Hettie on the shoulder.

Wescott walked out of the house with Blount, looking less than thrilled. After a brief exchange of words, he sent his valet away. "He's going to advise Police Inspector Stamford to have a word with Mrs. Avery, although I doubt she'll ever betray Devereaux. She seems completely besotted with the man."

Jenny brought Mary outside to them; she'd draped a blanket around the girl's shoulders. Mary pointed to the plane tree behind the washing lines. "That's where Ramu killed Jedidiah. Mrs. Avery was there. Where is Ramu?" Mary looked around anxiously.

"He can't hurt you, Mary," said Jane, and reached for her hand reassuringly.

Wescott looked around uncertainly. "What will we do with her now? We have to hand her over to the police so they can take a statement from her."

Jane shook her head vehemently. "Do you have any family, Mary?"

"I have a brother, ma'am, but I don't know where he is."

"Then she's coming with me. If someone needs her statement, I'll go along with her," Jane said.

In the week after that memorable night, Wescott and Jane barely exchanged two words. He was still terribly angry with her. Mary was examined by a doctor, who reported that the abuse she'd suffered was exclusively external. He ordered peace and quiet and some decent food.

Everyone in the townhouse lavished attention on the shy orphan girl. Josiah especially seemed smitten with Mary, and loved reading stories to her. But the girl's greatest enjoyment came when Polly's book was returned to her.

When Jane sat down at the breakfast table one morning and opened the newspaper, she sniffed indignantly and murmured, "Two inches in the margin, that's all! That man must have some extremely influential friends."

Wescott entered the dining room and sat down across from her without a word.

Jane set the paper aside and said, "Good morning. Or aren't you speaking to me at all?"

Wescott said nothing.

Jane drummed her fingers on the article in the newspaper. "Have you read this? A few measly lines about the overnight disappearance of one of the richest men in London. Nothing else, and no background. A suspected unhappy love affair. They have got to be kidding! Won't there be a trial? Devereaux could be tried in absentia. That's been done before."

Sullenly, Wescott said, "Yes, it has. But those cases could be prosecuted because there was tangible evidence. We have a statement from an orphan who had been locked up and beaten, neither of which is a punishable offense. Oh, and the same girl witnessed a murder committed by an Indian man. The murderer has disappeared, and the body, too. If the next flood washes up a decomposing male corpse, it still won't help. Mrs. Avery is keeping tight-lipped. I think it's fair to say that every servant in Devereaux's house agrees that she is a despicable woman, but she's done nothing she can be charged with. Polly ran away and died, as we know, which makes her no use as a witness."

"What about Ledford? Mary said she thought that Cooper was behind Gaunt's murder."

Wescott ran one hand through his hair. He looked tired. "The grounds of Ledford's property in Newbridge have been searched, and the teacher's personal items turned up. Ledford will do time, that much is certain. We have proof that he sold children, and I'm confident he's one of those who'll talk sooner or later. He's already identified one of the intermediaries, a ship's chandler in Plymouth. And we've arrested a madam named Lulu at a brothel here in London. Inspector Stamford is confident that he'll be able to bring in a few more helpers and go-betweens. Oh, yes, there's also an aid organization called Friends of Wayward Girls in Need that was under Devereaux's patronage. We'll be taking a very close look at that."

"That's perverse . . . Friends of Wayward Girls in Need!" said Jane indignantly. "But even with all of that, it's not enough?"

"No. Devereaux set everything up very cleverly. All of the threads seem to lead in one direction, then they get tangled into a knot of middlemen and abettors who vanish as soon as you get too close. Thomas and I fear there's someone at the top pulling strings. They seem to be a step ahead of us at every turn."

"What are you implying? The royal court?" Jane leaned forward excitedly.

"Jane, I want you to leave things as they lie. I can't always arrive in the nick of time to save you from some absurd or ridiculously dangerous predicament. That goes beyond my powers and tries my patience! Besides, you put your own maid in harm's way. What if something had happened to her? Is that what you want? Does something serious have to happen to make you see what you're doing?" Wescott's eyes burned with anger, and his scar flushed red.

Jane sighed. "I'm sorry. That's not what I wanted. But—"

Wescott slammed his hand onto the table, and the teacups rattled on their saucers. "No buts! Use your wits. You still have them, at least!"

Jane smiled sweetly. "Thank you. I'll take that as a compliment, even if it wasn't meant as one."

The muscles in Wescott's neck tightened and he stood up. "I'd better go. Before I forget myself."

After their conversation, if she could call it that, Jane left the house to pay a visit to Alison. She was so upset that the moment she was alone in a room with Alison, she threw her arms around her friend's neck and burst into tears.

"Jane, what's happened? I mean, well, plenty has happened, but . . . Is it Mary?" Alison stroked Jane's hair and led her to a sofa. "Sit down. We'll have a glass of port."

Jane obediently lowered herself onto the sofa and drank the glass of port that Alison handed her. It reminded her of her uncle, and she felt more miserable than ever.

"Well?" Alison asked, looking at her sympathetically.

"Mary's a wonderful girl. She's recovering, and her hair is growing back slowly. She says she's looking forward to going to school. When she's really feeling well again and feels strong enough, I'll go around with her and we'll look at schools together. Sometime in the future, she can visit Polly's grave in Fearnham. We'll have Polly's name engraved on the stone."

"That sounds lovely, Jane. But that's not what's making you so sad, is it?" said Alison gently.

"It's Wescott! To the devil with him! We actually talked to each other this morning for the first time since Mary's rescue, and all we could do was fight! He could at least admit I was right about Mary," Jane complained. She took a deep breath and looked accusingly at her friend.

Alison, looking as enchanting as ever with her blond hair and wearing an airy summer dress, began to laugh. "Oh, you really are too much!"

"For goodness' sake, Ally!"

Her friend wiped her eyes and blinked impishly at Jane. "Why do you two make your lives so hard? You love each other! A blind man could see that."

"Don't talk nonsense. The moment he sees me, he starts criticizing me or accuses me of something. No, wait, today he actually praised the continued existence of my wits—but only to advise me to use them. You call that love? Leave off, Ally." But deep down, Jane had long suspected that Alison could see what she couldn't quite admit to herself.

"Actually, yes. That's love," said Alison. "You have no idea how frantic he was the night he was here with Thomas. I knew you were planning something mind-bogglingly mad, but I didn't want to be disloyal to you. I trust you, you know." She smiled lovingly at Jane. "Unfortunately, men find it hard to trust women with any more than the standard wifely duties. At most, something artistic. You understand that. Wescott was out of his mind with worry about you. I only told him where you were when I feared he would drag me off to a magistrate if I didn't."

Jane took the carafe of port from the table and poured herself another glass, which she swallowed quickly. Then she said, "I still had my knife. But there was no harm in him being there, too."

"You two are made for each other, Jane. Believe me. Now pour me another port, too."

"Assuming what you say is true, then there's still a major hurdle to face."

"And that would be . . . ?"

"He has a lover. And I will not accept that."

Instantly, every trace of merriment vanished from Alison's eyes. "Talk to him! Thomas thinks very highly of him. He's an honorable man, and he won't lie to you."

"Hmm." Jane hesitated for a long time before she said, "I won't take the first step."

Alison rolled her eyes. "Then you'll just go on collecting orphans and trying to save the world."

"What's wrong with that?" replied Jane, archly.

With a look of pure innocence, Alison replied, "Nothing. Nothing at all. But will that be enough in the long run, I wonder . . ."

38.

Mulberry Park, September 1860

"Rufus!" Jane turned her horse down the steep cliff path and then let the mare gallop on the sand. The Great Dane ran wildly beside them, barking all the way.

Jane had been back for a week and was enjoying every minute that she spent outside. Toward the end of the London Season, she had been counting the days, cursing every appointment she had to keep. But she understood her obligations and obediently spent the days and weeks in endless trivial babble about Paris fashions, and the weather—a perennial English topic that foreigners would never understand. Then there were topics like horses, wagers, parliament, the prime minister, the Queen and her ailing husband—one could only feel sorry for the poor woman—and so on, and so on . . .

Wescott barely showed his face at home. He accompanied her to important receptions but otherwise always seemed to be needed elsewhere. She never asked what kept him away, and this seemed to suit him, for his expression was invariably closed and somber. Even when Mary decided on a school in Kent, all he said was that he was happy for the girl. If Alison's suspicion was correct, and he truly had another woman, then Jane could forget about love. She met with Violet on several occasions; the woman looked up to Jane as if she were a charity icon. With Violet's help, Jane financed a new orphanage in Lambeth and organized a new teacher and a doctor, who would check on the children twice a week. The work gave Jane a sense of fulfillment, but she often had the feeling that there had to be more. She longed to go on a long trip. Perhaps she and Hettie could travel to India in winter. Her courageous maid had earned that, and it would invigorate Jane as well.

Floyd had recovered to the point where he could run the household properly again, as a butler ought. Mr. Roche continued to take care of the house and grounds, and Mrs. Roche had transformed Mulberry Park into a livable home. The new cook, a woman from Edinburgh, had been chosen with care, and her background had been thoroughly checked. Jane insisted only that Scotland's national dish, haggis, be banned from the menu.

A number of open wounds remained. One of them was Mary's beloved brother, Tim, who could not be found, and her friend Fiona, who had been sent away to Australia. Such things took time, and one could never give up hope. The body of the missing teacher, Mr. Gaunt, was found. Cooper saved himself from hanging by disclosing the location of the grave; in exchange, his sentence was reduced to life in prison. They were not able to prove him guilty of murder because he offloaded all the blame onto his dead brother, Jedidiah.

The ocean that day was choppy and the wind strong, and the salty spindrift sprayed Jane's face. As her horse galloped over the wet sand, she let the wind blow past her and savored the taste of salt on her lips. The clouds were gathering, and the dark wall looming in the west did not bode well.

"Come on, Rufus. Time to head home, or Floyd will start complaining."

Several times, on her extended rides, she had been surprised by squalls and cloudbursts, and each time Floyd had worried himself sick. The poor man had been through enough on her account, and it would help no one if she came down with some self-inflicted lung infection and had to spend weeks in bed. Jane pulled the hood of her cape over her head. The first heavy drops of rain were already falling.

And there was another threat hanging over her. Since her last visit to Rosewood Hall, her cousin Matthew had not been in touch again. Yet she knew he was obsessed with driving her out of her beloved home. She checked the post every day, looking for anything that might be officially certified or written in her cousin's hand, but so far she had been spared any more bad tidings.

She jumped her mare over a wall, then trotted across the fields. A herd of sheep was huddled against a hedge for protection from the impending thunderstorm. The wind freshened and became gusty, driving a broken-off gorse bush before it. Branches bearing tiny yellow flowers swept through the air. *The summer is coming to its end,* thought Jane, and spurred her horse onward. In the distance, a bolt of lightning flashed. The storms that rolled in from the sea were powerful, but passed over quickly. Finding yourself caught in the middle of one, however, was no picnic.

Jane was lucky. The storm took its time, and most of the dark mass of clouds stopped and hung over the river's mouth. On the other side of the river lived Doctor Westwood, whom she had not yet seen since her return. Perhaps she should visit him soon. After all, Floyd owed his full recovery to Westwood's medical skills. The mare trotted briskly around the last curve just as Rufus began to bark and charged ahead.

"Come on, old girl, let's go see what's going on." With light pressure from Jane's legs, the horse covered the final stretch to the house at a canter.

When Jane saw the two horses in the yard, she felt hope and fear grapple inside her: the fear that Matthew had brought a court order together with a bailiff to enforce it, and the hope of seeing Wescott again. Despite everything, she missed his company, his surly expression that could give way to a warm smile from one second to the next, and their arguments. There was simply no one that she loved to argue with more than him, and that in itself was remarkable.

Barely had her mare's hooves rattled the pavers in the courtyard when she saw Blount and Floyd coming around the corner of the house. The two men were chatting away amicably as if they had been best friends for years. Jane did not wait for one of them to help her from her horse, but jumped to the ground on her own. She was wearing riding breeches, boots, and a robust tweed jacket beneath her rain cape, which she now untied and tossed over Floyd's arm in passing.

"Nice to see you, Blount. Is the captain already inside?"

"Yes, ma'am." As usual, the valet was wearing his brown suit, but today there was the trace of a smile on his face.

Jane thwacked her boots with the riding crop and then ran up the front steps with Rufus at her side. Only when she opened the door did she realize that her hair, disheveled from the ride, must be a terrible sight. Her cheeks were certainly red from the wind, and she looked like anything but the image of a lady of rank. But to blazes with that. Who cared about convention!

With a spring in her step, she entered the hall. The heels of her boots clacked loudly with every step. When she pushed open the door to the library, she found Wescott standing at the window. He looked at her with an unfathomable expression.

"Jane." His voice was hoarse.

"What a greeting. I'm touched. How are you? Keeping well? What are your plans? Are you going to let me in on them, or are you just here to check that everything's in order? Not to worry. I have very little opportunity out here to compromise either of us." She dropped the crop on the table and pulled off her gloves.

"Finished?" He reached into the pocket of his jacket and withdrew a bundle of letters.

"What's that?" A dark suspicion rose inside her when she recognized the familiar handwriting on the envelopes.

Wescott approached until he was standing just an arm's length away. He handed her the bundle. "My wedding gift."

"Your . . ." It was true. He had not given her anything for the wedding. Everything had happened so abruptly that they had just exchanged rings, and then he was gone again. She ran one hand gently over the letters, in which she found her father's promissory notes. Her eyes filled with tears.

"That's why Matthew never got in touch again. How did you get your hands on them?" she whispered.

His dark eyes sparkled, and he gave her a knowing smile. "Didn't I tell you that you could trust me?"

She nodded.

"But you didn't." He took the letters out of her hands and set them on the table. Tenderly, he stroked her wind-tousled hair and placed one hand around her waist.

Jane breathed faster. She could easily let herself be seduced by him. He knew it and was playing with her yet again. "Don't!"

But Wescott did not release her. He pulled her closer to him, so close she could feel the beating of his heart through the woolen material of his jacket. "I want to terminate our damned contract."

"Excuse me?" She found it hard to think clearly so close to him, but she was not about to let him ride roughshod over her like she was some idiot farm girl.

He sighed. "Oh, Jane. I can practically read your thoughts."

"No, you can't. Unless you're a medium with supernatural powers at your command! You want to make things easy for yourself. You lead your life in London, in the clubs, amusing yourself with other women, and now you want a warm bed at home, too, but that's not—"

That was as far as she got, for Wescott closed her mouth with his own lips. His kiss was extremely convincing, and for a long moment, Jane gave herself over to the feeling. As his lips glided over her cheek and down to her neck, she leaned away from him spiritedly.

"Thank you for this sample of your talents, David. But I can agree to the cancellation only on one condition."

"And that would be . . . ?" He stroked his hand a little lower over her back. "I can't get the sight of you in trousers out of my head."

"No other women."

He looked at her earnestly. "There have been no other women since we've been married, Jane."

"But Alison saw you!"

"All purely professional."

Jane pursed her lips.

"It won't work without trust," he said.

She smiled at him provocatively. "I'll remind you of that the next time I need you to help me break into a house at night."

Wescott pulled her close and laughed. "The moment I met you, I knew I was in for trouble."

About the Author

Annis Bell is a writer and scholar. She has lived for many years in the United States and England and currently divides her time between England and Germany.

For more information, please visit www.annisbell.com.

About the Translator

Australian by birth, Edwin Miles has been active as a translator in the literary, film, and television fields for nearly fifteen years. Widely traveled, he has worked, among other things, as a draftsman, teacher, white-water rafting guide, and seismic navigator.

After undergraduate studies in his hometown of Perth, he was awarded an MFA in fiction writing by the University of Oregon in 1995. While there, he spent a year working as fiction editor on the literary magazine *Northwest Review*. In 1996, he was short-listed for the prestigious *Australian/*Vogel's Literary Award for young writers for a collection of short stories.

After many years living and working in Australia, Japan, and the United States, he currently resides in his "second home" in Cologne, Germany, with his wife and two very clever children.